Billy Love's
Secret Crusaders

To Donna!

Enjoy

Dr. Jean Wolf

Jea Wolf Logan
5-29-19

Cover Art: Pam Burton
Editor: Terrie Scott

ISBN #: 978-0-359-30516-2

Printed in the United States of America

Dedication

This book is dedicated to the memory of my great-grandmother May Carris Phillips who with great determination and courage superseded tragedies in her life. I like to think these qualities spilled over to me…whether through the gene pool or through her nurture of my soul in my early childhood.

At the ripe old age of 45 she became a nurse—at a time with the profession mandated twelve hour shifts and duties encompassed much more then tending to health care needs. There was cooking and cleaning and taking care of an endless stream of infants.

Gram as she was called colored the character of Nurse Phillips in this book—an advocate for mental illness, a researcher, a person who stood up for herself and others. Someone who was a change agent and a strong woman. And yet, outside of her professional role she found time to give me dancing lessons, plant my own flower garden and slide down the bannister without fear of reprimand from my parents.

And so, thank you for the inspiration Gram. For your brilliance, your role modeling and your impact on me—guiding and supporting and believing I could do anything. Even write books.

May Carris Phillips (Pictured Left)

Acknowledgments

Billy Love's Secret Crusaders is the final book in the trilogy of *Billy Love Novels*. I am grateful for my extended family of Wolfs, as this book is loosely based on some of the personalities of my own family. Generations of Wolfs lived in Darmstadt, Germany before immigrating to the United States.

I want to recognize Pam Barton, who designed the fabulous black and gold cover art for all three of my novels. She is a high school classmate of mine, a friend but also a colleague in my journey through the publishing world.

My husband, Tom Logan became my business manager. I am grateful for his support always.

I never could have published any of my novels without the funny, witty and insightful editor Terrie Scott. Per her instructions: "Now get writing. I believe you have enough material to pursue historical novels well into the future."

To put it succinctly, there is nothing Ms. Scott cannot accomplish: editing, formatting, publishing, marketing. She is the total package and I am lucky to have found her.

She has been my support and inspiration from the minute I met her—knowing when to push and knowing when to praise. We simply mesh.

Finally, to all of the people affected by the Cold War that dominated for decades—this novel serves to showcase women working together to effect peace in a world bent on violence and dominance.

CHILDREN'S RELATIONSHIP TREE

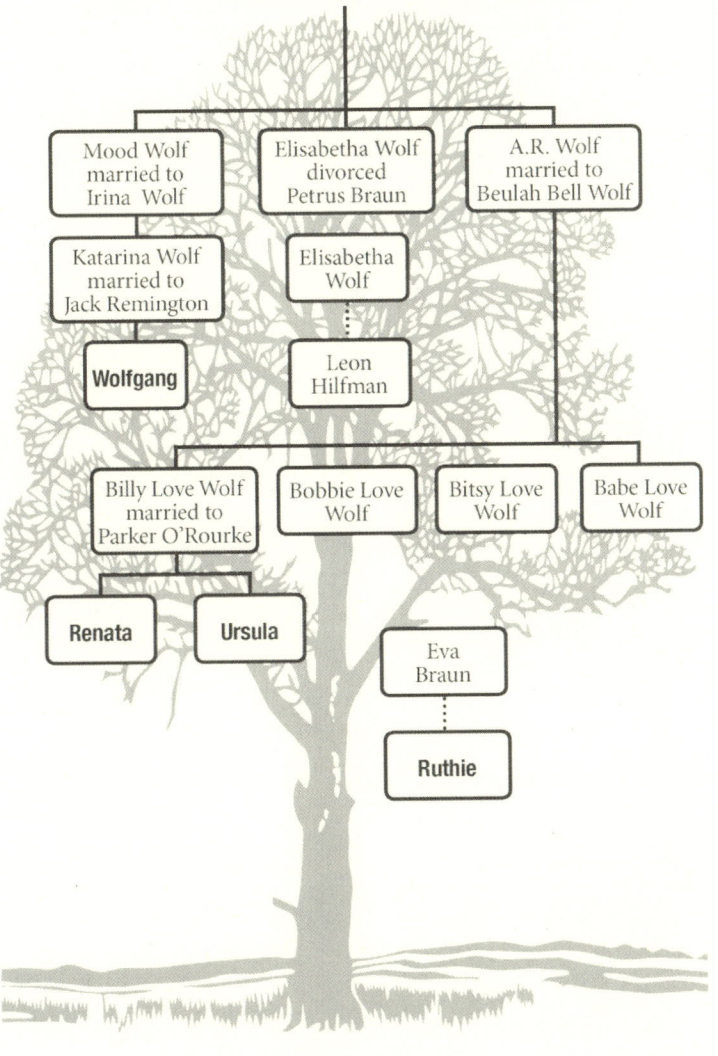

Mood Wolf married to Irina Wolf

Elisabetha Wolf divorced Petrus Braun

A.R. Wolf married to Beulah Bell Wolf

Katarina Wolf married to Jack Remington

Elisabetha Wolf

Wolfgang

Leon Hilfman

Billy Love Wolf married to Parker O'Rourke

Bobbie Love Wolf

Bitsy Love Wolf

Babe Love Wolf

Renata

Ursula

Eva Braun

Ruthie

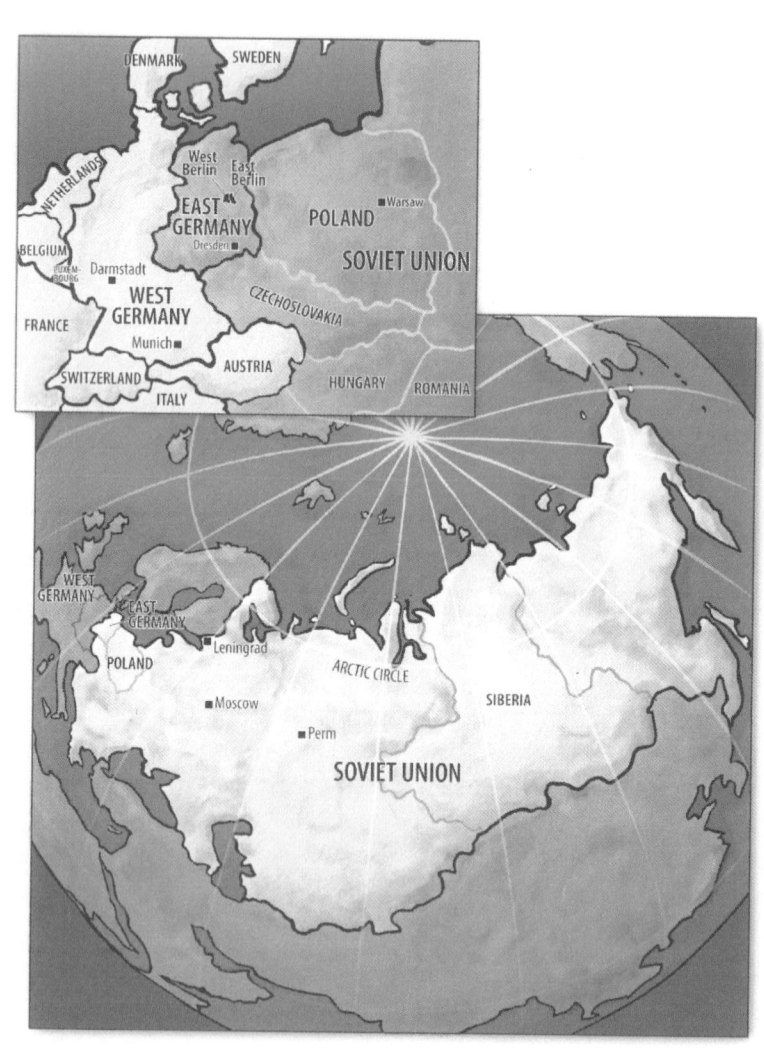

Chapter 1
Bellevue Psychiatric Hospital

I can promise you that women working together—
linked, informed, and educated—can bring peace and
prosperity to this forsaken planet.

~ Isabelle Allende

New York City
1950
Billy Love

I slumped against the cracked leather chair, feeling dejected and defeated. I knew I appeared disheveled and unkept—I had hurriedly dressed in old jeans and one of Parker's plaid flannel shirts this morning. There was an urgent need to transport Ursula to the hospital, for she had started self-mutilating herself, taking scissors and cutting at the tender tissues on her wrists.

Admittedly I had not handled Ursula well. I was faint at the sight of all the blood spilling onto the white carpet, staining it ruby, then seeping and spreading throughout the bedroom. I had screamed at Ursula, startling her as I grabbed clean rags and placed pressure over the slashes—trying to stem the bleeding. She fought me at first thrashing and moaning, until she finally became slack, her eyes vacant as she played into her own head game.

Now I was in the emergency waiting room replaying my daughter's situation that devastating day in the crematorium of Dachau Concentration Camp—when we learned from Samuel that her birth father was executed with a bullet to the head and her mother was raped to death. Ursula had been an eye witness to the carnage. Would she ever be able to overcome the hideous pictures filling her mind…seemingly an endless reel of images?

Whatever the health professionals told me I knew she would have to be admitted to the mental health ward for inpatient treatment. Parker and I could not cope with her acting-out behavior and it was unfair to Renata, who needed some semblance of a calm stable home.

Parker and I had tried therapist after therapist to no avail. There had been very little improvement in her behavior and she was failing in her school studies. Now that she was nine-years-old, she was harder to control—she was bigger and stronger, and she could land a punch to the face or groin with skill. Her outbursts became a daily occurrence. And I felt like we were in a constant battle zone.

I was against giving Ursula medications but in the end, we relented and filled a prescription for the antipsychotic drug Thorazine. Within days of taking it however she became a shell of herself, drooling and wetting herself as she sat in the corner and stared at nothing for hours on end. Renata would huddle with Ursula, draping her arm around her shoulder as she cooed positive messages. It was a heart-breaking sight—the two of them hunkered down which reminded me of when I first met them at Aunt Liz's house. Renata was Ursula's protectress—always there for her.

In the end we refused to refill the Thorazine prescription and Ursula's violent behavior returned with a vengeance. I looked around the waiting room and noticed other parents with their heads bowed as they waited for a miracle to make their kids *normal* again. But what was *normal*? One thing I knew Ursula was NOT normal, and I was mad at God. Why was Ursula exposed to such horror, a horror so great that it would prohibit a healthy happy childhood?

I frowned and furrowed my brow. What was taking them so long? A lone tear slid down my cheek…a handkerchief floated into my lap.

"Honey, is this your first time at Bellevue?"

I turned to the diminutive young woman sitting beside me.

"Yes, it is. My daughter is very ill," I said with my eyes filling again.

"Let me give you some advice. Most of the people who work here want to help our kids but there are a few sinister people you need to avoid. And whatever they tell you, never consent to a lobotomy procedure," the woman said as she lowered her voice and leaned into me conspiratorially.

8

"A lobotomy?"

"Yes, they cut into the brain and separate the lobes. It makes the person into a senseless blob," she said as she sat back and crossed her arms.

I paused uncertain what to say to this unwelcome information from a stranger.

"Well, my husband and I would never approve such a barbaric procedure. But thanks for the advice about the people who work here. I will be vigilant regarding Ursula's care," I said as I looked at my watch. Surely, they were done evaluating her by now.

"Mrs. O'Rourke?"

A nurse encased in a head-to-toe starched white uniform stood in the doorway of the examination room. A white bonnet-cap was perched on her gray-streaked tresses. She had a serene look to her that instantly calmed me.

"Yes, you can call me Billy Love," I said as I stood and walked toward the nurse.

The nurse seemed older around forty-five, which was unusual as most nurses these days were giddy, single young women searching for husbands. When the nurses found mates they typically retired to the mundane life of a housewife.

I found the nurse's demeanor professional and confident. It was clear that Ursula was in good hands. I relaxed a bit.

"My name is May Phillips, Nurse Phillips if you wish and I am taking care of Ursula today. We are getting the paperwork ready to admit her to Bellevue. Will you come with me now? I need to get some history from you," she said as she turned and strode down the hallway in her sturdy white polished shoes.

"Thank you, Nurse Phillips my husband is on his way here," I said.

"Let's sit down and visit for a few moments before seeing Ursula," the nurse said.

I liked the lilting tone of her voice. I felt myself trusting her.

Nurse Phillips pushed her round wire-rim glasses up on her nose and grabbed a clipboard containing Ursula's chart.

"It took us quite a while to dress her wounds. She would not let us near her. We finally had to restrain her and inject her with a

9

sedative—now she is sleeping. What can you tell me about her background? She is adopted, right?" Nurse Phillip asked.

"Correct. She and her sister were discovered hiding in the bombed-out area of Munich after the war in 1945. We did not discover their circumstances until 1948, when a survivor of Dachau came forward and shared his story," I said.

The nurse scribbled copious notes as I relayed Ursula's history.

"Has Ursula had violent behavior from the beginning?" she asked.

"Yes, and we believe it stems from witnessing the deaths of her birth parents at Dachau. Her father was an SS guard and the family lived on the grounds of the camp. The American army unit that liberated the camp...well, in the chaos they delivered fatal injuries to many of the guards and their families."

"Oh, my goodness dear, I can think of no greater horror for a child to witness," she said patting my hand.

The door opened and Parker stood hat in hand as he adjusted to his surroundings.

"Oh, Parker, Ursula cut herself. It was horrible," I said raising my voice. I ran across the room and wrapped my arms tightly around him.

"Darling, let's take some deep breaths. She is safe now and in the best possible place for her," Parker said in a calm sure voice.

I looked up at him and nodded. Always my rock, I was more confident when he was by my side. He still had a bit of a boyish look to him with his sprinkle of freckles and his sandy wind-tossed hair.

"Come, Parker I want you to meet Ursula's nurse. We were just going over her history."

"Parker, nice to meet you. I will be Ursula's long-term nurse and I will manage her daily care," Nurse Phillips said stretching out her hand to Parker.

"Like-wise. I am sure Ursula is in good hands," Parker said to the nurse. He grabbed a chair and sat down beside us.

"Now, where were we?" Nurse Phillips asked.

"Ursula has been violent for many years but never before has she cut herself. Why...why would she do such a thing?" I blurted out before I could stop myself.

10

"Billy Love, there is a theory in psychiatric circles that when people feel extreme anxiety, the act of cutting themselves and the resulting pain and bleeding reminds them that they are still alive," Nurse Phillips said.

"Oh," I said. I tightly gripped Parker's arm.

"Another theory is that when people cut themselves it is like popping a balloon—all of the air is released—when the blood flows the anxiety flows away with it. Until their apprehension builds again," the nurse explained.

"Then what?" Parker asked.

"Then they will slash again. We found a pocket-knife in her bathrobe. Ursula knew that the fear would come again and overwhelm her," Nurse Phillips said arching her eyebrows.

"Please, make her better," I said in a small voice.

"Nurse Phillips, how long will she be hospitalized?" Parker asked.

"I will need to consult with our lead psychiatrist Dr. Andrews, but I believe a three-month-stay is standard."

"Three months?" I asked flooded with relief that I might get a long stretch of respite—but I simultaneously felt guilty as a mother for abandoning my child to someone else.

"Billy Love, you know Ursula needs the routine and the long-term medical help. And Renata needs our undivided attention for a sustained period of time," Parker said.

"Let me get us some tea. I think we need a break from this intense conversation," Nurse Phillips said as she motioned to the aide peering through the window. I sat back and tried to clear my mind as we waited for the refreshments.

I watched the steam rise from the teacup and smelled the spiced tea. As I sipped the liquid I felt my spirits lift.

"Nurse Phillips, what is your background?" I asked taking the focus off Ursula for the moment.

"I know it is a bit unusual, but I became a nurse at age forty. Nursing was always a profession I thought I was suited for and after my divorce I pursued my dream."

"Why did you decide upon mental health?" Parker asked.

"I did a rotation here at Bellevue as a student nurse and I fell in love with the children, most of whom are on public assistance.

There are so many children who fall through the cracks," Nurse Phillips continued.

"You know I forgot Bellevue was a public hospital," I remarked.

"Indeed, the first building went up in 1796 not long after our country was founded," she explained.

"There is another reason I came to Bellevue. One day a week I am assigned to the medical research laboratory. Our research team receives government funding to collect information on the effectiveness of new psychiatric medications and procedures. It is fascinating work—and the results could very well help people in the future."

"How interesting," I said. Parker nodded in agreement.

"I am very content. Now, let's get back to Ursula," Nurse Phillips said in a no-nonsense voice. She looked down at her notes.

"Why do you think Renata has adjusted to life in your family and Ursula has not?" Nurse Phillips continued.

I sighed. "Renata was in the cottage at the time of the camp liberation. Only Ursula witnessed the killings."

"Samuel said that Ursula screamed like nothing he had ever experienced, then she tore through the camp grounds until she reached Renata. She could not have been more than three or four years old at the time," Parker explained.

"Research shows us that even very young children can have flashbacks and terrifying dreams because of traumatic events. I suspect that is what has been going on with Ursula—the memories keep coming in waves," Nurse Phillips said. She put down her clipboard and fluttered her hands in the air.

I leaned back and concentrated on the information given to Parker and me about Ursula. I understood what had to be done. I moved forward and quickly signed the admission papers.

"Nurse Phillips, I enfold my precious Ursula into your care. My forsaken child," I said. My eyes welled yet again and my voice cracked.

Parker helped me out of my chair and we moved toward the door.

"Let's go see her. I can explain to Ursula why she is staying with us for a while," Nurse Phillips said.

"Thanks, Nurse Phillips, but I need to tell her myself," I replied.

Together we slowly walked down the hallway until we stood before Ursula's barren room. We peered into the small window. She sat on the mattress legs crossed staring blankly at the gray walls.

I approached her and sat next to her. She scooted away and pulled her legs up under her chin, refusing to give me eye contact.

I decided to keep my conversation short. "Ursula, Nurse Phillips will take good care of you here at the hospital. Daddy and I want you to get better. We will visit often."

Nurse Phillips gently pulled me to my feet and led Parker and me from the room.

"I will be by Ursula's side throughout her journey toward recovery," Nurse Phillips said. She held Ursula's chart to her chest and leaned against the cold stone walls.

Something flickered inside me. Hope.

Chapter 2
The Brandenburg Gate

Berlin
1950
Katerina (Kat)

Papa and I stood with arms linked and marveled at the imposing structure before us—the Brandenburg Gate. I knew something of its long history…that it was built as a military symbol of peace and unity.

What a joke! I thought as I raised my eyes to the fluttering Soviet flag planted on the top of the neoclassical sandstone beam. In fact, the gate divided Berlin to such an extent that armed Soviet guards scrutinized the comings and goings of everyone who came through it.

I frowned squinted and raised my hand over my eyes blocking out the sun to get a better look at the edifice. It had been repeatedly bombed during the war and was heavily damaged but not destroyed. However, the sculpture atop the structure which had once consisted of Athena, Goddess of Victory, driving a chariot with four horses was mostly abolished.

"Papa, I wonder how the Gate is still standing after so much destruction around it," I said.

"Well, my dear it took years to build it, so it will take more years to tear it down. I reckon it will last a few hundred more years. Look at those massive Doric columns. You know it was modeled on the Athens Acropolis, right?"

"No, I was unaware of the history," I said as I turned to face him.

I studied my father. It had been five years since he returned to Darmstadt, Germany and helped to rebuild the Merck Pharmaceutical Company and the city itself. People there called him *the mayor*. And he was happy, robust even—content with his marriage to Tilly.

I leaned my head on his shoulder and snuggled as I reviewed my life over the past two years. The terrible reveal about the fate of our children's birthparents at Dachau was heartbreaking but also a chance for new beginnings—a starting point to move forward. Just last month Papa called me in New York to inform me that the American Embassy had finally issued a visa for Wolfgang to immigrate to America.

"Papa, do you think Wolfgang is ready to leave you and Tilly and come live with Jack and me?" I asked. I lifted my head to make eye contact with him.

"As long as he can take the dog I am confident he can adjust," Papa said. He gave my shoulder a little squeeze.

"Of course. Schnitzel, his precious wiener dog," I laughed.

"Wolfgang is doing much better in school these days and he is making friends. And I have been giving him English lessons every day," Papa noted.

"Papa, does he ever talk about his birthmother? He was a bit older than the other children when the camp was liberated," I said.

"Not a word. I believe that is his way of coping—to block everything out. I think with time he might reveal what he saw and heard," Papa said.

"Yes, people cope in different ways. I was thinking about Mama and how young she was when she died in childbirth with me. I felt some guilt as a child so I pretended that she never existed. That was horrid of me," I said.

I tightened my trench coat as the wind came up and swirled through my thick, dark hair. I paused as I stared through the Brandenburg Gate and conjured up pictures of Russian women. One of them could have been my mother.

"Now, you were but a wee child," Papa admonished me.

"I realize that and now that I am adult about to marry Jack and adopt Wolfgang I want to know more about Mama," I said.

Papa pushed his round glasses up and ran his fingers through his wispy gray hair.

"Let's go across the plaza to the café and get some tea to warm us up. I can tell you what I know about your mother, the beautiful Irina," Papa declared.

I took one last look at the massive structure with its five walkways and six columns—a structure that divided east and west Berlin. It represented the tensions between Europe the United States and Russia. Why did humanity never learn?

I turned away and Papa and I strode briskly toward the comfort of the café.

****

We were shown to a small table in the corner of the smoky restaurant. I slid out of my coat and pulled a compact from my purse using the mirror to reapply my deep red lipstick and smooth my hair in place. My turquoise eyes stared back at me. I knew it was unusual to have an olive skin tone and dark hair paired with blue eyes but somehow it worked for me marking me as a unique woman. Jack had commented on their color the first day we met.

"Katerina, every time I see you I picture your mother with her twinkling blue eyes," Papa remarked as he sipped his tea and broke off a corner of a scone.

I sat back in my chair and waited for him to continue.

"Your mother was a joy. Why, she could light up the whole room," Papa said. He sat back and grinned.

"I know you met her at the Merck factory where she was working on the morphine production team. And I am aware that she was surrounded by a group of other Russian women but what else do you know about her history? Where did she come from? Why did she end up in Darmstadt?" I asked rapidly ticking off question after question.

"Hold on, Katerina let's take this conversation one step at a time," Papa said. He leaned toward me in a conspiratorial manner.

"Sure, Papa I am so eager to hear about her. I got ahead of myself."

Papa lowered his voice to almost to a whisper.

17

"To be truthful Irina was mysterious about her past even around me. I met her in 1911, we married shortly after we met and then she died in childbirth with you in 1912," Papa explained.

"What part of Russia was she from? I assume she at least told you that."

"She did. She grew up in a remote part of the Soviet Union in the Ural Mountains—a city called Perm," Papa said.

"Perm? I have never heard of it," I responded.

"In 1940 the city was renamed Molotov. It is known as the doorway from Eastern Soviet Europe to Asia," Papa said.

"But what about her family?" I asked.

"There were four children and she was the oldest. She never revealed how her parents made a living. Maybe she didn't know. It seemed secrets were all around her. She did describe a picture of an idyllic childhood to me. She lived in a mansion overlooking a beautiful park. The city had erected statues on wide-avenue street corners…there were cultural events nightly such as the ballet and symphony. There were many vocational educational opportunities," Papa said.

I watched his eyes dance. He was visualizing my mother in another life.

"But why would she pick up and leave that life at seventeen-years-old?" I asked.

Papa frowned and motioned the waitress for more tea.

"I never got it out of her. She must have been sworn to secrecy by someone in her family. It was if they threw a dart at a map and it landed on Darmstadt. Irina boarded a train and took nothing with her except a small suitcase—when she arrived in Germany she found a women's boarding house where she could live and started work at Merck," Papa said.

"Papa, did you ever consider going to Perm or Molotov as it is called now and trying to discover Mama's family?" I asked.

"Well yes, but remember I raised you from birth as your sole parent. Then I was conscripted into the army as a medic during World War I and when I returned from the war, I was tired. Around that same time in 1917 the Bolsheviks came to power and there were riots throughout Russia. It was too dangerous to be in Russia. People were being beaten and starved to bring them in line under Lenin and communism. Foreigners were not welcome," Papa explained.

"Wow I wonder if Mama's family was somehow under siege. Someday I am going to find out," I announced as I clasped my hands together.

"Katerina, you should *let a sleeping dog lie*," Papa said with an edge to his voice. Papa loved to use proverbs.

"For now, I will let it go as I have a wedding to plan and a need to get Wolfgang settled in New York," I said.

But I thought to myself—I would get to the bottom of this mystery even if it took years.

Papa smiled at me.

"Katerina don't look so smug. I know what you are thinking. You can't hide anything from me. After all I am a master-schemer myself. I was a key player in helping Eva Braun escape from Hitler," Papa said.

"Okay, Papa you know me too well," I said.

I gave him a sly look as I contemplated finding my Russian heritage.

"Let's switch the subject. You look lovely today in your high-waisted ruby red skirt and black turtleneck blouse," Papa announced in a loud voice. Those around us swiveled in our direction.

I blushed and deflected the conversation.

"What time is Babe Love meeting us tonight for dinner?" I asked.

"Around seven but I have a surprise. Elisabetha and Leon are coming, too!" Papa boomed.

"How wonderful. I am so pleased for them as a couple. I understand that Aunt Elisabetha is planning to sell her house in Munich and move to Berlin," I said.

"Yes, her life has been difficult the last few years. She had the bout with tuberculosis and then Petrus left her. What a dolt…so for her to find love again makes me happy for my sister," Papa remarked.

"And remember she was raising Ursula and Renata for six months before she got sick and had to go the sanatorium," I said as I reminisced.

Papa nodded.

"That reminds me Papa, Billy Love called me last week. Ursula is mentally unstable. She had to admit her to Bellevue Psychiatric Hospital for a three-month stint. Ursula started *cutting* herself!" I said. I placed my hand over my mouth horrified by the story. Reliving my conversation with Billy Love.

"Oh, my," Papa replied. His eyes widened and he raised his eyebrows.

"Billy Love and Parker had no choice but to admit her. Ursula is very ill and she needs treatment," I said.

"I understand the facility is top notch," Papa said matter-of-factly.

"Yes, and there is an older nurse who will be taking care of her every day so she will have some stability, Papa."

"Well, the truth be told Parker and Billy Love will be able to spend more quality time with Renata."

"After I get back to New York I plan to visit Ursula. Maybe my presence will take some of the stress off Billy Love and Parker. When Billy Love told Ursula that she would be staying at Bellevue for months Ursula would not let Billy Love touch her. She is so angry," I explained.

"I am sure that was hurtful, but they are doing what is best for Ursula," Papa replied.

I squeezed a lemon into my scalding tea and sipped it slowly tasting the bitter liquid. I stared out the window of the tiny café and once again viewed the mighty Brandenburg Gate. What would be the fate of the Russian people who were being brutalized by the Stalin regime? Did I have cousins or other relatives on Mama's side of the family who were under communist rule? Someday I would find out—I was determined. I would *leave no stone unturned.*

Chapter 3
Babe's Boyfriend

West Berlin
1950
Elisabetha (Liz)

"Leon, did I tell you that Babe is bringing her new boyfriend to dinner tonight?" I asked as I sat at my dressing table and ran a wide-toothed comb through my thick gray-streaked tresses.

"No, where did she meet him? Oh, and she doesn't go by Babe Love anymore—just *Babe*?" Leon asked. He pulled a crisp white shirt from the closet.

"She thinks going by her first and middle name is a typical Oklahoma give-away. She feels it is ridiculous and makes her look like a hick. So, she dropped the middle name—not that she really likes going by Babe but for now changing her first name would be too much for people to handle. I mean would she waltz into a meeting and announce she was Anna Wolf?" I asked.

I laughed at the thought.

"Okay, Babe it is. Liz, what about this so-called new boyfriend?"

"His name is Hans Fischer and he works for the Deutsche Bank," I replied.

I arose from my dressing table and strode to my closet where I disengaged a pale pink cashmere sweater set from the hanger.

"Where did they meet? I must admit I have been so busy with my UNICEF responsibilities that I have paid little attention to Babe's private life lately," Leon confessed.

"They met at the Highlife Lounge a few weeks ago. It's where all the young people gather these days. For them the war years were especially difficult with all of the bombings and horror and constant fear," I explained.

"I am happy for Babe. I sense she has been lonely the past couple of years. And her job at UNICEF is not easy. There have been countless situations where children have been abused, neglected and abandoned throughout Europe. Babe has been privy to all of those frightful conditions," Leon commented.

"I remember when you and Babe went to Copenhagen to bring supplies to the mistreated children and helped to rescue the sickest of them—Babe was so amazing when she cared for and rocked the little girl. That child died in Babe's arms," I said. I shook my head and frowned.

"It was something I will never forget, Liz."

I switched the subject.

"But we can't be late. We need to arrive at Riehmers Restaurant by seven p.m.," Leon said. He pulled on a dinner jacket and winked at me to lighten the mood.

"You are right. I am excited to see Kat and Moody, too. It has been too long," I said. I shook off any negative thoughts.

I fastened my pearl earrings and brushed my lips with a pink lipstick. I glanced at my reflection in the mirror. What I saw was a small-boned woman who looked well preserved for someone who had been in the German resistance during World War II.

Leon bent down and kissed my neck. I loved everything about him—his energy, his craggy expressive face, his curly locks. My life had never been better.

Leon and I entered the restaurant and spotted Kat and Moody standing near the tall bank of windows. I had never been to Riehmers and I marveled at its beauty…the cream-colored walls housed contemporary brightly colored original paintings. I noted one in particular. A painting by Picasso hugged the wall above the baby grand piano. I momentarily studied its cubist elements before turning to greet my niece and brother.

"Kat, Moody, it is so good to see you," I declared. I kissed them each on the cheek.

"Aunt Liz, Leon, it has been too long," Kat noted.

"Let's sit down. I want to get caught up on your wedding plans Kat, and I understand Wolfgang's visa was finally approved so you can take him to New York. By the way Babe called and she and the new boyfriend are running late—said we should go ahead and order drinks and appetizers," I said.

"Whoa, Aunt Liz, slow down. We will have plenty of time to catch up. And don't grill Babe's new boyfriend. My cousin might never bring him around again," Kat said as she peeled with laughter.

"You never know these days with Russia sitting right next door. Perhaps we *should* grill Mr. Fischer—the newspaper reports there are unexplained incidents where everybody suspects each other of wrongdoing. No one trusts the other," Moody said in a solemn voice.

I ignored my brother's chatter and followed the waiter through the restaurant to our assigned table which was adorned with crisp linens and scented candles. The dark polished chairs gleamed against the cream-colored walls.

"Kat, sit next to me. My hearing is not as good as it used to be," I said as I patted the chair.

I studied Kat's profile. She was in her upper thirties now—a self-assured woman who had accomplished much with her singing career. And she and Marlene Dietrich had traveled all over Europe during the war entertaining the American troops. The pair had received an award from the United States Army with a top-ranked general thanking them for their service. I was so proud of my niece.

Katarina Wolf was a woman everyone noticed and tonight was no exception. She was exquisitely attired. Perfectly tilted on her glossy dark tresses was a black-felted cloche hat. She wore a black tailored wool suit and an emerald green rhinestone brooch was pinned to the jacket—it was a perfect accessory. She crossed her long slim legs and reached for a silver cigarette case. She tamped a cigarette removed it and lit it in swift movement.

We ordered cocktails. Leon and Moody started a side conversation about the allies' efforts to rebuild Darmstadt and Berlin.

I turned to Kat. "Tell me about your wedding plans."

Kat blew smoke out of the side of her mouth and watched it curl in the air.

23

"I have some exciting news. You will recall the big family fight that Jack had with his brothers and father because they found out I was Jewish," Kat said.

"Oh, my yes I do," I said.

"Well, the men are not invited to the wedding. Jack has washed his hands of them…they are no longer considered part of his family. So, the wedding will be fairly small but of course my relatives will attend along with Marlene Dietrich and Audrey Hepburn."

Kat continued. "We scouted a number of hotels in New York City, but nothing felt right to Jack and me. Then one day Jack got a phone call from Walter Annenberg."

"Who?" I asked.

"Walt owns Triangle Publications and he knows Jack's family. He and his soon-to-be wife heard about Jack's fight with his family and offered their mansion in Philadelphia as a location for the wedding. He is Jewish and he was appalled at the anti-Semitism shown against me by the Remingtons," Kat explained.

"Even today in 1950 I can't believe the slurs from ignorant people that occur so often. And all because of ethnic background or faith," I said with a distinct edge in my voice.

Kat nodded. "I am so lucky to have found Jack. Did you know that Papa set us up together? After the war Papa kept running into him around Darmstadt and Jack kept asking about me. We finally went on a date. It was a low-key picnic up by Frankenstein's Castle and really Aunt Liz, the chemistry was instant."

"That date turned out to be wild, though. Didn't you discover Wolfgang in the castle?" I asked.

"Yes, and the way Jack handled Wolfgang—he was exceedingly kind and calm. He lifted Wolfgang and climbed down the ladder with him. Wolfgang was filthy and he had a wound that was badly infected. He reeked, but Jack showed no emotion of disgust. I knew Jack was the right man for me. On the first date no less," Kat said.

"Wonderful, Kat, I look forward to hearing more about the wedding," I said.

"There is Babe and her boyfriend now." I stood and motioned them toward our table.

Babe appeared radiant as she crossed the room. She was so petite and small-boned with her pale-pink complexion. Standing not more than five-foot two. She was built like her mother Beulah Bell. There was no resemblance at all to her father, A.R.

I guffawed. Why, the milkman could just as well have fathered her!

Babe had recently cut her white-blonde long tresses to a stylish short curly look, which paired nicely with her yellow silk floor-length dress. I stared at the man glued to Babe's side. He was over six foot two—an imposing figure who was impeccably dressed in a brown pin-stripe suit. His arm easily encircled Babe's waist as he drew her to him possessively. He was the ultimate man's man…clean shaven with a square face, broad shoulders and a narrow waist. His thick dark brown hair was neatly combed and parted on the side.

His gray eyes bored into Babe's as they reached the table together.

"Hi y'all. I want you to meet Mr. Hans Fischer," Babe drawled as she drew out each syllable. I smiled. You couldn't take the Oklahoma girl out of Babe even if she lived in Berlin.

Moody and Leon stood as Hans unfurled his hand from Babe's waist and firmly shook each of their hands. He tipped his head toward Kat and me and acknowledged us. He was measured—cautious really. Then he turned on the charm.

"Why, Babe you did not tell me how beautiful your aunt and cousin are," Hans said as he pulled out a chair and seated my niece.

Kat blushed a little, but I remained impasse. All of the years I owned the nightclub in Munich had made my weary of certain men. There was something about Hans that seemed forced—a little off-kilter.

I admonished myself. I needed to put my instincts aside. Perhaps I was wrong: I would give him a chance. Babe clearly adored him. She was smiling as she placed her hand over his and squeezed it.

The waiter dressed in a black tuxedo approached the table. Hans motioned him to his side.

"I'd like to order a bottle of your finest champagne to celebrate this great family and my brilliant beautiful girlfriend, Babe," Hans said in a take-charge tone.

"And put it on my bill," Hans continued. He had a smug look on his face.

I sat back and said nothing as the waiter returned popped the cork and poured the bubbly into each of our flutes.

Hans stood and raised his glass.

"To the Wolf clan. I look forward to our future gatherings together," Hans remarked. He leaned down to kiss Babe gently on the lips and clinked his glass with hers. Hans circled the table and one by one made sure everyone interacted with him.

"Darling, you have a great family," Hans said as he continued to dominate the conversation.

Darling? I thought to myself. Hans and Babe were a new couple. To my knowledge they had only been dating for several weeks. But Babe must feel strongly about him if she brought him to meet the family so soon. I assigned a word to him—*shyster*.

"Kat, I asked Hans to attend your wedding with me. I hope that is agreeable with you," Babe remarked. She looked up at Hans with an adoring look on her face.

Kat looked a little startled—she paused for a few seconds. I could tell she was searching for her response. "Why certainly, Babe. Hans is welcome."

I watched the reaction of the rest of group. Their faces were unreadable. Each of them knew how to keep their emotions in check but I sensed they were feeling the same reaction to *smooth Hans Fischer*. There was too much bravado and not enough humility. We were all instantly wary.

"I am famished. I think we need to order," I said as I motioned to the waiter.

The Riehmers was known for its sumptuous menu...we ordered a variety of dishes from the famous Beef Tafelspitz with root vegetables to the Pink Duck Breast with red peppers and potatoes.

When the meals arrived, we all dug in and said little as we savored the perfectly prepared dinner. After we ate we ordered coffee and relaxed. I noticed Hans and Babe were holding hands.

Hans certainly was a showman of affection I thought to myself. I would be keeping an eye on this one. My instincts kicked in again and I felt a strong dislike for him. I sat back and folded my arms. I narrowed my eyes. He was sly.

A secret is a kind of promise...
It can also be a prison.
~ Jennifer Lee Carrell

Chapter 4
Wedding at the Annenberg Estate

New York City and Philadelphia
1950
Katerina

I looked out the bedroom window onto the busy streets of New York City. "Jack, Billy Love called. Parker is not coming to the wedding—he is staying home to monitor Ursula's progress and visit her at Bellevue Hospital. Billy Love my matron of honor will be traveling to the ceremony with Renata," I said.

"It has been a month since they hospitalized Ursula. Is she making any progress?" Jack asked as he finished brushing his teeth. He ran a comb through his tousled reddish-brown hair and splashed on some cologne after he finished shaving.

I inhaled Jack's masculine scent and thought about encountering him for the first time. I had been disheveled and sweaty the day I arrived in Darmstadt and all I wanted to do was get away from the persistent army officer. I had to hand it to Papa, though. From the beginning he sensed Jack and I were a match for each other.

I came out of my trance and answered Jack.

"Ursula is really angry at Billy Love right now and she refuses to talk to her when she visits. But there has been a break-through. Nurse Phillips has gained her trust. She got Billy Love's permission to take Ursula on a couple of outings to her small home where the nurse sectioned a corner of her flower garden—just for Ursula."

"Really? How wonderful," Jack responded.

"Yes, Billy Love said Nurse Phillips let Ursula pick the packets of seeds and they planted them together," I said. I smiled remembering.

"I am a bit curious. What flowers did she pick?" Jack asked.

I waved my hands expansively. "Daffodils, purple iris, and red tulips. What a wonderful gift to Ursula!"

"She chose the vibrant flowers, didn't she, Kat? In her drab little world there can be some bright spots," Jack said. He sat down beside me on the quilted bed cover.

"And guess what else? The nurse and Ursula plan to make weekly trips to weed the garden and when the flowers are in full bloom, Ursula can pick anything she wants…make a bouquet," I explained.

Jack took my hand and kissed my palm. "I would like to meet Nurse Phillips. People underestimate the effect nurses can have on people's health especially in the case of mental illness. It's pretty remarkable how she approached Ursula. She combined a bunch of therapies—she guided Ursula into the sunshine and fresh air on a spring day. She created a unique enjoyable activity and she gave Ursula some control by allowing her to choose her own flower seeds."

"Indeed, Jack, I had not really thought about it like that but you hit the mark. Billy Love said Nurse Phillips shared that Ursula in their very first outing to the garden actually smiled as she selected the packets of seeds. And the nurse reported that Ursula made sustained eye contact with her which indicates a level of trust," I said.

"It will be a long journey but from what you report there is a glimmer of hope. Ursula is so very ill. I am sure Billy Love and Parker are relieved she is in safe capable hands," Jack replied.

"Yes, Jack. And Renata has gained her parent's full attention. The three of them have been on several outings as a family—the circus, a Broadway show, picnics," I said.

Jack nuzzled my neck. "The wedding will be fun for Renata and Wolfgang. And I can't wait to marry you my darling Kat."

I smiled. "I have my final fitting for my dress tomorrow. It seems everything else is done. The Annenbergs have been lovely calling their caterers and florists in Philadelphia. And of course, Marlene has offered to pay for all of the decor."

"I love Marlene. She makes any party worth attending just by her presence."

"Yes, indeed." I picked up a picture of Marlene and me at a USO event in Europe. There we were dressed head to toe in white matching gowns with furs draped around our shoulders. We had a special bond created by our German roots and nurtured by our hatred of the Nazi regime.

"We are lucky that the Annenbergs offered to host the wedding. When I had lunch with mother last week she shared that my boorish father and brothers are unhappy we are having the wedding in Philadelphia," Jack said. He chuckled.

"Well, they are unhappy that you are marrying me the *Jewish woman*," I said. I playfully slapped Jack's arm, a habit I picked up from the Wolf clan.

"Yes, siree, that is why they are not invited. If they don't accept you then they reject me too," Jack said. He stood up winked at me and strode to the door.

****

Wolfgang was playing on the floor with Schnitzel when the doorbell rang. I anticipated it would be Eva since she was to accompany me to my gown fitting.

"Come in, darling. I will get my purse then I am ready to go," I called out.

Eva edged the door open as Schnitzel promptly jumped up at her and wagged her tail ferociously. Eva bent over and petted the dachshund on the neck. She noted that Wolfgang was hanging back with his head bent downward. It had been many months since he had seen Eva and he remained shy.

"Wolfgang, come give Auntie Eva a peck," Eva said as she held her arms open for my boy.

Wolfgang paused…but then he threw himself into her arms and cuddled with her.

"Wolfgang, you have certainly grown a half foot it seems," Eva remarked.

31

I crossed the living room and grabbed my coat from the hall tree.

"Wolfgang, Ruthie and Renata are coming to the wedding. Now that you are settled in New York City, Eva, we can all see each other more often," I said.

"What about Ursula?" Wolfgang asked his voice suddenly sullen.

"No, she won't be coming. She is in the hospital," I said in a sharp tone.

Wolfgang's face reddened.

I sighed. I realized that Wolfgang had been on the recipient end of Ursula's violence, but I couldn't help but sympathize with her predicament. She had seen both of her parents killed in such a brutal way at the Dachau concentration camp. There were shocking scenes that must play over and over in her mind—scenes that took control of Ursula's behavior and compelled her to lash out at others.

Jack strode across the room whistling as he so often did. He tried to lighten the mood.

"Eva, you make sure my woman is radiant in her wedding dress. I am counting on you," Jack said. He kissed her affectionately on the cheek.

"She really doesn't need me, does she? Everyone knows Kat has excellent taste," Eva said.

"Remember Jack, it's the final fitting. Eva already was wonderfully helpful when I found my perfect dress," I said.

****

My wedding gown was already displayed in the fitting room— I marveled at the regal nature of my dress as I encircled it. It was white satin with long sleeves and a floor-length skirt that ended in a four-foot train. The sweetheart neckline was encased in illusion and there were covered buttons that met the start of her train. The veil was gently laid on the floor. It was magnificent with its full flowered headband and fingertip netting.

"Eva, it is as beautiful as I remembered it," I said. Awe crept into my voice.

"Of course, it is Kat. Let's get the sales clerk in here to help get you into it," Eva instructed.

A small, pinched woman hustled into the room. She seemed all business as she removed the dress from the hanger and motioned for me to step into it.

I complied and she zipped me up…then she placed the veil on my dark tresses with streaks of ginger.

"Miss, can we have a few minutes before we come out before the mirror for the fitting?" I asked. My voice was thick with cloying sweetness.

The clerk abruptly turned and left the room as Eva and I tried to stifle our laughter.

"Eva, I wanted you to myself for a bit. With all of the hustle and bustle of the wedding, I want to know about you. How have you been?"

Eva stood still looking as beautiful as ever. She appeared to be a high-fashion model with her elevated cheekbones and chiseled chin, the result of the plastic surgery she had endured. The operation disguised her appearance and saved her life. Her new face was her ticket out of Nazi Germany and the clutches of Adolf Hitler.

I noted her blonde loosely curled hair-do was perfectly coiffed and her understated matte makeup made people take notice of her beauty. But I knew the real Eva beneath the façade of glamour. She was still finding her place in the world after years of abuse and uncertainty.

"Kat, after your papa's book signing when that awful man came at me with a pipe. I will admit I was shaken. And of course, it was reported in the New York Times. I am confused. Some people think I am a hero for leaving Adolf and sharing his evil secrets with the American government and military—others right here in New York still act as if the Nazis are in power. I have received nasty letters accusing me of being a *Jew-lover* and threatening to harm me. They know about Ruthie and I am scared

33

for her. It's the reason I am going to have to give up my adoption quest," Eva said.

Emotion clogged her voice and she abruptly stopped speaking as a tear slid down her cheek.

"Oh, Eva, a child was all you ever wanted. Are you sure you must give up Ruthie? There are ways we can help you—after all you are part of our family. I will call Parker and see if he can put a detective tail on you and find out who is causing all of this trouble for you," I said.

"Kat, let's get through the wedding first then we can all meet and discuss what can be done. I am not welcome back in Germany and it seems the same is true in the United States of America," Eva said.

"Eva, you know the Wolfpack will always be here for you along with Marlene and Audrey, right?" I implored.

"Yes, Kat, you have saved my life in more than one way," Eva said. She quickly changed the subject.

"Now let's see how you look in your gown."

I lifted my sumptuous skirt and glided toward the elevated platform where I viewed my mirror image. A magical reflection stared back at me.

The clerk scurried over and started pinning the dress to enhance my shape. I knew I was no longer a young woman especially in the year 1950 when the average bride was twenty-one years old. Yet there were no gray streaks in my tresses and the only lines in my face were laugh lines from many good times with Jack.

I turned toward Eva and thought about the relationship she had with Warren Grant. He was a good man, but he was not ready for marriage. I silently prayed that Eva would find a new mate. Maybe at the wedding? It was a perfect place to meet other single people. I closed my eyes and smiled. Yes, I would be examining the guest list myself. There had to be some friends of Jack's looking for a perfect mature woman—someone like Eva Braun.

The day of Jack's and my wedding was upon us and the whole clan was gathered downstairs at the Inwood Mansion home to Walter Annenberg. The attendees were in the large living area with floor-to-ceiling French doors that led out to a broad expanse of lawn. The sun was shining and the weather was ideal. Guests moved out onto the grounds as they mingled and drank cocktails. Maids served appetizers on gleaming silver trays.

I was in the large third-floor bedroom in my red silk robe as I waited for Billy Love to help me into my wedding gown. I leaned out the window and surveyed the guests. Uncle A.R. and Aunt Beulah Bell were having an animated conversation with Papa, who looked handsome in his tuxedo. Papa kept running his hand through his wispy gray hair. Aunt Elisabetha had her arm around Renata—I could see her affection for my child…a child Elisabetha had first discovered in a bombed-out apartment building in Munich. Leon stood nearby as he stared pensively across the massive lawn perhaps thinking about his time in Nazi Germany as a resistance fighter.

Wolfgang stood off to one side; he was aloof and not really paying attention or interacting with the other children. He badly needed a haircut, but I had not pressed him on this. It was not a priority. He was still acclimating to life in America where everything was strange and up-ended. There was no resemblance to his life in the filthy and crowded concentration camp, his experience living in an abandoned castle, and then his move to Tilly and Papa's house in the leveled to the ground Darmstadt Germany.

Once Wolfgang arrived in New York City the one bright spot was that Papa taught him English every evening. He was able to transition from German to English.

I pulled my gaze away from Wolfgang and focused on other guests. By the carved fountain there were four young men smoking cigars. I knew they were Jack's friends from college. Would one of them be right for Eva who was chasing Ruthie across the lawn? Eva had kicked off her pumps and peals of laughter emitted from their throats. I noted one of the men turned his head and smiled in Eva's and Ruthie's direction at the commotion they made. I made a mental note to ask Jack about him.

Babe and Hans stood closely together by the garden wall, entranced. Their hands were all over each other—highly inappropriate for a mid-day wedding I thought. I noted Uncle A.R. scowled at them as if trying to send a telegraphic message to cease and resist.

Bitsy emerged from the mansion and waved toward Babe and her boyfriend Hans. I could not believe my eyes. The twins were dressed in almost identical floral linen dresses. Of course, I remembered Bitsy was the loud twin. I could hear her every word as she shouted to Babe.

"Sister, it has been too long. Now I want to have some twin time with you today," Bitsy said. She grabbed Babe and swung her around.

I watched Hans as he stared in astonishment at the twins with their impossible white-blonde hair, turquoise eyes and their tiny five-foot two frames.

Bitsy stuck out her hand and introduced herself. Confidence oozed from her.

"I'm Bitsy, the oldest twin and believe it or not Babe and I had no idea what the other would wear today."

I could see Hans was taken aback and I knew what was in his mind. What if he mistook Bitsy for Babe? It wouldn't be the first time the twins were mistaken for each other that was for sure.

Marlene and Audrey were holding court with Walter Annenberg and his soon-to-bride, Lee at his side. I knew Marlene had just wrapped *Stage Fright* which was directed by the irritating and bloated Alfred Hitchcock. And Audrey Hepburn had completed *We Will All Go to Monte Carlo,* a foreign language film. I had a strong feeling that Audrey would hit her prime in the 1950s—she had the presence and beauty to attract audiences world-wide.

"Kat, we are going to be late. Get your head out of the window and let me help you into your wedding dress," Billy Love said as she admonished me.

I giggled and reluctantly withdrew from the window. I turned around and encountered my cousin Billy Love. She looked stunning in her-floor length burgundy crepe gown. Her hair was piled high on her head and held back with a headband made of delicate flowers.

"Too bad Parker had to stay behind with Ursula," I said my eyes dancing.

Billy Love said with authority in her voice. "Kat, I know most of my time lately has been focused on Ursula...I have dressed in anything that comes to the surface of my closet. I am hoping now that Ursula is in treatment that Parker and I can have some dates to rekindle our relationship. But enough with me, today is your day,"

"Yes, I have waited for this moment for a very long time, Billy Love. I could not be where I am today without the support of our family. Thank you from the bottom of my heart," I said.

Billy Love pulled the satin gown from the hanger and hiked it up over my silk stockings delicate panties and lacy brassiere. Then she took a crochet hook and fastened up the myriad of covered buttons.

Slowly she turned me around toward the full-length mirror.

I liked what was reflected back. My dark hair was pulled into a low bun and the netted veil sat securely on my head complimented with the floral headband. I studied my features—I could see my father's dark complexion and the startling blue eyes inherited from my Russian mother, Irina. I wished Irina was here to see my today...I hoped someday to find out more about my mother's family and why they sent her to Germany.

"Kat, pull out of your daydream. They are all waiting for you on the lawn," Billy Love said.

I put my thoughts on hold slipped my feet into satin pumps and pulled the rose-scented bouquet from the water pitcher.

"Come." Billy Love picked up my train and we floated down the stairs to where Papa was waiting with a smug smile on his face. After all he had been persistent in setting Jack and me up on that fateful picnic trip to Frankenstein's Castle.

"My darling Kat, I am blessed to accompany you to meet your groom," Papa said as he held out his arm.

The music from the string quartet was drifting through the door as we made our way through the living room and out on the patio and the broad lawns stretching before us. There was a chuppah adorned with thousands of deep burgundy roses. Even though I didn't actively practice my Jewish faith I still relished the traditions and values embodied in the religion.

A protestant minister and a rabbi were waiting to greet us. I noted Jack's mother, seated by herself looking forlorn. I made a note to myself to introduce her to other members of my friends and family. After all she had stood up to her husband and her sons and supported me.

Jack stood waiting for me smiling and confident in his three-piece dark brown suit. I reached him and Papa kissed me then left to be seated.

Then Jack did something unexpected—he motioned toward someone. I turned to see Wolfgang with his head bowed as he entered the canopy. His shy smile moved me to tears.

"Before we begin the ceremony I would like to make an announcement," Jack said. His voice was thick with emotion.

"Katerina and I are not only in love with each other, but we deeply love our son, Wolfgang. For five years we sought out a visa to bring him to the United States. Unfortunately, the State Department put obstacle after obstacle in place to prevent immigrants from entering our great country. To what end and why the discrimination? We are a nation of immigrants and it is wrong to deny defenseless children entry into the best country in the world."

I held out my hand. Jack could pontificate like no one else. But I instantly recognized the truth in his words. Last week the newspaper blared propaganda.

We can delay and effectively stop...the number of immigrants into the United States...by simply advising our consuls to put every obstacle in the way...and to resort to various administrative devices which would postpone and postpone and postpone the granting of visas.

~Breckinridge Long, State Department

"And so, today is a celebration of Wolfgang's journey to join our family. In the next month we will hold a party back in New York to celebrate and you are all invited," Jack said as I reached down and tousled Wolfgang's long locks.

The guests seemed momentarily astonished but then they stood and vigorously clapped. Jack and I gazed into each other's eyes and returned to the ceremony with Wolfgang centered between us.

After we were pronounced husband and wife Jack let Wolfgang try to break the cloth-covered glass to no avail. The crowd laughed in a good-natured way. Jack finished the deed as he stomped his foot squarely down on the glass.

I smiled to myself and thought about the symbolism of breaking the glass—*the absolute finality of the marital covenant.*

"Mazel Tov!" the guests shouted.

The ceremony was completed and Jack I milled around the grounds greeting our guests. The high-topped tables were piled with smoked salmon, vegetable kabobs, and other finger food items.

Walter Annenberg stood to one side looking dignified and impeccably dressed. His arm was draped around Lee, his soon-to-be wife.

"Mr. Annenberg, we are so grateful to you for offering us your estate for our marriage," I said.

I looked up at the 18-room, thirteen-acre baronial estate that resembled a Scottish Castle. It was located on a long stretch of what was known as *Phillie's Protestant Old Money*. Of course, Mr. Annenberg had deliberately selected the *Inwood Estate* as his abode knowing that he would be the only Jewish owner on the street.

The estate was flush with amenities—from the greenhouse to tennis courts and topped off with a 3-hole golf course. I was eager to explore it with Jack and Wolfgang tomorrow when the guests departed.

Jack and I would spend the night in the large bedroom where I had dressed for the wedding. Tilly and Papa would take the room next to ours and watch over Wolfgang.

"Why, Mrs. Remington Lee and I were delighted to host you and your family today. You have a most unusual and interesting collection of guests who attended the wedding," Walter said as he pointed toward Eva, Marlene, and Audrey.

"Yes, almost everyone here was part of the resistance against Nazi Germany before and during World War II. They are special heroic people. One day when there is more time to spend in conversation I will provide the details," I said.

"You all have our eternal gratitude, Kat. There is still a great deal of Jewish discrimination, even right here in Philadelphia," Lee noted as her voice hardened and her eyes narrowed.

"Here and throughout the world, Kat. My father was a Russian Jew who lived in Kalvishken, a small town by the Baltic Sea. The anti-Semitic Czar Alexander III drove the family out. Fortunately, father somehow made his way to the United States," Walter declared.

"My mother was Russian, but I am not clear why she was sent to Germany," I added.

The vibrant band could be heard tuning for the forthcoming dance.

"Now you two, skedaddle no more talk about politics or war. It is time to celebrate," Lee said.

Jack and I drifted onto the wooden floor ready for our first dance. Out of the corner of my eye I noticed Hans guiding Babe across the lawn toward the distant greenhouse. He possessively clutched her waist and it seemed that he purposely veered toward an unforeseen location.

Everyone else in attendance at the wedding was focused on Jack and me but I was alert and worried about my younger cousin. Somehow their relationship seemed contrived. Aunt Liz was right.

Hans was sly alright—and I strongly believed he was not a good influence on Babe.

"Darling, look at me. Don't I deserve your full attention tonight?" Jack crooned.

I turned my head back toward my new husband

"Of course, my love, I'm sorry. You have all my attention," I said as the instrumental version of *All My Love* filled the air. I felt Jack encompass me in his arms and I relaxed.

Tomorrow though I thought—there would be no escape for Babe. Something was off about Hans Fischer and I was determined to delve into his background. What was his scheme? My intuition was on high alert…and it was almost never wrong.

Chapter 5
Nurse May Phillips

New York City
1950
Billy Love

Cousin Kat's wedding was over and I was back to somewhat of a routine in New York City. It had been six weeks since Parker and I committed Ursula to Bellevue Psychiatric Hospital. Today I would receive a progress report from Nurse Phillips. I was not the praying sort but anything that would make Ursula well, I reckoned I would try. My stoic Oklahoma background had gotten me through many traumatic events, but it wasn't making a dent in my relationship with my troubled daughter.

When Ursula turned to cutting herself to release her pain I wanted to fling her away. Put her in a box. Escape from the sight, smell and memories.

But then the guilt took over. There had to be a way to get through to her and reduce her suffering. I focused my hopes on Nurse Phillips.

Nurse Phillips phoned this morning. She asked me to pack a basket with Ursula's favorite foods. We were going on a picnic— into the real world. I eyed the items laid out before me. There was fried chicken with the dark meat of the leg and the wing that Ursula loved. Mixed berries lined a plastic bowl and there were potato chips and roasted peanuts. I threw cans of root beer into the basket then lovingly placed a chocolate cream pie on top.

"Parker, Nurse Phillips asked me to bring some play clothes for Ursula. Can you dig out the denim overalls for me?" I called out.

"Sure, Love. It will be nice for Ursula to get out of those *prison clothes.*

"Parker, they are not *prison clothes*. You know as well as I that when you have suicide precautions there can be no strings or buckles of any kind allowed that could be used to harm patients."

"I know but it seems so cruel," Parker said as he brought the requested clothing into the kitchen and laid the overalls on the table.

"Nurse Phillips and I will be with her at all times during our outing so just this once she can be a normal child and wear play-clothes. Or at least she can pretend to be normal," I said.

"When can Renata visit Ursula? She has been asking about her for days," Parker remarked. He lightly scratched my back and bent down to kiss my neck.

"Nurse Phillips does not think she is ready to interact with other children yet. She is keeping Ursula isolated most of the time in her cell. When she is escorted to the dining room Ursula has screamed and hissed at the other children. Her behavior frightens them," I said.

"For now, I see her point about keeping Renata away. Ursula needs to become stronger and less reliant on her sister—and Renata should focus on her school work and…just being a child. From the time we first met the girls Renata hasn't had a stretch of time when she hasn't felt the urge to protect and mother Ursula."

"Parker, I saw glimpses of Renata in just the past few weeks where I can visualize her as a healthy well-adjusted young adult."

"Me too, Billy Love."

I was reminded of the depth of my love for Parker. He was truly my life-partner. Always perceptive and intuitive in caring for our children's emotional demands. And my needs too.

I heaved the picnic basket off the table and stuffed Ursula's clothing into a duffel bag—I fidgeted and tapped my foot impatiently. I mustn't be late for my appointment with Nurse Phillips.

But Parker wasn't finished with our conversation. He wanted to talk about our precious girls and I would accommodate him. What would it matter if I was a few minutes late? I took some deep breaths and regained my composure. I sat on the straight-back chair and took Parker's hands in mine willing him to continue.

"Billy Love, I am so impressed with Ursula's nurse. The fact that she took her into her home and planted a garden with her is really something. Ursula is in good hands…I have a lot of faith in Nurse Phillips.

"Me too. I am interested to hear more about the research she is conducting in the lab. She said something about Ursula visiting the lab, too," I said.

"Really?" Parker asked.

"Yes, apparently Ursula has her own set of test tubes and pipettes in the corner of the laboratory. Nurse Phillips received permission from the director of the laboratory. As long as May is directly supervising Ursula she can experiment to her heart's content."

"I never thought Ursula cared a whit about science or experiments," Parker declared.

"Me neither but Nurse Phillips must have discovered some hidden part of Ursula's personality that draws out her investigation skills—maybe she will become the female Sherlock Holmes," I said. I was grinning.

"I believe you might break through some of the barriers in Ursula's mind today, Billy Love. I trust you will be open to whatever the brilliant May Phillips suggests," Parker said. He picked up the heavy picnic basket and hauled it toward the front door.

I trailed behind him. Stay positive. Stay positive. Stay positive. The reel in my head played over and over. I was ready for something—anything that would point to progress for Ursula.

****

I poked my head into the day room. Nurse Phillips was concentrating on Ursula's chart. She flipped impatiently through the pages as if preparing for a major report not just an update for a child's parent. She was intense—I liked that about her. Her no-nonsense yet sympathetic approach was reassuring to me.

45

My voice echoed through the stark room. "Hello, Nurse Phillips."

"Aw, Billy Love, come in. I want to share some news about Ursula before we visit her."

I placed the picnic basket and duffel on the floor and sat close to her so that I could view her chart.

Nurse Phillips peered at me from her eyeglasses perched on the end of her nose.

"Billy Love, tell me about your cousin's wedding," she said.

Hmm, what would she care about the wedding? Was she trying to distract me and psych me out? There was no need for me to speculate. I should just answer her with a simple statement so we could get to Ursula.

"It went very well, thank you. Kat and Jack included Wolfgang in the ceremony. It was very sweet," I remarked.

"Ursula talked about Wolfgang, Billy Love," Nurse Parker responded in a calm voice.

"She did? I can't believe it."

"I think sometimes you don't give Ursula enough credit. We were walking to my house and a neighbor was out exercising his dog which happened to be a dachshund. She stopped abruptly and pointed. Then she said *Wolfgang's Schnitzel* and leaned over and petted the dog."

I put my hand over my mouth and tried not to audibly gasp. I had never heard Ursula talk about Wolfgang. It was if he didn't exist. But now she had acknowledged him and his dog to boot. I felt my heart skip a beat.

"There is more. Ursula has asked to go with me to my house—actually she starts out every morning now wondering when we can go there again. She has gone from a trembling bundle of nerves to glimpses of the little girl she could become."

I was silent. There was a huge lump in my throat. Nurse Phillips handed me a Kleenex.

"Now, Billy Love these are baby steps. She does not know you are coming with us today. Give her a lot of space, don't try to hug her unless she approaches you and let me control the situation. Are you comfortable with those instructions?"

"But she didn't know I was coming?"

"Sometimes surprise is a good thing. She will still have resentment toward you since you involuntarily hospitalized her. But on the other hand, she desperately wants you to love her. Ursula still has a lot of confusion and conflict. Let's just see how the story unfolds today. Give me her clothes. I will dress her and then bring you in after I have informed her of your presence—you can tell her about the picnic and the special treats you brought her," Nurse Phillips said in a matter-of-fact manner.

Nodding my head, I gave Ursula's nurse tacit permission to proceed with her plans.

Without another word Nurse Phillips snatched the duffel and marched toward Ursula's room.

I put my head back and closed my eyes forever grateful for the guidance and skill of nurses like May Phillips. I may even have said a little prayer.

****

Nurse Phillips was smiling when she returned to the day room less than thirty minutes later.

"Come, Billy Love. Ursula is waiting for you," she said.

I arose and timidly followed Nurse Phillips' rustling starched skirt down the hall.

Ursula was standing in her spartan cell with her back to me as she stared out of the barred window. Her hair was neatly braided into two long plaits that hung down almost to her waist. Her familiar denim overalls landed above her ankles an indication she had grown in the month since I had seen her. I wanted to run and sweep her into my arms, but Nurse Phillips had been emphatic. Caution was in order.

"Ursula, your mother is here."

I took a step forward and waited for my child's reaction. I noted the bouquet of red roses and purple dahlias arranged in a vase on her nightstand. The aromatic smell wafted through the air. Ursula turned slowly and narrowed her eyes at me. For an instance I was scared she would reject me but then she gave me a slight grin and I relaxed.

She pointed to the flowers and said in a breathy voice. "Nurse Phillips and I picked them. They are from my own corner of the garden. So pretty don't you think?"

"Oh, yes, darling they are beautiful," I breathed.

I started to relax. Optimism radiated through me.

Nurse Phillips left us alone while she went to change into civilian clothes.

Ursula perched on the bed…her spine was rigid. I sat down a few feet from her and remained silent giving Ursula time to collect her thoughts.

She murmured something that was unintelligible.

"Ursula, I need for you to repeat yourself. I couldn't understand you."

Ursula scowled but then she said in a clear enunciated voice, "Renata."

I froze but then chastised myself…I was the adult here and this was my child. I needed to answer her.

I moved my hand inches away from Ursula and waited for her reaction. Her face was expressionless. I cleared my throat and chose my words carefully.

"Ursula, Renata loves you so much. Nurse Phillips thought it best for her to wait a few more weeks before visiting. But I have a gift from Renata especially for you," I said.

"A gift? For Me?" Ursula's eyes were brimming with unshed tears. I reached into my pocketbook and pulled out the velvet satchel. I dropped it into Ursula's lap.

Ursula fingered the midnight blue bag and then cautiously opened it and poured the necklace into the palm of her hand. She held it up and studied the shape of the charm dangling from the chain. It was the gold horse charm I had given Renata the night we attended *Oklahoma!*

Ursula clutched the necklace to her chest and rocked back and forth.

I watched her reaction unsure if I had done the right thing.

"Please, can I wear it?" Ursula whispered.

"Yes, darling every time we have an outing with Nurse Phillips I will bring it and you can wear it. When I go home Renata will wear it and it will be something special just the two of you will share."

I held up the gold chain and clasped it around Ursula's neck. I understood that Ursula could not keep it in her room at Bellevue—it was too dangerous for her and the other children if Ursula chose to use the sharp edges of the charm as a weapon.

Ursula fingered the charm examining every inch of it. Then she reached over and momentarily placed her hand over mine. The brimming tears had overflowed onto her cheeks and were dripping off her chin. I handed her a handkerchief but knew I could not embrace her—she was not ready. But that was okay.

My mind swirled with a myriad of thoughts. I had witnessed a breakthrough with Ursula, and I owed it all to Nurse Phillips and Bellevue Hospital. I was ecstatic and could not wait to inform Parker and Renata of her progress.

I understood that Nurse Phillips had left us alone to see if we could rekindle our relationship. How did she know what Ursula needed? She simply did—her years of experience and her commitment to troubled children made her expertise something to behold. I would be eternally grateful to her. Our family had suffered for years and she was turning Ursula around…into a child of possibilities.

Ursula and I both turned toward the hallway where we could hear Nurse Phillips addressing someone.

"Dr. Bender, I am taking Ursula out of the hospital today to get some fresh air. Her mother is here and she will be accompanying us."

"I would like to speak to her mother about a treatment I have planned for Ursula," the doctor replied.

I was alarmed at the tone of Dr. Bender's voice. It was clear that she was determined to impose her will upon my child. And she was putting Nurse Phillips in the middle.

I closed Ursula's door and strode confidently into the dingy hallway.

Dr. Bender held Ursula's chart and was flipping through it. Nurse Phillips was glaring at the doctor—who touted herself as the premiere children's neuropsychiatrist.

"I am Billy Love O'Rourke, Ursula's mother," I said in a firm voice.

"Oh, yes, Mrs. O'Rourke I have diagnosed your daughter with schizophrenia and have scheduled her for several treatments of ECT which stands for Electro-Convulsive Treatment," she said. She did not bother to look at me and assumed I would acquiesce.

I observed the woman. She was mannish, with a broad nose and wide forehead.

"Let's get something straight DOCTOR, there will be no ECT for my daughter. It is barbaric and I have been warned about the horrible aftermath of such treatment. I will discharge her immediately if there is any indication that such a procedure would be carried out!"

Nurse Phillips tapped her foot and gave me a smug smile.

"Furthermore, Nurse Phillips has made tremendous strides in helping Ursula. I am requesting that she approve all of the psychiatrist sessions with Ursula," I said.

"Now, Mrs. O'Rourke nurses do not approve treatment, they are to follow the doctor's orders," Dr. Bender said peevishly as she pulled the chart to her chest.

"By far this nurse has had the most positive influence on Ursula's behavior. If you do not follow my wishes I will take her home immediately and employ Nurse Phillips in a private duty capacity," I was yelling now. My voice ricocheted off the hallway walls.

Dr. Bender took a step back as I took a step forward until I was but inches from her. I could see the cowardice in her beady eyes. I yanked the chart away from her and slammed it shut.

"I want a note on this chart. This are to be no ECT treatments or experimental drug treatments unless Nurse Phillips and I have approved them, do you understand?" I was shaking with anger now.

"Alright, I understand, but I will consult with the chief medical officer at Bellevue," she said not wanting to completely give up the fight.

"You do that and have him call me tonight. If you will excuse us, Nurse Phillips, Ursula and I have a date and we are already late due to your meddling," I said lowering my voice but still conveying my distaste for the doctor.

Dr. Bender scurried down the hall.

"Shall we get out of here?" I declared.

"Yes, indeed. I feel a renewed commitment to our dear Ursula and first up is a picnic fit for a princess," Nurse Phillips said.

We flung open the door to Ursula's room. Nurse Phillips oohed and awed over the horse charm necklace nestled in the hollow of Ursula's neck. Then we were on our way out of the crazy joint.

****

We exited Bellevue with Ursula situated between us. Black clouds roiled the sky and pregnant drops of rain started splattering on the sidewalk. Nurse Phillips opened her gigantic black umbrella and the three of us pressed together as we hung onto the handle. I felt Ursula create space between us as she wedged her pointy elbow into my side.

I clutched the groaning picnic basket and cursed the weather. Why did it have to rain on the one day that was supposed to be a glorious reuniting of mother and daughter?

I gave myself a reality check. Who was I kidding? Ursula was still a shell and although I had seen glimpses of a hidden personality I knew that there was still much work to be done.

Ursula made little mewing sounds as the slanted rain stung her face. Undaunted and determined Nurse Phillips marched with purpose.

"We are going to have a picnic in my living room, Ursula," she announced with aplomb.

Ursula looked up at the nurse. "But picnics are outside, Nurse," she declared. She strained her neck to tilt her face toward the sound of Nurse Phillips' authoritative voice.

"Why picnics can happy anywhere...anywhere at all," she replied. "Come, quickly, it is almost time."

"Time for what, Nurse?" Ursula asked with curiosity in her voice.

Nurse Phillips ignored us and pulled a golden key out of her pocket. She inserted it into the front door of the brick bungalow and pushed inside.

Ursula shook herself like a wet dog and looked around.

"Why, I have been here with you before, right Nurse Phillips? You gave me a lemonade and then we went into the garden."

Ursula ran to the window and surveyed the magnificent blooming garden. Her face was awash with wonder.

"Look, there is my own patch of earth!" Ursula shouted and pointed. I joined her at the window and was careful to keep my emotions in check. I didn't want to break the spell.

Nurse Phillips was busy pushing the couch and chairs against the wall to create a space for the indoor picnic. The checkered blanket floated to the floor and the nurse plopped herself beside the basket and pulled out its contents.

"Oh, Ursula, look what we have here, crispy fried chicken and it's the dark meat just like you wanted."

I observed Ursula as she reacted to Nurse Phillips' voice. There was a strong connection with her, a bond I had never experienced. I was grateful beyond words—I just hoped that at some point in the future it would be possible for me to forge a similar relationship with my daughter.

Ursula ran across the room and lowered herself to a sitting position just inches from Nurse Phillips. She pulled apart the succulent chicken wings and sucked them into her mouth. I had never seen her eat so fast or so much. She downed the chicken with sweet tea and then sat back and licked her fingers. She sighed with contentment and leaned against the nurse's chest as she pulled the napkin out of her overalls. She fingered her horse charm.

In a quiet voice she turned to me. "Renata come next time?"

"I think so darling, but it is Nurse Phillips' call."

Ursula stared intently back and forth from my face to her caretaker.

"If you keep making progress we will make sure Renata comes to the next picnic. And maybe we can have it outside," Nurse Phillips said.

"Oh, Miss May thank you! I miss my sister so," Ursula said clapping her hands.

I repacked the basket and got ready to depart.

"Before we go, Ursula I have a surprise for you," the nurse announced.

She stood up and went to a leaded glass bookcase. She withdrew two books and returned to her seat on the blanket.

"These are yours Ursula. We will take them back to Bellevue and read from them every day."

I was curious.

Nurse Phillips laid the books side by side.

Alice in Wonderland by Lewis Carroll English Version

Alice in Wunderland by Lewis Carrol German Ausführung

Of course, I had read these silly books as a child but how could they help Ursula? I raised my eyebrows at the nurse. She caught my eye but ignored me. I would just have to wait and discover how she would proceed.

Ursula picked up each book and studied the drawings on their covers.

"Ursula, it is important that you are a proud German and you can read and write the language. But now that you live in the United States English is just as important. So there are two books. There are lessons to be learned from Alice and her adventures. Shall we start today?" Nurse Phillips asked.

"Yes, Miss May." Ursula nodded and eagerly handed the book back to the nurse.

Nurse Phillips began in a sing-song voice.

Alice was feeling sleepy when suddenly a White Rabbit with pink eyes ran close to her. There was nothing so very remarkable in that; nor did Alice think it so very much out of the way to hear the Rabbit say to itself, "Oh dear! Oh dear! I shall be late!" But when the Rabbit actually took a watch out of its waistcoat-pocket, and looked at it, and then hurried on, Alice started to her feet, for it flashed across her mind that she had never before seen a rabbit with either a waist-coat, or a watch to take out of it, and burning with curiosity, she ran across the field after it, and fortunately was just in time to see it pop down a large rabbit-hole under the hedge. In another moment down went Alice after it, never once considering how in the world she was to get out again.

The nurse snapped the book shut and looked expectantly at Ursula over her glasses. Ursula's eyes were wide and luminous. She was already in another world. There was something in her facial expression I had never seen before.

Ursula grabbed the book and clutched it to her chest.

"Thank you, Nurse Phillips. Danke, Krankenschwester Phillips," Ursula repeated dutifully in English and in German.

Nurse Phillips pulled Ursula to her and kissed her forehead.

I was jealous. Would I ever have a relationship with Ursula that even begins to echo what she has with her caretaker?

"My little bear, Ursula you think about this story of Alice and the Rabbit. We will talk about its meaning later," Nurse Phillips said.

Silence hung in the air...it was a good silence. Something important had transpired in the moment when the spine of the book was cracked.

I was encouraged. I anticipated progress with my Ursula. It had been a very good day, rain included.

I looked out the window at the garden. The flowers glistened and a gentle breeze ruffled the dewy petals. I could not wait to relay the whole story to Parker. Nurse Phillips, god-send.

****

"Parker, I am exhausted, but my visit could not have gone better if I had planned every detail myself. At last I think we have found some effective treatment for Ursula," I said.

Parker handed me a martini with double olives and I stretched out on the chaise lounge and tried to relax.

"Bellevue is the place for Ursula and Nurse Phillips is the key to her mental health," I noted. The vermouth slid down my throat. I tasted its bitterness and coughed a little.

I continued. "However, there are some awful experiments being championed by a Doctor Bender at the hospital. I had to put a note on Ursula's chart declaring her exempt from treatments, especially ECT."

"ECT?" Parker asked. He was alert—He leaned forward and clasped his hands together. Then he looked at me expectantly.

I cleared my throat as I prepared to tell Jack about a young boy who was hospitalized at Bellevue. His mother had been sitting in the waiting area with me. I started the story.

"There was a mother of a six-year-old boy who had been diagnosed with schizophrenia and Dr. Bender convinced her that *Electroconvulsive Therapy* was needed to straighten out his brain and tamp down his hallucinations. She told me that she reluctantly agreed to the procedure since nothing else had been effective for her young lad," I explained.

Parker was silent.

"Parker, she looked like an elderly woman even though she could not have been over thirty. She was slumped over and she put her hands over her face. I waited with trepidation—it seemed like hours before she spoke again. She said she insisted that she remain in the room with her child. It was unusual for parents to observe such a procedure. But I guess Dr. Bender reluctantly agreed to let Mrs. Miller stay.

I observed Parker. He swallowed and gazed at me intently.

"Go on, Billy Love."

"According to Mrs. Miller, the treatment was akin to Frankenstein's experiments where the scientist ran a current through the brain to jump-start activity. A horror to behold. They dragged little Jimmy into the room—he was kicking and screaming because this was his third treatment and he knew what was about to happen. They placed a straight-jacket on him to restrain him. He twisted his head from side to side as they applied the gel and electrodes on either side of his temples. They forced a rubber bit into his mouth so that he would not sever his tongue."

"Oh my God, what did Mrs. Miller do?"

"She ran to her son and tried to remove him from the table, but two thugs pulled her back and put her in the corner of the room. She watched with hysteria as they set the voltage machine on high. Then with no anesthesia they shocked her son until he screamed and convulsed."

"Billy Love, that is barbaric. Is this what we have come to in 1950? The era of modern medicine, phooey. Clearly ECT is torture of the worst kind and to use it on innocent children," Parker said as his voice trailed off. He stood and paced back and forth across the room.

I continued in a flat voice. "Mrs. Miller fainted as her son convulsed. When she regained consciousness, her son was lying listlessly on his side with his eyes unfocused. She gathered him into her arms and carried him out of the room.

I drained my martini and held the glass out to Parker. I needed a refill.

"Dr. Benson tried to tell me Ursula is schizophrenic. But Nurse Phillips knows better—she clearly believes the trauma of seeing her parents killed induced her behavioral changes. Ursula does not have delusions or hallucinations…she has memories that emerge again and again to create chaos in her life. And those memories derail her ability to form meaningful relationships with other people."

"Ursula is bonding with the nurse?" Parker asked.

"Clearly."

I described our outing to Nurse Phillip's house…recounting the joyful expression on Ursula's face as she gobbled my fried chicken and pointed out her little garden patch to me.

"Truthfully Parker, I can't remember the last time I saw our *little bear* smile."

"Me neither. It is a relief for sure."

"What's in the package?" Parker asked.

"Something for Renata. I picked it up on the way home."

At the mention of her name Renata sauntered into the living room, snacking on popcorn and apples.

Parker and I looked at her expectantly. She was twelve now— and adolescence was just around the corner. She had grown three inches in the last year and could look me in the eye. Her breasts were budding and her waist had narrowed. She flipped her shiny dark-brown hair over her shoulder and smiled at us. Was she wearing lip gloss? I was aware she had been making stealth visits to my make-up table.

"Renata, Ursula and I had a very good visit today. She loved wearing your horse charm necklace and she asked about you. Nurse Phillips said if she keeps making progress you can come with me the next visit," I explained.

I held out the package to Renata.

"This is for you. Ursula has the same book."

Renata removed *Alice in Wonderland* from the paper wrapping and stared down at it.

"But this is for children. What do I need with this silly tale?"

"Ah, Renata, but it is not only for children. I want you to read the first chapter and write a response to it. There is not a right or wrong answer. Just record what you felt when you read it. React to it," I said.

Parker had moved to Renata's side and stared down at the White Rabbit and Mad Hatter illustrations. He arched his eyebrows at me.

"You have to trust the process," I said. "You will see. The meaning will emerge."

Chapter 6
The Trunk

*Three things cannot long stay hidden:
the sun, the moon, and the truth.*
~ Buddha

*New York City
1950
Katerina*

"Jack, I got a letter from Papa. It is very curious. Let me read it to you."

"In a minute, Kat," Jack called out.

It had been a month since our beautiful wedding at the Annenberg Estate in Pennsylvania. I daydreamed about our perfect day. Most of the important people in our lives were there to celebrate with us—Billy Love, Babe and Bitsy Love, Papa, Uncle A.R. and Aunt Beulah, Aunt Elisabetha and Leon. Our great friends Eva Braun, Marlene Dietrich and Audrey Hepburn added to our joy. And of course, the children, our precious children completed us: Renata, Wolfgang and Ruthie.

I was sad that Ursula was hospitalized in New York and Parker was compelled to stay behind to care for her. But I understood that Ursula was desperately ill and extreme measures were necessary to help her. I knew Billy Love and Parker were grateful for the expertise of an older nurse and I hoped to meet her one day.

My thoughts turned to my German child. Jack and I had an appointment with the lawyer in mid-town who would finalize Wolfgang's adoption. The arduous process had taken five years due to all of the State Department delays. But we would sign the papers today which made it official…Jack and I would become Wolfgang's legal parents.

There had been an investigation into Wolfgang's possible biological father. At Dachau Concentration Camp Samuel had indicated that Prince Phillipp Von Hessen was identified as his father—however, the prince denied any relation to the child and in the end his parental rights were terminated which allowed Jack and me to formally adopt him.

It was ironic that I knew little of the roots of my own mother and maternal grandparents. The connections were lost when my mother arrived in Darmstadt, Germany. My papa discovered her working on the assembly line at the Merck Pharmaceutical Company and within months they were married. Papa claimed Mama refused to discuss her history—and he was so in love with her that he never pressed her. Then she died giving me birth to me and it seemed that chapter of my life was closed forever. I had accepted Papa's reticence about Mama's secrecy, but today's letter changed everything.

I examined my face in the bathroom mirror. The only feature that identified me as Russian were my brilliant blue eyes. All of my other attributes reflected Papa's side of the family: the olive skin, the full lips, the dark, curly hair.

Wanting to look my best for the adoption hearing, I captured my curls away from my face in a red satin ribbon and stroked my lashes with a black shiny mascara. I looked in the full-length mirror. The crisp white blouse and the red circle skirt accented with the black rick-rack trim made me look youthful. I slipped my feet into patent leather flats and selected an alligator purse.

Then I picked up the hand-written letter lying on my dressing table and read the address again.

Mrs. Jack Remington
16 Harkin Street
Apartment 6B
New York City, New York

I was sorry to relinquish my maiden name, Katerina Wolf. *Wolf*—I liked the sound of it. With my marriage to Jack I had lost part of my identity. I would make sure Wolfgang knew about my background and the meaning it held for me. He also needed to know about my cabaret days, my recordings and my relationship with Marlene Dietrich when we entertained the American troops.

Part of me was conflicted though. Wolfgang's childhood was clouded by Nazi Germany—his formative years were spent in the Dachau Concentration Camp which was a horrifying experience. Was it therapeutic for him to relive his early childhood or should I push back and shroud his past in secrecy? Wolfgang himself never mentioned his time in the camp so maybe that was his way of coping. Or was there something else he was hiding? Now was not the time to be obsessing over Wolfgang's past.

I cradled the letter from Papa and entered the kitchen. Jack stood at the counter with his back to me. He held a whisk and he deftly swirled the eggs and milk into a mixture. I admired his muscled back and broad shoulders. He had on a frilly apron to protect his worsted wool pin-stripe suit which looked ridiculous. Smiling I snuck up behind him encircling his waist and kissed his neck. He turned around and responded to my romantic gesture, then pulled away.

His eyes bored into mine with serious reflection.

"Kat, I am impatient to hear what your papa has to say. Come on, don't keep me waiting."

"Okay, okay."

I led him to the Formica kitchen table and we both sat down. I smoothed out the letter cleared my throat and began.

My Darling Katerina,

Last week I received a call from a former neighbor of ours, Heinrich Müller. He is a city inspector hired by the city of Darmstadt to forage in the rubble and ashes of our citizen's homes. As you are aware your childhood home, along with thousands of others was relentlessly bombed by the British Airforce during the war. Most of the wooden homes caught fire and burned to the ground. I saw the destruction with my own eyes. There was nothing left. When I moved in with Tilly I put that part of my life out of my mind.

Henrich was charged with notifying former owners that their land would be cleared so that rebuilding could occur. I will receive some meager compensation for the property.

But here is the curious thing. Heinrich discovered the stairwell to the basement was partially intact so he made his way into the cellar to look around. In the corner shielded by a concrete barrier, he discovered a small metal chest. It was locked.

I knew instantly that it was your mother's. Forgive me, for I had forgotten about it. When I left Germany with Eva and arrived at my brother's ranch in Oklahoma, I tried to make a new life and put the old one behind me.

Your mama never told me what was contained in the trunk and I respected her privacy. I am not sure Irina herself was aware of the contents—no key accompanied it and your mama seemed uninterested.

It was 1912 and your mother died giving you the gift of life. I was inconsolable at the time. But now I have the wisdom and clarity to realize the importance of history. I am deeding you the trunk with all of its contents and clues about your rightful heritage.

I am sending it to you unopened. You will probably need to get a locksmith to unfasten the lock. And whatever you find may it give you peace and answers.

Your ever-loving,
Papa

I folded the letter and got to my feet...my legs were wobbly.

"After all of these years, Jack. What is the likelihood that I might reconnect with my mother and grandparents?"

Jack poured me a steaming cup of coffee and pulled the letter from my hands. He slowly reread it and returned it to the envelope.

"Kat, 1911 and 1912 was a time of great unrest in Russia. I wonder if your grandparents sent Irina to Germany because the family was in danger. The Bolsheviks were wreaking havoc everywhere, especially in the rural areas where the country estates were located."

I had done some reading about the communists.

"It is true by 1917 the Bolsheviks had taken over the country. Lenin ruled with an iron hand and many people were sent to the gulags, even children. My mama was only seventeen at the time—were her parents protecting her by sending her out of Russia?"

Jack smiled wanly as he attempted to lighten the mood. "Kat, let's not speculate on what we will find. Let's wait for the trunk to arrive—we can examine it contents together to help piece together your past life. It is an interesting family combination you have my little Katerina. *German Jew* and the possibility of *Russian Aristocracy*…both groups persecuted and discriminated against by others eager to gain control."

I was solemn. Jack made an important point. Why do humans prey on other humans? To what end? Power, enrichment, or something else? There had to be answers.

A crusade is, simply put, something that's bigger
than you are. It's a "cause" with an impact that
reaches beyond your personal wants and needs.
~ Arthur L. Williams, Jr.

****

There was a loud knock on the apartment door. I was startled as I was not expecting visitors. Wolfgang was at school and Jack was at lunch with a Harold Hanover. Mr. Hanover was overseeing the creation of city council districts—and Jack was interested in running for election in the Manhattan borough. It was ironic that if Jack was elected he would promote policies in direct opposition to those proposed in the state legislature by his nasty brother.

"Coming, give me a sec," I yelled.

I clicked off the modern turntable which was playing my latest album *Katerina's Love Songs* and padded to the door.

"Who is it?"

"Mrs. Remington, package for you."

Cautiously I cracked open the door and found a uniformed postal worker holding a cardboard box.

"Come in and put the box on the dining room table," I instructed.

The postman hoisted the box onto the table and handed a clipboard to me.

"Sign here," he instructed.

My heart was pounding as I signed the document and hurriedly escorted him from the apartment.

I secured the locks on the front door then stood still and stared across the room at the package holding court on the polished table. I knew what it was…Papa's return address was stamped in bold letters.

Should I wait for Jack to come home before I discovered it contents?

The suspense was too much. I had been waiting my whole life to make connections with my Russian family. Jack would find out soon enough and I had no will power. Ha!

I rummaged in the kitchen for a box knife then I carried the tool back to the box and sliced open the packing tape.

The cardboard fell away revealing a dust-covered metal trunk measuring two feet by four feet. Just as Papa indicated it was locked up tightly without a key provided that could open it. I needed to call the old locksmith Mr. Smith who lived a few blocks from us. He made house calls.

As I waited for the locksmith I picked up the trunk. It probably weighed twenty pounds which included the hinged trunk itself. Patience was not a virtue of mine—I paced the apartment and circled the trunk over and over imagining its contents.

Finally, the old locksmith sidled into the apartment. His large circle of master keys clanked as he stiffly walked. I escorted him to the awaiting trunk where he methodically inserted each of his keys into the odd-shaped keyhole.

After thirty minutes he stepped back and stroked his white handle-bar mustache.

"Mrs. Remington, none of my keys will open your trunk. I suggest we jimmy it open with a crowbar."

I was short with the man. "Whatever you need to do."

He opened a black bag pulled out the crowbar and inserted it in the crack of the trunk. After a swift movement the lid of the trunk creaked open.

I hurriedly pressed money into the locksmith's leathery hand and showed him the door. I wanted my treasure all to myself.

The metal chest beckoned to me and I was momentarily mesmerized anticipating its contents. A musty smell wafted from the container—I peered in and discovered disintegrating muslin which separated several items.

Be cautious, Kat I admonished myself. Do not disturb or harm anything.

I grabbed a flashlight then went to the bathroom medicine cabinet and pulled out tweezers. I gathered a crisp white sheet from the closet and laid it next to the trunk.

Taking a deep breathe I began my examination of the cargo.

I lifted the first layer of muslin and found a faded birth certificate. I carefully pinched the tweezers and lifted it onto the white sheet. It read:

Irina Maria
Born July 1, 1893

Parents: Aleksandra and Dmitri
Record of St. Stephen Russian Orthodox Church
Perm, Russia

I stepped back and stared. There recorded in black ink were the names of my Russian grandparents and the location of my mother's birth. I clapped my hand to my mouth as I processed the information. Then I wrinkled my brow in puzzlement. Why was the surname omitted? It seemed highly suspicious that a birth certificate would lack such vital statistics.

At least I had documentation of the city of Mama's birth. After Papa wrote me the letter revealing the existence of my mother's trunk, I studied maps of Russia in the late 1880s. I had imagined Mama was born in Moscow or St. Petersburg the so-called glamour cities of the Russians. However, I also studied the eastern territories of Russia and was aware of the existence of Perm known as the gateway to Siberia. Papa had mentioned Mama's family was connected to Perm and that Mama had lived there as a child.

So, Mama not only lived in Perm as a child she was born there 900 miles from Moscow in a city found deep in the Ural Mountains. The knowledge was a surprise. I could not picture her life in an industrial city where most workers mined minerals, oil and timber. But I also understood Perm to be an interesting city filled with culture and the arts. It was somewhat of a paradox.

I shook my head and reached for the next layer of deteriorating muslin. Underneath was a letter written in Russian. It was from my grandmother Aleksandra addressed to my mother. Papa had made sure that I had a grasp on the Russian language so I was able to interpret the contents of the letter.

My Darling Irina,

Know that your papa and I had no choice but to send you to Germany. It was too dangerous for you to stay in Perm or even in the country for that matter. There is much unrest and upheaval here.

We know that you can have a life without scrutiny and fear of retaliation. Germany is a welcoming country and many of our relatives reside there. For now, however, it is my wish that you become anonymous. We have secured a factory job for you at the Merck Pharmaceutical company and you will live with Miss Hinders who runs a boarding house for single women.

*Your sisters Olga and Viktoria, along with your brother Maxim are too young to travel...we must keep them with us for now. Someday we might be able to shepherd them to Germany so that you can keep them safe. The Bolsheviks are causing havoc, burning down country estates and looting properties. They are determined to destroy **Imperial Russia.***

Papa and I are needed here. We are a source of strength and inspiration for our extended family. We are chafing against the masses as they plot to control the running of industry and society. Lenin and his great socialism experiment are ruining the great Russian culture we have come to know and believe in.

We trust you will make us proud.

We lovingly let you go.

Mama

With a thud I sat down on the wooden chair and re-read the letter. Everything I had known about my mama was turned upside down. I had two younger aunts? A young uncle? What had become of them? Why was my grandmother emphasizing **Imperial Russia**? There were still so many unanswered questions. Would I discover solutions from the remaining items in the trunk?

I took a break went to the decanter on the side table and sloshed liquid into a glass. I threw my head back and gulped two shots of straight whiskey down my throat. It burned but I was numb. I knew

I couldn't continue without Jack by my side. I shakily picked up the phone and telephoned Mr. Hanover's office.

I shouted. "Jack, I need you." My voice broke as I struggled to convey my thoughts.

"Hold on, Kat, I will be there as soon as I can," Jack said.

I dropped the phone and it skidded across the room. I didn't have the strength to further explore the contents of the trunk. For I had seen something gleaming in the deep recesses of the trunk and whatever it was, I needed my husband to support me.

****

The whiskey had made me woozy and I knew I needed to sober up. I managed to fix myself a cup of tea with lemon as I awaited Jack's return. I sank into the chaise lounge and pulled a blanket up to my chin. This was what I had been waiting for but was I really prepared to finally discover my Russian heritage? It all seemed surreal.

My hands shook and the teacup rattled in its saucer as I reached for the hot liquid. My mind wandered. As I approached forty I thought I knew most of what there was to know about life. But, of course I was wrong. New discoveries could twist our lives in directions in which we never could have dreamed.

Questions filled my mind. What if Eva Braun had stayed with Adolf Hitler? What if cousin Billy Love as a young woman had never stepped foot in Germany? What if Aunt Elisabetha had never discovered Ursula and Renata in bombed out Munich? What if Papa failed to play cupid with Jack and me? What if Jack and I skipped the exploration of Frankenstein's Castle and Wolfgang had never been found?

What if Mama's trunk had never been discovered?

I came out of my fog and threw off the blanket. With renewed resolve I walked to the table and place my hands on either side of Mama's container which held her treasures.

The door clicked open and Jack entered the living room, removing his hat and coat and hanging his items on the hall tree. Relief washed over me.

He came to me and encircled my waist.

He peered over my shoulder. "Kat, I am here for you. I love you—we will get through this. Now, let's see what else is in the trunk."

I relaxed a bit and leaned into him as together we examined the interior. I could visualize an object beneath the next layer of muslin which separated its contents. It appeared to be approximately 18 by 22 centimeters in size.

With trepidation I carefully removed the cloth. I gasped. Staring up at me was an oil portrait of a young girl. Her strawberry blonde wavy hair was pulled back from her face and secured with a magnificent tiara consisting of diamonds and pearls. She had brilliant wide-spaced blue eyes and a shapely pointed nose. She posed with a demure smile that beckoned the viewer. Clasped around her swan-like neck was a simple string of pearls and on her ears were drop-like matching pearls.

"Kat, I believe this is a painting of your mother. Turn it over—let's see if there is an inscription."

"Jack, it says *Irina age 16, Perm Russia.*"

I lifted the picture and placed it on the pristine white linen sheet. Beside the portrait laid my mother's birth certificate and the letter from my grandmother. I surveyed all three items and watched Jack's expression…I tried to gauge his opinion.

"Kat, you understand that your mother in that painting—The tiara indicates that she was part of a royal family and your grandmother's letter confirms that you descended from Imperial Russia."

I was quiet as I absorbed the impact of my treasures. What else would we find?

"There are couple of more items in the bottom of the chest. Do you think you can continue or do you need to take a break?"

"Jack, I have waited long enough for knowledge of my mother's side of the family. Let's see what other treasures…" my voice trailed off as Jack lifted out a 12-centimeter-tall lacquered doll painted head-to-toe in a brilliant red.

"Papa told me about these dolls. He gave me an inexpensive set when I was six."

"Dolls?"

"Yes, they are called stacking dolls or nested dolls. Look, you take them apart and they get smaller and smaller until you reach the last tiny figure. Inside there might be a treat."

"These dolls look to be hand-painted," Jack said. He turned the largest doll over and studied her features."

"Jack, this is called a *Matryoshka* doll which is a symbol for the Russian *babushka*—the matriarch of the family."

"Can we take them apart? I am curious as to what we will find."

"It might be empty, but there is always anticipation when each doll is taken apart." I said. I carefully took the doll and used my fingernail to gently pry her apart at her mid-section. I continued to open eight dolls with each one progressively smaller than the last one.

I held up the final figurine and gingerly shook it.

"Jack, there is something in it. Do you want to guess what it contains?"

"I have no clue. Open it, Kat the anticipation is killing me."

I eased the doll open and gently removed the lid.

"Oh, my goodness!" I cried out as I almost dropped the doll with its encased treasure onto the floor. I steadied my hand and rescued the tiny figurine.

I looked down. Nestled in the doll was a diamond ring…but not any diamond ring. It was a multi-carat brilliantly cut stone. The sterling silver mounting lifted the diamond on a pedestal where it threw off light in a million different directions. Pave diamonds were embedded on each side of the large diamond which added to the ring's opulence.

I slipped the ring on my finger and watched the light dance off the diamonds. It was a masterpiece. I knew instantly that the ring represented a piece of the puzzle related to my heritage.

70

Jack jaw dropped. He could not stop staring. "Kat, it is magnificent."

"Yes, it is," I replied. I stacked the eight dolls in descending order of size next to each other on the linen. I slipped the huge diamond from my finger and placed it in its original container... doll number eight.

I stepped forward and gripped the table with both hands. The ring was treasure enough. What else could there be in the mysterious trunk?

Jack angled the flashlight into the rusty trunk and gently explored its bottom.

"Kat, there are two more items."

There was more? My eyes were welling now. It was a lot to take in after a lifetime of secrets locked away in an obscure metal trunk.

Jack wiped my tears. "Kat, darling look at me. Whatever we discover consider the findings a treasure, a connection to your soul. Your grandparents wanted Irina to keep her heritage alive. I think Aleksandra and Dmitri understood that your Russian family was in grave danger. They needed Irina to smuggle the valuables to a safe place—that place was Darmstadt Germany," Jack surmised. He grasped both of my hands and held my gaze.

"Jack, do you think Irina, I mean Mama knew what her parents had placed in this beat-up looking trunk?"

"I'm not sure. But I would guess that they didn't want to burden your mother with that knowledge on her trip west... it would have placed her in a position of always looking over her shoulder at the authorities and hoping they would not search her trunk."

"Come, let's unwrap the last two items." Jack said as he withdrew a black velvet bag riddled with moth holes.

He wrapped both of his hands around the heavy item and loosened the draw-string.

I couldn't breath—I knew immediately what it was—one of the *Imperial Faberge' Easter Eggs*. It stood ten centimeters in length with its shell a gleaming pink color. It was intricately decorated with gold leaf which crisscrossed the egg in a harlequin pattern. Diamonds were encrusted along the harlequin repeat of the markings. Even after being tucked away in darkness for almost forty years the sparkle of the egg's diamonds ricocheted off the dining room walls.

"Let me see it, Jack." I reverently took it from him and studied it intently turning it round and round trying to absorb its beauty.

"Papa read me a book about the Faberge′ eggs. They were commissioned for the royal family starting with Tsar Alexander III. The tsar had the Hen Egg created for his empress—he gave it to her for the festivities celebrating Easter in the Russian Orthodox religion. The unique object opened yielding a surprise in the form of a gold yolk. Embedded in the middle of the yolk was a chick."

"How clever. I can't imagine the hours and hours of intricate detail work it must have taken to create each one," Jack said.

I examined the hinge in the middle of the egg. My fingers itched to open it.

"Each egg revealed a surprise inside," I said as I gingerly tilted the top of the egg. "Let's see what might be in this one."

Jack's voice cracked. "Katerina, oh my Lord. It's a bird made of solid gold."

He could not contain his excitement in finding the exquisite hand-crafted metalwork tucked inside the royal egg. Jack shuffled his feet in a dance move and whistled a tune--which was quite unlike the reserved Jack I knew.

I was stunned and speechless. How could I be the recipient of such magnificence?

My thoughts turned to Papa. He was so practical…he probably thought the old metal trunk contained pictures and other worthless keepsakes. I couldn't wait to reveal its contents to him. Yet something held me back. My instincts urged me to keep my findings secret from everyone—at least for now.

"Kat, come out of your trance. There is one more object."

"It couldn't be any more exquisite than the Faberge′egg, Jack."

Jack mockingly bent at the waist and bowed before me. "Nothing would surprise me, Katerina of Imperial Russia."

"Stop that, Jack. This could all be a hoax for all I know," I said.

"Unlikely Kat. There are too many pieces of the puzzles that fit together," Jack said. He raised his eyebrows at me and urged me to continue the treasure hunt.

I withdrew the final velvet bag from the trunk and placed it gingerly on the white linen sheet.

"I can't open it, Jack. Will you do the honors?" I asked.

I sat down and drew out a long breath of anticipation. I needed a cigarette to calm my nerves. Maybe I could sneak one on the balcony later—Jack hated my smoking habit so I hid it from him as much as possible.

I tried to imagine what we might discover but my mind was refusing to focus. I was scattered and all over the place…waiting.

Jack slowly edged a piece of jewelry from the bag and placed it the palm of his hand.

It was a brooch composed of a round four-centimeter sapphire center surrounded by a halo of pave diamonds. Exquisite was the only word to describe it. I reached over Jack and gently traced my finger over the sapphire's smooth center.

"Jack, it seems like a miracle that my grandparents were able to send these priceless jewels out of Russia undetected."

I studied all of the paperwork and objects laid before me: my birth certificate, the letter from my grandmother, the stacking dolls—the smallest of which contained the two-carat diamond ring, the magnificent Faberge' Easter Egg, and the sapphire and diamond broach.

Who was I really? I knew the secrets from the Wolf side of the family—I had discovered my Jewish heritage and my father's connection to the F.B.I. But now a new mystery swirling about my Russian roots was emerging.

Why was my surname excluded from my birth certificate? What happened to my Aunts Olga and Viktoria and my uncle Maxim? Why was there no documented trail leading to my grandparents Aleksandra and Dmitri? Why was my mother sent to Germany? Was I really connected to Imperial Russia or was this part of a giant hoax?

Grandmother said we had relatives in Germany. Who are they—and where are they? Do they have royal connections?

I had more questions than answers. My sense was Perm, Russia held the central key to my history. I needed to travel to the city, but would a communist country approve my entrance? And if admitted would I be subject to interrogation or worse? It would be a risky move as the Cold War raged around us and The Bolsheviks led by Stalin opposed the west at every turn. But the quest to uncover my heritage was rooted in my soul and I was determined to succeed.

Jack looked at me. He knew exactly what I was thinking. He knew me too well.

Chapter 7
Pursuit

Munich
Late 1950
Billy Love

"Aunt Liz, come into the living room. I want to give you a present before we visit Ursula today," I called out.

I held out a brightly wrapped package to her—she picked it up and held it to her chest.

"Oh, Billy Love, you shouldn't have," Liz said.

"It is a small but mighty gift. I call it a therapeutic gift. Everyone in the family is getting one," I explained.

"Now I am curious. Can I open it now?"

"Please do."

Aunt Liz tore off the paper and gazed at the object before her. She looked puzzled.

"Yes, a children's book *Alice in Wonderland*. It is your very own copy. Look, here is Parker and my copy."

I pointed to the side table where multiple book marks found their way onto the pages of *Alice*…documenting parts we deemed important.

"I see," Liz said not really seeing!

"Rennie has the book in her room and Ursula is reading the book in the hospital."

"Rennie?"

I smiled. "Why, yes, now that she is on the verge of becoming a teenager she informed Parker and me that Renata is an old-fashioned name and we should never mention it again. I am certainly willing to comply with her wishes. It is a small request."

"Rennie it is—now tell me why we have these books?"

"Aunt Liz I am so impressed with Nurse Phillips and her relationship with Ursula. I trust her judgment so if she says we should all read a children's book…we should do what she says."

Liz patted her hair and smoothed it back toward her severe bun. I noted it was one of her nervous gestures—she was unsure of what to make of the book.

I settled my book on my lap. "Nurse Phillips is assigning Ursula and Rennie certain passages in the book. They are to read it and then write down the meaning for each of them in a diary. We will be meeting with the nurse to review Ursula's response prior to seeing her today."

"And this interpretation is supposed to help her cope with all of her demons?" Liz remarked as she pushed her glasses up on her nose.

"It's a start. And really, Ursula has made so much progress with Nurse Phillips' guidance. Look at it as a tool. I, for one, am really interested in both girls' interpretation. Turn to page seven Liz. The first assigned passage is *Alice's encounter with the white rabbit as she fell down a very deep well—the rabbit hole entrance to Wonderland.*

"Billy Love, this book-reading sounds rather unconventional. But nothing else has been effective with Ursula and you seem very sure of Nurse Phillips."

"I certainly do. And Rennie has agreed to send her own interpretation along with us today to share with Nurse Phillips. I have not read it and have assured Rennie that I would wait until we met with our nurse."

"Now I am intrigued," Liz noted.

"So am I. There is more to *Alice in Wonderland* than just a silly children's book. Even Parker is finding the assigned passages intriguing."

"On another note Billy Love, I believe it was good for Parker and Ursula to have some one-on-one time while you and "*Rennie*" attended Kat and Jack's wedding."

"For sure, Liz. Parker and Ursula laughed together and had so much fun. She told him about the indoor picnic at Nurse Phillips' house and he mimicked holding the tea cup with his pinky finger extended while sitting cross-legged on the blanket. It was a rare light moment for Ursula. Parker even held her hand for a couple of seconds and Ursula let him into her world."

Rennie skipped into the room and climbed on Aunt Liz's lap. She was growing up; yet she was still a little girl when it came to showing affection. Liz kissed her on the cheek and pulled her close.

"Mommy, when can I see Ursula?"

"Rennie, Nurse Phillips said very soon but she wants to see how Ursula does with this first assignment in *Alice*.

"Okay but read Ursula's writing first before you read mine," Renata said as she handed me her precious diary.

"Darling, of course you have my word."

"And mine, too," Liz said.

"Oh, and Mommy since I'm *Rennie* now, maybe we should call my sissy *Ursie*!"

"What a good idea. Deal."

****

Liz and I arrived at Bellevue Psychiatric Hospital amidst a driving rain that attempted to turn our umbrellas inside out. We stamped our wet feet on the well-used mat, removed our plastic rain hats and entered the waiting area together.

I noted a new sign on the drab wall. *Push the buzzer for assistance.*

The waiting area was over-crowded with anxious parents who were fidgeting and pacing. I had read in the newspaper that the children's psychiatric beds were full—tots were virtually sleeping on cots in the hallways. I felt lucky that Parker and I could afford a private room for Ursula.

In a low voice I murmured. "Aunt Liz, there is the woman who warned me about the dangers of lobotomies and Electroconvulsive Therapy."

Liz turned her head toward the woman slumped in the corner with her knees drawn up to her chest.

I crossed the room and gently placed my hand on her head.

The woman looked up at me with a vacant expression. Clearly, she did not recognize me.

"We met when my daughter was admitted to Bellevue. You were very kind to me, offering me advice and a handkerchief for my tears."

The woman mumbled and turned away. Then in a swift movement she was on her feet addressing the whole room.

"Beware!" the woman screamed. "They will take your child and turn him into a monster! My Jimmy, oh my Lord, my Jimmy. He's only six. They strapped him down on a cold table and jammed some rubber in his mouth. Then the old doc shocked him. Nothing for pain, nothing at all. Now my Jimmy's mind is gone, my sweet Jimmy is gone!"

I arose and cradled the distraught woman in my arms as the others in the room stared and pointed.

"Shh, it will be alright. Be firm…do not allow any further experiments on your boy. Here, ask for Nurse May Phillips. She will know what to do for your Jimmy—I scribbled down the nurse's telephone number on a scrap of paper.

The sobbing woman clenched the note and sat back down. She rocked back and forth and appeared forlorn. Was it too late for her child? I sincerely hoped it was not the case.

I looked up. Nurse Phillips stood in the doorway. I had not even pushed the buzzer yet here she was…with her calm reassuring demeanor. As usual she was impeccably dressed head to toe in her starched white uniform.

"Mrs. Remington, please come with me," she said in a quiet voice.

Liz trailed me through the heavy metal door. We walked through several interlocking doors until we reached a small cubicle—Nurse Phillip's makeshift office.

"This is my Aunt Liz. After the war she discovered Ursula living in a bombed out building in Munich. If not for my aunt's rescue Ursula and Renata surely would have perished from malnutrition and rampant disease," I explained.

"I am pleased to meet you. I believe Ursula mentioned your name once or twice—at random moments. She remembers someone rocking her. It is a very soothing memory for her," Nurse Phillips explained in her calm voice.

"I am so grateful. Really the whole family is indebted to you. I was resigned that Ursula would never recover from the trauma bestowed upon her at such a young age," Liz said.

"Billy Love and Liz, caring for ill children is not just a job for me it is a calling, a vocation. Now let's talk about Ursula. I believe she has made a lot of progress although she has a long way to go. She will require intensive outpatient treatment after she is discharged from the hospital."

I nodded.

"I see you each have your copy of *Alice in Wonderland*. We will focus today on Ursula's interpretation of the first assigned passage," Nurse Phillips said as she opened a notebook containing Ursula's diary.

"I brought her sister's writings also," I remarked.

"Very good. Ursula is aware that I am sharing her diary with you. Shall we get started?"

Liz and I both gripped our children's book and leaned forward expectantly.

"Let's review the excerpt, shall we?" Nurse Phillips traced the passage with her index finger as she read aloud in a clear voice.

Alice was feeling sleepy when suddenly a White Rabbit with pink eyes ran close to her. There was nothing so very remarkable in that; nor did Alice think it so very much out of the way to hear the Rabbit say to itself, "Oh dear! Oh dear! I shall be late!" But when the Rabbit actually took a watch out of its waistcoat-pocket, and looked at it, and then hurried on, Alice started to her feet, for it flashed across her mind that she had never before seen a rabbit with either a waist-coat, or a watch to take out of it, and burning with curiosity, she ran across the field after it, and fortunately was just in time to see it pop down a large rabbit-hole under the hedge. In another moment down went Alice after it, never once considering how in the world she was to get out again.

"Here is Ursula's interpretation," Nurse Phillips said. She placed Ursula's writing in front of us and waited as we silently read.

Rabbit ears big and tall and stiff hear everything screaming and screaming loud noises Boom boom boom pop pop pop!

Rabbit Pink eyes turn red blood will flow down fur and soak his waist-coat. Rabbit looks at watch. Time to hurt people. Watch glass cracks. Time stops Screaming and screaming

Rabbit mean puts Alice in hole and darkness. Alice falls and falls. She Scared of darkness. Everything black. Rabbit makes Alice out of control.

Alice wants her mommy and daddy. Only Mommy and Daddy can help Alice. Mommy and Daddy are gone. Daddy and Mommy on ground. Alice run and run and run but Rabbit finds and thumps Alice with his big Foot.

Alice cries and cries but no one hears.
Rabbit B A D!!!! I hate Rabbit. Alice will never get out of Rabbit Hole. She stuck in black hole forever.

I shuddered and my shoulders heaved. Tears ran down my cheeks in torrents and cascaded off my chin soaking my blouse. I couldn't look at Aunt Liz but I could hear her keening sounds of distress. I reached over and clutched her hand.

Nurse Phillips stood over the two of us and put an arm around each of our shoulders. She quietly handed us tissues to staunch our emotional outbursts.

I was not capable of speaking. My throat was buttoned-up tightly which prohibited even a peep of sound from emerging. I observed Nurse Phillips in my peripheral vision. She had her eyes shut perhaps envisioning Ursula's trauma. Or maybe something else was traipsing through her mind? I couldn't read her.

Nurse Phillips waited a few minutes letting Liz and me absorb Ursula's reaction to the passage. She pulled out Renata's notebook.

"Shall we examine sister's writings?" she asked.

Both Liz and I gave taut grimaces which indicated our agreement. The gestures were all we were capable of doing at the moment.

Nurse Phillips placed Renata's entry before us.

"Here it is. I will give you a few minutes to absorb it. Then I want you both to re-read Ursula's interpretation and we will have a discussion."

I cleared my throat, wiped my tears and peered down. I began reading.

Alice is bored. There is nothing to do, when suddenly life becomes exciting. A big white fluffy bunny has entered her world and turns it upside down. Alice can't wait to follow him wherever he goes! And he talks and wears a coat and can read time! He is a remarkable rabbit, unlike anything Alice has ever seen. He is "late" for what? I hope it is a party or some other great adventure. Alice is revved up. She gleefully runs after the rabbit trying to

81

catch him and tame him as her pet. He disappears into a large hole and Alice doesn't even stop to think. She plunges after him and finds herself in a magical place. Even though it is dark in the hole, she floats down, almost like she has on a puffy parachute. Alice is not afraid of what she might find at the end of the tunnel. She trusts the rabbit. He is her friend. What else will she find in this land of wonders?

Nurse Phillips placed the two writings side by side and stood silently and patiently—waiting for our reaction.

Aunt Liz spoke first after what seemed like hours although it was only a few seconds. "It is like Ursula and Renata read two completely different stories."

I shook my head, giving Liz tacit agreement.

Nurse Phillips gazed at us and responded. "I have given many children this assignment and have studied their reactions. Renata's is typical of a well-adjusted child. She views the story positively within the world of make-believe. She understands it is a fantasy and plays along with it. She is eager to find out what is in store for Alice."

I leaned in and pointed to Renata's story…I finally found my voice. "I can clearly understand her connections to Alice and her realization that the story is a fantasy."

"I agree with Billy Love about Renata's interpretation, but it takes all of my strength and effort to re-read Ursula's remarks," Liz said as she stuttered with emotion.

Nurse Phillips unexpectedly grabbed Ursula's comments and clutched them to her ample bosom.

"I know you see nothing but darkness and fear here, but I consider this to be Ursula's cry for help. She craves assistance in coping with her flashbacks and she has been swirling in murky memories for many years with no resolution. In the recent past her coping mechanisms included harming others and herself in an attempt to make sense of her feelings. Finally, she identifies the terror of seeing her mother and father killed."

"Do you think she relates the *bad rabbit* to the soldiers who killed her parents?" I asked.

"Yes. Has she ever mentioned *Mommy and Daddy* to either of you?" Nurse Phillips probed.

"Never," Liz and I said in unison.

"But her story does make sense. She captures the essence of what happened to her birth parents that dreadful day in the concentration camp. She described how she felt as the rabbit *thumped* her emotionally and caused her to flee from the carnage— to run and run and run," the nurse explained.

Liz smiled wanly. "So, Ursula is starting to make sense of what happened to her that dreadful day."

"Definitely. There will be other passages for her to interpret from *Alice* and I fully expect Ursula to make progress in her recovery from her psychological trauma. It will take time including much outpatient therapy, but I am encouraged. I believe Ursula has a core of inner strength that will shepherd her through therapy."

I could feel a weight lifting off my shoulders "Nurse Phillips, how can we ever thank you?"

"Ursula is not out of the woods yet, Billy Love. There will be setbacks, but I am optimistic," Nurse Phillips said.

She continued. "I have a surprise for her. We can give it to her today when you and Liz visit. I want it to be a joint gift from your family and me."

I was startled. "What is it?"

The nurse pulled out a cardboard box from under her desk…then she lifted out a red lacquered box and placed it before us. My mind was racing.

What new tricks did Nurse Phillips have up her sleeve? I had never met anyone like her. She had an intuitive knowledge of my precious Ursula that I had never before seen displayed by any of the myriad number of professionals Parker and I had consulted in the past.

I held my breath, then slowly relaxed. I knew I needed to trust her judgment.

Nurse Phillips thrust open the lid. The velvet-lined container revealed a set of hand puppets representing all of the main characters from *Alice in Wonderland—Alice, White Rabbit, Mouse, Puppy, Cheshire Cat, Caterpillar, Mad Hatter, Queen of Hearts, Flamingo, Mock Turtle, Lobster.*

"Oh my!" Liz exclaimed. Her eyes widened as she picked up each puppet and studied its features.

My eyes watered and I quickly brushed the tears away. "Nurse Phillips, will you give me a few minutes to compose myself?" I asked. I turned away and clutched my pocketbook.

"Certainly. Take all of the time you need. I have a short appointment with someone in the research laboratory. I shall return and we will visit Ursula."

Nurse Phillips' sturdy shoes clicked across the room. She pulled on the heavy door and swished through on her way to yet another appointment.

"Billy Love, Nurse Phillips is a miracle-worker. How did you ever find her?"

"It was pure luck, Liz. She was my first contact when I brought Ursula to Bellevue. I was a mess because Ursula had cut herself. I was beside myself and in the chaos Nurse Phillips appeared. There is something to be said for the older more experienced nurses. They know how to navigate the system while advocating for the patient. No matter who tried to bully her—and believe me I saw a number of belligerent doctors who tried to tell her what was what—she never backed down. Ursula was always her priority."

"I think Nurse Phillips treats the whole family not just the patient. Why, just look at what she has given us today. We have the resolve and patience to keep the faith—that Ursula is worth all of our efforts to bring back her memories from the past and help solve issues in the future," Liz commented.

I powdered my nose and reapplied lipstick. I was composed and ready to visit with Ursula.

There was a commotion in the hallway. A loud female voice boomed. Liz and I leaped to our feet and approached the glass-paneled door.

We peered out and were met with an ugly scene. I recognized Dr. Bender, the doctor who recommended Electroconvulsive Therapy for Ursula and who had treated Mrs. Miller's son Jimmy with the treatment.

"You will NOT interfere with my relationship with Jimmy Miller!" Dr. Bender shouted.

Nurse Phillips replied with a calm yet firm demeanor. "Mrs. Miller has requested my assistance with her son and she will not allow any further ECT for Jimmy."

Dr. Bender seemed undone as she pointed her finger in the nurse's face and threatened her. "I will report you to the chief of staff. You are nothing but a lowly nurse."

Nurse Phillips did not respond—she understood she had the upper hand. None of the awful Dr. Bender's antics would sway her.

Liz and I jumped away from the door and feigned ignorance.

Nurse Phillips unlocked the heavy door and charged through it oozing authority.

"Ladies, I took care of some important business," she said giving us knowing glances.

We all laughed for the first time. "You certainly did, Nurse Phillips, you certainly did," Liz declared.

****

I carried the puppet box into Ursula's room and placed in on the bed beside her. Ursula looked up at me and gave me a questioning look. She was dressed in her beloved overalls and her dark hair was neatly braided in one plait down her back.

Nurse Phillips addressed her. "Ursula, you have visitors."

Ursula studied Liz as if she didn't remember her.

I let it go. I admonished myself. Let the nurse steer the situation.

"Ursula, this is a gift from me and your family. Why don't you open it?" Nurse Phillips said as she directed the conversation.

Ursula sat the package on her lap. Her eyes were wary, but she proceeded to do as instructed. She tore off the paper and lifted the hinges of the large box. She paused then raised her saucer-like eyes and peered at each one of us.

"It's all the characters from *Alice in Wonderland*," she said quietly.

Ursula lifted the *Rabbit* puppet from the box. I saw her eyes become stormy.

"BAD RABBIT!" She cried. She threw *Rabbit* across the room where it hit the wall and slid down landing in a crumpled heap. Its glassy eye stared up at us.

Ursula pulled the *Alice* puppet onto her fist and addressed the *Rabbit* puppet.

"I *thumped you bad Rabbit!*" Ursula called out in a strangled voice.

Nurse Phillips nodded in approval. Ursula was exacting revenge on *Rabbit*.

Ursula raised her fist containing Alice and motioned toward the *Bad Rabbit*. One small victory was at hand.

Memory is not really in the past.
It is helping you act appropriately in the future.
~ Eleanor Maguire

Chapter 8
Containment

West Berlin
1951
Elisabetha

"Leon, I talked to Babe today. She tells me that the Russia government has forbidden UNICEF to provide relief to thousands of Russian children whose parents have disappeared under Stalin's reign of terror. They won't let the workers step foot in the country."

Leon looked at me and smirked. "Sure, they disappeared. For the slightest infraction or criticism of Stalin their parents were arrested and sent to the so-called labor camps, where they were shot or tortured."

"Why is it always the children who must pay for adults' sins? History repeats itself. The German children paid a high price for World War II and now the Russian children are experiencing the same fate. Russia has forsaken them and the innocents battle every day for survival. Stalin rivals Adolf Hitler with his cruel tactics," I said.

Leon raked his hands through his tangled curly hair and stared into space. He paused.

"Liz, there are some days when I would like to have a nine to five job, perhaps as a banker...something mundane with little responsibility and no worries about how to solve the problems of a cruel world."

I picked up the brown bag lunch-sack filled with the bologna sandwich and chips and handed it to my love. My thoughts churned. Leon had served his entire life aiding the downtrodden—first in the Nazi resistance helping persecuted Jews flee the country and now as the German director of UNICEF, the United Nations International Children's Fund.

"Leon, you could never be content as a stuffy old banker. You do not have the constitution. Besides, you and I are alike in that we thrive in chaos."

Leon polished his round glasses and perched them atop his head.

"Liz, your life certainly has not been conventional. You carried German war secrets, which were instrumental in defeating the Nazis, to the United States government. For God's sake under threat of torture and execution you spirited Eva away from Hitler's clutches. It was perhaps the rescue of the century. So, give yourself some credit. You are a hero."

I smoothed my drab woolen skirt and tucked a stray strand of gray hair into my severe bun. I knew I should acknowledge my role in fighting the Nazi regime. I had medals of honor proudly displayed on my fireplace mantel that documented my bravery. But to the passersby on the streets of West Berlin I was just a grandmotherly type who faded into the sea of the German population. And I liked it that way. There was no reason for me to draw attention to myself.

I got humanitarian missions done under the radar—with persistence and patience and perhaps a stroke of luck. But also, with the help of my trusted family and friends. That bond could not be denied.

I looked questioningly at Leon. "Do you see any possible inroads…of getting assistance to the children of Russia? I understand that the city of Perm is particularly overrun by abandoned children."

Leon snorted. "Of course, Stalin situated one of his worst gulags in Perm. Every day children are ripped from their parents who are then worked to death in the camps. Malnutrition and disease continue to kill prisoners every day."

"Why do the Russians call the camps *gulags*?"

Leon sniffed and spoke with distain. "Stalin specifically created them for political prisoners. Anyone who opposes him, speaks against his ideas or is even slightly suspicious gets sent to one of his many camps. It doesn't matter if you are a distant member of the royal family, a white Bolshevik or even a high official in Stalin's government who is imagined to have betrayed the mighty leader."

He sprang to his feet. He quickly crossed the room and stood before a giant map of Europe and the U.S.S.R.

"You don't hear much about what goes on in Perm. It is so far away from civilization—it is like an outpost. Moscow and Leningrad dominate the news cycle," I said.

"Of course, you don't hear anything. Look at the map, Liz. You will notice that it is located on the eastern most part of the European continent. It's hidden in the Ural Mountains—there it is the mighty gateway to Siberia." Leon remarked stabbing his index finger on Perm's location. "I am highly suspicious that Russia is amassing military vehicles and weapons in the mysterious city."

"Leon, it seems there is very little available published information on Perm. It is almost like it doesn't exist."

"The Russians like the secrecy Liz. They want the rest of the world to think they have this ideal utopia—a society where everyone is on equal footing—when nothing could be further from the truth!"

I turned to the sink and started to hand-wash the breakfast dishes. The morning routine was a distraction from the uncomfortable conversation. I swished the soapy water and continued the difficult discussion.

"I know Russia was considered our ally during the war. They did help us defeat Germany but now there is no trust between Western Allies and Russia. It seems that Russia wants access to nuclear weapons and has plans to expand their influence to Asia."

"Yes, Russia wants to spread communism throughout Eastern Europe, Asia and Africa. That is why the United States enacted the *Containment Policy.*" Leon said.

"Ah, the Cold War. The world has no appetite for another world war so we fight with threats of nuclear weapon attacks to try and block Russia from gaining control over other countries," I added.

Why does one major conflict get resolved while in another part of the world there are struggles simmering and ready to burst into flames?

Leon struck a match and lit a cigar. I waved the acrid smoke away. I was not going to change his one bad habit.

I switched the conversation to more positive thinking.

"Perhaps we could make some headway for UNICEF at the German fundraiser next month. Babe said some of the allied occupying force generals will be attending. They might have some influence on rendering aid to the Russian children."

"It's a long shot, Liz."

"We have to try. There is no choice."

****

"Babe, what exciting news!" I shouted into the telephone.

What? Leon mouthed.

I raised my eyebrows at Leon and continued talking.

"Audrey has agreed to make an appearance at the UNICEF fundraiser? And to think that we got her to come to Berlin when she has been so pre-occupied shooting the screen test for *Roman Holiday*."

"Yes, I love her new pixie cut too, Babe. Everyone in the States is copying it—I believe Audrey is on her way to becoming a major movie star. But the fact that she will graciously take time out of her busy schedule to support UNICEF. I am delighted."

Leon edged closer to me as he tried to make out the conversation from Babe's end.

"That's a shame Babe. Are you sure he can't get out of it? No, well we will carry on without him. He is not directly involved anyway. We'll talk soon. I will help you figure out how to work Audrey into the program."

I hung up the phone and turned to Leon.

"Let's start a fire. It is so damp and dreary outside."

I nudged toward the window and watched the heavy white flakes float to the ground. Already the snow accumulation was waist deep. Germany was in the throes of a harsh winter.

Leon tossed the scented pine logs onto the hearth and lit a match. He flipped it onto the logs and they burst into high flames.

I handed him a hot toddy and pulled a crocheted afghan over our laps.

Leon scowled. "Liz, you are keeping me in suspense. What did Babe have to say about that scoundrel Hans Fischer?"

I slapped him lightly on his arm. "Leon! You don't know him well enough to make such a harsh judgment."

"Well?"

"Babe said he would be unable to attend the UNICEF event with her…something about a banker's retreat that weekend."

"Phooey, if he really cared he would accommodate her. It seems like he is always begging off, especially on the weekends. Didn't he bail for dinner last month?"

"He has a lot of responsibility at the bank," I announced. I felt the heat rise in my cheeks—why did I always defend Hans? Probably because Babe adored him and I wanted her to be happy. But Leon was onto something I couldn't put my finger on. Hans lavished Babe with attention one minute and then was peculiarly absent the next, with little explanation.

"Ha, Liz, you should know better with your instincts and sleuthing skills. When has Hans ever invited us to his apartment or to meet his friends or family? Does he have any friends other than Babe? It is quite curious."

"For now, Leon, let it go. However, we know contacts in Berlin who could be employed to find out more about our elusive Hans," I said.

Leon brooded silently.

"So, isn't it great news about Audrey? The great Audrey Hepburn! She is gaining popularity throughout the world. But Leon, she remains so humble—I am so impressed that she continues with humanitarian work even with her horrendous film schedule."

"She will draw a crowd…that's for sure. UNICEF needs money for all of the relief efforts it provides for children across the world."

Leon folded his arms and leaned back.

"I almost forgot, Leon. Babe also informed me that the East Berlin diplomat representing the Stalin Regime has indicated he will attend our fundraiser."

"Really, Liz was this your idea? Allied generals and Russian diplomats at the same event?"

"I can handle it, Leon. I have a plan."

"I'll bet you do, Liz and it better be a doozy. I don't want an altercation at a UNICEF fundraiser to be the impetus for World War III!"

"I can get them to play together in the sandbox—and Audrey Hepburn will be my secret weapon."

I lazily stretched my legs and looked at Leon. He stared back…I knew he would figure out my scheme. What was that old saying? *The left hand knows what the right hand does.*

****

The UNICEF fundraiser was tomorrow night and I was assigned to pick up Audrey Hepburn at the West Berlin airport and take her to our home in West Berlin. I shifted gears and lurched forward in my 1945 German Audi. My driving skills were subpar—there had been little access to automobiles during the war—therefore I was clumsy as I tried to navigate the foot feed the steering wheel and the gear shifts.

I parked and thought about my good fortune to know the young actress. I had no doubt that Audrey was on her way to becoming one of the biggest stars on the planet—and she was only 22-years-old! I was anxious to hear about her screen test for *Roman Holiday*. Did she feel any chemistry with her co-star the handsome Gregory Peck?

I chided myself. Why was I concerned about the frivolities of Hollywood movie stars? I supposed Marlene Dietrich had gotten me interested in all of the efforts that went into film- making. But, really in the end wasn't it all about fantasy? An escape for movie-goers from the perils of everyday living?

Marlene's face floated into my mind. She was a unique woman and that quality served her well as she rose through the ranks as one of the world's top entertainers. Katerina had spoken endlessly about the U.S.O. events throughout war-torn Europe. The tours where Marlene defied dangerous conditions to sing for the allied troops.

Babe had invited Marlene to West Berlin for the fundraiser. She wanted Marlene to headline the event along with Audrey Hepburn. But Marlene had immediately declined…she did not trust the German people to embrace her. There still existed clandestine Nazi supporters who resented Marlene for her relentless criticism of Adolf Hitler and the fascists…even before WWII broke out. And Marlene detested the Nazi regime every day until its demise.

Marlene the movie star was an enigma and often difficult to understand. While she refused to step foot in her native country of Germany she idolized the Russians by claiming she had a Russian *soul*. Many times, I overheard her extolling the virtues of Russian writers and composers and praising them for their anti-fascist views. But whatever her views in life she would forever be a friend to our Wolf clan.

I pulled my warm woolen hat over my ears and belted my long coat tightly. Then I plunged into the stinging sleet and trekked into the airport—Audrey Hepburn awaited. Marlene Dietrich was but a memory.

****

In the spare bedroom Audrey unpacked her suitcases, pulling out elegant ensembles one after another and placing them on hangers. At a very young age she was already becoming a style icon in Hollywood. I marveled at her ability to distinguish herself from the hundreds of ingenues arriving daily in the city. They flooded the movie industry…those young women who were trying to break into the tight-knit world of acting for a living. Most would be turned away—their dreams dashed.

"Liz, this is the dress I wore for my costume test for *Roman Holiday.*"

Audrey held the midnight blue satin dress against her waif-like frame and gazed in the full-length mirror. It had a halter neck-line and stand up collar which enhanced her delicate facial features and highlight her strong eyebrows.

"Audrey, it is divine. Your style is impeccable. I don't know how you hit the mark every time."

"I have some designers I am very fond of—and they make suggestions. I make the final decisions though. It is important to have a certain image."

I gently picked up a red silk floor length sheath covered with hand-sewn floral embroidery. "Is this the gown you will wear tomorrow night?"

"Yes, it is—what do you think of it?"

"I believe it is perfect. Every man there will swoon."

Audrey furrowed her brow and shook her pixie-shorn head. "Liz, I am disappointed that James is unable to attend. He is so busy globe-trotting and promoting his businesses that I hardly ever see him."

I remained silent…I was not fond of James Hanson. He seemed like a self-centered man who wanted a beautiful woman on his arm but who was unable to put work into a meaningful relationship. But Audrey seemed determined to make their partnership work. They were engaged to be married and she had already ordered her custom wedding gown.

Finally, all of the suitcases were unpacked. Several rows of shoes were precisely lined up by color and style from espadrilles to high-heels.

I sat down in a straight-back wooden chair and surveyed her wardrobe. "Audrey, it looks like you are staying for a month rather than just a few days." I pointed to the jammed closet.

Audrey's laugh tinkled. "Oh, Liz I am having a ball. During the war years in Amsterdam, I had two thread-bare dresses that I rotated. I dreamed of a better life. But I never imagined this." She swept her arms in the air indicating the breadth of her clothing and accessories.

I smiled. "Leon is awaiting us. He has hot toddies ready and the whiskey will warm us up. Then we want to hear what you have planned for your speech tomorrow night."

Audrey and I descended the stairs together. Leon kissed me and handed me the beverage. I sipped it and felt the liquid sting my throat ending up spreading warmth into my belly.

We were seated around the heavy-oak dining room table. Audrey spread a sheath of papers in front of her. I knew they housed her UNICEF speech.

"Leon, Liz, my speech may raise some hackles tomorrow night," Audrey announced.

"What do you mean?" Leon looked surprised. He refilled our glasses with the gut-warming drink and sat back looking intrigued.

Audrey's face lit up. "It is my understanding that there will be some Russian officials at the fundraiser. And it has come to my attention that the Russian government is being obstinate—refusing to allow UNICEF into their country to help the thousands of children who need assistance… whether it be nutrition, medical supplies or clothing needs."

"Go on," Leon said as he warily stared at her. I knew he was not keen on agitating the Germans OR the Russians. Clearly, he didn't want the UNICEF organization sullied.

Audrey pulled out a black cigarette holder and flicked a lighter, making the tip of the cigarette glow. She inhaled deeply then blew out the acrid smoke. She glanced down at her prepared speech. "Let's just say I will challenge the officials of Stalin's regime to reconsider their position."

I laughed but Leon was more cautious with his reaction. He was poker-faced.

I could convince Leon to go along with Audrey's speech. I was certain of my persuasive ability. After all, we were both aware that the UNICEF event would be covered heavily by reporters throughout the world. The Russians would not escape notice. No sir, Audrey would have them cornered.

"Go after them Audrey! You will have them at your mercy," I exclaimed.

Leon nodded giving tacit approval to the planned speech.

With the discussion over, Audrey calmly gathered up the sheath of papers and applied a paperclip."

She put the papers aside and leaned forward toward Leon and me. She spoke conspiratorially. "Now that my speech is approved, let's move on to more important items. What do you hear from the Wolfpack—my dear Katerina and Billy Love?"

Leon and I raised our eyebrows. Where would we begin?

****

The UNICEF fundraiser was to be held in the Kempinksi Hotel, an elegant structure newly opened in West Berlin. It symbolized the restoration of post-war Berlin—which had been flattened by bombing from the western allies but now stood proudly as evidence of victory over the Nazis.

Leon and I arrived early to check on the details of the evening. I spoke with the banquet staff as Leon looked over the guest list. From a distance I watched as Leon became agitated. His voice rang out across the ballroom…I excused myself and made my way to his side.

"What is it Leon?"

"The Russians have added another diplomat and his wife, Ambassador Ilya and Karina Petrov."

I looked over his shoulder. "Why is this a problem?"

"Because I didn't clear them ahead of time. There could be trouble between the American and British diplomats and these new additions. I don't like surprises…and there is no documented background check on them," Leon said.

"Let it go. Perhaps they have a real interest in the children of Russia and we can use their assistance in gaining access to them,"

I said with reassurance.

"I am not convinced but I will have one of the West Berlin police assigned to the couple. He can follow them and make sure they don't cause trouble."

"Quit being so negative. Look, the guest list says the ambassador represents Perm Russia of all places. Rearrange the seating and place the couple next to us," I said.

"Now Liz, are you sure? It is just like you to ingratiate yourself with our enemies no less."

"I don't view them as enemies, Leon. They could be a vital link—communication is key."

Leon looked at me and frowned. I knew he was hesitant yet he trusted my judgement. He took a grease pencil and circled the ambassador's name. "Move them to table 8, to the right of Liz and me…and for God's sake get rid of that snide Mrs. Gunner who was slotted to be seated at our table. She gives me a headache just thinking about her."

I smiled and turned away. My attention was needed for other things. Where was Babe? It was not like her to be late to an important event.

Audrey was already ensconced in the dressing room reviewing her speech. I could always count on her to be impeccably groomed and ready for her starring role. Leon and I had reviewed her speech—it was a rousing message and I was certain that the evening would be a success. I stopped to inhale the sweet aroma of pink roses amassed throughout the ballroom and the polished scent of the gleaming cherry-wood furnishings. The guests were chattering as they entered the multiple doorways to the ballroom and made their way to their assigned seats.

I scoured the room looking for Babe…there she was, greeting the American ambassador and his wife. She looked sophisticated and confident in her floor-length midnight blue velvet gown. Everyone was in their place.

Showtime.

"Leon and Elisabetha, may I present Ambassador Ilya Petrov and his wife Karina?" The hotel official announced as he guided the couple to their assigned seats.

I looked up at Ilya. He looked every inch the official Russian Ambassador—tall, broad shoulders, his thick dark hair swept back with his bushy eyebrows framing his eyes. The mustache and clipped beard completed the look. His black woolen tunic was adorned with metals and a red sash traveled diagonally across his chest. He stood out. There was no question about it.

In contrast his wife Karina was barely noticeable. The mousy woman stood barely five-foot and was wrapped in a shapeless gown. Her hair was pulled back in a severe bun and her only jewelry consisted of a gold wedding band.

I commiserated with her to a degree. I had recycled the gown that I wore to Katerina's wedding. It was simple—a black beaded column, but much more elegant than that of Mrs. Petrov.

The ambassador kissed my cheek and seated his wife directly to my right. Good, I thought, maybe I can glean some information about Perm from her. I knew there was more to her than first met the eye.

Audrey was about to be introduced by Babe who seemed calm as she glided across the stage and stood before the podium. Her embroidered red satin dress shimmered creating a light show in the ball room. The guests loudly applauded her entrance.

Babe stepped to Audrey's side and spoke into the microphone. My niece was so beautiful with her white-blonde coiffed hair and her intense blue eyes. Indeed, all of my nieces were beautiful in different ways: Billy Love and Katerina with their dark curly tresses. Bobbie Love, the sophisticate who graduated college and moved to Los Angeles (although we never heard from her—she was not involved with the Wolf family in any manner). And finally, Bitsy Love, Babe's identical twin who now worked for Marlene Dietrich and kept our family's vibrant connection to the actress alive. I was blessed to have them in my life.

My attention returned to Audrey as she delivered her speech which focused on advocating for the multitudes of suffering children in the world. At its conclusion she recounted her time in Amsterdam as a child when she suffered malnutrition at the hands of the Nazi regime.

"And now in 1951 we must continue to help the defenseless children of the world, for they are our future wherever they are located." She stepped away from the microphone to sustained applause from the audience.

I looked over at the Russian ambassador. He was scowling and staring straight ahead with his arms folded across his chest. His tiny wife kept her hands in her lap but glanced at me sideways as if to give approval for Audrey's speech.

I nodded slightly, acknowledging her.

I scooted back my chair and arose. "Leon, I am going to the powder room."

"Oh, Elisabetha may I accompany you? I was unable to use the restroom before the banquet," Karina said quietly.

Leon and Ilya were left to stare each other down as Karina and I made our way to the back of the ballroom. I was quite certain that the attitude between the two men would remain downright chilly. Maybe they would bond over the vodka I had Babe send to the table? It might loosen them up and help distract them from the absence of their wives.

The ladies room was deserted and I casually glanced under the stall to confirm that Karina and I were alone. I observed my Russian guest. We were almost the exact same height and stood nose to nose with our five-foot frames. Small but mighty? There was something about my counterpart that triggered my intuition— I instinctively understood that Karina would become an important fixture in my life. How or why was less understood at the moment. I waited for her to speak.

I took a brush out of my purse and smoothed it over my short graying locks. Karina momentarily ignored me as she applied matte red lipstick over her thin lips.

Karina spoke in a low monotone voice. I had to strain to connect with her words. But when I deciphered her message I became dumbfounded.

"Elisabetha, I read your brother's book *The Escape of the Century: Eva Braun*. I had to buy it on the black market and keep

99

it hidden in the apple cellar to keep it secure."

"Go on." My mind was racing as I tried to make sense of Karina's words.

Karina snapped her purse shut and made intense eye contact with me. "I was intrigued as to your role and Moody's role in sweeping Eva Braun out of Germany and into America before the war started."

"Yes, and…?"

"I was particularly interested in the life of your niece Katerina Wolf and her relationship with her father, Moody."

I leaned in close to Karina and spoke conspiratorially.

"What business do you have with my beloved Kat?"

Karina assuredly grabbed my hand and held it against her chest.

My mouth was cotton-dry as I waited for her to reveal her connection.

The Russian ambassador's wife whispered in my ear. I jumped back against the wall as the impact of the information fully registered in my brain.

"Can you repeat what you just said? I need to hear it again."

Karina paused as a long silence hung between us.

Finally, she repeated her message.

"I knew Katerina's mother Irina. We went to school together in Perm back in the days before the Revolution," Karina said as she arched her eyebrows and simultaneously rummaged through her purse.

I tried to process what I had just heard. After many years with no connection to Irina's family, finally there might be a breakthrough! I staggered forward and embraced Karina.

Karina pushed me away. "Elisabetha, you must never reveal you have any knowledge of my relationship with Katerina's mother. It is extremely dangerous especially since I am married to a Russian ambassador. Any leakage of information to the West no matter what its subject could be construed as treasonous and my entire family could be sent to the gulag."

I nodded as I tried to process everything I had heard. Was there espionage involved somehow? Or was this simply a family matter...an attempt to determine the roots of Katerina's Russian family? I had so many unanswered questions but now was not the time to pepper the ambassador's wife. Ilya and Leon would be wondering what was keeping us.

Karina shoved a sealed envelope into my hands.

"Here, Elisabetha, deliver this directly to your niece, Katerina. Do not break the seal and read it. You are better off not knowing its contents. Tell Kat to read the letter memorize it and then destroy it. It is imperative that it cannot be traced back to me. Do you understand?"

I stared at the letter unable to tear my eyes away.

"Quickly hide it in your purse."

I shook my head and sprang into action. At the same time, I admonished myself. You are a seasoned F.B.I. agent Liz! Get a grip and comply with Karina's instructions. I shoved the letter deep into the recesses of my purse and composed myself.

A gunshot rang out. Karina and I jumped...people screamed.

****

We pushed open the powder room door and made our way through the chaos. Berlin policemen were snaking through the crowd, pistols drawn, trying to determine the direction of the gunfire.

I was grateful for the distraction whatever it was for it provided a good cover for Karina's and my interaction. I clutched my purse to my side and spied Leon and Ilya in the distance. They appeared to be yelling at each other and pointing across the room. Karina separated from me and reached Ilya and Leon first.

I watched as Karina spoke to her husband and firmly pulled him away from Leon. Ilya's face was red but he acquiesced to his wife. Karina swiftly took Ilya by the elbow and led him from the ballroom.

They were gone.

I reached Leon's side and searched his face.

"Damn Russians. They are so arrogant. Apparently one of the other Russian ambassadors got into an altercation with the West German ambassador and became gun-happy, shooting his pistol in the air to make a point! Don't they know how dangerous that is in a ballroom with hundreds of guests?"

"What were you and Ilya discussing?" I asked as I tried to remain calm.

"He was pontificating and using the typical communist propaganda to make his point. He told me that the children of Russia had no need for UNICEF's services. That the children were doing just fine living and working in communes."

"Leon, calm down. We will have to keep reaching out to the communist government to make inroads. After all the children are our priority. We can't give up because adults are fighting."

Leon gripped my shoulder and I winced. I understood his agitation and knew that he would come around to my viewpoint. Maybe.

I observed the flash of lightbulbs and the scribbling of frantic reporters trying to document the altercation between East and West. My thoughts turned to my brother A.R. and his career as a reporter for the L.A. Times. I grinned. He would have had a field day at the dinner.

He might have even brandished his own pistol in an attempt to invoke order.

"Leon, let's go home. We made our point. Clearly there is a need for UNICEF to help the Russian children."

"Not as long as Stalin rules with an iron hand," Leon muttered.

I said my goodbyes, but my mind was entirely filled with imagining the contents of the letter addressed to Katerina. I was burning with curiosity. But I knew my assignment: getting the correspondence into my niece's hands. I was already planning the delivery. But it was not my place to read the message…I was just a courier.

Chapter 9
Russian Ties That Bind

New York City
1951
Katerina

Aunt Liz was being evasive, there was no doubt about it. When she called last week to give me an update on the UNICEF fundraiser in West Berlin I could sense the hesitation and maybe something else in her voice—fright. I knew her too well and we had been through so much together, from concealing Eva Braun's existence from the world to the discovery of the roots of our German children's duress as World War Two came to an end in 1945.

It was not like her to conceal anything from me. After all I had been trustworthy to a fault in keeping *her* secrets. But I had a niggling feeling she had some information about my Russian side of the family. And I was wary. What could she know or did she know?

Could her knowledge be connected to the old trunk? I thought not--no one other than my husband Jack was cognizant of the treasures we had discovered in the rusty old trunk. We had kept the beautiful items top-secret. Papa knew we possessed the trunk but curiously he had not inquired about our findings…which for now was a blessing.

I was concerned about protecting my heritage and I needed time to uncover the meaning of the antique trunk and its possessions. I burned with questions.

Why was the trunk sent to Germany with my mother? Who else besides my grandmother was aware of it? What happened to my grandparents and my two aunts and uncle? Why had my Russian family seemingly disappeared? What was the origin of the treasures found in the trunk--were they inherited, stolen, a payment for services rendered?

Apparently even my own mother Irina was unaware of the trunk's contents. She either was not interested or she was told to hide it away from prying eyes and not risk discovery…pretend it never existed. Perhaps to protect someone from tyranny.

My mind ricocheted back and forth from the past to the present.

I was a voracious reader of the New York Times and I was already aware of the altercation between the Russian ambassadors and the American ambassadors at the fundraiser. The Russians in particular had not been receptive to an international organization like UNICEF interfering with their approach to raising Russian children. Their attitude was yet another component of the Cold War between the east and the west—an attitude that had far-reaching effects on the world of politics.

The newspaper also reported that Leon and his staff were lucky in that no one was injured when the pistols suddenly rat-a-tat-tatted and ended the party. West Berlin police broke up the fight and the night ended. There was no resolution to the plight of the Russian children, however. Thousands still roamed the countryside, pushed from their home with their parents arrested for unknown infractions.

I recalled last week's conversation with my aunt.

"Kat, I am sending you a package," she said as she carefully selected her words. Her voice was soft making it difficult to understand her. I pressed my ear against the receiver and strained to hear her.

"What is it?"

"Just wait. It should be arriving by courier in a few days. I can't give you any further explanation as I myself am unaware of its contents. Keep it in a safe place," Liz said. And then the phone was dead.

I replaced the receiver in its cradle.

What could be so important? I couldn't imagine but I would find out soon enough.

Wolfgang would be home from school in an hour. I bent down and scratched Schnitzel between the ears. Then I scratched my own head and pondered. Why was my life always somehow turned upside down, roiling with one adventure after another? How about some old-fashioned boredom?

Part of me was open to adventure and the other part of me wanted a serene existence. But I knew I couldn't have both. It must be my fate. I needed to be open whatever befalls me.

****

I went to the back of my closet, pushed aside the sliding panel door and reached into the black space. I hastily rubbed my hands along the rough trunk as if to reassure me it was still there.

Jack had suggested the creation of a false panel which could hold the trunk and its contents. He had the skills to build the hidden space and I encouraged him. We knew the treasures within the battered trunk were invaluable and we needed to keep them hidden for now. But the story of their origin was still a blank slate.

I lifted the trunk onto the bed and carefully withdrew the letter from my grandmother. I felt tears welling up and then spilling down my cheeks. Flicking the streaming tears away I was careful to keep my grief from spoiling the spidery handwriting dominating the yellowed pages. As I composed myself I looked out the window and imagined what might have happened to my grandparents and the rest of my Russian family.

There was a loud banging on the door. I hurriedly closed the trunk and shut the bedroom door then crossed the living room wiping my eyes and attempting to smooth my messy curls. I knew I was not presentable, but I also was aware that a package from Aunt Liz was awaiting me.

I unlooked the bolt on the door and flung it open, startling the tall uniformed man standing before me.

"Yes?"

"Are you Katarina Wolf Remington?" he asked in a stern voice.

"Yes," I stammered as I straightened up and tried to keep myself together.

He pushed a clipboard toward me.

"Sign here, Lady."

I grabbed the pen and scribbled my name. Then I clutched the satchel to my chest and slammed the door.

I latched the lock and stood with my back against the heavy door as I tried to catch my breath and calm myself.

I admonished myself…where had all of my resolve gone?

What was in the satchel? I had an urgency to find out.

I re-entered the bedroom and drew the curtains.

Was there a connection between the trunk and the satchel?

Why did Billy Love suddenly float into my mind? Billy Love, my closest friend and cousin. I had not spoken to her in weeks. Why had I neglected her? I needed her and she needed me.

Billy Love had a strength that I could draw on—and vice versa. Right now, she was preoccupied with her precious Ursula who was hospitalized for an illness unimaginable for the vast majority of us. Billy Love said she was making progress, but yet I was selfish…consumed with my own issues. I had not even visited the child at Bellevue Psychiatric Hospital. I vowed to call my beloved cousin soon. I couldn't keep putting it off.

Taking a deep anticipatory breath, I gently placed the satchel on the bed beside the trunk and flipped open the leather binders holding it shut. I reached in and withdrew a wax-sealed envelope. There was no indication indicating who it was from—just a name in large block letters. KATARINA.

I placed the new letter next to my grandmother's weathered correspondence and stood back scrutinizing them both in anticipation of finding out some meaningful information.

What was I waiting for? I jolted myself out of my stupor and picked up the delivered letter.

I gently broke the waxed seal and edged the letter out of the envelope. As I smoothed it out, my eyes darted to the closing remarks. There was no signature. Whoever wrote this wanted to remain anonymous.

Disappointed I nevertheless was curious about its message. I sat on the bed and began reading.

Dear Katerina,

You don't know me, nor shall I reveal my identity to you. It is much too dangerous for both of us.

I can reveal that I was a classmate of your mother Irina, back in the days when life was good for a significant number of Russian people.

Let me give you some history. At the turn of this century the nobility was comprised of almost two million people which translated to about 1.5 percent of the population of the Russian empire.

Your mother was part of that privileged class, but yet her life was not one of the idle rich. Indeed, her family was considered a "service" class tapped to work for the princes and tsars at court, in the military, in cultural affairs or in administrative roles. For almost a thousand years these nobles were called "the white bone" and they were the creative forces behind the palaces of St. Petersburg, the poetry of Pushkin and the music of Rachmaninov. They kept the Russian society afloat with their intellect and dedication.

These nobles were scattered throughout Russia some of whom served in the cities while others resided in rural estates.

For all of their usefulness to the princes and tsars the nobles eventually became branded as consorters with Tsar Nicolas II. Unrest erupted in 1905 as the peasant class demanded concessions from the tsar and burned the countryside in retaliation when the tsar refused to capitulate.

There was some panic within the noble realm. Most of them wanted to stay in Russia to support the tsar and protect their status and riches but others were alarmed and began to make plans to leave the country. The violence between classes continued and became worse every year after 1905. But the tsar continued to crack down on the peasants through the use of brutal armed forces he sent to quell the dissent.

The revolutionaries fought back. Between 1908 and 1910 alone thousands of attacks and killings of noble families occurred. But by pretending nothing was happening many nobles continued their glittering lifestyles, reveling in balls and luxury and lavish parties.

Your mother and her sisters continued to attend school. They were quiet and unassuming and attempted to avoid being singled out. Irina especially was cautious pulling her blonde hair back in a severe bun—and dressing in drab cotton apparel.

One day in 1910 Irina failed to come to school. That's when I knew...she had been sent away by her parents. She, as the oldest child would carry the burden of the family and stake a claim in another world. But even her sisters were bewildered as to what had become of her.

Five years passed and then one day your mother's entire family disappeared. We never heard from them again.

Please do not contact me or question how I knew where to find you. Just know that your grandparents loved your mother very much and did what they thought was best for her and the family.

As you are aware the Bolsheviks took over Russia in 1917 after killing Tsar Nicholas and his family. In some ways our society is better off with its socialist underpinnings; yet in other ways we have ignored the needs of thousands upon thousands of children.

I wish you well, Kat. Keep the Russian spirit that holds your heart.

I folded the letter, brought it to my chest and began singing the

Russian song that I always recalled when I thought of my mother.

We fall asleep when we hear…
We fly away when we hear…
We travel far when we hear…
When we hear the Russian lullaby.

Papa always sang the song to me in his gravely deep voice. I would laugh at his attempts to stay on key—for sure I had inherited my alto pitch from Irina's side of the family. In many ways however, I was grateful to Papa for insisting on daily lessons in reading and writing the Russian language. It was so foreign from German and English yet now I welcomed my education…thus I was able to translate the letter from the unknown classmate of my mother.

The new letter answered a few questions about my heritage, but it also raised a barrage of additional inquiries. Why did my family disappear? Where did they go? Were they able to escape the violence rocking Russia? How did the treasures found in the old trunk relate to my family's disappearance? Were we really part of Russian royalty or was that scenario a mirage?

I unsteadily arose from the bed and walked into the bathroom where I secured a cold compress and pressed it onto my forehead. Returning to my bed chamber I laid on my back and stared at the ceiling. Thoughts hurtled through my brain like an avalanche out of control.

So much evil existed in the world. One conflict was resolved and then another popped up. It was akin to squeezing a tube of toothpaste on one end which resulted in a mound somewhere else. The world had defeated the Nazi regime only to confront the consequences of war—thousands of young Germans forcibly conscripted into the army and killed on the front lines, concentration camps housing and working to death anyone who did not fit the Aryan profile, hundreds of thousands of Jews sent to the gas chambers, and abandoned children roaming the country as they succumbed to disease and malnutrition.

And now the Western allies were embroiled in a cold war with Russia. Why? Because of the Bolsheviks' urge to maintain power and control. The once great Russian empire was determined to rise again...but without the Russian monarchy. They wanted access to nuclear weapons because of fears that West Germany with help of its allies would invade their country once more.

Josef Stalin might be the most ruthless dictator ever to exist and he would do everything possible to stay in command. Could there be anyone more abhorrent than Adolf Hitler?

I drifted off into a restless sleep. I awoke to Jack's voice echoing through the apartment.

"I'm in the bedroom, Jack. I have something to show you."

Jack strode into the bedroom and clicked on the overhead light. I winced as the light flooded into the room and bore down on me making my headache worse.

"Kat, can we talk later? I just received a call from the school."

I arose on one elbow and tried to make sense of what Jack was saying.

I scowled. "What, Wolfgang should be home by now."

"Listen to me, Katerina. Wolfgang was beaten by a bunch of thugs. We need to get to the Bellevue Emergency Room."

"But why? Wolfgang is so gentle," I implored as I arose from the bed and threw my arms around Jack.

"They called him a filthy Russian Jew!"

I started to sob as I leaned against Jack. My tears soaked his dress shirt. An innocent child was sullied and broken solely because he was born Jewish and Russian. Jewish from my father's German roots and Russian from my mother's family.

How did those bullies even know this about our son? The shackles of discrimination were difficult to shed. Instead they tethered us to unfounded notions of what it meant to be human and indeed, humane.

All thoughts of the anonymous letter skittered from my brain. My only thought was to rush to my darling defenseless Wolfgang. My parental instincts were howling—howling like a wounded Wolf who caught its paw in a trap.

Chapter 10
Labyrinth

New York City
Bellevue Psychiatric Hospital
1951
Billy Love

"Rennie, are you ready? It's time to go," I declared as I stood by the front door with coat and hat in hand. I tapped my foot impatiently. Teenage girls were always primping at the last minute. Who exactly they were trying to impress? After all we were embarking on a trip to the psychiatric hospital—not exactly a place where a style maven would take up residency.

"Billy Love, there is plenty of time. Let Renata be…it is the first time she will visit with Ursula in two long months…I suspect she is a bit nervous," Parker said.

I arched my eyebrows. "What do you mean? Ursula is all she has talked about for weeks."

"I understand. But picture the last time she saw Ursula. It was a pretty gruesome scene she walked into. Blood splattered the walls and carpet and all she heard were the screams coming from you and her sister. She is probably wary of how Ursula will react to her today. She is stalling and probably for good reason," Parker said.

I dropped my voice to a whisper.

"Parker, you are so wise. Of course, Renata has reservations about interacting with Ursula. I need to be more supportive and less selfish."

Parker kiss the top of my head.

"You have every right to be selfish. You have devoted yourself to our girls for the past six years."

"I would commit myself to both of them all over again. And Ursula has made such progress under the watchful eye of Nurse Phillips. We are extremely lucky I know that. Renata will see for herself once we get to the hospital," I said.

Renata emerged from her bedroom searching my face for approval and I willingly gave it to her. There was a break in the New York winter weather and she had taken advantage of it. Rennie looked like a typical young teenager, gawky yet beautiful. Her thick chestnut-colored hair was held back from her face in a ponytail and she had on the uniform of the day…powder-blue pedal pushers and a flowered, ruffled blouse. Her long coltish legs stretched forever.

I smiled remembering the long-ago days of my own teenage years when I was a school girl in Enid, Oklahoma. All I cared about was riding horses on the ranch and playing the viola in the orchestra. Renata was so much more sophisticated than me at her age.

"I'm sorry I took so long, Mommy," Renata said as she reached me and looked into my eyes.

Mommy!

I treasured motherhood and her endearments. I knew it couldn't last much longer. The insolence of the teenage years would eliminate any affection. But for now I welcomed the notion.

"I have my *Alice in Wonderland* book and my diary, Mommy and Daddy," Renata said as she tightly clutched the dog-eared volume.

"Good. What was your assignment this week?" Parker asked. He was quite curious as to how reading a seemingly silly book would be helpful to Ursula's recovery. His practical side raised doubts.

"It was about Alice and the *Pool of Tears*," Renata said.

"You know I read that book as a child and it seemed rather ridiculous," Parker remarked as we entered the hallway and called for the elevator.

"Oh, Daddy, no. There are hidden messages. You just have to

concentrate and believe in imagination," Renata lectured with a great deal of aplomb.

Parker dipped his head toward me and gave me a look. I knew he was playing along with Renata. Humoring her.

"Parker, Nurse Phillips thinks a good part of Ursula's progress has revolved around her interpretations of the book and her play therapy with the wonderland puppets," I explained.

"Yes, Ursula wants to play with the puppets today. Mommy told me so—even though I am getting a little old for puppets and dolls and such," she declared. She put her nose in the air and walked ahead of Parker and me showing off her independence.

I grinned. There was no doubt that my little mother took her role as Ursula's protector very seriously. She had from the very beginning. I was sure she had done her homework and written down her interpretation of the *Pool of Tears* in her diary. I was also certain that her version would be completely different from her sister's thoughts. Which was the whole point of therapy—giving Ursula the tools to grow and re-wire her brain, if not to erase horrific images then at least gain a sense of closure.

After we arrived at the hospital the plan was that Nurse Phillips would meet with the three of us first and then Renata and Ursula would re-connect. I was extremely interested in Ursula's writings and how she was progressing. Over the telephone Nurse Phillips had mentioned that if Ursula continued to make strides in her treatment she might be discharged to home—well enough to begin outpatient treatment at Bellevue. But she did warn me that Ursula would have set-backs…some of them would be severe. She would probably need some form of therapy for the rest of her life.

I hoped to host a small party for Ursula after she was discharged home. It had been ages since the family had been together—the last time was at Katerina and Jack's wedding in Pennsylvania. And I knew my family would nurture Ursula.

I frowned as a delinquent thought crossed my mind. Kat had seemed distracted when we last talked. It was unlike her to ignore Ursula. But there had been an incident with Wolfgang at his school…something about bullying and name-calling. She didn't get into the details with me, but I knew her well enough to know my cousin was very distressed. I needed to make more time for her. She was living in the city now. There was no excuse.

We arrived at Bellevue. I looked out the cab window and marveled at the building's façade. Built in 1933 and taking seven years to complete, the city had spared no money. Its eight elegant stories modeled in the Italian Renaissance architecture resembled a hotel rather than a mental institution.

Parker sniffed. "I can't understand why the city poured unlimited funds into a building such as this. It cost the taxpayers a fortune."

I reached across the cab seat and grabbed his hand.

"Parker, let it go. It is marvelous that the people of New York have access to this magnificent building and the treatment that it offers."

"Okay Billy Love, I apologize."

"Renata, let's go see your sister," he said.

Renata's eyes were blazing. "It's the longest I have ever been away from Ursula," she said. She held her hand over her heart.

"I know Renata, you will finally get to reunite with little sister. Come," I said.

****

The three of us walked hand-in-hand through the halls toward Nurse Phillips office. There were punctuated screams and cries as we neared the children's wing of the building. Tiny voices rang out seemingly in unison. *"Help me, Mommy!"*

Renata's eyes rimmed with tears, but she stared straight ahead and became stoic. I put my arm around her shoulders and guided her toward our destination.

Nurse Phillips seemingly appeared out of nowhere and motioned us into her office. She was serene and composed as usual. She immediately pulled up a chair for Renata and seated herself across from her.

114

"You must be Renata, Ursula's big sister," she said in a gentle reassuring voice.

"Yes, ma'am," Renata replied politely.

"Now, darling, you are to call me *May*. I see you brought your diary and I want to thank you for participating and helping Ursula."

"She is my sister. I would do anything for her," Renata replied.

"Of course, you would. Now it has been a long time since you have seen Ursula. What are your concerns? I know you are the big sister, but you might be a little afraid, right? My job is to help you with her. You can lean on me," Nurse Phillips said.

Renata straightened her spine and handed her diary to the nurse.

"Here, May. I wrote about the *Pool of Tears*," she said.

Nurse Phillips gathered up Renata's writings and set them unopened on the table beside her.

"Let's all look at the book passage together, then I will show you Ursula's diary and how she reacted.

May began reading in her clear authoritative voice.

Alice had shrunk "and things are worse than ever, for I never was so small before, never!
And I declare it's too bad, that it is!"
As she said these words her foot slipped, and in another moment, splash! She was up to her chin in saltwater. Her first idea was that she had somehow fallen into the sea. However, she soon made out that she was in a pool of tears which she had wept when she was nine feet high.
"I wish I hadn't cried so much!" said Alice, as she swam about, trying to find her way out.
"I shall be punished for it now, I suppose, by being drowned in my own tears! That will be a queer thing, to be sure! However, everything is queer-to-day."
Just then she heard something splashing about in the pool a little way off, and she swam nearer to make out what it was. She soon made out that it was only a mouse that had slipped in like herself.

"O Mouse, do you know the way out of this pool? I am very tired of swimming about here, O Mouse!"

The mouse looked at her rather inquisitively and seemed to wink with one of its little eyes, but it said nothing.

I had read this particular passage over and over, but it had never seemed particularly noteworthy to me. Somehow when Nurse Phillips read it though, I could sense a connection to Ursula's feelings right away. Parker looked at me and nodded his head, giving tacit approval. I could see he was pondering the reading's meaning himself. He ran a hand through his sandy hair and flicked it out of his eyes.

"Nurse, do you wish to read my interpretation?" Renata asked shyly.

"Rennie, that's the name you go by now, right?

"Yes," she said expectantly.

"I would like to save your thoughts and have you share them with Ursula later," Nurse Phillips said.

She opened Ursula's diary and moved her index finger to the dark, thick writing. "Ursula is aware I will share her ideas with the family, so sit back and listen," May instructed.

May moved her glasses down to the tip of her nose and tilted the diary toward her.

I am tiny, like a bug you could step on and eliminate from the world. Just squish me and I am gone forever. I like the darkness where no one can see me. But then someone yanks my hair and throws me into a bottomless black sea with lots of danger. No one taught me how to swim. I thrash and prepare to die. My head is thrown back as far as it can go and I taste the salty tears as I start sinking like a huge stone going down, down, down. I gulp water and cry like never before—I don't want to leave Renata and my family.

But drowning is not so bad. It will take away all of my pain. I never have to think about the mean people again. But I cry so much that the saltiness of my tears lifts me onto my back and I am floating. The sea stinks of evil and blood and pee. There is still danger.

I quiver when mouse swims by—for mouse is not what he seems. He pretends to ignore me, but I know he wants me dead. The slimy tail of mouse wraps around my body and squeezes my stomach until I throw up. Then mouse squeaks in a loud voice and he lazily swims off and abandons me. He doesn't care about anyone but himself. He is bad just like Rabbit. I hate him!

Mouse is gone for now. But what else is lurking in the sea waiting to suck the life out of me? It is too much. I can't talk anymore. It is done.

MOMMY!

Renata's voice rang out. "Nurse, Ursula is not thinking straight, is she? Alice is on an adventure and she is smart and silly and can make fun of people and the talking animals. Why would she think she is going to die? Why would she…?"

Nurse Phillips snapped Ursula's diary shut and turned to Renata. "Honey, this is an important breakthrough for your sister. She is finally putting her thoughts to words. She spent the last six years of her life keeping the terror inside her, only letting it out through violent actions—harming other people and cutting herself. You must view her musings as a victory of sorts."

Parker and I were silently weeping. It was so difficult to absorb the depths of Ursula's distress, yet now we had a starting point.

Nurse Phillips would probe and push our daughter into realistic thinking with the end goal of healing and leading a productive life.

"Renata, why don't you go to the cafeteria and get yourself a Coca Cola. I want to talk to your parents. When you return we will go visit Ursula," Nurse Phillip explained. She held out some coins to Renata.

Renata stood and accepted the coins putting them in the pocket of her pedal pushers.

"And one more thing Renata. I want you to know that you are not Ursula's mother, you are her sister. It is not your job to look after her. That is your parent's and my job. Got that?" Nurse Phillips said pointedly.

"Yes, Ma'am."

"May to you, remember that. Now shoo."

Renata glanced at Parker and me for reassurance. I motioned toward the door and tried to smile: I admonished myself to think positive. After all Renata's well-being was just as important as her sister's.

"Thank you May," Renata called out as she exited the office.

Nurse Phillips turned back to us.

"Now Parker and Billy Love, I want to stress to you the progress Ursula has made up to this point. For the past month there have been no violent outbursts against other children or the staff. She has been cooperative and has regularly attended our inhouse school. Her teachers tell me the drawings she created early on which included crude pictures of her cutting and stabbing herself all over her body, have slowly evolved and now include images of her playing with Renata. Although I must say that she still separates herself from her sister with various objects. Just last week she drew a barbed wire fence. She is not ready for close physical relationships yet."

Parker pulled a pipe out of his suit coat and tamped the tobacco into the bowl. He lit it and pulled the stem into his mouth. Inhaling deeply, he then let the scented smoke swirl into the stagnant air. I understood his smoking habit was a coping mechanism for him. It calmed him and I would give him the one bad habit.

Nurse Phillips stood and smoothed her starched pristine skirt.

"Are you ready to see your precious daughter?"

"Yes," Parker and I replied in unison.

May opened the heavy glass door that led to the narrow hallway.

Life could become normal again, couldn't it? But who knew what was normal.

****

Nurse Phillips took Renata's hand and together they marched down the hall toward Ursula's room. Parker and I trailed behind as we anticipated the reunion of our daughters. May suggested we linger in the hallway while she escorted Renata into Ursula's spartan room.

Parker and I waited anxiously.

Within a few seconds, we heard squeals of delight and peals of laughter tumbling into the hallway. As the high-pitched voices echoed off the cement block walls nearby staff members turned toward the unfamiliar sounds and smiled. It was clear that there were few causes of celebration within the purview of Bellevue Psychiatric Hospital. And the sounds were welcome.

May came out of Ursula's room and shut the door behind her. She smiled serenely…there was a glow of satisfaction surrounding her—a presence that could not be measured.

I stepped forward and clung to Ursula's savior.

"How can Parker and I ever thank you?"

"Billy Love, it is my job and I love it or I wouldn't be doing it," Nurse Phillips replied.

"Come, let's view the girls' interaction with each other." She crooked her finger and motioned us to move into a room adjacent to Ursula's space.

We entered the cramped cubicle which was outfitted with a large picture window. There vividly displayed were the two girls. Their arms were entwined around each other and Ursula's head laid on Renata's chest.

"This room is outfitted with the latest equipment. It is designed so that we can hear and see the children, but they are unaware that we are observing them. It is most useful when we are assessing what children do when they think no one else is looking," Nurse Phillips explained.

We sat down on straight-backed chairs and watched. I could hardly believe what I was seeing and hearing. Was this my Ursula with her black moods and ugly behaviors?

Ursula was downright giddy. She took her sister's hands and danced backwards across the room. She hummed *Frere Jacqui* her favorite tune from when she was but a wee girl.

"Rennie, I love you so much it hurts!" Ursula shouted as she threw her head back and laughed. Her pigtails swished and bobbed around her head.

Ursula laughed!

Renata picked Ursula up and swung her in a circle. "Ursie, should I call you Ursie? I missed you so much. You are a part of me—I was so sad without you," Renata declared.

"Me too, me too, me too," Ursula sang with exuberance.

Nurse Phillips turned to Parker and me. "I must say I have never seen anything quite like the bond Ursula and Renata have for each other. They are glued together."

"Yes, it was apparent from the very beginning that we could never separate them. They were a package deal," Parker said. His eyes twinkled with tears of joy.

"Let's give them a few moments and see if Ursula shows Renata her the *Alice in Wonderland* puppets. I hope Renata will share her interpretation of the *Pool of Tears* reading and see how Ursula reacts."

I glanced around Ursula's room. It was then that I noticed the *Wonderland* puppets lined up meticulously on her dresser in the order in which they appeared in the book. I suspected Ursula might have a bit of Obsessive Compulsive Disorder. There they all stood waiting for Ursula's attention—in readiness for her hand to encase their forms and bring them to life:

Alice

White Rabbit

Mouse

Puppy

Caterpillar

Cheshire-Cat

Hatter

Queen of Hearts

Flamingo

Mock Turtle

Lobster

Parker and I exchanged glances. We read each other's thoughts: please, don't let there be a repeat of out-of-control behavior. At our last visit Ursula had tossed White Rabbit across the room as she screamed *Bad Rabbit!*

Nurse Phillips was silent anticipating the girls' next interaction.

Renata released Ursula from her affectionate grip and held back as she waited for her sister to make her next move. Ursula looked at Renata her huge chocolate eyes awash with intensity as if begging for her sister's approval. Then she turned and skidded over to her dresser where she tapped each of the puppets on the nose and recited their names in order of course, beginning with Alice.

Renata stood behind Ursula.

"Ursie, let's play *Pool of Tears*. I will play Alice and you will be Mouse."

Ursula nodded her consent while she jammed her fist into the furry puppet.

"Ok, Rennie Mouse is ready."

Renata gently picked up the Alice puppet and reached her hand into its lining. Her fingers worked the puppet's arms and she placed them around Ursula's fist which contained Mouse.

Ursula tilted Mouse so that its shiny glass eye seemed to wink at the Alice puppet.

"Now Mouse, we are swimming in the *Pool of Tears* today. I know you can't swim but I, the mighty Alice, will protect you and keep you safe. You can climb on my back and I will do the breast-stroke. Mommy taught me to be a strong swimmer and there is no use being scared," Renata said in a high-pitched falsetto voice.

Ursula shook Mouse to simulate fear. "But Alice, why is there a *Pool of Tears*? Tears means sadness and death. Mouse could die. The evil ones will suck Mouse to the bottom of the swimming hole and pin him there never to see the light of day again."

"Oh Mouse, that is where you are wrong. For I am powerful and I have the magic secret if you will only trust me," Renata replied.

I watched intently as Renata's confidence grew. She was an excellent story-teller!

"I trust you Renata, I mean *Alice*. Shall I climb on your back now?"

"Yes, please oh Mouse. For I need you to help me later when I get into a tussle with the Queen of Hearts."

Ursula moved her puppet onto the Alice puppet's backside and they glided seamlessly together across the room where they landed on Ursula's bed—the pretend shore of the *Pool of Tears*.

"We made it didn't we Alice!?" Mouse cried out in Ursula's girlish voice. Ursula moved Mouse's head vigorously up and down.

"You bet we did and oh Mouse you were so brave, not knowing how to swim and all," Renata said as her Alice grabbed Mouse and they danced together messing up the bed sheets.

"Yes, I was brave, yes, I was brave. Mouse was brave," Ursula said over and over again in a sing-song tone.

Ursula abruptly stopped and peered up at Renata.

"And *Mommy* thinks I was brave too didn't she Renata?" Ursula asked as she removed Mouse from her fist then tangled her fingers in her sister's hand squeezing tightly until both of their pink complexions turned white.

"She sure did, Ursie."

Ursula leaned on Renata's shoulder and shut her eyes. Her mouth turned up slightly. Was she chiseling away at the brutal memory of her birth mother's gang rape during the liberation of Dachau? I hoped she could one day completely repress the visualization—keep it deep within herself and never again bring it to the surface to relive it over and over again. Find some other memories that could fill her with joy.

Our Ursula!

I couldn't help myself. My *Pool of Tears* had become pure emotion—I was filled with a reaction so intense I leapt from my chair kissed the two-way glass and leaned my forehead against the cool glass.

Then I was back in Oklahoma again, reflecting upon the care-free endless summer days of horse-back riding and rodeo training. It was a time before I knew Cousin Katerina and Aunt Elisabetha even existed—I was in a bubble of an idyllic childhood. A bubble from which Renata and Ursula were excluded.

Parker pulled me away from the glass and folded me in his arms. I relaxed…thankful that my husband loved the children as much as I did.

Nurse Phillips broke the emanating silence that surrounded our reaction to the play therapy.

She was her usual unflappable self. I marveled at her professionalism and dedication.

"Today was a major breakthrough for Ursula. And her sister's performance was a major reason for her growth. I quite believe Renata may have some acting chops," May said. She flipped through Renata's chart and made several notations before closing it and standing up.

123

"I have another appointment. But you are welcome to stay and visit with Ursula. Perhaps you could take the girls down to the cafeteria for supper."

"Nurse Phillips, Billy Love and I can never thank you enough," Parker said as he stretched out his hand to shake May's hand.

"I am afraid I don't shake hands Mr. O-Rourke. Too many germs can lead to disease and heaven knows, a hospital is the worst place to be...but *Danke* for the compliment Parker and Billy Love."

Danke? German?

There was more to Nurse Phillips than met the eye. Hmm.

****

Parker and I watched Nurse Phillips briskly walk away from us and stride down the long windowless hallway. She checked the time on her watch and picked up her pace. It was apparent that she was late—and the particular appointment was too important to miss.

As she retreated, her shoulders were arched back. Her body language indicated a determination, a mission from which she was seeking a solution. She was the epitome of a picture-perfect nurse with her white starched uniform and the accompanying cap centered perfectly on her gray-streaked hair—which was pulled back into a severe bun at the nape of her neck.

I idly noted how the seam up the back of her white hose was meticulously lined up. She was a no-nonsense sort yet she managed to be the consummate caring professional. Certainly, she was more knowledgeable and kinder than most of the so-called doctors who were more concerned with trying new invasive treatments than getting to the root of what was causing children's mental pain.

No, Nurse Phillips was not a typical handmaiden at the beck and call of arrogant physicians. That was apparent from the very first visit to Bellevue Hospital. She had an independence rarely

124

seen in the modern woman. In some ways she reflected my own personality—a risk taker who rarely took no for an answer.

Parker and I turned to leave the observation room. It was then that a squat Dr. Bender looking unkept appeared in the hallway. She peered straight ahead and did not acknowledge our presence.

There was something sinister about her. I disliked her intensely ever since she had argued with Nurse Phillips and me. Insisting that Ursula should receive electroshock therapy. She obviously wanted to run her experiments without thought about the damage it might do to hundreds of children…including my precious Ursula.

"Parker, I think Dr. Bender is following Nurse Phillips and I believe she is up to no good. You go ahead and visit with the children. I am going to travel behind her."

Parker lowered his voice and spoke into my ear. "Billy Love, really? I thought your scheming days were over?"

I pulled my sweater around me and straightened up. "Not by a long-shot. Now I better get going if I am to determine where she is going and why she is interested in Nurse Phillips."

Parker knew me too well. He was aware that he couldn't stop me…so he accepted my sleuthing.

I stepped into the hall and squinted at the retreating figure of Dr. Bender. I was aware that the multiple buildings contained throughout the Bellevue properties were connected with a maze of twisting hallways and corridors. Where would they lead me?

Nurse Phillips had disappeared from view and Dr. Bender was just a speck on the horizon. I picked up my pace to almost a gallop (if you thought in horse terms) to keep her in my sight-line. Thankfully I had worn comfortable tennis shoes that were noiseless, the rubber soles absorbing the sounds of my steps.

The filthy paint-peeling underground tunnels stretched endlessly before me its walls impregnated with a combination of the smells of urine and musty dirt. Pipes above me belched with steam heat which then transformed into droplets coating the walls. Compared to the magnificent architecture of the exterior buildings of Bellevue these passages were an abomination. No wonder the public was cordoned off from them.

I wrenched my sweater off and stuffed it into my bag. I perspired profusely and side-stepped a family of rats scurrying through the passageways. Not far behind the rodents was a stealthy cat waiting to pounce on his dinner for the evening. I drew closer to Dr. Bender. But I kept close to the walls and tried to remain in the shadows.

A balding man bent over a cart approached me. He concentrated on keeping rattling test tubes upright and paid me no heed. There must be a laboratory located in the vicinity I thought to myself. I knew Nurse Phillips spent part of her time assisting with research experiments. Was she headed into one of the myriad of doors scattered throughout the maze?

I almost tripped over a snoring old man propped against the wall in front of me. I had recently read a story in the New York Times about the city-like atmosphere of Bellevue, with its interconnecting buildings and its seventy-five exits. No wonder the homeless accessed the tunnels seeking warmth and safety within the bowels of the so-called city of Bellevue. Security was impossible. The open doorways served as a sieve for people to come and go as they pleased.

I rounded a corner in the tunnel maze and suddenly stopped, ducking into a stairwell so as not to be seen. Dr. Bender stood silently glaring at Nurse Phillips who had her back to the doctor and was rapping on a heavy metal door.

I was close enough that I heard a clicking sound. The door creaked open revealing a glaring white light-filled space. I heard Nurse Phillips speak but was not close enough to make out her words--they were muffled.

Someone opened the door wide enough for May to squeeze through. I observed a glint of shiny metal and heard the squeak of something moving within. The door slammed shut swallowing Nurse Phillips within.

Dr. Bender crossed her arms and nodded her head, as if she had caught Nurse Phillips in an indecent act. She studied the door intently as if to memorize its location. Then she turned abruptly and started walking back toward me.

I shrunk back into the shadows of the stairwell. The doctor was frowning and talking to herself.

She raised her fist in a menacing manner and spoke to herself. "Damn that nurse! I will get even with her for making me look like a fool in front of the head of the medical staff. What can she possibly know about electroshock therapy? This is MY area of expertise and I won't allow my important research to be sullied."

The homeless man snapped awake at the unexpected tirade from the doctor and tried to raise himself up on his elbows.

"What?" he croaked in his drunken voice.

In an instant, Dr. Bender reached the old man and viciously kicked him in the lower spine. "Listen old man, you piece of shit, get out of here! We don't need the likes of you stinking the place up."

The man screeched with pain as Dr. Bender, the doer of good works Ha! continued to kick him in the abdomen and around the head.

She gave him one final kick which left him trembling and hunched in the fetal position. She picked up the half empty whiskey bottle and slammed it against the fetid walls spraying its contents everywhere. Shattered glass shards rained down on the beaten man.

I cursed the doctor silently and impatiently waited for her departure.

"Sir, let me help you," I said as I stepped out of my hiding place.

I took his arm and helped him to his feet. He was whimpering, and his gait was unsteady as I wrapped my arms around his waist and escorted him to one of the many exits. I gently pulled open the door and led another soul into the open air of New York City. He disappeared into the night mist.

Slick with perspiration and a pounding frontal headache, I tried to gain my bearings as I pondered the return path to the Bellevue children's psychiatric ward.

One thing I understood. I had more questions than answers about the complex Nurse Phillips and her presence at Bellevue Hospital. She was clearly an enigma. And I intended to find the answers to my questions no matter what it would take.

The Wolfpack floated into my mind…Aunt Liz, Cousin Kat the (famous or infamous?) Eva Braun and me, Billy Love Wolf. We were a fearsome group of four women whose life experiences across the globe gave us the tools to solve problems within society—a society fraught with secrets and espionage. It seemed like for all our attempts at normalcy, there was nothing "normal" about any of us. But as a group the clan gave me energy and a renewed purpose.

I straightened and began my determined trudge back through the labyrinth. Parker would be worried about my prolonged disappearance and I needed to get back to my children, precious Ursula and Renata.

Suddenly I had clarity—I had plunged down the Rabbit Hole and had entered *Wonderland*. Where was White Rabbit when I needed him, but then again who needed *Rabbit* when I could rely on *the Wolfpack*?

Chapter 11
Two Worlds

East Berlin and West Berlin
Germany
1951
Elisabetha

Thanks to the Marshall Plan West Berlin continued to make progress in cleaning up the massive destruction created by allied bombing at the end of World War II. However, East Berlin which was occupied by Russia wallowed in the rubble of fallen buildings. It was clear that the Russians wanted to punish the defeated people of East Germany and suppress any hint of an uprising against the Bolshevik nation.

East Berlin was maligned and singled out for the wrath of Russian officials. At the Brandenburg Gate barbed-wire divided the city and served as a reminder of Russian power over its defeated German constituents.

Yet the barbed wire was but an artificial symbol that failed to deter those determined to embrace the holism of their chosen city. Though Berlin had been carved up among the allies and the Russians most people ignored the borders and freely roamed the entire city.

Residents of East Berlin commuted west to the vibrant part of the city via an urban railway and subway and, in turn, West Berliners streamed to East Berlin's opera houses and dined at their up-scale restaurants—all for rock-bottom prices.

In the aftermath of the war Berlin was the subject of world-wide interest with many reporters flocking to cover the ever-evolving politics between East and West. For even though the city itself lay deep in east Germany territory the Americans in particular were adamant that they control the western part of the city—preserving German culture was paramount. But the Russians were highly suspicious of the American motives and chafed at the thought of acquiescing to them.

Hence the tensions of the *Cold War* hostilities played out on a daily basis in the city of *The Bear,* an emblem of strength. What was propaganda and what was truth? It was difficult to discern.

Leon and I recounted the posturing between nations that occurred at the UNICEF dinner held in West Berlin.

"Liz, I think the Russian ambassadors were all bluster. They shot their pistols in the air to create a scene, but they were just showing off while trying to impress the crowd."

I shut my eyes and conjured up the whole episode which ended the glamorous evening.

My voice reflected disgust. "Yes, those idiots created a scene at the expense of all of those innocent Russian children who are lingering in the gulags…which by the way are not dissimilar to Hitler's concentration camps."

I continued. "It was like watching little boys in a pissing match! Excuse my language but really it's not all about decorated old men," I erupted.

Leon gave a short staccatoed laugh then tipped his chair back on two legs and withdrew a cigar from his pants pocket. He struck a match and sucked on the blunt end of the cigar then watched as the acrid smoke curled in the air. Usually he talked in short bursts but tonight he chose his words more carefully as he spoke.

"Well, Audrey essentially saved the night—she is quite the humanitarian, isn't she? So much more intelligent than most of those air-head Hollywood starlets. Miss Hepburn uses her celebrity status and helps others to the fullest extent."

I nodded in agreement. Audrey Hepburn was just out of her teens, yet she was making an impact on what transpired among nations. She would never forget what happened to her when the Nazis occupied Amsterdam—and she would remind the world what had occurred every chance that she got. The brutality of the third Reich created misery and destruction that should never be erased. And Hitler's army not only terrorized people of the Jewish faith, the entire occupied population was starved and treatment for disease and illness were withheld.

Why were humans always looking for the next fight, the next country that would succumb to the threat of annihilation by evil forces? I understood I was being philosophical, not practical but when would peace prevail? Never? Sometimes I was discouraged beyond what words could describe. And the great United States was not without fault itself.

There were many examples. My darling niece Katerina was subject to discrimination from her own in-laws. And recently she and Jack were summoned to Wolfgang's school…He was beaten and called a dirty Russian Jew! He, only in his early teens. A child still. And yet when Kat called she informed me that the school brushed the incident aside after insinuating that Wolfgang had provoked the attack. Shy long-locked Wolfgang who loved his dog Schnitzel and would never initiate a fight with a gang of bullies.

I shook my head and came out of my trance. Leon was talking to me.

"Liz, did you hear me? We must continue UNICEF's efforts to reach the thousands of isolated Russian children. I think the next step is to secure a meeting with the Russian officials to discuss Audrey traveling into the country, perhaps in the guise of starring in a new Hollywood movie that could be filmed there?"

"Leon, do you think it is a possibility? I mean if there is any way we could make inroads into getting the Russian children assistance. Using a glamorous star as a cover…." My voice trailed off as I considered Leon's proposal.

I stood and walked over to the giant map which took up one wall of the conference room. There were pins placed in the various countries where UNICEF was currently in action. Leon watched me intently as I read the plaque that stated UNICEF's mission.

To advocate for the protection of children's rights, to help meet their basic needs and to expand their opportunities to reach their full potential.

I flicked my hand over the map which contained the world's geography. There was one location where there was a distinct absence of markers.

"Look at the tremendous expanse of land in Soviet Union. It is a shame, Leon, a shame that children are not receiving help from UNICEF there."

"Liz there is no need to dwell on the situation. We need to take action."

Leon stood up and adjusted his red suspenders then reached for the black rotary phone.

I watched him as he dialed an unknown number. What was he doing?

"Marlene, is that you? I need a favor." Leon turned his growly voice down a notch to prevent the staff from eavesdropping on the phone call.

Marlene? Yes, Marlene. The ballsy Hollywood star who was a *Russian* at heart. She could be the key to our success.

Marlene's sexy voice emerged from a staticky speaker phone.

"Anything for you Leon, you know that."

"Marlene, can you get one of those directors interested in making a movie in Russia?" Leon asked as his voice rose in anticipation of her response. He leaned forward so that he spoke directly into the speaker.

"OOOOh, darling, of course. Let me work on the situation right away."

"Audrey Hepburn will need to star in the movie of course, and we wouldn't be making any firm commitments. It would be a preliminary meeting with interested Soviet officials and then perhaps a journey to possible locations."

I smiled slyly. I was quite sure Marlene could influence a Hollywood director to bring an entourage to Russia to explore movie locations. And the group needed to include Audrey and my Katerina who had strong Russian connections. Why else would the ambassador's wife ask me to deliver a secret letter to Kat? I knew Kat's mother was Russian—there had to be a link. For now, I needed to concentrate solely on how to get UNICEF into the Russian world.

I sat back in my chair and crossed my arms. The official meeting with the Soviets would include Mrs. Ilya Petrov, the wife of the Russian ambassador Petrov…who so nonchalantly shot up the room at the UNICEF fundraiser. I was absolutely sure of it. And she would have suggestions as to the best location for an American movie.

My mind traveled to possibilities. I would advocate for Karina Petrov to be our guide into Russia. Her appointment would be a perfect solution. She was the key to making clandestine moves. After all wasn't she the mysterious courier who brought the sealed letter to me—destination Katerina Wolf Remington?

Leon hung up the phone and looked at me with a smug expression.

In return I raised my eyebrows giving him tacit approval for the Soviet scheme.

Somehow Marlene Dietrich always emerged as a key player in our lives. Whether she could be trusted to keep our secrets was open to debate. But one thing I understood—Marlene may have German roots, having been born and raised outside Berlin but her loyalties stood with Americans. Ironically Marlene also harbored a penchant for everything Russian. Hence, she had one foot in the west and one in the east. Would she be the right person to bridge the two worlds?

There came a time when the risk to remain tight in the bud was more painful than the risk it took to blossom.
~ Anais Nin

Chapter 12
Mohonk

Upstate New York and New York City
1951
Katerina

"Jack, I am so angry right now. Why does violence keep rearing its ugly head? What did my precious Wolfgang possibly do to provoke such an attack? I want to do something. Take a hammer and smash out all of the windows at the school."

I paced back and forth throwing out questions and demanding answers. I understood I was being irrational. But I had had enough—I was intolerant of the intolerant. It was 1951. Discrimination against people simply for the color of their skin, their religious beliefs or their country of origin was antithetical to human morality.

"Kat, keep your voice down. Wolfgang needs to rest and heal. He doesn't need to relive his experience right now," Jack said as he seated himself at the kitchen table and poured himself a finger of brandy.

I picked up the decanter and sloshed golden liquid into my own glass. Then I tipped my head back and gulped the burning liquor down my throat. I wiped my hand across my mouth and trembled.

My mind raced. I would not sit back and become a party to such an injustice. Anger would propel me to take action.

Jack covered my hand with his.

"Give yourself a day or two to process everything. Try not to act rashly," Jack said in his usual calm voice.

I pulled my hand away from his and looked down at my soaked jacket—Wolfgang's head had lain against my chest—and imprinted the fabric with blood.

"No, Jack I will scream and rage and scratch out someone's eyes. It is our child, Jack. And you sit back and make light of the situation," I railed.

"And what right did those hooligans have shaving off my boy's curls? They are despicable!" I added as I slammed my empty glass down on the table.

"Honey, I do understand your frustration completely. But it doesn't solve any problems."

Glaring at my husband I stripped off my ruined jacket and skirt and flung them in the corner of the room. "Wolfgang will take a long time to heal and I am not sure he can ever go back to that school," I said as I pulled on a terry-cloth robe.

Jack stood up and walked behind me. He wrapped his arms around my waist and tucked his chin into my neck. I inhaled his musky scent and tried to relax as I unclenched my jaw. It seemed like every time Wolfgang made progress there was another set-back. I was weary of it all.

"I will start looking for another school right away. In the meantime, why don't you take Wolfgang and Schnitzel up to Eva's farmhouse for a few days?" Jack asked as he tried to placate me.

Eva was fed up with New York City and all of the constant probing questions about her past, especially her relationship with Adolf Hitler. A few months ago, she had sublet her apartment and abruptly moved to the country where she was living a relatively quiet life. She spent her days tending her garden and raising chickens. Her lifestyle was a far cry from the lead up to the Second World War where treacherous days were spent with the Führer...and followed by years hiding out on Uncle A.R.'s Oklahoma ranch.

A visit to Eva's rural abode might be what we all needed. Wolfgang and Schnitzel could spend hours running and playing together. After all Eva lived close to 40,000 acres of unblemished forest in the Hudson Valley. A paradise! Dachshund Schnitzel might catch a rabbit or two and Wolfgang could explore uninhibited by stranger's stares as he healed from his bruises and pummeling by classmates. I in turn relished time away from the city. Long quiet walks treading on pine needle pathways leading up the mountains were what I needed to clear my head—to provide me with think time.

In the last few months *The Wolfpack* was juggling multiple incidents: Billy Love's decision to place Ursula in the psychiatric hospital…the arrival of my mother's old trunk and the treasures it held…the letter revealing information about my Russian grandmother…Wolfgang's trauma at school…Aunt Liz' work with UNICEF and her efforts to help children in Bolshevik-controlled Russia…and Eva's move to the rural New York in an effort to start a new life of sorts, one with more fulfillment and less stress.

Getting Wolfgang out of the city and away from taunting classmates was key to his mental health. But I also wanted the chance to have Eva Braun all to myself. To relive our golden years when I was recording sultry records and she was working the cameras for the Hollywood studios under the alias *Giselle Gregor*. It would be good to reminisce.

And then I was keen to receive an update regarding her efforts to adopt little Ruthie. The red-tape from the American Government was beyond imaginable. There was a new excuse every day. *Eva was unmarried. Eva was German, not really an American. Eva could not be trusted to raise a child. Eva was Hitler's mistress! Eva might still be plotting against America!* The messaging never ended and was yet another example of obstructionist behavior that placed an innocent child in limbo. Little Ruthie who had flourished under Eva's care was being denied a loving home—Eva Braun's loving abode.

****

Jack had arranged for me to rent a gleaming-red Super Buick for our road trip upstate. I walked around the vehicle admiring it and running my hands over its features.

"Kat, you had better get going if you are going to arrive at Eva's before dark," he admonished me. I pretended to ignore him as I opened the trunk and gently piled the suitcases on top of each other.

137

I understood that Jack would utilize his time wisely while Wolfgang and I were away. He had been called to Washington D.C. to head up a special project for the government. It seemed that our family had an endless penchant for secrecy on all fronts— His new job had something to do with security now that the Cold War between the east and west was raging.

When I returned from my trip I would press him on the job's details. There was no conceivable excuse for keeping me in the dark…after all, we had a partnership that depended on honesty.

I slammed the trunk of the car shut and kissed Jack goodbye as I climbed into the driver's seat. I shifted the car into gear…we all waved to each other and I set out to navigate the heavy traffic of the city.

Wolfgang and Schnitzel snuggled up together under a blanket in the backseat and promptly went to sleep. Both of them emitted soft snoring sounds. I pulled on over-size sun glasses, rolled down the window and headed out of the city feeling the early spring breeze riff through my curly chestnut hair. As I became closer to New Paltz the road steadily climbed into mountain country taking unexpected twists and turns as the car traversed into higher altitudes. The views became spectacular and the aromatic smells of spring flowers and fresh pine needles wafted into the car filling it with a natural perfume. I could understand Eva's decision to move to the country.

Wolfgang poked his head out of the blanket and rubbed his eyes.

"It smells so good," he said with a lop-sided grin, the first sign that Jack and I had made a good call in taking Wolfgang out of the city.

I glanced into the rear-view mirror and grimaced at what I saw. Wolfgang's injuries were still healing. His inky black eyes had gradually turned to violet and then to a yellowish-green. He wore a stocking cap pulled low on his brow to conceal his jagged hair which when revealed made him look like a scare-crow. A sling encased his left arm—to support the sprained limb that resulted from the bullies twisting it behind his back.

I became enraged all over again. Damn those privileged boys who thought they ruled the world through their obnoxious and violent behavior!

Why was Wolfgang a target over and over again? He was a gangly teenager now and I often wondered how he endured the first years of his life sequestered in the harsh life of Dachau. Samuel, a concentration camp survivor had revealed that Wolfgang's mother was sent to the concentration camp by his own biological father, Prince Von Hessen when he found out she was Jewish.

How does a child reckon with such a terrible scenario? For Wolfgang he must have suppressed his dire circumstances for he rarely asked any questions about his parental heritage. And Jack and I agreed that we would be patient with our son. There was no reason to inflict additional psychological harm—he was not ready to know about the father who had abandoned him. The father who continued to live in relative comfort within Germany and who was responsible for sending his mother to the gas chamber.

I sighed and straightened my shoulders as I kept both hands on the wheel and concentrated on the journey up the mountain. There would be time later to process with Eva. Eva—my sister in spirit.

Glancing at the map spread on the seat beside me I pinpointed Eva's house. My eyes shifted to the left of her location where I noticed just a few miles away from her abode Lake Mohonk and the towering Victorian Mohonk Mountain House dominated the map. I was curious—Eva planned for us to hike over to the beautiful lodge which over the years had hosted dignitaries from all over the world—and housed a plethora of secrets. What would we discover?

I folded the map. A small white two-story farm house with several outbuildings came into view.

"Wolfgang, Schnitzel, here we are!" I called out.

Schnitzel emerged from the blanket and yapped seemingly delighted to be on an adventure. She lifted her front paws onto my head rest and panted. I gently pushed the dog down and honked the horn announcing our arrival.

The screen door opened and Eva Braun strode out of the paint-peeling house. Although she would turn forty soon she was still glamorous with her high cheekbones and pointed chin courtesy of plastic surgery that once concealed her identity from the world and kept her safe from the clutches of the Nazi regime.

Her blonde hair was swept up out of her face and even wrapped in a burlap apron she radiated personality and glamour.

"Darling Kat, here you are and Wolfgang oh, and Schnitzel," she laughed as she clapped her hands.

I opened the back door and Schnitzel bounded across the gravel drive-way landing in Eva's lap and almost knocking her over in the process.

"Schnitzel, no, down," Wolfgang yelled as he leapt after his dog.

"It's okay. She will calm down after she gets used to the place. And there are some big cats for her to chase too," Eva replied.

I watched Eva and Wolfgang's affectionate interaction as I opened the trunk to retrieve my suitcase. I felt a twinge of guilt. I had a child and Eva did not. The absence of Ruthie hung thickly in the air and I made a vow to dig deeper into the orphanage's denial of Eva's adoption of the young girl. The rebuke was yet another form of discrimination…Why not give Ruthie the loving home she deserved with a mother who was deeply attached to her?

Eva patted Wolfgang on his stockinged head and handed him a bucket. She made no mention of his appearance. I was appreciative of her sensitivity. Another reason to cherish our friendship.

"Here is some grain. Why don't you feed the chickens, Wolfgang? It will be fun. Then you can collect the hens' eggs and bring them into the house. They will be delicious for breakfast, no?"

Wolfgang nodded grabbed the pail and marched toward the low building. I could hear the hens cackling and the flapping of their wings as he yanked open the door to the shed.

I lifted the trunk and grunting I hauled the heavy suitcase across the gravel driveway. Tucked inside wrapped in reams of protective tissue paper rested the nested Russian dolls. I had yet to decide if I would reveal them to Eva or even hint at their connection to my mother. Jack was unaware that I had taken them from the trunk and although I felt a bit guilty about my deception, in the end it was my decision—it was my heritage after all. I would share my secrets with whomever I wished.

My earlier thoughts about Jack's new job popped into my head. I had just vowed to be honest with him and now I was considering sharing my Russian treasures with Eva—and keeping the knowledge from my husband. Guilt assuaged me, but I brushed it away for now.

"Let's hope Wolfgang doesn't get pecked Eva," I called out.

"Nonsense. He can take care of himself Kat."

I set my suitcase at Eva's feet and reached to hug her tightly.

Switching abruptly from English to German I asked.

"*Wie geht es dir?*"

Eva replied, "Mir geht es gut Ruthie."

"I understand. You are well in mind and body but not in spirit. When you have Ruthie with you then you will be healed in your spirit," I interpreted.

It was so reassuring, easy to slide into my native German language. Fluent in three languages I was certain that my Russian skills would also be useful in solving the unexpected mysteries placed before me.

"Come, let's catch up," Eva said as she held open the screen door and Schnitzel leapt up the stairs before us into the kitchen.

I reached for the handle of my suitcase and pulled it up. What would people think of the glamorous Eva Braun living life in a farm house? It wasn't such a stretch. After all she lived on a ranch in Oklahoma for years. Maybe it was a desire to return to her roots. Really it was no one's business, was it? Except for members of *The Wolfpack* of course.

****

It was early…five in the morning. We were up and dressed and ready for our hike to Mohonk Mountain House. It was chilly even though there was no wind and the skies were cloudless. After all we were 1200 feet above sea level.

Eva had fixed us a hearty breakfast of scrambled eggs, bacon and wheat toast. Our bellies were full and would sustain us on our journey through the wooded mountains.

Wolfgang and Schnitzel were still asleep, tangled together on the twin bed in the guest room. Wolfgang had elected to stay behind at the farmhouse—he was not ready to display his injuries—and so he and Schnitzel would explore the area uninhibited and freed from the shackles of stares.

Eva and I sat on a heavy oak bench and pulled on rough-soled boots. We were prepared for the trek decked in tweed sweaters and woolen head scarves.

Wolfgang appeared at the top of the staircase with his saw-toothed hair in full display.

"Ta Ta Wolfgang, we shall be back in late afternoon," I said.

He smiled shyly and waved us good-bye.

Eva and I locked arms and began to pick our way through the thick forest, where sun-light randomly dotted the pine-laden path.

As we moved steadily toward our destination I reflected. We had stayed up late talking and relaying idle gossip but not addressing the primary reasons we had come together—Wolfgang and Ruthie. We needed one night free from problems. And one day of a hiking adventure that would lead to what the locals called *The Victorian Castle, Mohonk.*

We moved steadily toward our destination.

"Eva, tell me about this magical place we will visit."

"I don't know too much about the place. Just that twin brothers Alfred and Albert Smiley built it as a sort of retreat where people could go to connect the mind, body, and soul. There are beautiful gardens, hiking trails all throughout the many acres, a horse-riding barn, and beautiful tall hedges of interconnected mazes. Mohonk Lake sits in front of the lodge. Perhaps we can even paddle a rowboat out on the water this afternoon."

"It all sounds heavenly, Eva. I can see why you are enamored with your life up here."

Eva nodded. We continued in silence as we soaked in the stillness of the environment. It was punctured once in a while with the caws of crows and the scurrying red-tailed squirrels leaping from one branch to the next, sassing at each other, nuts buried deep in their cheeks.

Above us in perfect v-formation was a flock of geese winging their way south, making their way from Canada to warmer climates. I watched as one of the geese moved out of position and approached the leader in the nose position. Deftly the goose nudged aside the other goose and replaced him, giving him a rest.

It was a remarkable gesture illustrating how the birds worked together for the good of the group. It was notable how components of nature are often repeated in other settings—similar to our *Wolfpack*. Sometimes it was imperative that you confide in each other and work together…to make the whole family stronger.

I thought again about the nesting dolls. My urge to confide in Eva as to their existence became stronger—almost urgent. I was still uncertain though. Jack trusted me to remain silent. The secrets of the trunk must remain hidden. For now.

****

Eva and I stood before the magnificent lodge and shielded our eyes from the glaring sun that backlit the building. It was like a mirage with its Victorian turrets red-tile roofs and dormer windows dominating the sky-line. Adirondack rocking chairs dotted balconies. With the shimmering Mohonk Lake cloaking the hotel in its forefront and the majestic forested mountains framing its backdrop it represented a beauty like none other I had experienced—even the castles of Germany could not compete with its majesty.

Eva's spoke quietly.

"Katerina, do you understand what I meant about this place? You have to experience it to understand how such an oasis could even exist."

I continued staring trying to take in the scenery and searing the picture into my mind.

Smiling broadly, I tossed my head as if to make sure the image was not imagined.

"Eva, thank you for bringing me here. I feel like I am floating—all of the problems and evilness in the world are gone or at least hidden from view."

"Indeed. This place can heal the soul. Come, I see Mr. Smiley out front. He is waving his hat at us."

"Mr. Smiley?"

Eva waved back acknowledging the gentleman.

"His family owns all of this magnificence. They are truly stewards of the land and committed to living in peace and harmony. They are Quakers," Eva explained.

My brow furrowed as we began our decent toward the lodge.

"Quakers?" I asked.

"Yes. The way Mr. Smiley explained it to me is, to quote him. *'A way of living in the world so that the world is more just, loving and peaceable by his or her presence.'*"

"Is it a religion?"

"Most people who identify as a Quaker believe understanding and experiencing God leads to a rich life."

"And all of this is dedicated to the Quaker beliefs?"

"Yes Kat, and I have decided to dedicate my life to being a *Friend.*"

"Why Eva we are already friends right?" I was confused.

"It has a new meaning for me now. I grew up Roman Catholic and while that religion comforts a great mass of people, for me I needed something different. I am surrounded by fellow *Friends.*"

I needed more clarity but for now I would follow Eva's lead and absorb the whole *Mohonk* experience.

"Come on, Kat. Mr. Smiley will explain more when he tours us through the hotel."

We picked up our pace and finally stepped on the rough-hewn dock that jutted into the lake.

Mr. Smiley grinned and gently hugged Eva. He shook my hand with a reassuring grip.

I took in his appearance. He was a slight man, with a receding hairline that culminated in thinning gray hair. There was a presence about him that I sensed. He was sure of himself, yet he was warm and engaging—interested in others.

Mr. Smiley's eyes twinkled.

"You are Katarina Wolf, part of the famous *Wolfpack*, huh?"

I bantered with him.

"Aaah, Eva has told you about our unique clan, has she? My cousin Billy Love and my Aunt Liz along with some of my other relatives retrieved Eva from some unpleasantries so to speak."

Eva rolled her eyes and snorted. "Something like that Katerina."

"Kat, we here at *Mohonk* are well aware of your family's role in helping Eva. We have your papa's book in our library. And by the way call me Bert. Mr. Smiley sounds like my father."

"Bert it is then."

"*Friend* Braun, I have you scheduled to address the Quaker's conference coming up. Is that agreeable with you?"

Conference? Whatever is going on with Eva? She seems to have more surprises than me. Now my curiosity was spiraling out of control. When Jack suggested this trip might do me some good he had no idea where my adventures might take me. And *Mohonk* would play a central role I was sure of it.

Mr. Smiley led us into the massive wooden beamed lobby. An eight-armed chandelier dominated the ceiling and the nature-like red floral wall-to-wall carpet completed the picture. Black and white photos lined the walls…some of them clearly revealing Victorian era gatherings.

"I want to take you into our dining room first. It was completed in 1893."

We followed him into the formal room with windows overlooking the lake. In the far corner of the room a massive stone fireplace stood as if waiting for frigid winter temperatures to

145

employ its use. Wooden tables draped with pristine white linens dotted the room.

Once again, the walls were filled with photos dating from 1895 to the early 1900s.

"Kat these photos are very important to the legacy of Quakers," Mr. Smiley said.

I edged closer to scrutinize the photos which were group pictures of mostly men.

"My family initiated the International Arbitration Conferences to seek solutions to global, national and local problems. Specifically, the focus was on peace—a cause that Quakers support," Bert lectured as he walked and pointed to each photograph.

My eyes started to glaze over as the group photos became monotonous. They all looked the same...the men all dressed in three-piece suits and Bowler hats.

The three of us turned a corner and I abruptly halted as I came face to face with a portrait that dominated an entire wall. I gaped.

It was a portrait of Czar Nicolas II, the last Russian czar of the Romanov family.

What was its meaning? I stepped closer to examine it.

The painting was completely out of place, disconnected from the other ordinary gray photos. And it was prominently placed so that most of the diners had a clear view of the oil painting. The czar was depicted in full midnight blue military uniform with golden shoulder epilates and multiple medals pinned to the coat's bodice. A light blue sash traversed diagonally across his chest. With his slicked back dark hair and his thick mustache and short beard he looked every bit the regal king.

My Russian mother Irina floated into my mind blocking everything else out. I thought about my conversations with Papa...he had mentioned the possibility that my mother may have had royal connections. And once again I was reminded of the contents of the old trunk—the letter, the Fabergé egg, the nesting dolls, the diamond ring and the painting of my mother wearing a tiara and garbed in a beautiful gown.

Eva and Bert walked up beside me and stood on either side. They waited for my reaction not wanting to intrude on my thoughts. But what were my thoughts? I was perplexed.

"Kat, let me tell you about this portrait. You seem to be very intrigued," Bert said.

I paused then blurted out. "My mother was Russian. She was sent to Germany when she was seventeen, but my papa had no explanation as to why she was exiled. At the time there was a lot of unrest swirling around the Romanov family and about Czar Nicholas in particular. Uprisings among the peasants were common and members of the royal family were targeted with violence. Some were driven from lands they inhabited for generations which left them destitute."

"Kat, I believe there were many sides to the czar. History labeled him as a weak leader and that was the explanation as to why the Bolsheviks were able to overthrow him and his regime, thus ending the monarchy. But here at *Mohonk* we keep his portrait as a reminder of how he tried to broker peace in the world whatever his motives may have been," Mr. Smiley explained.

"Why is it that people are unaware of this? It is a remarkable story," I said. I leaned in to examine the portrait more closely.

"Yes, it is and we have original correspondence between Alfred and Albert Smiley—who initiated the World Peace Conferences—and Czar Nicholas. My relatives encouraged the czar to further initiate peace talks at The Hague in the Netherlands."

Bert continued as he took my arm and guided me to the next room where I encountered another large oil-portrait—that of Albert Smiley. It was dated 1911.

"You see, Czar Nicolas II and Albert Smiley had a common cause in the early 1900s. World peace—to *make the idea of universal peace triumph over the elements of trouble and discord.*"

How had the world moved so far away from this philosophy? How could it be, that in 1951 following a horrific World War II experience, we were embroiled in the Cold War between East and West?

147

Eva clutched Bert's arm and turned him toward her. Her blue eyes bored into his.

"But Bert the peace movement was going so well. Wasn't the czar nominated for the Noble Peace Prize? I don't understand how he could have moved from peace broker to declaring war on Germany in such a short period of time."

"Most people believe he was unduly influenced by his generals who in 1914 felt Russia must invade Germany in order to survive as a nation—in order to protect the monarchy. He probably was given no choice," Bert explained as he led Eva and me across the dining room and into an original parlor.

My mind was spinning. All of the propaganda about the Romanovs had pointed to a power-hungry monarchy. The Bolsheviks portrayed the royals as one-sided evil rulers who must be overthrown so that the common people could reap the benefits of a fulfilling life. But in reality, dictators had taken over the vast regime and ruled it with an iron hand. Any dissent from the masses resulted in massive crackdowns trips to the gulags torture and murder. Lenin followed by Stalin—one after the other.

"Bert, I am amazed about the connections between your family and the czar. So important—why does the rest of the world have no inkling about your efforts to promote harmony?" I asked.

"Our family desperately tried to influence the leaders at the time, but World War I broke out and the peace efforts were buried. It was a sad time in history."

Eva looked down at her feet deep in thought. I was awash with emotion, unable to describe my feelings—guilt, sadness, anxiety, anger?

Bert broke into our thoughts.

"Let's have some tea and refreshments before I take you on the rest of the tour." He motioned to the waitress who promptly returned with a large porcelain tea pot and matching cups.

We sipped the steaming brew.

"Kat, this is where the hub of activity takes place at Mohonk," Eva explained.

"Right, there are music events, evening song, and all sorts of entertainment. And papers are read here," Bert said as he pointed to the elevated stage.

"Papers?" I asked as I wrinkled my brow.

"Anything from poetry to political position papers Kat," Bert said. "Eva will be reading her paper here at the conference."

"Eva?" I turned toward her.

"Kat, I will fill you in when we get back to the farmhouse tonight."

Bert deferred to Eva but did not divulge the topic of her presentation. He knew exactly what she would reveal.

I put the knowledge of Eva's paper aside and we spent the next hour examining the nooks and crannies of the rambling lodge.

"Ladies, let's finish our tour with a boat ride across the lake, shall we?"

We walked back to the docks adorning the tranquil Lake Mohonk, stepped into a row boat and seated ourselves on the wooden benches. Bert grabbed the oars and pulled them steadily through the waters. He pointed out the bull snakes sunning on the stone façade of the buildings and the deer chasing each other throughout the lush grounds.

I sat back and enjoyed the sun on my face. I could stay here forever tucked away from the world. Reveling in the quiet atmosphere. You could sense a commitment to Quaker values: simplicity, peace, integrity, community, and equality.

People must do justice, love mercy,
and walk humbly with the God who cherishes all.
~ The Prophet Micah

****

"Wolfgang we are home," Eva called out.

I trailed behind Eva and watched the sun descend behind the mountains. The sky was a mixture of pinks, yellows and oranges caressing the sky.

I pondered my hiking trip to Mohonk Mountain House. I had discovered a full dose of history—and it had prompted me to consider new ways of thinking about my own story. The entanglement of the Germans and Russians and Americans, the influence of religion and philosophy, the struggle for world power. The absence of black and white...the gray smudging decision-making.

Most people never stopped to consider the complexities of our very existence.

My thirst for learning would thrust me forward in my life journey. Thank goodness I had the love and support of *the expanded Wolfpack...*

Chapter 13
The Queen of Hearts

New York City
1951
Billy Love

"Parker, Ursula and Renata have one last play session at Bellevue Hospital today. If Ursula continues to make progress she will be discharged to us soon."

Parker ran a comb through his thick hair and splashed on aftershave. "Billy Love, Nurse Phillips is a savior. Ursula never would have blossomed like she has without her."

"I am so grateful that Ursula will be able to continue outpatient therapy with her at Bellevue and at Nurse Phillips' home."

"Do the medical administrators at Bellevue realize that Ursula is making frequent visits to Nurse Phillip's residence?" Parker asked.

"No, and I will not tell those people who think they know what is best for our daughter. They understand that May takes Ursula on frequent outings, but they think she is taking her to a park. At her home there is privacy...Ursula is free to frolic and play and be a kid away from the regiments of institutional life."

"Ursula thrives on the environment Nurse Phillips has created for her, Billy Love. She established Ursula's own flower garden and encourages her to pick bouquets whenever she pleases which is quite often I must say. Ha! She lets her slide down the curly-cue bannister and eat messy fried chicken while lounging on a blanket thrown upon the floor. Nurse Phillips ignores greasy hands and all semblance of decorum. She created a child's utopia."

Parker turned toward me and smiled broadly. The trademark dimple in his check became prominent.

I concurred with Parker's sentiment...we were a lucky family.

"On another note Parker, Nurse Phillips wants us all to meet her husband."

"Her husband? I had no idea she was married. Why have we never met him?"

"I'm not sure Parker, but May has decided now is the time to introduce him and we should accept her decision."

Parker nodded his assent.

Renata knocked on the door and pushed it open without waiting for our response.

"Is it true Mommy? Is Ursie coming home soon?"

"Yes, Rennie depending on how the session goes today."

"I am so happy!" Renata said as she skipped and twirled across our bedroom. She clutched *Alice in Wonderland* to her chest.

"And Mommy, you look so pretty today. Ursie will love your outfit. Pink is her favorite color."

I smiled and winked at Parker. Truly, the change in Renata had been as remarkable as Ursula's transformation. She was happy and care-free. Renata had experienced the burden of perceived responsibility for her sister shift to a healthcare professional, a caring therapeutic nurse. Renata was able to become a giddy soon-to-be teenager.

I attempted to hug Renata, but she pulled away asserting her independence. I wouldn't have her to myself for long. She was changing and growing toward an adult life of her own. For now, I would treasure our relationship.

"I see you are ready to show Ursula your diary," I said pointing to her book.

"Yes, this story is the hardest one yet," she announced as she opened the book and pointed to Chapter Eight.

"The Queen of Hearts wants to behead Alice all for some silly antics," Renata said as she showed the pictures of Alice holding the flamingo upside down. The bird served as her croquet mallet.

"Renata, thank you for helping Ursula by playing with her and encouraging her. You know we couldn't have done it without your help. You are the best sister anyone could ask for," Parker said.

He playfully grabbed her and swung her around until she was giddy and dizzy. He released her suddenly and her legs wobbled as she tried to straighten up.

She giggled. "Daddy, thank you."

Renata suddenly looked grown up. I could picture her in the future…with her delicate features, dark eyes and hair—her blossoming lithe figure. I knew she would become a grounded, compassionate adult who reached out and helped people from all walks of life.

I cleared my mind and returned to the present.

I was dressed in a pale pink cashmere sweater set. Looking in the full-length mirror I smoothed my pencil skirt and fastened the single strand of alabaster pearls around my neck. My dark tresses were knotted into a low bun and I had tied a pink satin ribbon around it. It was important to me that I looked pulled together. These days I rarely had the occasion to dress up so I took advantage of the opportunity. After all, Nurse Phillips had invited our family to meet her mysterious husband.

Behind me, Renata's reflection appeared in the mirror.

She pointed to her feet and laughed.

"What's so funny?" I asked.

"Won't Ursie be surprised when we give her the gift?"

I glanced over at the gayly-wrapped package sitting on the bed. Inside it nestled a brand-new pair of black and white saddle shoes. They were the latest fashion rage.

"Indeed, she will," I answered.

Gleefully Renata called out. "We will be alike now, like twins. And Ursie and I shall wear them to the Queen of Hearts croquet game!"

"Well, now we shan't be late madam or the party might start without us. Come," Parker said.

He picked up the package on the bed which contained the saddle shoes and made a swooping gesture.

"Ursula and the king and queen await our arrival."

Renata and I fell in line behind Parker make-believing our own royal processional…then we headed to *Wonderland* and Miss Ursula Remington who resided at Bellevue Psychiatric Hospital.

****

153

Ursula sat on the edge of her spartan-like iron bed and swung her legs rhythmically back and forth. She smiled shyly and stared at the shoes adorning her feet.

"Rennie, we match, don't we?" Ursula asked.

"We certainly do. These shoes will help us when we confront the evil Queen of Hearts, Ursie," Renata said.

She sat beside Ursula on the bed as they kicked their feet in unison and admired their polished saddle shoes.

"We even have on our overalls, today don't we?" Ursula asked.

Renata grabbed Ursula's hand and squeezed it possessively.

"We sure do. Now let's get the puppets out before Nurse Phillips gets here."

The girls climbed off the bed and made their way to the table housing the *Wonderland* puppets. Parker and I stood in the back of the room. We were silent as we watched the girls interact with each other.

After a few minutes of careful consideration Renata selected The Queen of Hearts and White Rabbit. Ursula hastily gathered up Alice and Flamingo.

They laid the puppets on the bed and patiently waited for Nurse Phillips' arrival knowing she would appear without warning to commence reading the chosen passage.

Ursula seemed calm. She understood how story-telling worked now and she trusted the process.

May strode the room carrying the bookmarked *Alice in Wonderland*. Always encased in her crisp white linen uniform with the cap pinned tightly to her scalp she commanded attention in her no-nonsense way.

My heart quickened. I yearned for a positive outcome—for both my girls.

Nurse Phillips had chosen a violent passage from the book. (I wondered as to the intent of author Lewis Carroll—it was a children's book after all. Did he mean to scare youngsters? But then, he often threw in silly escapades that made the rantings of the characters seem ridiculous).

Renata showed Parker and me her written response last night. We were eager but on edge to discover Ursula's reaction.

"Parker, Billy Love why don't you leave us while I spend a little time with the girls," she announced in an authoritative voice.

Parker and I understood that she meant for us to go to the observation room connected to Ursula's bedroom. She didn't want the children's reactions to be influenced by our presence.

I got up and took Parker's hand. We vacated the room and entered the observation room with the one-way mirror.

Why, we were Through the Looking Glass, I thought. How ironic!

I sat on the wooden bench and leaned forward.

Nurse Phillips wasted no time…She sat down in the straight-backed chair, made intimate eye-contact with the girls snapped open the book and began reading.

Her voice paused and swooped with high and low modulations making the story crackle with inflection.

Come on, then! roared the Queen, and Alice joined the procession, wondering very much what would happen next.

It's—it's a very fine day! Said a timid voice at her side. She was walking by the White Rabbit, who was peeping anxiously into her face.

"Very," said Alice. "Where's the Duchess?"

Hush! Hush! Said the Rabbit in a low, hurried tone. He looked anxiously over his shoulder as he spoke, and then raised himself upon tiptoe, put his mouth close to her ear, and whispered. She's under sentence of execution.

"What for?" said Alice.

"Did you say What a pity!?" The Rabbit asked.

"No, I didn't," said Alice. I don't think it's at all a pity. I said What for?

She boxed the Queen's ears—the Rabbit began. Alice gave a little scream of laughter. "Oh hush!" the Rabbit whispered in a frightened tone. The Queen will hear you.

"Get to your places!" shouted the Queen in a voice of thunder, and people began running about in all directions, tumbling up against each other; however, they got settled down in a minute or two, and the game began.

Alice thought she had never seen such a curious croquet-ground in her life; it was all ridges and furrows; the balls were live hedgehogs, the mallets live flamingoes, and the soldiers had to double themselves up and to stand on their hands and feet, to make the arches.

The players all played at once without waiting for turns, quarreling all the while, and fighting for the hedgehogs; and in a very short time the Queen was in a furious passion, and went stamping about and shouting Off with his head! Or, Off with her head! Aboutonce in a minute.

Alice began to feel uneasy: to be sure, she had not as yet had any dispute with the Queen, but she knew that it might happen any minute, and then thought she, what would become of me? They're dreadfully fond of beheading people here: the great wonder is, that there's any one left alive!

She was looking about for some way of escape, and wondering whether she could get away without being seen.

May closed the book and gazed intently at each girl trying to discern their reactions. Renata seemed to be in a trance with her glazed eyes and subtle up-turned smile. It was if she was envisioning herself in the make-believe croquet game, egging on the Queen of Hearts.

Ursula was motionless with her head down, her arms clenched to her sides as if locking herself away from an intense evil.

Had Nurse Phillips gone too far? Taking Ursula to the brink of her memories? I was suddenly unsure—what if all of the progress made over the course of several months became unraveled? I stood up, intent on returning to Ursula's room.

Parker restrained my arm and put his finger to his lips. He patted the bench and urged me to return to my seat.

I angrily pulled away but acquiesced, conceding that Parker might be right.

Nurse Phillips paused then knelt before Ursula and gently lifted her chin. Her eyes made contact and she spoke quietly.

"Ursula, you are safe here. I am here. Your sister is here. Your family is near. We will all protect you. Do you understand?"

Ursula made a choking sound and then she lunged toward Nurse Phillips flinging her arms tightly around May's waist. Tears flooded in rivers down her cheeks as the wailing began—a scream so acute so intense it seemed as if she had left her body.

Nurse Phillips held Ursula tightly. Renata knelt behind Ursula and leaned into her completing a human cocoon. Ursula shook and shook and shook. She cried until there was nothing but a silent scream left.

Slowly, Nurse Phillips lifted Ursula up pulled out a white kerchief and swiped at her stricken face.

Nurse Phillips handed Ursula a notebook. Ursula hiccupped.

"Ursula, I want you to go first. Do you think you can do it?"

"I'll try Miss May," she said in a barely audible voice.

Renata encouraged her. "Little Bear, I know you can do it. I will be right here. I can even read for you if you can't finish."

Ursula pushed herself away. She sat upright with her legs crossed over each other and opened the diary.

"I can DO it!"

People started to gather in the hallway, murmuring among themselves as they tried to discover the cause of all the commotion. Nurse Phillips stepped out of the room and admonished the crowd.

"Ladies and gentlemen, there is no need for all of your gawking. We are in a hospital after all and treatments are taking place. Give us some privacy, now shoo." She made an elaborate sweeping motion.

The crowd retreated intimidated by her demeanor.

"Please Ursula, begin," said May.

Ursula straightened her spine and cleared her throat. She became resolute.

Soldiers began marching in a line one after another, like robots. They were scary and mean. Someone was yelling through a horn, giving orders.

It was the Queen of Hearts—but she had no heart, Someone cut it out of her.

Someone slapped the Queen in her ears and now Queen would kill people who did this to her. People tried to run away from the Queen. Ursie was running and running too and people were bumping into each other and falling down.

Ursie held MOOOOMY's hand, but suddenly MOOOOMY wasn't holding Ursie's hand. Ursie was standing in the middle of the ground looking around.

White Rabbit was there, but he was too timid, a scaredy cat! He did nothing to help Ursie.

Queen of Hearts said start to play the game, but this was not a game it was Real Life. She pretended hedgehogs and flamingos were real but they were not real—

No, what was real? The soldiers were real.

The soldiers twisted themselves around and around and stamped around the Grounds as the Queen shouted again and again "Off with their heads!"

The soldiers made people die. They obeyed the Queen—they shot them all in the head. Their heads were gone. DADDDDY!

Ursula was all alone looking around. Ursie shut her eyes. She did not want to look around. The Queen of Hearts was evil. Soldiers were everywhere. Ursie had done nothing wrong. Ursie needed to escape. Ursie found Renata and they ran and ran and ran.

MOOOOMY! DAAAADY! HELP ME!

All of us were stunned. We remained motionless as if suspended in another universe. Never before had Ursula been able to articulate what had happened that fateful day as the American soldiers liberated the concentration camp—the day where overzealous forces changed the narrative from joyous occasion to mass carnage.

And the defenseless children were left with memories so horrific that they spent years burying the visualizations. The concealing of memories itself was so harmful that the only emotional outlet led to tantrums acting out and harming themselves and others. To quell the pain.

Even May seemed a bit rattled by Ursula's written expressions. She pulled her round glasses off her face and rubbed the handkerchief round and round as she tried to wipe clean the smudges.

Nurse Phillips gesture was symbolic perhaps? Even though Parker and I understood what had happened at Dachau on the day of allied liberation we had never before pressed either girl to confront their memories. It had been six long years—and finally, a break-through.

Renata was staring at Ursula, beginning to understand the significance of what her sister had experienced.

She moved to glue herself to Ursula's side. She ran her hand affectionately through Ursula's hair and brought her head to her shoulder. "I am sooo sorry, Sissie."

Ursula silently handed her diary to Nurse Phillips, who then slipped it into a satchel on the floor. We all waited expectantly for Ursula to say something.

Ursula squeaked in a tinny voice. "Please, no puppets today okay Miss May?"

"Okay Ursula. No puppets. And no more Queen of Hearts either."

"The Queen is dead isn't she Nurse?"

"Indeed, she is, Ursula, indeed she is."

Nurse Phillips looked up at the window where Parker and I were viewing the interactions.

She spoke in an authoritative voice.

"Billy Love, Parker. It's time to take your precious Ursula home."

"Mommy, Daddy, I want to go home."

My heart pounded and I couldn't breathe. Never before had Ursula spoken endearments about *us, Parker and me.*

I joyfully collapsed into Parker's arms. *Mommy and Daddy* would be taking their youngest daughter home.

****

We packed Ursula's suitcase and waited for the discharge orders. Nurse Phillips had been gone a long time—I was anxious to take Ursula away from Bellevue. I understood that Ursula would need outpatient treatment but to have her home and established in somewhat of a routine of school and family life seemed like a luxury.

Someone was speaking to Nurse Phillips. They had her backed up against the dimly light hall. I strained to her what was being said and realized that Dr. Bender was speaking to her in a loud belligerent voice.

"What gives you the right to say when a patient is ready for discharge? You are but a nurse and are here to take doctor's orders. I say when she is ready to go home."

Nurse Phillips peeled with laughter.

"Now, now Dr. Bender, I kept you informed the entire time Ursula was here. And today there was a breakthrough."

"Whatever do you mean?" Dr. Bended demanded as she stomped her foot and yanked Ursula's chart out of Nurse Phillips' hands.

"Read it. I am not going to debate you standing in the hallway where others can listen. There is such a thing as patient confidentiality."

Dr. Bender pulled her ratty lab coat around her and flipped through the chart.

I raised my eyebrows at Parker…once again I was grateful that we had a nurse who championed the care for our daughter. As far as I was concerned Dr. Bender was a sadistic quack and I intended to write a note to the Chief Medical Officer outlining my concerns.

Parker winked at me and gave me encouragement. I stepped into the hall.

"Dr. Bender, you will immediately approve Ursula's discharge or Parker and I shall take the matter up with your superiors."

Dr. Bender snorted and scribbled her signature on Ursula's chart. She turned on her heel then yelled over her shoulder as she traipsed down the narrow hallway. "Nurse, you will report to me later this afternoon for another discussion about your insolent behavior."

Nurse Phillips was dismissive. "You can't teach her anything. She knows nothing about children and how their minds work. She clings to outdated and egregious therapies and actually creates more harm than good. Come, let's get Ursula out of here."

Parker nodded. "Our family is ready to be together again."

All the pretentiousness Nurse Phillips had exhibited with Dr. Bender was gone. Her voice was warm with emotion. "Speaking of family, my husband is anxious to meet you all. And he is an excellent cook. After you get Ursula settled at home and into a routine, would you kindly come to dinner at our abode?"

There was commotion as Renata and Ursula holding hands skidded into the hall. Their saddle shoes clomped in rhythm with each other.

Ursula halted in front of us and looked up expectantly at Nurse Phillips.

"Rennie you will love Nurse Phillips' house. She lets you do lots of stuff that Mommy and Daddy won't allow," Ursula said.

Nurse Phillips smiled slyly and peered at me sideways out of the corner of her eye. She said nothing.

I let go. I let it all go. I experienced emotions that had been submerged and now were lifted out of my being: joy ecstasy bliss contentment love. For my family and especially for my dear children.

"We are delighted to be invited to your home," I said.

Renata kissed her sister on the cheek as Parker picked up Ursula's suitcase and herded Renata and Ursula toward the waiting cab.

I lingered.

"Nurse Phillips I need to discuss one more important thing with you," I said.

"Oh?"

"My cousin Katerina's son, Wolfgang. He is a Dachau concentration camp survivor and is being bullied by bigger boys. Last month they beat him up and cut off his hair. I believe you can help him. He has such low self-esteem."

"Have your cousin call me to set up a consultation. I will talk with him—see how he views his past. I am sure we could arrange some outpatient therapy sessions."

"I will ring her up. I wonder why the children of the world are cast away almost as if they are replaceable."

Nurse Phillips squeezed my arm in a gesture of comradery.

"So do I, Billy Love so do I."

Chapter 14
Visit to the Brownstone

New York City
1951
Billy Love

Ursula's last session had been difficult for all of us yet paradoxically it was the most joyful as Ursula was free of the Bellevue Hospital confines. She was adjusting relatively well to being home. So far there were no night terrors or acting out behaviors on her part—and Renata was unwaveringly kind to her sister.

Last night the girls cuddled up to each other in Ursula's bed and Renata read aloud the ending of *Alice in Wonderland*. Parker and I were seated in the living room relaxing and reading the day's news when we heard Renata begin in her high-pitched teen-age voice.

Alice sat on, with closed eyes, and half believed herself in Wonderland, though she knew she had but to open them again, and all would change to dull reality—the grass would be only rustling in the wind, and the pool rippling to the waving of the reeds— the rattling teacups would change to tinkling sheep-bells, and the Queen's shrill cries to the voice of the shepherd boy—and the sneeze of the baby and all the other queer noises, would change to the confused clamor of the busy farm-yard—while the lowing of the cattle in the distance would take the place of the Mock Turtle's heavy sobs.

Lastly, she pictured to herself how this same little sister of hers would, in the after-time be herself a grown woman; and how she would keep, through all her riper years, the simple and loving heart of her childhood: and how she would gather about her other little children, and make THEIR eyes bright and eager with many a strange tale; perhaps even with the dream of Wonderland of long ago; and how she would feel with all of their simple sorrows, and find a pleasure in all their simple joys, remembering her own child-life, and the happy summer days.

There was a pocket of silence before we heard Renata speaking in a whisper to her sister.

"Don't you see Ursie? It was all a dream for Alice...a silly weird dream. Sometimes dreams are important to remember and sometimes they are not. If you want you can erase them, or if you choose you can hold on to them and pass them on to others."

"Rennie, I didn't like the Queen of Hearts. I will forget about her!"

"I agree! Let's get rid of her forever, shall we?"

"Yes."

The girls pealed with laughter. We heard the book slam shut and thud against the wooden floor of the bedroom.

I folded my newspaper and rose to sit on the arm of Parker's chair. Sighing with contentment I leaned in to kiss my partner. It had been a very long time since I felt so connected to him, to the whole family. We were finally on the right path to living a fulfilling life for me, Parker, Renata and especially my precious Ursula.

Nurse Phillips was the lynchpin that held us all together—And Parker and I realized how lucky we were… we received the best care for Ursula because we had the financial resources to do so. So many children without champions were experimented upon. Lobotomies were performed that reduced them to lumps of clay. Electroshock convulsive treatments that resembled a Frankenstein experiment passed currents from one side of their brains to the other without medication that could control the pain. Ice baths that turned children blue. Travestries.

****

Renata and Ursula in their matching denim overalls, sat in the back seat of the cab silently kicking their saddle shoes in sync with each other. We were in route to a working-class section of Manhattan where May Phillips lived with her husband Jay. Her house was close to Bellevue Hospital…I was aware that she walked the eight blocks to work daily regardless of the weather.

The driver passed several blocks of reddish-brown brick row houses butted up against each other. People crowded the streets as they scurried to unknown destinations. Finally, the cabbie pulled up to 125 Rosebud Street. He blared his horn and squeezed into a narrow space in front of the address.

Parker handed him a fistful of bills and the four of us climbed out and stood before the building.

"Look, Ursula, there is a pink balloon tied to the front railing," I said.

Ursula shyly nudged forward and nodded, indicating her pleasure at the welcome sign.

"Come, Ursie," Renata called. "Let's skip." She grabbed Ursula's hand and led her up the stoop to the front door.

"Renata, you know I have been to Nurse Phillips' house before," Ursula said a bit smugly as if she was the anointed one.

I smiled at Ursula's verve. It was astonishing to observe the confidence of my forsaken child. Her broken body and mind had been replenished by a caring nurse. I understood that there would be many set-backs but Parker and I also realized that Ursula was on the road to a productive and satisfying life enveloped in the arms of her family—our family.

"Yes, Sissie you can show me around. I can't wait to see your very own flower garden. Now ring the bell. I can smell something delicious coming through the front screen."

Ursula confidently stepped forward and pressed her finger against the tinkly bell.

"Just a minute," a deep voice responded.

The screen door was pushed open and the girls jumped back to make way for a man seated in a shiny silver wheelchair.

"Come in and welcome. Follow me. I am Jay, May's husband. Do you like how our names rhyme?" he chuckled in a gravelly voice. His facial features were all broad angles and sharp edges— a specimen of masculinity.

His hands gripped the large wheels on the sides of the metal chair and he used his heavily muscled forearms to propel himself along the hardwood floors.

"May, our guests are here," he called out.

Nurse Phillips appeared at the top of the stairs. Her starched uniform was gone but her civilian clothes were as crisp as a professional uniform. From top to bottom she was impeccable, with her gray-streaked hair coiled into a neat bun at the nape of her neck and her short-sleeved deep plum mid-calf dress swirling with each step as she descended the staircase. Why I noted she was even wearing a bit of powder and lipstick.

Ursula's eyes lit up. She ran to May and hugged her affectionately.

"You all have met Jay, right?" she said as she motioned toward her husband.

We all nodded.

"Mr. Jay why do you have to sit in a wheelchair?" Ursula blurted out.

"Now Ursula, it is rude to ask such a question," Parker admonished apologetically.

Jay was unfazed by the question.

"Ursula, Renata come over to me. I want to show you something."

Ursula and Renata cautiously walked together toward Jay.

"Now, you see how my feet are on these pedals? The pedals support my feet. I have no feeling or ability to move anything below my waist. The only way I can move my legs is if I lift them using my arms. See."

He grabbed his upper thighs and lifted his feet off the pedals and onto the floor.

Jay motioned. "Here you girls try to put my feet back onto the foot rests."

On one side Renata promptly lifted his leg back onto the pedal and Ursula followed suit on the other side.

The girls stood back.

"But Mr. Jay why can't you move your legs by yourself?" Ursula asked.

"When I was twenty I had polio," he said in a matter-of-fact manner.

"There was a girl at school who had polio. She has to be in a wheelchair too," Renata offered.

May, ever the teacher approached Jay and laid her hand on his arm.

"You see polio is a very nasty virus that destroys nerve cells along the spinal cord. When those nerve cells are destroyed paralysis results and your muscles get very small because you can't move them. Look at the difference between Jay's arm muscles and leg muscles."

May pulled up one of Jay's pantlegs and pointed.

"Your legs are so skinny—like twigs," Ursula said.

"Yes, they are and they will always be like this," Jay explained.

"But is there no cure?" Renata asked.

"No, darling there isn't but one day there will be a vaccine that will prevent other people from contracting this terrible disease," Nurse Phillips said. "I am sure of it."

"Don't go feeling sorry for me," Jay said. "I get around pretty good."

He flexed the biceps and triceps in his arms.

"Look I have built up my strength in my upper body so that I can control my lower body."

"It balances out doesn't it?" Renata asked.

"It most certainly does. Let's get on with Ursula's celebration. Isn't that what this day is all about?" Jay asked.

I was impressed that Jay and May were so open about his condition and treated his situation with aplomb. It was just one more example of May's philosophy of life—live it to the fullest no matter the obstacles that are placed in front of you.

Ursula ignored talk of celebration and moved directly in front of Jay. She rolled up both sleeves to her elbows. Her voice trembled.

"See here Mr. Jay, these marks are where I cut myself."

Jay reached out and gently traced the silvery furrows covering her arms.

"Ursula, thank you for showing me. You can't change your scars. But you can make them part of your story, right?"

Ursula smiled shyly and nodded. She rolled her sleeves back down and fastened the buttons at her wrists.

May patted Ursula's back and pulled her away from the wheelchair. She led her into the kitchen supposedly to help prepare the meal—to distract her. I could hear the two of them rattling the dishes as they pulled them from the cupboard.

Parker and I wiped away our tears sniffed and tried to curb our emotions. Today was supposed to be a party. Let's get on with it!

I lingered in the hallway examining the beautiful décor that set the stage for Ursula's party. The brownstone was strewn with pink bouquets of every type of flower—roses, tulips, carnations, peonies—everywhere you looked they covered every surface. And the fragrant smell permeated the air which created an inviting atmosphere.

Parker and Jay stood by the leaded glass window and conversed about current events and work-related news. Jay had questions about Parker's research at Columbia University. Parker in turn tried to discern if and how Jay was connected to Bellevue Hospital. But Jay quickly diverted Parker from any discussion of the psychiatric hospital and instead turned the conversation to what was happening in East and West Berlin.

For once I was uninterested in adult conversations…especially when they revolved around the Cold War between Russia and the United States.

My thoughts turned back to the amazing party May had prepared. The area rugs were rolled up and sat quietly in a corner as if their usefulness had run out—indeed, the hardwood floors in the living room seemed primed for dancing and the upright piano beckoned as if daring someone to tinkle the keys.

I watched Renata as she wandered around examining every knick-knack and cubby on the first floor of the brownstone. She was a curious young woman which was a trait that I shared with her along with Cousin Katerina and Aunt Elisabetha. Her mind was full of questions and she didn't hesitate to voice them.

May's voice rang out from the dining room.

"Come on everyone let's eat before the meal becomes cold."

I motioned to Renata and we entered the dining room and sat down. May reached across the table and placed a steaming plate of dumplings before us.

"Nurse Phillips, why do you have a bandage on your arm?" Renata asked.

"Yes, Nurse Phillips, what happened to you?" Ursula asked. She pointed to the large dressing peeking out from under the capped sleeve of May's dress.

I scowled at the two of them and warned. "Girls it is really not any of your business."

"Now, Billy Love, fiddley dee. They are just curious. I was out in the garden picking roses and I inadvertently bumped up against some thorns. They scratched me and drew blood so I needed to cover them up. It is nothing."

Ursula and Renata seemed satisfied with May's answer and the men were distracted—they were busy scooping the succulent pork roast onto their plates. To me something seemed odd about Nurse Phillips' response. The bandage was very large and bulky for a thorn prick. I knew I needed to let it go. After all I was not a health professional so who was I to judge? Why does my brain never shut off?

May passed platter after platter of food around the table family-style. We polished off the roast and accompanying fried apples then dug into German Chocolate Cake topped with homemade ice-cream.

We leaned back in our chairs. We were sated and aware that we had eaten too much.

"Girls why don't you explore the gardens and the house while your mother and I clean up?"

"Yes Ma'am," they said in unison.

Renata and Ursula got up from the table held hands and ran to the back door leading to the flower gardens in the yard. I heard them laughing as they trampled down the steps and found themselves surrounded by the brilliant atmosphere of colorful overgrown flowers.

May and I washed the dishes and stored the porcelain in their glass cases. We flung off our aprons and returned to the dining room. Jay poured the adults scotches. Then the four of us clinked glasses and in unison downed the burning liquid in one gulp.

"To my beautiful Ursula. May God protect her and keep her on her healing journey. Amen," May said with her head bowed.

We were silent for a few seconds until my daughters burst into the house. They waved to us adults then exited the dining room and climbed the narrow stairs to the upper floors of the brownstone.

"Nurse Phillips we are looking for treasures in the attic," Ursula shouted over her shoulder.

They disappeared and were gone for a length of time. They finally clattered down the stairs and stood before us. Each of them held a small painting which they held out for inspection.

I was repulsed. Ursula's depicted a grotesque war scene with dead soldiers and decomposing bodies. Renata's picture revealed a street scene where crippled and disfigured war veterans begged for food.

"I am surprised you found those paintings. I thought they were hidden away in a secret location," May said as she took the paintings from the girls and laid them side by side on the table.

"One day these paintings might be worth some money. They are certainly infamous. Look, they are signed by the artist Otto Dix. When the Nazis seized power in the 1920s they banned Dix's work and burned many of his paintings because they were deemed *degenerate*. In 1932 I managed to buy these two paintings in a small gallery in Dresden."

Parker interrupted. "Dresden, is that where you are from May?"

"Yes, I lived in that city my whole life. I even survived the horrific bombings in 1945 but that is a story for another day, Parker. Let me get back to the paintings by Otto Dix."

"After I purchased them I hid them away in a safe place because I felt they were important. War is terrible—and these paintings reminded me of the chaos and impugning of humanity."

I looked at Ursula and noted the look of dismay on her little face. I could tell she was churning the paintings' images around and around in her mind and connecting them to her experiences with her birth parents. I turned them face down on the table.

Renata seemed unfazed by the disturbing pictures in the paintings. She was impatient and muscled her way into the conversation.

"Mr. Jay, Ursula and I tried to go down the basement but there was a padlock on the door. What is down there?"

"Girls, that is the one place in our home that is off-limits."

"Why?" Ursula asked.

May spoke. There was an odd detached tone in her voice. "There is no suitable explanation. Just know that it must remain a secret for now."

Ursula and Renata seemed satisfied with May's answer, but I was troubled. First there was that bandage and now there was a room filled with mysteries. Parker and I exchanged glances. He was curious too, but for now we needed to let it go.

It was Ursula's party. And we needed to dance.

Chapter 15
Devil's Hill

East and West Berlin
1952
Elisabetha

> *Lying to ourselves is more deeply ingrained in us*
> *than lying to others.*
> ~ Fyodor Dostoyevsky
> Russian Novelist

"Leon, it has been a full year with little progress made in getting supplies to the Russian children who languish in the gulag camps," I said. My voice radiated with discouragement.

We were preparing for a strategy meeting at UNICEF headquarters. Babe Love and other staffers would be joining us.

I plugged in the old coffee pot and waited for it to percolate. It was chilly in the office...I pulled my woolen sweater around me and contemplated the stalemate that had arisen between the Soviet Union and the Western Allies.

Leon picked up the West Berlin newspaper and spread it across the table.

"Liz, here is the transcript of a diplomatic note dated March 10, 1952. It was sent by Dictator Stalin to the U.S., British, and French governments. The thought of him proposing a peace treaty with Germany on the basis of neutrality! He is a God-damned liar." Leon scooped the newspaper off the table crinkled it into a ball and angrily threw its contents into the wastebasket.

"You are absolutely correct. Stalin has no wish to reunify Germany, Leon. He can't be trusted. Surely the allies are aware of his deceptive ways. His proposal to eliminate East Germany in order to reunify Germany insults Western intelligence. It is merely a propaganda move on the part of the Russians. If he was sincere there would be more concern regarding the people who are trapped in the Eastern Soviet block of nations…people who languish under his cruel rule…people who are sent to hard labor camps for publishing literature against the Bolsheviks and for other minor infractions."

Leon tugged on his goatee and frowned. "And the greatest impunity is the neglect of the Russian children, whether they be offspring of the bourgeoise, the poor or the imprisoned. The children who suffer from wide-spread communicable disease and malnutrition. It is déjà vu—what happened to the German children immediately after World War II is almost identical to the plight of children throughout the Soviet Union now."

"We must find some way to break through the barriers of the Stalin regime and help the children. I have called Katerina and encouraged her to come to Berlin to help us. She speaks fluent Russian and I believe she could serve as a liaison to the Russian ambassador's wife—you know, the one from Perm."

"I think that proposition is a long-shot considering how the banquet ended with the Russians and the Western ambassadors getting into an altercation by shooting their guns in the air and causing havoc. They were all spoiled brats," Leon spat.

I put my hand on Leon's arm, my signal to him to calm down.

He pulled away, but I knew he would respond to me. We had an intuitive relationship from our history serving in the Nazi resistance together. Leon understood that his explosive angry outbursts solved no problems.

We needed a strategy. I believed Leon had some plans he had not yet revealed. We would wait for an opening that would allow UNICEF to pry open the cracks of the Bolshevik façade. In order to reach our goals, which were always centered on the innocent children.

I sipped my steaming coffee and sat down notepad in hand. Where was everyone? It seemed like the young people were always late. Whatever could they be doing? Time was important.

My exasperation vanished when my beautiful blonde niece swept into the room and kissed me on the cheek. She looked as pulled together as ever with her elegant white-blonde hair swept into a French twist.

"Darling Aunt Liz can I have a cup of coffee?"

Babe's voice tinkled. I marveled at her positive outlook on life.

On a darker note I wondered about that scoundrel boyfriend of hers. What was he up to? He seemed to be absent from Babe's life most of the time. But he would pop up unexpectantly as he had last week…and promptly ensconce himself at Babe's cottage. Did they make passionate love to each other this morning thus delaying Babe's arrival? I would be meeting Babe at the Tavern later this evening and I was determined to grill her about Mr. Hans Fischer banker extraordinaire. Hah—a joke!

Babe stood with her hand on her hip as she studied the giant wall map strewn with push pins. It included all of the Eastern Bloc countries along with the vast Soviet Territories which included Leningrad and Moscow in the west and Perm the established gateway to the east. Siberia laid mostly north of the Arctic Circle.

"Aunt Liz, it seems overwhelming to try and make inroads helping Soviet children when there is such a huge territory to cover."

I walked over to the map and traced my finger along the area that traversed Moscow and Berlin.

"Here lies one of the most devastated areas in the world, Babe. At the very end of the war when the Russians advanced across the frozen earth toward Berlin scarcely anyone survived. Almost every man, woman and child in their path was killed. It looked like an apocalypse. A wasteland."

Babe raised her eyebrows as she pondered the almost unthinkable situation.

I paused as Leon crossed the room and stood beside me as the rest of the small staff filtered into the room and sat down for the meeting.

"Hello everyone. I'm glad you could make it," he said. He scowled and looked intently at his watch.

The young staff looked down and their faces reddened. They understood they were being chastised.

"All of you. Be aware that everything discussed today must be kept top-secret. I don't care if sweet-nothings are whispered in your ear or you are offered a million marks. Your lives and the lives of innocent children and families are at stake. Do you understand?" Leon's coal black eyes surveyed the room. Heads lifted and responded with nods.

"We are entering a new era. Anyone who is fearful or disagrees with our mission should leave right now," Leon said as he pointed to the closed door.

A small-boned man spoke up.

"Leon and Liz, when we joined UNICEF it was our understanding that we would do what it takes to get assistance to the suffering children of the world. The iron fist of Stalin should not become a barrier to our mission."

The man scoured the room with narrowed eyes. "Who is with me?"

Six hands shot up including Babe's.

"Alright then," Leon said. "You all will sign an oath of secrecy…and be aware that your actions will be monitored, perhaps by me and perhaps by other more sinister people.

"Leon, what do you mean?" Babe blurted.

"I mean there are spies everywhere in Berlin on both sides of the Cold War. The person next to you in the coffee shop could be listening to your conversations. The dentist could be a courier. Even children could be unwittingly drawn into missions. No one should be trusted outside this room."

"We have waited long enough—let's get on with it," Leon concluded.

He walked to the map. "Perm is the symbolic gateway to the East and home to one of the worst Russian gulags in existence. This is where we will concentrate our efforts to help the Russian children."

I looked at Leon. He must have made a snap decision about Perm. I could understand his logic. Focusing on Perm might solve two problems: getting children supplies and medications and gathering information on the rumored missile production plants hidden in the forests surrounded the mountains.

If we approached the United States Air Force with the plan they might agree to supply a spy plane equipped with the latest technology. And we would have the added support from the military. We understood the addition of a military tactic would be risky, but it was a calculation we needed to take.

We would keep the military mission hidden from the UNICEF staff. The fewer people who knew about documenting Soviet missile production the better...the chance for leaks would be diminished. Leon and I would keep this secret between us and the United States Government.

"Is everyone clear?" Leon boomed.

"Yes sir," the group echoed back to him.

"Liz and I need some time to put the operation together. You will not know the date until we show up on your doorstep and utter the code word. You will all go immediately to the warehouse and gather up the supplies. At that point we will reveal the location of the plane that will embark to Russia."

"Sir, who will travel on the plane?" one of the women asked.

"I will designate those people immediately before the plane embarks. So, all of you should be prepared to go. If you are unsure tell me now and I will drop you from the assignment."

The staff murmured and shook their heads.

Babe spoke for everyone. "We are all committed—every one of us."

"Good, then this meeting is over. I will see you tomorrow," Leon announced.

I stood and watched the young people leave the room. Babe trailed the group.

I pulled her back tugging her arm as I whispered. "See you tonight. And don't bring Hans."

Babe gave me a dirty look as if to question my judgement, but I didn't budge. Something was very wrong with Mr. Fischer. And

I didn't intend to include him in any conversations that had to do with UNICEF.

****

I was getting ready to go out to meet Babe when the black Bakelite telephone rang.

"Liz, it's Billy Love," Leon said. He held out the receiver to me.

"Billy Love, it has been much too long."

I tucked the receiver under my chin as I pulled on sensible sturdy walking shoes.

Billy Love's voice came clearly through the line.

"Aunt Liz, I wanted to give you an update on Ursula."

"And?"

"Well, the news is mostly good. She continues to see Nurse Phillips on an out-patient basis at Bellevue Hospital. She is able to attend school and is cooperative most days. Her outbursts have slowed to a minimum so Parker and I are encouraged."

"You and your family have certainly been on a long journey."

"We are not the only ones. You can't imagine the number of children who are being treated at Bellevue for psychiatric problems…everything from depression to mania to schizophrenia. I have to gird myself every time I enter the facility."

"I understand Kat has connected with Nurse Phillips and has brought Wolfie under her care?"

"Yes. In fact, we schedule back to back appointments for Ursula and Wolfgang. It gives Kat and me some time to catch up with each other. Typically, we stroll the grounds of the hospital together. It has been interesting. As you know, Wolfgang was weary of Ursula and her violent outbursts—he would cringe when she was around him. But in the last year they have found a way to relate to each other. I am encouraged."

"Billy Love, it is important to remember the chaotic circumstances that the children experienced. I have flashbacks to the day we stood in the crematorium at Dachau and Samuel

178

revealed the fates of our precious ones— Wolfgang, Ruthie, Ursula and Renata."

"I know. It seems like yesterday, yet it was so long ago."

"Is it any wonder the mental wounds from war linger well beyond the physical healing?" I remarked.

There was momentary silence.

"How is my sister?" Billy Love abruptly asked as she switched the subject.

I lowered my voice to a whisper.

"Babe? Frankly I am worried about her relationship with Hans. Of course, he is devilishly handsome and fawns over her. He treats her like a perfect gentleman but there is something off-kilter about him. He is absent for days at a time and then when he returns he never has a sufficient explanation. Listen I was in the FBI and I understand deception…Mr. Fischer is not to be trusted in my opinion."

"Keep monitoring the situation Aunt Liz."

"Will do, and Billy Love give my love to Katerina."

"Of course."

There was a long pause. Billy Love's tone changed—she became evasive. Something was brewing with Kat…I intuitively felt it.

****

I pulled a light sweater around my shoulders kissed Leon and headed into the street toward The Tavern. Ahead of me stood the Brandenburg Gate which represented the divide between East and West Berlin.

Glancing around at my surroundings I note construction in West Berlin was everywhere…evidence that the Marshall Plan to rebuild West Germany was working. I was ensconced in an oasis in the midst of communist rule. Just beyond the Brandenburg Gate lay piles and piles of rubble. Almost no progress had been made in rebuilding East Germany. There were rumors that the Russians were punishing the Germans who resided there in an effort to oppress them and prevent them from rising again against Russia.

The Tavern was bustling with activity. Young people were relishing their social lives chattering loudly into each other's ears. I noted the ripe smell of stale beer and cigarettes permeating the air…I was put off by it. Hanging out in bars was for the younger crowd. I needed a quiet life. Ha! Wouldn't Leon chuckle if he could read my thoughts? Especially as we plotted the UNICEF mission to Russia?

I looked around the gloomy bar and spotted my niece. Babe motioned to me from her seat at the bar. She stood out among the patrons even dressed in dungarees and a flannel shirt with her hair pulled back in a ponytail.

Several men were attempting to chat Babe up and buy her drinks. But she easily batted them away pulling a cigarette from her purse and lighting it. Her red fingernails clicked on her glass of bourbon as she took a long drink.

I kissed her cheek and slide onto the stool beside her.

"Your sister called."

"Billy Love? How is she? We haven't talked in ages."

"She's okay. The children keep her busy." I raised my voice—practically shouting as the big band tuned.

I turned toward the noise and noticed a handsome man in a three-piece suit standing by the stage. He stared intently in Babe's direction as if he recognized her.

"Babe, a gentleman is coming over to us. Do you know him?"

Babe swiveled her stool around. She examined the man and then ignored him as she turned back facing the bar.

"Babe, you are being rude!"

"Aunt Liz, it is none of your business!" she retorted.

The man was undeterred as he sauntered up beside us. He smiled revealing his even white teeth.

"Hello there Ms. Wolf. How are you doing?"

He spoke in English with a thick German accent.

"Ernst," Babe replied making no eye contact with him.

I stuck my hand out and he shook it.

"I am Elisabetha Braun, Babe's aunt."

The gentleman never took his eyes off Babe.

"Nice to meet you."

A red flush crept up Babe's neck. I could tell she was flustered and uncertain as to her next move.

"I work at the bank with Hans." He brushed a curly lock of hair out of his eyes and waited for Babe to respond.

Babe was silent.

"Where is your beau tonight? Surely after he was away for such a length of time on business he would want to escort his girlfriend out on the town?"

Babe scowled. I was aware that Ernst was baiting her, hoping for a response.

"That Ernst, is none of your business. Why don't you find someone else to irritate?"

He laughed and put his hand on her shoulder. She flung it off and stood up.

"How dare you! Come on Aunt Liz, let's get out of here."

She grabbed her purse and strode toward the exit. Her ponytail swished from side to side as I trailed behind her. I looked over my shoulder at Ernst. He was relaxed as he leaned back with his elbows positioned on the bar and grinned from ear to ear.

There was no question in my mind. Mr. Hans Fischer was not going to stand in Ernst's way. Ernst planned to seduce Miss Wolf. And my niece knew it.

****

"Babe, what's your hurry?" I called out. I was relishing the game that was playing out between Ernst and Babe. Anything that might throw a shadow on the relationship between Babe and Hans Fischer was a step in the right direction…which in my opinion was wiping Hans clean out of her life.

Babe flew out the door and stopped abruptly. I came close to crashing into her backside—I could tell she was very angry. She snapped open her purse and rummaged through it. At last she

181

removed a package and removed the final cigarette. She crumpled the package into a ball and hurled it at the ground then twirled around to face me.

"Aunt Liz, I don't appreciate your interference in my love life."

I remained silent and allowed her to vent her frustrations.

Tears welled in her brilliant blue eyes. "All my life I have been treated like the baby of the family—unable to make adult decisions. Well I don't deserve that treatment. Haven't I proven myself? I came to Germany to start over, away from my twin and the monotony of ranch life in Oklahoma. I feel I make a difference—I am helping innocent children through my work with UNICEF and I have a boyfriend who treats me like a queen. Why can't you be happy for me?"

Babe lit her cigarette with trembling fingers and inhaled as she tried to regain control over her emotions.

"Babe, you know I love you. You are like a daughter to me. But you must understand that I have years of experience in the underbelly of life. People are not always how they appear to others. Many hide their pasts with elaborate schemes and disguises. I just want you to be cautious, will you give me that?"

Babe threw her cigarette to the street and stubbed it out with her shoe. She glared at me but then her expression softened.

"For you, Aunt Liz, I will make an effort to be cautious, maybe not so trusting."

"Thank you, Babe. That is all I ask."

I attempted to tamp down my alarm about Hans. But I needed to warn her.

"And Babe, do not, in any circumstances mention our UNICEF plans to anyone. We might have to abort the mission if our enemies get wind of it." I was careful to leave Hans out of the conversation. For now.

Babe nodded.

"Let's walk up to Devil's Hill, shall we? The night air will do us good—get us away from all of the smells and sounds of the bar."

Babe scowled. "And get us far away from that horrible Ernst."

I ignored her comment. We started walking toward the beckoning Gruenwald Forest in which Devil's Hill was situated.

I spoke in order to change the focus of our conversation.

"Two years ago, the West Berlin Magistrate decided to open a rubble disposal site. The allies needed a place to store all of the debris left over from the bombings."

Babe was curious. "Why did he choose that particular site?"

"Two reasons. The Nazis had started building a military academy there prior to the end of the war. It was too expensive to demolish the structure so they decided to cover it up…remove it from people's minds. The second reason is that there was no other place suitable for the rubble. West Berlin was land-locked, surrounded by East German territory, so the decision was made to pile up the shattered bricks and make a hill."

"I had heard something about that Liz. Berlin as a city is flat so we were creating a man-made hill, right?"

"Correct. Every day you see *Rubble Women* as they are called hauling the wreckage and loading it onto dump trucks. Sometimes as many as 80 truckloads a day make the journey out to the site."

Babe and I kept walking toward the edge of the forest as I explained the history of Devil's Hill.

"It seems degrading to call them *Rubble Women*."

"I agree with you. But so many German men were killed. The country was decimated—and the women needed the work. There were no other jobs and many had young children who needed to be fed and clothed. They really had no choice, Babe. Some of them still don't even seven years after the Second War ended."

"War is horrendous. And to think I was so sheltered, living on a ranch in Oklahoma…roller skating and riding horses. Fighting with Bitsie Love over petty things. I am ashamed."

"Babe, your young life was idyllic in many ways, but now you are a strong determined woman searching to make a difference in the world. I admire you."

Babe was quiet as we traveled the dusty gravel road into the dense forest.

Within a few minutes we came to a clearing. There rising up before us was Devil's Hill. Even after a mere two years of piling rubble it was an imposing sight.

My eyes traveled to the top of the debris heap. A thought flickered across my mind—I couldn't wait to inform Leon.

Chapter 16
Secret People

New York
1952
Katerina

Hidden in each of us is a secret person,
often unknown even to ourselves.
~From the Movie *Secret People*—1952

"Jack, Audrey has been chosen to model for Givenchy the fashion house that just opened in Paris. She sent me the proofs and she is absolutely stunning in a strapless white ballgown. That pixie haircut of hers and her pale delicate face peering up at the camera. My goodness. There will be an avalanche of young women trying to emulate her."

"Audrey has certainly acclimated to the Hollywood scene, hasn't she? To think she was but a teenager when the war ended— isolated in Amsterdam," Jack said. He struck a match and lit his fancy pipe.

"Yes, Marlene has been instrumental in opening doors for her. Now Audrey is in London filming *Secret People*. Audrey plays a ballet dancer and she actually gets to dance in the role," I explained.

Jack exhaled a cloud of smoke and gave a little laugh. "Isn't that picture about an assassin? It's ironic that the studio is making a film about someone who plots to kill their so-called enemies. They could substitute Stalin in that role."

Jack had returned from a government assignment in Washington D.C. and was unpacking his satchel. I understood his trip was connected to the stand-off between Russia and the United States over nuclear warheads. He was guarded about his role— which he should be. The stakes were high for all involved.

The dictator Stalin was causing havoc in Europe especially in Berlin. It was rumored that he was in poor health trusted no one, even those who supported the Bolsheviks, and was generally isolated. But his threat of loose-cannon orders to launch missiles at the United States was still causing wide-spread consternation in the west.

I sighed. "Do you think the civilized world will ever learn that war is not the answer to our problems? Now we are getting involved in Korean clashes. It's endless."

Jack ran his fingers through his thick hair. "As long as we allow those who are power-hungry to control the masses there will be conflict. Look at Hitler, Mussolini, Lenin, Stalin, Mao –all of them monsters and thugs."

"I don't want to know what your assignment entails, but I want you to be safe. Can you guarantee me that, Jack?"

Jack was exasperated. "Kat, really? How can you even bring up the subject? With all of your involvement during the Second War and in its aftermath…your efforts helping the abandoned children of Germany? You threw caution to the wind."

"Okay Jack you are right. I might be a bit head strong when it comes to causes that I support."

Jack snorted and gave a short deep-throated bark. "You think, my darling Kat?"

My face flushed. Jack knew me so well. I admitted to myself that he understood passivity was not in my nature especially when I felt injustices were being carried out against humanity.

I felt a bit queasy. I had secrets of my own that I was harboring with no idea where they would lead me—the Russian treasures in the trunk.

✳✳✳✳✳✳✳✳✳✳✳✳✳✳✳✳✳✳✳✳

Billy Love and I planned to meet at Bellevue Psychiatric Hospital as Wolfgang and Ursula had back-to-back appointments with Nurse Phillips. Many months had passed since we had a chance to spend time together: just the two of us. I missed her fiercely. She could always be counted on to give me good advice. And I certainly needed some wisdom.

I couldn't keep the secret of the old trunk hidden from her any longer. I knew Jack would not approve and I understood his concerns. But I trusted Billy Love with my whole being. She would not betray me under any circumstances.

I thought back to the time when I first met my cousin. We were young women—eighteen and nineteen years old. Billy Love had embarked on a trip to visit Aunt Elisabetha in Munich where I was singing in the cabaret known as *The Garden*. We instantly liked and connected with each other.

It was the end of the flapper era. Adolf Hitler and his goons were roaming the streets of Munich and Papa had come up from Darmstadt to see me perform. On that trip the seeds of the *Wolfpack* were sown as generations of the Wolf clan came together. Today we still stood as a family unit.

Looking around my bedroom I spotted the framed picture of Billy Love and me that sat on my nightstand. Our arms were around each other as we mugged for the camera. We looked remarkably similar with our dark chestnut hair, olive skin and lithe builds. The one discernable difference between us rested in my brilliant turquoise eyes, courtesy of my Russian mother. Billy Love's eyes were so dark the pupil blended with the iris.

I brushed aside thoughts of our youth and concentrated on Wolfgang. Where was he headed? What was his future? I ached for him.

He walked woodenly beside me as we entered the main entrance of Bellevue. At fourteen he had become a sullen teenager. Nurse Phillips had assessed Wolfgang and as a result understood that the approach utilized with Ursula was not effective with Wolfgang. Reading and analyzing youth books like *Alice in Wonderland* was not an option.

There were some glimmers of progress with Wolfie. He had switched schools and made a few friends, but he could quickly retreat into himself and brood in his room for hours. Sudden loud noises sent him into a tailspin and he could be destructive.

We arrived at the appointment prior to Ursula and Billy Love's appearance. Nurse Phillips was there to greet us. She clutched

Wolfgang's chart to her bosom and motioned for us to follow her down the hall. We entered her office and sat down on the cold wooden chairs.

Wolfgang looked down at his feet and refused to make eye contact.

"Wolfgang," Nurse Phillips began in her most authoritative voice.

His chin jerked up and his eyes narrowed into slits.

"I would like your permission to talk to your mother about your request."

I leaned forward. Request? What could he want? There was no warning.

"Okay," he said in a barely audible voice. His long thin face was unreadable.

I braced myself.

"Billy Love, Wolfgang has requested the name of his birth father. He understands that his name was revealed to you and Jack at the meeting held in Dachau at the concentration camp."

I trembled then tried to calm myself. I didn't want Wolfgang to know I was shaken. I nodded—unsure of my ability to speak.

"Wolfgang your father is Prince Philipp Von Hessen," Nurse Phillips proclaimed as she flipped open his chart and read from it.

Wolfgang's eyes widened and his pupils dilated. He tilted his head toward me as if to validate what he had heard. His father was alive? His father was royalty? His father never claimed him? I could imagine the jumble of questions that must be pummeling his brain.

Was I doing the right thing in allowing Nurse Phillips to reveal the identity of his birth father?

I reached over and touched Wolfgang's arm trying to be reassuring, but he angrily pulled away. What would happen next – now that the secret of Wolfgang's heritage had been revealed?

Nurse Phillips took charge of the conversation. She was calm yet commanding.

"Wolfgang, clearly you have a lot of questions about Von Hessen. I am going to ask that you settle back and for now let the information sink in. You and I will talk further about it together during your appointment today."

I abruptly stood up. Alarm bells were ringing in my head. I had waited years for Wolfgang to inquire about the prince. Now that time was upon us and I had no idea what came next for our family.

Nurse Phillips spoke to me, reassuring me. "Katerina, today's appointment will be extensive. We are running some tests and launching some other therapies. It will consume most of the day. I suggest you get out of the hospital—perhaps you and Billy Love can catch up together."

My voice trembled. "I appreciate your suggestion. She and Ursula should be here soon. I understand Ursula has some scheduled play therapy today. I will wait for them."

I turned and looked at my silent Wolfgang. He had retreated back into his shell.

"I love you." I pulled open the door and exited the cloying room.

I ran down the narrow hallway and ducked into the ladies' restroom. I yanked open the stall door and sat down on the toilet seat. My breathing was jagged and perspiration broke out on my forehead and neck...I struggled for control.

For I knew secrets about Prince Phillipp Von Hessen—dark secrets. How much should be revealed to Wolfgang? And would it make his psychological situation better or worse?

Hurry up, Billy Love. I need you.

****

Someone banged on the metal door.

"Kat, are you in there? Come out. Let's talk," Billy Love cajoled.

I unlocked the door and slid out of the stall wiping my eyes and nose. Billy Love pulled me to her and patted my back.

"Come on, our children are in good hands. Let's get out of here. We can walk to your apartment where we can grab a cup of tea and talk," Billy Love said.

"I'm okay. I just wasn't expecting the news today."

"You can tell me all about it after we leave Bellevue. Nurse Phillips mentioned you had something to share with me—of course she is so professional and confidential. She would never betray Wolfgang's confidence directly to me."

I reapplied lipstick and brushed my hair behind my ears. I had so much to tell Billy Love. Secrets were exploding inside me— about to burst to the surface.

The Germans and the Russians. The Russians and the Germans. Why was my life so complicated?

Billy Love and I pushed open the heavy metal door of the psychiatric hospital. We acknowledged the security guard standing at attention and climbed down the steps to the bustle of the New York street. We walked briskly and silently for several blocks. The air was heavy with humidity and the gray sky threatened rain.

Finally, Billy Love spoke. Her voice was gentle.

"Do you want to tell me what happened with Wolfgang today?"

I paused then haltingly replied.

"He finally asked about the identity of his father. Of course, when Jack and I first met with Nurse Phillips she asked about his biological parents. And we knew his history because Samuel shared it with us at Dachau, remember?"

"Yes, I clearly remember. How could I forget that day in the crematorium, Kat?"

"I was concerned that for so many years Wolfgang seemed uninterested. So why today out of the blue?" I questioned aloud.

"In my opinion Nurse Phillips opened the path for him to express himself. He kept his thoughts and feelings locked away for so long. It was a coping mechanism to shield his vulnerable side and now he feels ready to confront his past."

"But is he really ready?"

"Kat, I believe he is ready. And we all can help him. We are a team, right?"

"Billy Love, I feel ashamed that I have kept some information about the prince from Jack."

"Oh?"

"Ever since Samuel revealed Philipp's existence I have kept records of him—where he lives, how he spends his time, who he interacts with." ….my voice trailed off.

"And?"

"I sense Wolfgang will want to travel to Germany—to meet him," I explained.

"Do you think that is wise given that he sent Wolfgang's mother to Dachau and she was eventually chosen for the gas chamber?"

"Of course not! What do you think, Billy Love?"

"So sorry Kat, it was a thoughtless question. But it still must be addressed."

"I will rely on Nurse Phillips' recommendations. Does she think Wolfgang is strong enough to handle the truth? Right now, he is pretty fragile. I also must figure out how to inform Jack… and try to understand his position regarding the prince."

Billy Love paused. I could tell she was carefully considering her words. "Whatever decisions you and Jack make, know that the family will support you. Our childrens' lives are precious."

I squeezed her hand tightly as fat rain drops descended and deluged us. We had no umbrellas. We didn't care. We kept walking. Together. Wolfpack.

****

"Billy Love, catch. Towel off while I put on the teapot," I said.

"Thanks. I will rummage in your closet and grab a t-shirt and jeans," Billy Love replied.

I turned up the burner and filled the teapot with water. It had been quite the morning. And I had more information to reveal to Billy Love—namely the contents of the old metal trunk hidden in the back of my closet.

I placed the teacups and pot on a tray and brought it into the living room. Billy Love was stretched out on the overstuffed couch looking relaxed, her wet hair piled on the top of her head. I poured

191

the steaming black tea into the china cups and handed her one as I pondered how to tell her about the treasures in the old trunk.

Perhaps today was not a good day to reveal my secrets? No, it had been over a year since I had made the discoveries. It was not prudent to delay any longer. Billy Love might be able to help me make connections regarding my Russian roots. She had a knack for that sort of thing. After all her detective skills uncovered the scheme to bring Eva Braun to the Howling Wolf Ranch in Oklahoma.

I stood up and pulled Billy Love to a stand.

"Come cousin I have something to show you."

Billy Love looked puzzled, but she did as I instructed.

"What are you up to Kat?"

"Sit down. It is a surprise. Besides Jack, you are the only person privy to what I am about to show you."

"Don't keep me in suspense. Let me see."

I opened the closet door and pushed the hanging clothes aside. I pressed on the back panel of the closet and a secret door sprang open. Then I carefully pulled out the old metal trunk and placed it before Billy Love.

I spoke in Russian as Billy Love gaped.

"Kat you are scaring me a bit. Whatever do you have to reveal?"

I didn't answer right away. I inserted the key into the lock and slowly lifted the lid.

"Billy Love, my mother Irina arrived from Perm Russia with this trunk. She never knew what was inside and neither did my papa. She stored it in the basement and promptly forgot about it. When she died in childbirth with me, Papa was so overcome with grief he couldn't bear to open it. He actually forgot all about it— acted as if it never existed."

Billy Love interrupted my story.

"Let's get on with it. I am dying to know what is in there."

I withdrew the letter from my grandmother and placed it before Billy Love. I watched her face as she skimmed the letter—her eyes widened as she understood the importance of the document. She was quiet. She sat back and waited for my next move.

I reached into the trunk and carefully withdrew and unwrapped all of its contents: my birth certificate, the oil painting of my mother, the brilliant-red stacking dolls—the smallest of which I opened to reveal the two-carat diamond ring, the magnificent Fabergé Easter Egg, and the sapphire and diamond broach.

"Katerina, you know what this means right?"

I nodded.

"Based on my grandmother's letter, our family must have a close connection to the *Imperial* family of Russia. I still can't wrap my head around this whole world I never knew existed. In 1911 when my mother was sent to Germany by her parents, the Bolsheviks were busy destroying the treasures of the Romanov family…all throughout Russia from the country manors to the royal palaces. The treasures were a symbol of the perceived greediness of the monarchy."

"Your grandmother was brilliant in that she used your mother as a vehicle to secure these invaluable Russian pieces of art. She saved your mother from an almost certain death or hard labor in a gulag by sending her to Germany, didn't she?"

"Billy Love, it is complicated even further by the fact that the Bolsheviks were wreaking havoc at the same time that Russia joined the allies to fight Germany in the Great War."

Billy Love picked up the large broach and turned it over to examine the underside.

"Katerina, did you see this signature?"

"What do you mean?'

"Look! It's engraved. *To Olga from Nicholas*."

"Let me see!" I leaned over and studied the Russian signature. I had not noticed it before now.

"It's from the Czar to his sister Olga," I said in awe.

"And how did your grandmother come to possess it?" Billy Love asked.

"There has to be a connection to the Imperial family, but it remains unclear. Apparently, my grandparents along with my two aunts and an uncle vanished from the city of Perm one day. And they were never seen or heard from again."

Billy Love stood and paced the bedroom. I could see she was turning the findings over and over in her mind.

Finally, she spoke.

"We can't just sit on these discoveries can we Kat?"

I grinned for the first time following a very stressful visit to Bellevue.

"No, we can't Billy Love. No, we can't."

Chapter 17
Monkeys

New York City
1952
Billy Love

"Mommy, Nurse Phillips took me to the laboratory last week," Ursula declared.

Mommy! I loved it when she used that term. Many years had passed after she came to live with Parker and me before we ever heard Ursula utter the affectionate name. It was always unexpected yet so emotionally satisfying.

"What did you say Ursie?" I had turned on the mixer and the whirring sound blocked out her voice.

"The monkeys, Momma!" Ursula shouted in a voice that indicated I should have known what she was talking about.

"The Monkeys?"

Ursula rolled her eyes—as if I was a complete idiot. "Yes, in the laboratory."

I turned the mixer off and looked at Ursula expectantly.

She put her hands on her hips and posed. "They were cute and they screwed up their faces, Mommy, and their eyes crinkled and they chattered at me and Nurse Phillips."

I smiled at my curious child and felt an immense gratitude toward the hospital and Nurse Phillips in particular. Ursula would still be a husk of herself if not for the expertise of a wonderful skilled nurse.

"Well, what kind of monkey-business were they up to?" I asked playfully.

"They were eating bananas and one of them took away the other's food so the big one got swatted on the head. It was funny." Ursula came down from the step stool and rested her elbows on the kitchen table.

She untied her apron strings and became serious.

"But it was sad, too."

"What do you mean?"

"There were people in the monkeys' cage. They had on white coats and rubber gloves and they were pinching the monkeys and making them yell."

"Were they giving them shots?" I asked.

"I think so and there was blood too. And one of the monkeys in the corner of the cage couldn't move his legs. He was dragging himself around the cage on his elbows. He looked scared—I didn't want to watch that so I looked at the other monkeys who were playing instead."

"That was a good plan Ursula." I held the mixing bowl in one hand and used the spatula to transfer the batter into a baking pan. I pondered why Nurse Phillips would take Ursula into the Bellevue laboratory. Did she consider the visit a sort of explorative field trip or was there another motive?

"Mommy, my eyes were watering too. There was a very bad smell and I felt like I couldn't breathe. It gave me a headache. I told Nurse Phillips it was time to go. She gave me a handkerchief to put over my face."

I knelt down before Ursula and smoothed her hair behind her ears then cupped her little face.

"Ursula, sometimes they do tests on animals to see if they can discover treatments that can help people so that they don't get disease."

"I didn't like that part of my visit...where they hurt the monkeys. But I did like watching them play. Can we go to the zoo next week?" Ursula asked as if ready to move on to other topics.

"Let's get these cookies in the oven, shall we?" I asked.

We moved to the kitchen counter top and I removed a rolling pin from the drawer and handed it to Ursula. She grabbed the handles and smoothed the cookie dough until it was flat. Then she selected cookie cutters and sliced the dough with their edges.

"How did you know I liked animal shapes?" Ursula picked up the array of shapes: giraffe, lion and, sure enough a monkey.

"It was a wild guess. I had no idea you had visited the monkeys."

Ursula smacked her lips. "Rennie will be hungry for these cookies when she gets home, won't she? And they are my very favorite sugar cookies."

Ursula chattered as my mind wandered to Nurse Phillips. Clearly the monkeys were part of a large experimental study and she was part of the research team. I was intensely curious…but for now, she was apparently unwilling or unable to share any findings. My radar was up—I would be discussing my conversation with Parker when he got home. Perhaps he had some ideas…or maybe not. The mysteries kept unfolding.

****

The kitchen was filled with the aroma of fresh-baked cookies cooling on wire racks. Renata was home from her viola lesson and was ensconced in her room talking on the telephone to one of her new-found orchestra friends. She displayed typical teenage behavior--ignoring everyone around her except for her so-called friends. But her shift in attitude had allowed her to shed the burdensome responsibility of taking care of her sister, transferring it to Nurse Phillips Parker and me. Which was where the duty should lie—with professionals and parents.

Ursula played with her *Alice in Wonderland* puppets propping them up on the large footstool in the living room. White Rabbit was her friend today which was quite a turn-about from the first time she encountered him during play therapy when he was *the bad rabbit*! Ursula had the Alice puppet in charge of the show and as I stood in the doorway watching her it was clear to me that my daughter was enacting a scenario in which she was revealing a confident and positive young girl.

Ursula giggled. "White Rabbit don't be late. For we are going to a tea party with the silly Mad Hatter," Ursula proclaimed. The Alice Puppet patted Rabbit on the head. "I love you White Rabbit. You showed me how to have fun didn't you? Now let's go down the rabbit hole again."

The doorbell rang and Ursula dropped the puppets and skipped to the door. "Whoever might be at the door Mommy?"

I smiled for I knew it was Parker. He loved to pretend that he was one of the characters from *Alice in Wonderland*. Every day he would choose a different character, emulating their voices which made Ursula titter with glee.

"It is the Cheshire Cat. You must hurry and answer the door or I will disappear before you can even pull it open," he said in the sly voice of the Cheshire.

"I'm coming, please don't disappear, Cat."

Ursula yanked the door open and Parker swept in swooping Ursula up in his arms.

"Come on Alice, it's time to go down the Rabbit Hole."

I waited for the ritual Parker and I had adopted from my father back on the Howling Wolf Ranch in Oklahoma.

Parker threw his trench coat aside and settled on the couch with one leg crossed over the other forming an opening—the infamous rabbit hole.

Ursula was a bundle of energy now. She dove head-first through Parker's legs. Then she repeated the ritual again and again until she was spent. She looked up at Parker with adoring eyes and settled contentedly on his lap leaning her head against his chest.

"What do I smell Ursula? Did you and Mommy make cookies?"

"Yes, we did. Do you want one? I will bring you some milk to go with the cookies."

Parker nodded. Ursula slid off his lap and ran into the kitchen.

I approached my husband and he stood up and encircled his arms around me. He bent his head down and kissed me deeply cupping my bottom and pulling me toward him.

"Mommy and Daddy no hanky-panky now!" Ursula rolled her eyes as she stood holding the tray of cookies and milk.

Renata emerged from the bedroom when she heard the commotion. She grabbed a cookie off the tray and stuffed in into her mouth. Then she wagged her finger at us as if we were naughty lovers.

Parker and I ignored them both and kissed again thinking about making love to each other later in the evening. Our love had not waned over the years. It had grown stronger as we faced the many challenges in our lives.

"You girls shoo. I want to talk to Daddy and have some grown-up time."

Renata scowled at Parker and me. I knew she envisioned herself grown-up, but I knew better. She had a long journey to adulthood yet. Her teen-age years were just beginning.

"Rennie?" I asked.

"Forget it!" she exclaimed. She turned on her heel and flounced from the room slamming her door with a loud bang.

"Rennie is stupid," Ursula announced in a loud voice. She set the tray down in front of Parker and me and waited for our response…baiting us.

I tried to keep my face impasse, but it was impossible. My eyes crinkled and I burst into a wide grin. Parker gave her a tap on her rump and pointed toward her room. Ursula took the hint as she grabbed her puppets and retreated to her bedroom, cookie in hand.

I settled back on the plump couch.

"Parker, as we were making cookies Ursula told me about her visit to the laboratory with Nurse Phillips."

"What? She took her to the lab? That seems out of character for Nurse Phillips."

"I would have to agree. Lately she has seemed preoccupied and secretive. I sense something is going on with her—she didn't connect with Ursula in the warm welcoming way she usually does."

"Well, what did Ursula say about the lab?"

"To a certain extent she enjoyed the monkeys who were flitting about their cages raucously playing with each other. But I have to say she was also disturbed by what she saw. The way she described the scene research was being conducted—the were people in white coats drawing blood from and injecting the monkeys."

"Monkeys?"

"Yes, from what I have read primates are good candidates for testing the effects of various treatments."

Parker furrowed his brow and ran a hand through his thick mane. "Okay what else bothered Ursula? I don't want her to be negatively affected by this experience and have a relapse into negative behavior."

"I don't think that will happen Parker. She took it all in rather matter-of-factly. Ursula did complain about a strong smell. From her description I would say it was formaldehyde which is used to preserve samples of tissues and other body parts."

Parker wrinkled his nose. "Formaldehyde has a distinctive smell all right. You can recognize it with the assault on your nostrils immediately. When I visited morgues while conducting F.B.I. work it hit you the minute you opened the door."

"But we are getting off track. Should we ask Nurse Phillips not to take her to the lab again?" Parker asked.

"Let's sit on it for now. Perhaps it was a one-time incident."

I stood up and clicked on the radio. A voice boomed filling the room…it was President Truman addressing congress.

Americans are moving through a perilous time. We are confronted with a terrible threat of aggression. We must meet the communist challenge and take action in meeting that threat.

However, the Soviet Union is increasing its armed might and the Soviet acquisition of atomic bomb technology has the world still walking in the shadow of another world war.

Parker reached over and abruptly snapped the radio off. "It's endless isn't it? I'm not optimistic. One war ends and another immediately takes its place."

I took Parker's hand and drew it to my lips. "Just today I got a call from the government asking me to teach the school children how to *duck and cover* should there be an atomic bomb launched at the United States by the Soviets. I refuse to be their patsy! What

200

good would that simpleton gesture help when a bomb could wipe out an entire region? There is no reason to scare the children by putting them through futile drills."

"Billy Love, I completely agree with you. You have much better uses for your time."

"I want to discuss something else with you. Aunt Liz called today. Something is brewing with my sister Babe and her banker boyfriend. She wants me to come to West Berlin soon—to get my take on Mr. Hans Fischer."

"You have my blessing. There is something off about that guy. You have good instincts, Billy Love, so rely on them. I can handle Renata's and Ursula's schedule."

"Thanks, Parker. I knew I could count on you." I became quiet and a bit sheepish, but I knew I needed to inform him of all of my intentions. There were other reasons I wanted to travel to Berlin.

He nodded.

"Kat has been invited also. They need her to translate Russian messages into German—apparently UNICEF has been attempting to have conversations with Russian officials and the language barrier is an issue."

"What about Wolfgang with all of his problems? Can Kat leave him right now?" Parker asked.

"Jack has carved out some time to be home, not traveling as much with the government so that Kat can go to Berlin. And Wolfgang is being seen by Nurse Phillips at Bellevue on a regular outpatient basis so he is getting some help. But at Wolfgang's last appointment he asked about the identity of his birthfather and Nurse Phillips told him about Prince Philipp Von Hessen who still resides in Germany. Parker, this is the first time in seven years that Wolfie has requested information. And it came out of the blue. Of course, Kat was shaken up and luckily I was there to support her. We spent time processing together."

"I'm sure it was difficult for Kat. But will Wolfgang want to meet the prince? I can't picture that guy as a loving father. According to Jack he was a real asshole, collaborating with the Nazis when he thought it was to his advantage!"

"Kat seems to think Wolfie will want to travel to Europe at some point and meet him. I have to be honest with you. On our trip Kat and I plan to incorporate a visit to Kronberg which is where Philipp resides in a tower in the castle located there."

"Billy Love, please be careful. You never know what you might discover and it could be dangerous. I understand there has been a resurgence of the Royalist Movement in Germany. Philipp and others continue to share sympathetic views on National Socialism which was the Third Reich's position."

I stood and paced across the room.

"The prince need not know who we are. Kat and I will be disguised as America tourists who are interested in the castle and the art collection that Philipp curates."

"Jack told me that when Philipp was jailed in Darmstadt he was known to be bitter and cynical. Is Jack aware that Katerina is planning to visit Kronberg?"

I paused. "I'm not sure. I haven't spoken to Kat since Wolfgang's last appointment at Bellevue."

"Billy Love!"

"I know. I know. I will talk to Kat."

"You don't want to rile Jack up. He is usually calm as a cucumber, but his military instincts can kick in."

I went to the window and opened the curtains. Streetlights illuminated the mass of people hurrying through the crowded streets of my adopted hometown of New York City. I never could have imagined my life would end up here so far away from my roots in Oklahoma. Yet it was where I was supposed to be. I felt it in my very core. I slowly turned around and faced Parker.

"Come here," Parker said as he patted the seat beside him. "It appears that you and your family have been scheming behind my back. There will be payback in the bedroom, oh yes there will." He pulled the red ribbon from my hair and watched my dark curls cascade down my back.

Desire coursed through me as his slender fingers unbuttoned my blouse. I blushed and shot a glance toward Ursula's and Renata's bedroom.

Parker whispered. "They're too busy to notice."

We quickly moved toward the master bedroom. Our hands were all over each other as we flung off our clothes and coupled until we were both sated.

I flung off the covers and paraded my still taut body so that Parker got an upfront view.

"Babe, you still got it. I never get tired of looking at you," Parker said. He lazily lit two cigarettes and handed me one of them. I pulled on my satin robe and sat down in the window seat.

My mind churned with the conversation about my return to Germany. It was thrilling after all. And it had been too long. The sisterhood would be reunited: Aunt Liz, Cousin Kat and me.

It was time to be reunited. What secrets would be revealed and which ones would be kept?

Chapter 18
Eva's Diary

West Berlin
1952
Elisabetha

"Leon, Eva is begging me to come to upstate New York where she is living. It seems she has become heavily involved with the Quaker peace movement and has been asked to present a paper in a couple of months at The Peace Conference at Mohonk Mountain House. She wants my reaction and advice," I announced.

We had just returned from an exhausting UNICEF meeting in West Berlin where we wrangled with the German and United States officials about how to reach Russian children suffering at the hands of the Bolsheviks. There was very little support for our efforts from either country. We were frustrated and saddened at the cold-blooded responses—the use of innocent children as pawns was especially maddening.

I looked at my mate—he had grown a scruffy beard and his curly hair touched his shirt collar. He looked spent…there were black circles under his eyes and deep lines creased his face. "Liz, now is not a good time for you to be away. There is so much pressure on us from all over the world."

"We are at a stalemate Leon. It would do us all good to step back and rethink our strategies. Perhaps this peace conference at Mohonk will facilitate world-wide conversations about the plight of innocent children…give us some publicity and reopen conversations."

Leon snorted and slammed his hand down on the table. I jumped. I knew he meant well but he could be stubborn and insistent on doing things his way. I had learned how to give him time to consider my opinions—he usually came around to my way of thinking.

Ignoring him momentarily, I went into the kitchen and yanked open the drawer containing Eva's lengthy letter. It was still hard for me to comprehend the depth of what she had endured at the hands of Adolf Hitler. The fact that she had survived and now wanted to make an impact on the world was almost incomprehensible. I snatched up the sheaf of hand-written papers in one hand and the brandy bottle in the other. Leon needed a few nips and so did I…I hauled both items into the dining room.

"Here Leon, take a swallow," I said handing him a shot glass.

He put his hand on my shoulder kissed me on the cheek and tucked a strand of gray hair behind my ear. "Liz, I am sorry I was rude to you. I know how much you care and I never should have acted the way I did."

"Forgiven." I said as I downed my own glass of burning liquid. A sense of calm descended on me as the liquor did its job.

"Look at her letter. Eva sent me some excerpts from the diary she kept in 1935, right before Mood and I helped her escape to America."

"What, she kept a diary? How were we unaware of such a thing?" Leon asked.

"It is remarkable isn't it? None of us knew. She apparently hid it in the bottom of the suitcase."

"If the diary had been discovered I am sure she would have been sent to a concentration camp or worse."

"Indeed, there are some damning excerpts in the diary regarding her thoughts about the Fuhr. Leon, she was only seventeen-years-old when she met Adolf and twenty-three years old when she was whisked out of Germany."

"Alright, Liz, now I am curious. Read me some of what she wrote."

Leon tipped his chair back on two legs and crossed his arms as I picked up the first two pages of the letter. His craggy face was reflected in the dim evening light coming through the window.

Hiking my reading glasses into position on my sharp nose, I squinted at the paper and began.

October 1935

> *How could I have been so naïve as to the evils Adolf was espousing? One needed only to examine the writings from his book Mein Kompf in order to see how his mind worked.*
>
> *Here is Adolf's writing from his book.*
>
> *"Everlasting peace will come to the world when the last man has slain the last but me."*
>
> *What a horrible thought! How could I have been so smitten? Was it his power, his fame, a combination, or the idea that I could glom onto his coattails and ride to infamy myself? I am but an empty-headed girl who likes to take photographs, dance and wait around for whatever affection Adolf might dole out on any particular day.*
>
> *But here is the reality of my situation. When he says he loves me, it only means he loves me at that moment. Like his promises which he never keeps. Why does he torment me like this, when he could finish it off at once? I have made up my mind to take 35 pills this time and it will be 'dead' certain.*
>
> *If only I had not set eyes on him. I am miserable. I sat with him for three hours and we did not exchange a single word.*

I looked up from reading the letter and saw pain in Leon's eyes that matched my own. Eva was very young when she wrote these words. Yet, it would take great courage for her to renounce her association with Hitler in a very public way—at a peace conference many years later attended by world leaders!

"Liz, after hearing parts of Eva's diary I absolutely think you need to go to New York and visit her," Leon said.

I smiled grimly. "Thanks for your support, Leon, but I would have gone with or without your blessing. You know that."

I folded the letter and placed it back into the envelope. "Eva's journey has been difficult. She is not trusted by many Americans and by the same token she is shunned by her fellow German countrymen who are still secretly harboring thoughts of German Nationalism and what could have been."

Leon nodded in agreement. "I am curious as to what she will deliver at the peace conference. Do you think she will read from her diary?"

"I certainly think so—she needs to give concrete examples of a dictator's behavior. But beyond that I believe she will deliver a message that resonates with what is happening in the world today where countries remain in conflict with each other. Threatening missile-strikes and annihilation. There will be an emphasis on the children. I am certain of that."

I put the letter aside and sat silently with Leon. Kicking off my sturdy shoes, I placed my feet in his lap. He rubbed them absent-mindedly.

Finally, he spoke. "Not to negate the importance of the diary and the peace conference Liz, but I am curious about something else. Did Eva give you an update on her attempts to adopt little Ruthie? It seems she hit some roadblocks with that."

I spat out my words—riled up yet again. "I'm afraid antiquated laws are being used to deny Ruthie's placement with Eva. Apparently, you need to be a married white couple to be considered for parenthood. Single parents need not apply. Ruthie had been *selected* by several families and returned like an unwanted package when her behavior wasn't that of the perfect little angel. She was found by soldiers, abandoned in a field essentially naked—wearing only a diaper—Who knows what horrors she experienced and how that might impact her future behavior?"

"Can you talk with Parker and Billy Love while you are in New York? Parker seems to know how to pull strings."

"I can try, but it won't be easy. The government would rather let a little girl ping pong from one family to another and then land back in the orphanage rather than provide Ruthie with a loving, stable home with Eva. If we could get around the red tape not only would Ruthie have Eva, she would have the support of our loving family."

Leon looked up at me. Clearly his mood had lightened. He grinned—understanding what I was relaying to him. "You mean the Wolfpack, don't you?"

"Of course."

I dropped another bombshell.

"Billy Love and Katerina arrive in West Berlin next week. We need their help at UNICEF headquarters."

I didn't wait for his response. "One more thing…"

Leon looked at me expectantly.

"Wolfgang's birth father survived the war and Katerina and Billy Love plan to pay the scoundrel a visit. At his home at Kronberg Castle Germany. Where he apparently is living a quiet life tending to the family cemetery and attempting to recover the art collection that he contends was stolen by the Americans at the end of the war."

Leon shook his head and rolled his eyes. He knew there was no sense arguing with me. I would do what I wanted and I would get what I wanted when I wanted. And what I needed to get there was the presence of my nieces.

Chapter 19
Wolfgang

New York City
1952
Katerina

> *It was the secrets of heaven and earth that I desired to learn—whether it was the outward substance of things or the inner spirit of nature and the mysterious soul of man that occupied me.*
> ~Mary Shelly—Frankenstein

"Kat, yesterday when I was walking home from my *wonderful new school* I saw Nurse Phillips on the street corner," Wolfgang said. He spat out his words in a hard cadence.

Kat, he calls me Kat. Was his use of my first name a teenage rebellion or did he reject me as his mother? And what about his negative attitude regarding the school where we placed him following the beating he received from a group of bullies? He was clearly being sarcastic. I gripped the back of the chair and attempted to stay impasse.

"What? You saw Nurse Phillips? Did you speak to her?"

"Naw, she was headed in the opposite direction—didn't see me—and I didn't *want* her to see me. She had on street clothes, no uniform but I still recognized her. She has a certain way of carrying herself. I followed her for several blocks," Wolfgang said. He shrugged and tried to act nonchalant.

"Wolfie! Why did you follow her?" I cried.

"Why not, *Kat*? She seemed all mysterious and kept looking from side to side. And she carried a big bag that she protected."

I scowled. "It's really none of our business what she does outside of her work at Bellevue."

"Believe me, she is up to something. After I followed her for about six blocks she stopped at a phone booth. The phone was ringing, *Kat*! How did Nurse Phillip know someone was calling for her at 4 o'clock on a Wednesday, huh?"

I had no answers…I waited for him to continue.

Wolfgang picked up Schnitzel and positioned the dog on his lap absently rubbing his fingers behind her droopy ears. "I could clearly hear her speaking to someone. She spoke in German."

"German?"

"Yes, German I understand my native language even if I can't really speak it much anymore. I was seven when the camp at Dachau was liberated. I understand more than anyone knows."

"And what did you hear?" I couldn't help myself—I was becoming immersed in the situation. I was curious.

Wolfgang put Schnitzel down and turned to stare at me.

"Kat, she said something about a shipment that would be sent soon. I couldn't make out what was contained in the shipment, but Nurse Phillips was adamant that the situation was urgent. She was arguing with someone on the other end of the phone. Then she slammed the phone down and cussed."

"That does not sound like Nurse Phillips. She always presents herself in such a calm professional manner."

He didn't wait for my response. He grabbed Schnitzel's leash attached it to her collar and slammed out the door.

I tried to compose myself as I poured myself a large glass of white wine. I swirled the liquid around and around rehashing the conversation with Wolfgang. What kind of shipment? Why speak in German? Why answer a phone booth call? And what was in her bag? There was a myriad of unanswered questions. For now, I would put Wolfgang and his sullen behavior aside. My coping mechanisms were depleted.

Nurse Phillips had always had a bit of mystery surrounding her. Now the intrigue deepened. Later I resolved to call Billy Love as she had had more interactions with Nurse Phillips than me. Perhaps she had picked something up that I had failed to notice.

I crossed the room and put a record on the phonograph. Marlene Dietrich's deep voice crooned. Leaning back against the plump cushions of the couch, I became nostalgic thinking back to when Marlene and I recorded duets together before the start of the Second War. We made quite the pair. Both of us with our German heritages now fiercely embracing America.

Marlene could be quite the enigma. Recently she had agreed to record an ABC radio show in New York City called *Café Istanbul*. The show had some cockamamie story-line where Marlene played a nightclub singer in Istanbul and ends up being a spy—it was unclear just who she was spying upon.

I had seen the promotional pictures for the show—there was Marlene wrapped seductively in a fur coat standing before a microphone with her painted pouting lips and hat complete with black netting covering her perfectly oval face. Classic Marlene Dietrich.

Marlene called me last week with an enticing offer. I recalled her husky voice.

Kat Darling, the bosses called and they want you and me to record a duet for Café Istanbul. Mitch Miller composed it. I believe it would be divine don't you honey? And we can spend the whole afternoon together. The studio will provide us with libations. It will be like old times!

Laughing heartily to myself I pondered Marlene's request. Just like old times—right. If I was to take her up on her offer I had better start vocalizing and tune my voice up with some extra lessons. You didn't just pick up where you left off years ago. Professional singers were keenly aware that practice is imperative.

I rationalized that it would be good for me to deflect my thoughts from Wolfgang and his issues by teaming up with Marlene for her radio gig. I would accept her offer.

I finished my glass of wine and poured another as Jack swooped into the room returning home from his government consulting job. He took off his raincoat threw it onto the hall-tree and looked at me strangely. "I just crossed paths with Wolfgang on my way up in the elevator. He grunted at me and refused to look me in the eye. What's his problem, Kat?"

"Jack, I don't know what to think of him these days. He's a teenager, he's a concentration camp survivor, he's been bullied by school children…I'd say that's quite a list of achievements wouldn't you say?"

Jack raised his eyebrows acknowledging my assessment. He crossed his arms and waited. He understood I had more to say.

"Oh, and did I mention he has been following his therapist by traipsing across New York City, trying to discover her secrets?"

"Nurse Phillips?" he asked.

"You got it, Jack and Wolfgang may be on to something…he just might have made a discovery."

****

It was raining heavily as drops pinged against our apartment building. I pulled the curtains aside from the windows and peered out. The rain was driving side-ways and there was a mist coming up from the concrete streets—it obscured the view of the park directly across the street.

Wolfgang was difficult and reclusive. When he spoke to Jack and me it was always about his latest obsessions which these days revolved around Prince Philipp Von Hessen (*his birth father*), why the prince sent his birth mother to Dachau—and the novel *Frankenstein* by Mary Shelley.

He had read the entire book at least five times and the pages were dogeared where he had tagged certain passages. Wherever he went he carried *Frankenstein* in his satchel…and pulled it out to pour over its content whenever there was a spare minute. Nurse Phillips understood and encouraged Wolfgang to find meaning in the book—some connotation that might help mitigate his intense boiling anger.

At night we heard him in his room reading aloud in a quivering voice. It was always the same excerpt:

My abhorrence for this fiend cannot be conceived. When I thought of him I gnashed my teeth, my eyes became inflamed and I ardently wished to extinguish that life which I had so thoughtlessly bestowed. When I reflected on his crimes and malice, my hatred and revenge burst all the bounds of moderation. I would have made a pilgrimage to the highest peaks of the Andes, could I, when there, have precipitated him to their base. I wished to see him again, that I might wreck the utmost havoc on his head, and avenge the deaths of William and Justine.

Each time Wolfgang focused on this particular passage Jack and I discussed its possible significance. Was he equating the monster with his birth father Philipp? In his mind was he plotting to destroy Philipp for sending his mother away to one of the worst Nazi concentration camps of World War II? Solely for being Jewish? Did he consider himself an instrument for violent retaliation?

At the next appointment with Nurse Phillips I planned to discuss Wolfgang's reaction to *Frankenstein* with her. How did she interpret it in the context of Wolfgang's behavior? Was it therapeutic or did it arouse sinister feelings that drowned out any psychological progress he had made? Questions seemed to be replaced by questions. They were endless.

It seemed that Wolfgang had intertwined reality with fantasy as he pondered his place in the world. The other day he asked to make a pilgrimage of sorts to Frankenstein's castle—the ruins in Darmstadt where Jack and I first discovered him after the Dachau camp was liberated by the allies. I was not sure Wolfgang's fragile psyche could handle a trip back in time, but I planned to call Papa and get his reaction—he had a grandfatherly sensibility and from the beginning had made a strong connection with Wolfie.

Today Wolfgang was determined to go out—to the cemetery that lay adjacent to the park—to roam it for hours on end examining the tomb stones embossed with the star of David. It was a ritual for him—one that Jack and I failed to understand.

He was sullen and withdrawn coiled like a snake waiting to spring forward. I watched in dismay as he donned his bright yellow slicker and pulled the hood up to obscure most of his wan face.

I grabbed his shoulders spun him toward me and tried to hug him, but he brushed me aside.

"Don't touch me!"

Wolfgang shuddered and slumped toward the door. He looked like an old man fighting his demons. Then without looking back he slipped out into the hallway and ran toward the mist.

How many things are we upon the brink of
becoming acquainted, if cowardice or carelessness
did not restrain our enquiries?

~Mary Shelley—Frankenstein

Chapter 20
Respite in Palm Springs

California Desert
1952
Billy Love

> *I have an abiding faith in what women can do.*
> ~Franc Roads Elliott
> Founding Member PEO 1869
> Known as the girl with the far vision;
> for she was years ahead of her time.

How long had it been since the care-free days of our youth—when Katerina, Eva and I traveled to the land of milk and honey so to speak? Marlene had been adamant that it was time to rekindle relationships shorn of men and children. To support women who wanted to be together to be present with each other and to revel with each other. To unwrap the secrets and mysteries that tended to stress and age us before it was necessary. To fling off stereotypes of what women should want and be in the year 1952.

Of course, Marlene had never fit into any stereotype and never would. She represented herself as the woman who got what she wanted when she wanted and never regretted any decisions made. Although I was cognizant that Marlene Dietrich the movie star was often reckless, I also recognized that I often became engrossed in the everyday quagmire of my life and needed to refresh my spirit with Marlene's lit-up presence.

I pictured late night cocktails and swimming in her glamorous pool then wrapping ourselves in fluffy terry cloths robes sitting by the fire, sharing with my sisters. Heaven knows there were a million secrets floating about in each of our lives: Marlene, Audrey, Eva, Kat and me. How many of the confidences would be revealed and how many would continue to be submerged?

At Marlene's original cottage house nestled at the base of the desert mountains I imagined we would split into twosomes and then switch it up, discussing the intimate details of each other's lives and asking each other for advice—advice that we might internalize or toss out the window depending upon our mood. One thing I knew…our lives were tangled together but that was not necessarily a good or bad thing…it was omnipresent and none of us would want to change our trajectory.

It would be refreshing to get out of the constant noise and chaos that swirled in New York City for I viewed Palm Springs as a retreat a spa-like environment to unwind and be pampered. I smiled to myself though with the thought that Marlene would make sure that none of us would be bored. She would have *plans*.

****

Kat and I hauled our bags into the cab and departed for the airport. We were on the same flight which would give us a head start on catching up with each other. As the cabbie swore and honked in the snarled traffic we became giddy anticipating the trip to Palm Springs.

We arrived at the terminal and checked into our flight before boarding the plane. The perfectly coiffed flight attendant showed us to our seats. I secured my seatbelt across my lap and glanced over at Kat who was applying another layer of bright red lipstick to her plump lips. She winked at me and clutched my hand as the stewardess prepared the cabin for take-off.

My cousin remained one of my best friends—we had been through a life-time of ups and downs together. Our children, our greatest joy and our greatest challenge bound us together in a seamless way that could never be broken.

I shut my eyes and leaned back against the headrest as the pilot revved the engines of the plane. I thought about my girls Renata and Ursula—particularly Ursula—who now was making significant progress under the care of Nurse Phillips. Without feeling guilt, I could leave both girls for a few days of vacation.

When I returned from Palm Springs I had a treat planned for Ursula. There would be an outing for just the two of us to Sardis Restaurant and a Broadway musical much like I had done with Renata when she was Ursula's age.

"Billy Love, what are you smiling about?" Kat asked.

"How much love I hold for my girls. To be truthful I never thought Ursula would be able to enjoy life or even fit in anywhere after the horrific trauma of seeing her parents killed. But there is hope in the world isn't there Kat?"

"Yes, and there are people who genuinely care about our children's future. Jack and I remain concerned about Wolfgang though. He is lobbying us to travel to Europe—to meet his birth father the *prince*."

"For now, let's put our children in a box," I said. "We can take them out after we return to New York."

Kat giggled and said, "You were always good about compartmentalizing things, Billy Love. Alright let's be frivolous. What does your new swimsuit look like and who do you think Marlene is taking up with now a man a woman or both?"

"I heard through the grapevine that she was on the prowl for Yul Brynner who happens to be twenty years her junior. Just her type, young muscle-bound and handsome," I announced in a loud voice.

The stewardess heard our antics and smiling with her perfectly even gleaming teeth presented herself as she stepped into the aisle.

"Ladies can I take your drink orders?"

"We thought you would never ask," Kat and I replied in unison.

****

"My beauties, welcome to the desert!" Marlene exclaimed as she emerged from her cottage flinging a brightly-colored scarf across her throat. She was as glamorous as ever with her hair newly coiffed into close-cropped blonde curls and her makeup impeccably applied to highlight her cheekbones. She was movie scene ready…the mountains behind her cottage framed the landscape and the scent of the scarlet bougainvillea filled the air.

Kat and I kissed her on each cheek as she pursed her lips and blew smoke rings into the dry desert air.

I was giddy. "Marlene thanks for inviting us."

Marlene tilted her head toward the back of the house and replied in her husky voice. "It has been way too long. Now Eva and Audrey arrived a couple of hours ago and have already changed into their swimsuits. They are lounging on the patio and are on their second cocktail so you two are behind."

We dutifully trailed Marlene and entered the cottage where the décor was exactly the same as it was many years before when we visited—plump comfortable chintz chairs and couches in a cozy setting—relaxing with a touch of elegance.

Kat twirled in place and her blue eyes sparkled. In her emerald green cotton swing dress with a deep V-neck and décolleté she looked like she resided in the Hollywood community. And I had purchased a bright yellow floral print midi dress which swished around me as I walked. I felt young and fresh. This vacation was exactly what we all needed.

Kat and I hurried up the staircase to the familiar bedroom at the top of the stairs where we had stayed together years ago. We tossed our suitcases onto the bed extracted swim wear and changed.

Eva and Audrey were deep in conversation when Kat and I burst onto the patio giggling like school girls.

"Audrey, I adore your haircut. You are on the cover of every teen magazine. So stylish my dear," Kat proclaimed.

Indeed, with her baby bangs and pixie cut Audrey represented the epitome of stardom—her waiflike frame and luminous eyes contributed to the sublime picture. I leaned over Eva and Audrey's lounge chairs and simultaneously hugged them both.

Eva looked relaxed. The solitude of the farm in upstate New York had done wonders for her glow of health. I understood from Kat that Eva was working on a paper to deliver at the next Peace Conference to be held at Mohonk Mountain House. All of us were invited to the conference but for this trip I hoped to put the details aside.

Audrey sucked on an ice cube and looked me up and down.

"Lady, that red polka dot swim suit does wonders for your figure. And Kat, wow your navy striped suit makes the tatas stand up and salute!"

Kat and I laughed and placed our towels on the lounge chairs.

"You two got started before us, we're behind—so let's get this party going," I said.

Marlene rolled the drink cart to our side. It contained every type of liquor imaginable which was imperative when you were catering to a Hollywood crowd known for its wild parties.

"Now ladies I have invited a few neighbors over for drinks tomorrow night. It should be fuunn," Marlene said as she emphasized the word.

"Who?" Eva asked.

"Why Sammy Davis Junior and Dino Martin. We are all neighborly with each other. They are particularly interested in meeting you Eva."

"Why me?" Eva asked.

"Well, of course you are as famous as everyone else in Hollywood. The fact that you ditched Adolf Hitler and made a new life in America is fascinating to all," Marlene explained.

Marlene paused. "But you couldn't have done it without the help of our two beauties here…Kat and Billy Love."

"That's old news Marlene. Surely the stars can't be interested in the details of my journey…" Eva's voice trailed off as she studied her fingernails.

"Don't be silly Eva." Marlene said with an emphasis that ended the discussion.

"It's hot. I'm baking," Audrey said. She stood up and dove into the pool. Several seconds later she popped to the surface and surveyed the rest of us.

"Well? Come on now," she cajoled.

Eva, Kat and I held hands and jumped in together laughing uproariously. We felt care-free. At that moment there were no problems in the world. Just pure pleasure.

Thank you, Marlene.

****

Marlene's patio was brilliantly lit with string after string of crisscrossing lights that served to create ambience for the Hollywood welcome party. The outdoor serving table groaned with caviar, smoked herring and other delicacies including pastries and rich desserts. And the bar was stocked with every imaginable liquor that existed.

Marlene had just wrapped *Rancho Notorious* and Audrey was back in the States after completing *Secret People*. They were both ready to party and Marlene known as the Queen of Entertainment had gone all out.

Eva was nervous. "Billy Love I really don't want any attention tonight. I hope everyone will just let me blend in without any fuss." She sat at a dressing table and studied her features. Even now fifteen years after undergoing plastic surgery to disguise her appearance she seemed startled when she looked at her reflection in the mirror.

I edged silk stockings up my leg and attached a garter belt.

"Eva, everyone invited is famous in some way so I don't think you will receive undue attention. Just remember people will always be curious about your situation."

Eva nodded as Kat waltzed into the bedroom fully dressed in eveningwear. A sublime smell of gardenia perfume wafted around her.

"People will be here any moment, why are you two dilly-dallying?" Kat asked.

"Poo Kat. You are always early. And Hollywood stars are fashionably late," I said.

"I will have you know that Sammy Davis Jr. has already arrived and is holding court out by the pool," Kat declared.

"I can't wait to meet him. He is so interesting—I understand he is opening for Frank Sinatra in Las Vegas," Eva said as she abrupted stood flung off her robe and reached for the pink satin dress hanging in the closet.

"You two better hurry or you will miss out. I plan to monopolize him," Kat commented as she turned and swished out of the room—her high-heels clicking on the terrazzo floors.

Eva and I looked at each other then we laughed uproariously as we pictured *Miss Katerina Wolf Cabaret Singer* in all her glory at *The Garden*.

"Come on, Eva. We don't want to be upstaged by Kat," I said.

"Oh, Billy Love, I believe we have already been out maneuvered. The festivities are in full swing," Eva said as she opened the bedroom door.

We descended down the wrought iron staircase and observed well-heeled people on the patio by the pool—cocktails in one hand cigarettes in the other they stood chatting each other up. There was Marlene commanding attention. Kat draped herself on the bar thus cornering Sammy Davis, Jr.

"Come my darlings," Marlene shouted above the din. "You both look lovely."

I did feel attractive and seductive even although I would soon be turning forty. I glanced at myself in the parlor mirror. Dark eyes and smooth olive skin reflected back. My sapphire blue taffeta dress with the deep v décolleté hugged my still-lithe figure. I pulled away from the mirror and stepped onto the patio. Eva was right behind me.

People instantly recognized Eva and started pointing in our direction. I noticed Eva carefully ignored them and went to Marlene's side. Marlene put her arm around Eva protectively.

"Welcome to my little abode everyone. I would like to introduce you all to my house guests. Then we have a special performance before we get the party in full swing," Marlene said.

The crowd waited expectantly for the introductions.

"I call these ladies *The Wolfpack* because we all watch each other's backs. In the corner by the pool is Katerina, Kat if you will.

Beside me is Eva and next to her is Billy Love. Audrey will join us shortly. You know, Audrey Hepburn the chic upcoming movie star? Please. These incredible women are changing our world for the better and I hope you will get to know each of them."

People applauded. I frowned…we were supposed to be having a party not a gabfest about issues related to changing the world. I chided myself to let it go—Marlene meant well and she was so very proud of each of us.

"Thank you all," Marlene said expansively. "Now I have a treat. Katerina and I are going to sing a duet reintroducing a favorite song of mine that we will be performing on my New York radio show Café *Istanbul.*

What? I stared at Kat as she blushed and looked away. That scoundrel—she knew about this all along and had failed to share the secret with me! I couldn't be upset. It was a delightful surprise.

Marlene strode to Kat's side then guided her into the living room to stand before the baby grand piano. All of the windows and doors were open so that the sound could drift through the dry heat of the night.

A tall white-haired gentleman tinkled the opening notes. Then Kat and Marlene crooned in harmony to *Falling in Love Again* one of Marlene's favorite sultry songs.

I closed my eyes and concentrated on the duet savoring every note. Someone brushed against me and I looked up to see Sammy Davis Jr. also enjoying the moment. He was grinning and tapping his foot to the beat. Did he ever stand still?

Marlene and Kat finished the song and gazed at the crowd as applause rang out. They nodded to each other. Then in unison they switched to German and repeated the song. It was an acknowledgement of their German heritage, their upbringing…and a nod to their past. Even though the Nazis had torn out every stitch of national morality before and during World War II Marlene and Kat conveyed a renewed sense of comradery comeback and bonding that could ultimately triumph and mitigate some of the deep-held pain.

By the end of the song Marlene and Kat were both in tears. I looked over at Eva—she was openly sobbing. Memories had been uprooted and brought to the forefront. I pictured a transformed Eva Braun nee *Giselle* standing on the platform at the station in New York City waiting to board a train for a new life in Oklahoma. Desperate to leave her time with Hitler behind, yet fearful of the unknown undercover world she would need to live in for the next nine years—until World War II finally ended.

I cleared my head of negative thoughts and returned to the party atmosphere surrounding me. Sammy was tugging at my arm.

"Miss Billy Love is it? Pray tell, how did you get your name?" he asked smiling slyly.

"You had to know my parents, Sammy. Unconventional in every way. I think father wanted a boy—I was the first born, ha! Not only did he fail to get his wish with me—I was followed by three more sisters!"

"So, Billy spelled with a y," Sammy said as he took a long drag at the end of one cigarette and promptly lit another from its butt.

"Yep and our middle names are Love--so Billy Love, Bobbie Love, Bitsy Love and Babe Love. It's an Oklahoma thing. Everyone has two first names and I think my mother was too lazy to come up with something different for each of us," I said reverting to my familiar Oklahoma twang.

Sammy doubled over laughing. "I never thought I would meet someone as unique as me but now I have! Why look at me and look around. I'm pretty sure I am the only colored Puerto Rican Jew at the party."

Now it was my turn to laugh. He was right. There was not a lot of noticeable diversity within the confines of Marlene's party.

Kat was suddenly before us taking in our conversation.

"Mr. Davis, what did you think of our performance?"

"Marvelous my beautiful Katerina, marvelous," he said as he stubbed out his cigarette and took both of her hands in his.

"I overheard what you said to Billy Love about your background, Sammy. It seems the three of us have something in common—Billy Love and I are Jewish too. We didn't discover our roots until our parents informed us—we were adults."

Sammy and I nodded waiting for further explanation. But Kat veered off in another direction.

"My mother Irina was Russian. We don't know much about her in that she died giving birth to me. My lineage is a bit of a mystery, but it is rumored that there is royalty in my past. It is a shame that the damn Bolsheviks have ruined Russia!" Kat shouted trying to be heard above the din. I could tell that Kat was a bit tipsy. She weaved back and forth. I could smell the brandy on her breath.

I swatted Kat's arm and hissed in her ear. "Kat not now, not here. It could be dangerous for you with the intensity of the Cold War between countries going on. There are reports that Russian spies are everywhere—someone at this party could be undercover gathering information to use against you and your family. Please drop the subject."

Kat became sullen. Her jaw clenched. I knew she was unhappy with me but felt I had no choice. Years of experience had taught me that enemies could and would use information against you. It was of the utmost importance to be guarded.

Sammy had turned away from us…courted by other guests. With Frank Sinatra as his mentor it was clear he was on the road to stardom.

I stepped away from the crowd and locked myself into the first-floor powder room. I sagged against the wall as Kat's Russian treasures swam before my eyes—the Fabergé Egg, the Russian stacking dolls, the portrait of Irina, the jeweled brooch and the diamond ring. The cache clearly indicated Russian Royalty.

Jack and I were the only people aware of the contents of the trunk. Not even Uncle Mood had been told. But I knew Katerina was jittery and itching to tell others especially Eva and Marlene. And liquor made the tongue loose.

There were unknown dangers and consequences connected with Kat's discoveries. Were Kat's Russian relatives still alive hiding somewhere in the USSR or in exile in a foreign country, unaware of Katerina Wolf Remington's existence? I felt an obligation to keep the secret…but for how long and under what circumstances?

I straightened powdered my nose and tucked stray strands of my thick hair behind my ear. Then I pulled open the door and rejoined the gaiety of Marlene's party. Russian spies be damned.

Chapter 21
Betrayal

West Berlin and East Berlin
1953
Elisabetha

> *Betrayal can be extremely painful, but it's up to you*
> *how much that pain damages you permanently.*
> ~Emily V. Gordon

It had been six long months and Leon and I failed to make significant progress with our plans for UNICEF to air-drop supplies into Perm Russia—in a full-on effort to assist starving and disease-ridden children who were being persecuted by the Bolshevik regime. It was extremely frustrating especially for Leon who felt an urgency to act.

Lately he was moody and just plain crabby…not that I blamed him. I also was impatient with the sluggish movement of events. The United States Ambassador to West Germany was avoiding Leon's calls. There appeared to be a standoff between the east and western countries. Neither side wanted to take the first move to rock the boat.

There was a glimmer of hope however. The underground newspapers reported that the dictator Josef Stalin had suffered a stroke and was secluded near the Kremlin. Perhaps his demonic rule would soon be coming to an end—it was rumored that to consolidate his power he had killed between 10 and 20 million people! He had forced industrialization upon the nation, formed collective farms which created famine and, in his paranoia directed the secret police to inflict atrocities on his people which were beyond belief.

Leon railed. "Stalin's dictatorship is worse than Hitler's rule if that is even possible."

All I knew is that it was important to end the stalemate between countries and take action that would alleviate the people's unimaginable suffering.

I glanced out the bedroom window where frost was collecting on the pane. It was snowing and the wind gusts were picking up. I needed to end my inertia…gathering myself up I threw aside the woolen blanket and headed to the bathroom. Easing myself into the hot shower I soaped my sinewy body. Although folks thought of me as an older adult I knew I still had a physical strength and presence that served me well. My mind raced. I always did my best thinking as water streamed across my body.

Bitsy Love was arriving in West Berlin this afternoon. Lately she had telephoned me often to inquire after her twin Babe Love and Mr. Hans Fischer *the boyfriend.* Bitsy Love had implored me to keep her visit to Berlin secret from her identical sister. I was not sure what her intentions were but I was determined to find out. My nieces could be in danger.

It was well known that there were spies crawling all over in Berlin. Just this morning the West Berlin paper blared—*Two East Germans Arrested at the United States Embassy Spying for the Kremlin.* Although there were no details as to the nature of their activity it could be assumed that they were leaking information to the Russians related to nuclear war heads and other military information that fueled the Cold War.

I sighed, shut off the shower and hurriedly dressed in my drab uniform of gray wool trousers and cardigan. On my bedside table stood a picture of Bitsy and Babe Love Wolf standing together with their arms wrapped around each other, their identical brilliant smiles and sparkling turquoise eyes staring up at me. I picked up the picture and tried to discern differences in their features but it was impossible. They would have handily won a contest for *most identical twins.*

There was an insistent knock at the door. I went to the window and looked down to see a petite white-blonde woman dragging a large suitcase behind her—it was Bitsy Love. At least I thought she was Bitsy and not Babe. I smiled. It had been too long.

I threw open the door and hugged Bitsy Love tightly. Her floral scent filled my nostrils as I urged her to come into the foyer.

"Let me look at you my dear," I said.

"Auntie thanks for hosting me. I had an interesting train trip into West Berlin. At every stop along the route through East Germany Russian soldiers climbed on board and inspected our passports."

"Did they threaten you?"

"Not at all. I turned on the charm flirted with them a bit and they were like little puppies."

"Well, Bitsy Love they are not puppies. They could be bulldogs, spies or convicts so be careful."

"I intend to be careful. Where is Leon?"

"Let's get you settled in the guest bedroom and then we can start a fire and have a glass of wine. I want to hear all about your plans while you are here."

"Leon?" Bitsy Love repeated.

"He is at UNICEF headquarters. Always."

"Well he should take some time off, Liz. Lord knows he has put in his time—a true patriot."

I switched the subject. There was no sense defending him. He was going to do what he wanted.

We sat before the crackling fireplace in our bathrobes sipping white wine and making small talk about the family. I peppered Bitsy Love with questions. *What is my brother A.R. doing now that he was retired from the LA Times? Is your mother still cooking for the hired hands? Where is your recluse sister Bobbie Love?*

Finally, I directed the conversation to Babe Love and *the boyfriend.*

"What are your intentions?"

"What do you mean?" Bitsy Love said avoiding eye contact.

"Come on you are up to something," I said.

"Hans Fischer is not right for my sister. He is using her—for what I don't know but I am going to find out. I plan to infiltrate his world by pretending to be Babe."

I arched my eyebrows. I was suspicious even before she revealed her plan that she would impersonate her twin. As children they had easily fooled people as to their real identities.

"Spill it. How do you plan to approach Mr. Fischer?"

"While Babe is at UNICEF I plan to pay him a visit at the so-called bank where he works."

"You don't think he is legally employed by the bank?"

"I certainly do not. At Kat's wedding he was so shady and vague that I immediately flagged him as a liar. I have a strong intuitive sense when it comes to reading people—especially when it comes to Babe Love and her relationships with men."

"Now Bitsy I have gotten close to Babe these past several years while she has been working with Leon and me at UNICEF headquarters. She has blossomed and become a confident woman..." I trailed off waiting for my niece's response.

"I don't doubt that Liz, but she is blinded by Hans. He has her under his spell and she cannot see what I see."

"Bitsy I believe in you, but I don't trust what is going on in Berlin right now. It is highly dangerous. I would like to propose that I escort you to the bank and then stay hidden behind a large barricade across the street. I can watch you through the plate glass window. If there is any sign of trouble I can notify the German police."

"I think I can handle the situation Auntie but if you think it best to come along then very well," Bitsy said giving me a half-smile. Her blue eyes twinkled.

"What are you going to do?"

"I'm going to pick a very public fight with Mr. Fischer and watch how he reacts. I predict he will try to keep me quiet not wanting to attract any attention to himself. He would rather keep a very low profile in his shady world."

I stood and paced the room. I knew I was helpless to stop Bitsy, but she had complicated a precarious situation...I had both Babe and Bitsy to worry about now. I contemplated the stubborn nature of my extended family. We were all obstinate!

"And after you create a scene? What next?"

Bitsy laughed and wagged her finger at me. "I will huff off and wait for him to exit the bank. He will be shaken up and careless with his actions so I will follow him. It's Friday afternoon. Let's see where he goes—Babe tells me he always has commitments on the weekends. She hardly ever sees him which is suspicious in itself."

"Let's keep this between us Bitsy Love, shall we? There is no need to involve Leon."

I knew Leon would disapprove and attempt to intervene.

"I can keep a secret. Oh yes, I can. Here we come."

****

The snow continued to fall overnight and the streets of West Berlin were icy and slippery. My face was wrapped in a woolen scarf and my furred-hood fit snugly on my head. I peered across the street and watched Bitsy Love as she confidently grasped the brass handle of the Deutsche Bank nodded to the uniformed guard and eased herself into the lobby.

She disappeared from view for a few moments…I was momentarily afraid she would be discovered as an imposter and thrown out but then there she was leading Hans, who was dapper in his three-piece banker's suit, toward the imposing fountain that stood in the middle of the lobby.

Heads turned toward the handsome couple. Bitsy Love was striking in her crimson red woolen suit accented by her white-blonde hair which was twisted into a stylish bun. I observed her interactions with Hans. At first her body language indicated she was light and flirtatious as she smiled and leaned into him. Bitsy was a superb actress! Hans responded by taking her hands in his—his face impasse as he stared at her.

Bitsy suddenly ripped her hands away from Hans. I understood she was creating a scene. Hans face reddened. He scowled as he put his finger to his lips and tried to silence her.

Bitsy persisted with her act and strode away from him then spun around and returned within inches of his face. She sneered, raised her hand and slapped him hard across the face.

I watched Han's jaw clench as he struggled to gain control. He stood rigidly red-faced and for a moment I thought he might strike her back. It was clear he was taken by surprise—Mellow Babe Love had never acted like this before.

A guard rushed to the pair's side and attempted to mitigate the fight but Bitsy pushed him away turned her back and rushed through the lobby throwing on her winter coat as she made her way down the marble stairs onto the snow-covered streets.

She didn't look back.

Hans appeared dazed and stricken. He put up a hand as if to tell people to ignore what they had just witnessed. Then he rubbed his jaw and slunk out of the lobby.

Bitsy hustled down the icy street and I followed her a few paces behind. She entered a small crowded café and seated herself. I brushed the snow off my coat and joined her at the table.

I greeted her. "Babe Love, thanks for joining me today on your day off. This winter weather is really getting to me."

Bitsy's eyes sparkled momentarily and then she launched into her performance.

Her voice commanded the room. "Liz, I had the most horrendous fight with Hans. He is never around on the weekends and I confronted him about it at the bank today."

"Shh, keep your voice down," I said.

"I will not! I slapped him!"

"Babe what were you thinking to create such a scene?"

"I just can't take his behavior any more. He is a scoundrel—I think I may have to break up with him."

Bitsy made a sobbing sound and I handed her a handkerchief. She dabbed at her eyes as I held her hand. *This might be the act of the century! Babe was going to be furious at her twin if she ever discovered what her twin had done. And now I was an accomplice. It would be hysterically funny if not for the implications for Babe's relationship with Hans. Bitsy better be right about her so-called intuition.*

The waitress brought us some hot cocoa and made some clicking noises indicating we should quiet down and quit disturbing the other customers. I leaned over to Bitsy and whispered.

"What now?"

She winked conspiratorially and whispered as she sat back and folded her arms.

"Why we will follow him as he leaves the bank tonight. You and I are going to discover where it is he needs to go on the weekends—without Babe."

****

Mr. so-called *Hans Fischer* exited the bank and stood on the street corner. He looked to his right and left then stepped off the curve and strode briskly to the east. Bitsy and I trailed a block behind him keeping him in our sight-line but not appearing suspicious. To outsiders we were two women hurrying to warmth and the safety of shelter after a long week of inclement weather.

"Where do you think he is going?" I shouted as the wind carried my voice away.

"I have an idea but now we can validate it," Bitsy Love replied. She took my arm and urged me to increase my pace. Hans was striding rapidly and we needed to keep up.

The majestic Brandenburg Gate appeared on the horizon— once a symbol of peace it now represented the division between East and West and The Cold War. I shivered as the implications of what we were doing took hold in my mind.

Hans was intent on traveling to East Germany. We watched the Soviet guards interact with him—clearly, they knew him as they chatted him up and laughed at some unknown joke. It was apparent that he made the journey into East Berlin regularly.

I glanced at Bitsy. Her eyes narrowed as she processed the transaction between Hans and the guards. She subtly nodded at me

235

an indication that we should continue to follow him. Bitsy's intuition was bearing fruit. Hans was not who he purported to be.

Hans pocketed his papers. He tightened the belt on his coat and tied down the flaps on his fur-lined hat. Waving to the guards in a familiar gesture he continued on.

Bitsy nudged me forward. The soldier held up his hand and I handed him my identity papers.

"This is my niece who is visiting me from the United States," I explained as I tilted my head toward Bitsy.

The guard was young—still a teenager who barely had enough facial hair to shave. He stamped his feet to keep warm and rubbed his gloved hands together. It was evident he was under duress and did not want to be stationed at the gate. He barely glanced at my papers and failed altogether to ask for Bitsy Love's identification.

"Danke," I said quietly. We hurried through the checkpoint and again spotted Mr. Fischer purposely walking toward a massive cluster of concrete buildings.

"I know where he is going," Bitsy Love said as she pointed. "That group of buildings houses the East German Ministry for State Security."

"And?"

"Mr. Hans Fischer is seemingly a part of the organization—an organization known for sending its spies around the world to collect information for the Russians."

"Are you sure?"

"Yes, look at him acting so confident…right at home—smiling and laughing with the armed sentinel guarding the door."

We watched him open his briefcase and display some papers then he nonchalantly disappeared into building number 27.

"Now what, Bitsy Love?"

"We wait. Over there is a diner with a direct view of building 27. We will watch for him. I'm suspicious…he will surely be heading to another location soon."

"You seem confident."

"I am. Let's go get warmed up."

We ordered vegetable soup and drank hot tea as we waited. Neither of us spoke. My mind was jumbled. I should have informed Leon of Bitsy's intentions, but it was too late now. Here we were in enemy territory and if we were discovered we could be tossed in jail and never heard from again! I knew that scenario was unlikely but still…

The diner was deserted. We were the only customers and the waitress had disappeared into the kitchen. Bitsy snapped open her purse rummaged inside and pulled out a cigarette lighter. She discreetly stepped outside the eating establishment flicked the lighter igniting the flame and held it to the tip of a cigarette. She inhaled the smoke and blew it out into the frigid air.

I watched as Hans emerged from Building 27. Bitsy stubbed out her cigarette and lit a fresh one as she held the lighter up in the air. It was a strange scene. What was she doing? She lit several more cigarettes before she ducked back into the diner.

Bitsy smiled secretively and crammed the lighter back into her purse.

"Come on Liz. He's on the move again."

We pulled up our hoods and covered our faces with scarves to ward off the stinging snow and traipsed doggedly behind Hans. After several blocks he stopped before a drab apartment complex and looked up. I noticed a figure at the window—he waved and a petite woman waved back at him.

Bitsy tapped my arm and pulled me under an awning in the neighboring building. Once again, she pulled out her lighter tilted it toward the woman in the window and touched the fire to a cigarette. I heard a distinct clicking sound.

"What is that whirring sound?"

Bitsy Love ignored me and retorted. "He's a two-timer Liz. I knew it. I knew it!"

"You can't be sure, Bitsy Love."

"Just wait Liz. Look."

Hans Fischer was clearly outlined in the window of the apartment. The woman smiled as she greeted him. He removed his heavy coat and flapped hat and moved to her putting his arms around her waist and pulling her to him.

We watched them embrace and kiss. Bitsy lit yet another cigarette as we watched the couple…we were mesmerized by their actions. They both laughed with an ease that indicated they enjoyed an intimate relationship. He reached into his pocket and pulled something out—and fastened something around her neck. Then he picked her up and carried her out of the room.

"They're going straight to the bedroom," Bitsy declared. "It's clear to me she is his mistress or his wife."

I scowled. "Okay, so you have evidence on Mr. Fischer but it's your word against his. How will you prove it? How are you going to tell Babe? What will we tell Leon?"

"Aunt Liz, I have proof but right now I am unsure how I will proceed. Let's just say that the West German authorities will be interested."

"Bitsy Love, I do declare the capacity for espionage seems to run in the Wolf family doesn't it?" I took a deep breath and gave a little chuckle. "Let's get out of here. Leon will be frantic with worry."

"No worry, Auntie, no worry."

****

It was dusk when we crossed through the Brandenburg Gate and emerged into the safety of West Berlin. Our feet were frozen and our lips were blue as we wearily trudged through the ankle-deep snow-packed streets. My only thought was the urgent need to get home shed my wet clothes and bundle up before a roaring fire.

I whistled for a cab. It lurched to the curb where we were standing.

A friendly face called to us. "You ladies look beat. Come on, get in. Where are you going?"

Bitsy Love and I sank into the leather cushions and reveled in the warmth of the heated cab. I gave him my address and shut my eyes—I was bone tired. Maybe I really was past my prime when it came to espionage? My heart thudded in my chest and I forced myself to take some deep breaths. I chided myself. I would not allow Bitsy Love to draw me into such drama again. And now I had to contend with how Babe Love would react to her sister's exposure of *Mr. Hans Fischer*.

The cab screeched to a halt in front of my small brick home. Bitsy Love and I scrambled up the sidewalk and entered the foyer of the home. The smell of fresh-baked bread filtered through the air along with a spicy aroma of tomato sauce. Leon stood in the kitchen stirring a large pot with one hand and holding an ice-cube filled drink in the other.

He turned toward the two of us and raised his eyebrows. We looked bedraggled. He was silent as he waited for an explanation.

Bitsy Love spoke first, haltingly. Leon could be intimidating.

"Leon, I am so sorry for getting Aunt Liz involved in a situation, but we discovered some very important information."

Leon's voice was low and husky. "Babe Love called. It seems someone telephoned her this afternoon wanting to know all about the public fight between her and Hans that occurred in the lobby of the bank."

Bitsy Love looked down appearing contrite but when she lifted her head there was a steely look in her eyes. She was not going to retreat from her discoveries. I was sure of it.

"Babe told the caller it was only a rumor, but I knew right away—you were impersonating your twin. Why?"

Bitsy failed to answer his question. "I'm going to change." She hurriedly climbed the stairs and shut the bedroom door leaving me to face Leon.

I decided the best response was be honest.

I sat down at the kitchen table folded my arms and looked up at him. "Leon, we discovered some incriminating information about *Hans Fischer*. It appears he is an impersonator—somehow wrapped up in spying for the East Germans."

"You went into East Berlin? That was foolish, Liz."

"I have no doubt. But I also know that Babe Love is in danger if she continues her association with Hans. We watched him enter

239

the East German State Security building and we also followed him to a high-rise building where he appeared to be involved in an intimate relationship with another woman."

"But Liz it will be your word against Hans. And if you are correct, he surely has an alibi all set up."

Bitsy Love appeared in the doorway of the kitchen. "Oh, but Leon I have proof beyond our word."

What was she hiding from me? I had been by her side during the entire expedition. I put my hand on my hip waiting for an explanation.

"Let's eat. I'm starving and Leon, you are such a fantastic cook."

Leon scowled. "Bitsy Love spill it now…I want to know what proof you hold."

"Fix me a drink and I will share my secrets."

Leon made us both double martinis with double olives. Bitsy Love drained hers and held out her glass for a refill.

She sat clenching an object in her hand.

"What do you have?" Leon pressed.

She slowly opened her fingers to reveal a small brass cigarette lighter. She held it up to the lamp. "This is an Echo 8 manufactured in West Germany 1951."

Leon and I both were puzzled. So? She turned the lighter around and around.

"It's a camera. In order to snap a picture, you must light the flame."

I was amazed. "That was the clicking sound I heard when we were outside the apartment building?"

"Yes, it is rather ingenious isn't it?" Bitsy Love declared.

"Unbelievable," Leon said.

I nodded in agreement.

Leon knitted his caterpillar brows together. "And how did you gain access to such a device, Bitsy Love?"

Bitsy Love ignored the question and continued to speak. "The film is in the bottom of the case. I will take it to my source to get it developed tomorrow then you will have documentation of my sister's so-called boyfriend's deceptive ways," Bitsy Love said as she drained her second drink.

"Until we make sure that the pictures are clear I think it prudent that we keep the secret among us," I said.

"Agreed, there is no need to upset my twin until we develop the pictures."

"One thing I can tell you…it will not be a pretty scene when Babe Love is told of your deception," Leon said.

Bitsy Love slurred her words. "I understand but I had no choice. I couldn't allow my sister to ruin her life with that cheat! Let's eat before I pass out from those double martins, Leon."

We ate until we were sated.

Bitsy Love and I crawled into bed leaving Leon with the dirty dishes—we had completed one more adventure for the *Wolfpack*. We could only hope that it ended well.

****

Bitsy Love sat in the living room and held a manila envelope which contained the developed pictures. The small camera in the form of a lighter had exquisitely captured the images of Hans at the East German Security Building and in the apartment building with the mysterious woman.

"Your twin in on her way over and I can tell you that she is furious with you," I announced.

"What did you say to her, Aunt Liz?"

"What could I say? She is aware that you approached Hans pretending to be her and that you deliberately created a scene."

"I did what I had to do for Babe. My conscience is clear," Bitsy Love said in a calm voice.

She reached into the manila envelope and secured the pictures—fanning them out on the coffee table. "Look, the evidence is undisputable. I could have gone directly to the West Germany authorities, but I wanted to share information with Babe first."

"How thoughtful of you," Leon said facetiously. "You know this will break her heart. I think she intended to marry him."

"Babe Love would have eventually discovered his phony ways so it is better now than down the road when her life would be over."

"I'm pretty sure she will believe her life is destroyed, Bitsy Love," I said in a sharp tone.

The front door sprung open and Babe Love stood in the doorway unannounced. Her face was stormy. Angry tears rolled in waves down her face.

I stared unable to take my eyes off Babe and her twin. They were dressed as if they had consulted with each other—in red woolen sweaters and black pants.

"You BITCH!" Babe Love screamed. She charged across the room and tackled Bitsy, pinning her to the ground. The twins' white-blonde hair swirled and their arms and legs intertwined with each other as they fought, scratched and landed punches.

Leon grabbed the twin on top (I was uncertain which one) and pulled her to the side.

"Stop! You are acting like children. There is no need for this. You are sisters. Act like adults. Let's see if we can sort this all out."

"Bitsy Love, Babe Love, pull yourself together," I admonished.

Slowly they rose to a stand and stood side by side. Neither of them looked at the other. They were stony-faced.

Leon chewed on the end of an unlit cigar and cocked his head toward my nieces. "Let's be reasonable. Bitsy Love what do you have to say?"

"Babe, *Mr. Hans Fischer* is an imposter—he lied to you and betrayed you."

"No, you betrayed *me*. How could you have gone behind my back? I don't believe you."

I took Babe Love's arm and guided her to the couch.

"Babe, while I don't condone some of your sister's tactics the evidence is clear. See for yourself," I said.

242

Reluctantly Babe scrutinized the pictures scattered before her. There was Bitsy in the lobby of the bank creating a scene. There was Hans entering the East German Security Building. There was Hans with another woman, kissing her and bestowing jewelry upon her.

Babe brushed tears out of her eyes and reached across the coffee table swatting the pictures. They skittered to the floor and landed askew.

Recognition showed on her face. She wearily hung her head.

I patted her back as she spoke in a resigned voice.

"*Hans Fischer* isn't his real name, is it?"

"Probably not, Babe," Bitsy replied.

"I still can't believe it. I trusted him. He was always a perfect gentleman, bringing me flowers and taking me to expensive restaurants."

"But weren't you suspicious when he was absent every weekend?" Bitsy Love probed.

I addressed Bitsy sharply. "Now is not the time to question your sister in such a manner. She needs time to process everything. After all Hans has been a huge part of her life for the past couple of years."

"I'm so sorry Babe Love. I might have overstepped my boundaries but know I did it to protect you. Who knows what his ultimate goal was in establishing a relationship with you, but it was clearly wrong," Bitsy Love said.

Leon stooped and gathered the pictures together then carefully placed them back into the envelope as he spoke. "Bitsy Love has provided evidence. The next step is to contact the authorities. We cannot keep this information to ourselves. There could be clues contained in these pictures that lead to other connections, perhaps a ring of spies."

"And we must do so immediately before Hans returns from his weekend visit and discovers his ruse has been uncovered," I added.

Bitsy Love reached over and hugged Babe Love who then slumped against her twin…spent with effort.

"We're in deep together. And I intend to see this whole fiasco out until the end," Bitsy Love declared.

I watched my nieces as the unspoken connection between them wove them back into a tight-knit bond.

I had an intense urge to pick up the telephone and ring Billy Love. For even she—the oldest sibling with all of her past adventures—would never have imagined her sisters entangled in a situation of this magnitude.

Leon put a hand on my shoulder. I instantly knew the gesture was a sign of caution—*you've done enough for now, Elisabetha, you've done enough.*

I sighed. Leon was right. I had other issues to worry about starting with the push at UNICEF to deliver supplies deep into Soviet Union territory. I needed to let the twins take responsibility for their own actions. They were adults after all.

Hans' betrayal of Babe Love would not be taken lightly by the family, however. There would be revenge—of that I was sure.

Chapter 22
Romeo

West Berlin
1953
Elisabetha

We were exhausted—it was four in the morning and none of us had gotten any sleep. After Bitsy Love revealed the photos of the imposter *Hans Fischer* Leon and I felt it was urgent to contact authorities. But who could be trusted with the information?

With the number of spies and double agents casting their nets in Berlin it was almost impossible to determine which people would safeguard our information and take appropriate action. I dug out a telephone number of an old friend of mine from the F.B.I. who was currently residing in West Berlin and placed a phone call, not knowing if anyone would pick up.

A deep voice came on the line. "Yes?"

"*Coach*?" I questioned, trying his code name.

"Yes, *Wolfpack*," he answered back with my alias.

I experienced immediate relief. My contact was still current.

"I will meet you at 0600," he said then hung up. He understood at once that I had important information for him that could only be delivered in person. It was well known that most everyone's phone in Berlin was being tapped.

Coach knew where Leon and I resided and would make his way to us at the appointed time.

"Ladies we will have a visitor in two hours. Let's get the house picked up—and clean yourselves up while you are at it. You look disheveled from your tussles, rolling around on the floor like common criminals," I said.

The twins looked admonished. But I couldn't stay mad at them for long. They meant the world to me. I gave a little laugh—"Go on now, shoo."

They climbed the stairs to the bedroom arm in arm…sisters again sticking together.

Leon crossed his arms and arched his eyebrows. "Liz, the fixer. That's my new nickname for you." He nuzzled my neck and I kissed him gently.

"Leon, make a pot of tea. We all need to wake up and be alert when *Coach* gets here."

"Liz, you can't fool me. I know exactly who your contact is and I approve. He will know where to take the information along with the pictures."

Promptly at 0600 there was a knock on the door. I ushered the man in and took his coat and hat, then settled him on the couch. Neither of us had yet uttered a work. I brought in a tray containing hot tea and crumpets set it beside him then handed over the envelope of pictures.

He sipped the tea and leafed through the pictures. He had on his poker face, the mark of a professional. When he had finished examining the pictures he sat back.

"I would like to talk with Babe Love alone," he said quietly.

I nodded and went upstairs to fetch her.

Babe emerged from the bedroom. She had washed up, reapplied makeup and brushed out her tangled curls. She was presentable again…indeed, impeccable. You never would have believed she and her twin were engaged in a cat fight just a few hours prior. I pointed downstairs. "He wants to talk with you alone. Don't worry, I am certain he has your best interests at heart. Leon and I will be in the kitchen if you need anything."

"I'm a bit nervous Auntie."

"Don't be Babe, just tell him what you know. He will decide where to direct the information. You are but the conduit. You did nothing wrong."

Leon and I settled in the kitchen and waited. After an hour, Babe finally pushed open the door. She appeared relieved yet stressed. She motioned for us to return to the living room."

"Bitsy Love, come on down," I called up the stairs.

We all rearranged ourselves in the living room and looked expectantly at *Coach*.

"First, thank you for your bravery and for calling me about your situation," he said as he looked at each of us.

Coach was a non-descript average man. He could fit in anywhere and yet not be noticed—average build, average mousy brown hair, average light brown eyes. Not too handsome and not too homely.

"Bitsy Love, you took a big risk and while it was not advisable for you to spy on him, these pictures are invaluable. Let me start by telling you that *Hans Fischer* has been under suspicion for a period of time. We were close to arresting him but did not have definitive proof. Now we do." *Coach* patted the manila folder.

"Who is *we*?" I asked.

"Not important. We believe he is a *Romeo*."

"What do you mean, a *Romeo*?" Babe Love asked. She was fidgeting and perspiring. I handed her a kerchief and she pressed it to her neck.

"Hans is an East German officer whose job is to seduce women and get them to hand over secret documents that might help the communists. He was assigned to develop a long-term relationship with you—to fulfill his patriotic duty, Babe Love."

Babe Love gasped and put her head in her hands. "Is that why you asked me if Hans ever probed for information about the operations of UNICEF?"

"Yes, before he ever met you he had been handed a dossier about you. He was aware that you were American, single and worked for UNICEF…an organization that was planning a mission to drop medical and food supplies to Russian children."

"So, I was targeted? I must assure you that I never ever gave Hans any information about my work at UNICEF," Babe Love commented.

"That much is clear. Hans became frustrated with you, Babe. He courted you ardently with gifts flowers and attention yet you wouldn't reveal any secrets. His mission failed."

"I take my work very seriously. I would never reveal top secret information," Babe Love retorted.

"Of course, you do, Babe but many women have fallen for the so-called *Honey Trap*. These spies target lonely women and lavish them with attention. To get them to reveal government secrets that the Soviets can use. They are told to follow the three Ls: *Love, Lure, Lies*."

"This is unbelievable," Bitsy Love interjected. "Clearly the women who succumb to these so-called Romeos are weak."

"These women pay dearly for revealing government secrets to the Russians. They could be arrested for aiding and abetting the enemy. It is sad. Many lose everything--their livelihoods, money and family," Coach explained.

Babe Love said dryly. "Now that I think back to our two years together I can clearly see that my so-called boyfriend was not who he pretended to be. But I certainly did not picture another woman intruding in our relationship."

"I am quite certain these pictures are of his wife who also has no idea what Hans does or where he goes during the week. He has likely made up some elaborate tale with all its twists and turns. He is a master liar," *Coach* said as he pushed up his glasses and placed the packet of pictures inside his suitcoat. He stood up and reached for his coat and hat.

"Thank you for coming straightaway," I said.

"I will be in touch. Babe Love, in the meantime I think it would be prudent for you to stay with your Aunt and Leon for a few days until we take care of this matter, yes?"

Babe Love finally relaxed and smiled for the first time all night. "Yes."

Chapter 23
Ruthie

New York City
1953
Billy Love

I studied the colorful flowered dress Ursula had laid out on her bed in preparation for our night out on the town. As promised it was Ursula's turn to experience the glamour that comes from dining at Sardis and then taking in a Broadway show. I had been so sure this day would never arrive—Ursula's behavior was unpredictable and violent for many years...the screaming, the fighting, the cuttings, the rage. Her darkness had brought our family to the brink of separation and despair.

The Wolfpack itself had been part of the lead up to Ursula's recovery but we all understood that one person was primarily responsible for Ursula's turnaround—Nurse May Phillips. Her love acceptance compassion and intellect had encompassed my precious child and helped her cope with her demons in healthy ways.

My mind returned to the planned evening. I snapped open the small box and examined the silver charms that lay within. There were two tiny exquisite dancers with raised swirling skirts...Ursula would receive one and Renata the other. The charms were a tradition which started when I took Renata to the musical *Oklahoma.* At the time both girls were given a silver horse charm which they proudly displayed on a thin chain they wore around their necks. Neither one of them ever took the necklace off even in the bath. The jewelry represented the bond they had for each other. And now they would have an additional keepsake to add to their collection.

"Girls, come here I have something for you."

Ursula skidded into her bedroom exuding a bundle of energy. Renata walked in deliberately trying to act as if she was too sophisticated for all the hoopla. She was a teenager after all—above the fray.

I fished the dancer out of the box.

"Close your eyes Ursula. No peeking," I instructed.

Ursula squeezed both eyes shut and held out her palm.

I gently placed the charm in her outstretched hand.

"Open now," I instructed.

Ursula's eyes fluttered open. She clapped her hands and squealed in a high-pitched voice.

"Look, Rennie, it's a dancer. OOOH I can't wait to see *Can-Can!* Mommy help me put it on my chain. Won't it look peachy beside my horse?" Ursula asked.

Renata smiled. I could see she was remembering her own special night out. Now it was Ursula's turn.

Ursula stepped into her youthful dress and I buttoned up the back then clasped the necklace around her neck. She fingered the charms and looked into the mirror clearly pleased with the image that stared back at her.

Ursula was not a classic beauty like her sister but when all of her features were combined she was a striking young girl. I noted her large jet-black eyes and hair, her sharp nose and her pouty lips. My heart thudded with love.

Renata moved to her sister's side and put her arms around her. Renata—Ursula's protectorate. Even now she clung to her keeper role even if she had relinquished most responsibility to Parker and me. She was a special child. Always giving.

"Ursula, your godmother will be here soon. Finish getting ready. We have reservations at Sardis. Let's not be late."

Audrey Hepburn who had experienced her own trials during the German occupation of Amsterdam understood Ursula. She had experienced starvation and danger and knew how it felt to be scared all of the time. She could coddle and protect Ursula with unconditional love—leaving the discipline up to Parker and me, and Nurse Phillips of course.

I hurriedly twisted my dark curly hair into a side ponytail and clipped it in place with an ivory pin. I noted some scattered streaks of gray had begun to appear, but I didn't mind—it made me look more sophisticated. I touched up my makeup and reapplied red lipstick then shimmied into a form-fitting gray woolen dress. Turning to the side I examined my profile in the full-length mirror.

I could compete with Audrey but of course I would never have her waif-like figure which was okay. Parker thought Audrey was a bag of bones, but the camera loved her which was the ultimate status symbol of Hollywood royalty.

****

Cameras clicked and popped as Audrey stepped out of the cab. She was starting to emerge as a major new star. With her pixie hair-cut long lean legs and luminous eyes she cut a striking picture in her black and white dress with matching peep-toe heels. As her fan base grew people recognized her and clamored to be around her.

Ursula are I were content to follow behind her into the restaurant where we were greeted by the white-haired headwaiter.

"Mrs. O'Rourke and Miss Hepburn…welcome. And this must be Miss Ursula," he said as he stooped down to solemnly shake Ursula's hand.

The waiter held up his gloved hand and cautioned the crowd to move away from Audrey. "Before we seat you Miss Hepburn, we would like to have you sign the caricature of you created by our artists here at Sardis."

"My pleasure. Show me the way. Come on Ursula. I need you to help me."

Audrey swished across the room in her short dress and stood beside her portrait. She signed it with a flourish and stepped back to study it.

"My neck seems a bit long doesn't it?" she asked as she laughed. The dining crowd surrounding us tittered with delight. I smiled as I watched Ursula and Audrey interact together.

"Audrey, there is Marlene's portrait. Look over there," Ursula said as she pointed across the room.

I looked in the direction Ursula pointed.

Suddenly I felt faint and I tasted bile as it rose in my throat. A curtain fell over my eyes and I struggled to focus.

There seated at a table in the middle of the dining room was Ruthie—our dear sweet Ruthie. I wanted to look away but I was

251

drawn to her. She stared back at me—recognition appearing on her face followed by an expression of utter despair.

The adults at her table carried on a loud conversation as Ruthie and I continued to wordlessly connect. They ignored Ruthie's presence.

In an instant Ruthie sprang from her chair and charged across the room.

"Billy Love! Billy Love!" she screamed over and over again.

As soon as she reached me she threw her arms around my waist. I held her sobbing against me as she shuddered and quaked. The room grew silent as heads turned toward us. I ignored the snooty people…my only concern was Ruthie. I sheltered her and pulled her into an alcove as I spoke softly to her.

"Darling Ruthie it's okay."

"No, it's not. No, it's not. I hate them. Why didn't Eva want me?"

"She did precious girl. She did," I murmured.

I looked up. A tall thin woman had arisen from her seat. She walked toward Ruthie and me. It was clear from her ominous expression that she was furious.

"Ruthie!" she hissed. "I will not allow you to make a scene."

Ruthie burrowed against me and refused to make eye contact with the woman.

The woman dripped with sarcasm. "Is this the reward we get for plucking you out of the orphanage and giving you a good home? You are a little wretch—truly ungrateful."

I was astounded. What was I hearing? Clearly this obviously wealthy woman thought she could save the world by taking in an older child—a child who had been through unspeakable circumstances, abandoned in a field in Germany after the war—at two years of age sent to the Dachau camp with thousands of other dislocated people and then finally housed in an orphanage in the Bronx. Parentless.

I pictured Eva at the orphanage holding and rocking little Ruthie. And I was overwhelmed with emotion. I slumped to the floor pulled Ruthie onto my lap and gripped her tightly. I flashed back to the listless little girl with the hollow eyes. Her emaciated body wracked with disease and malnutrition.

The woman sneered. "Ruthie you will quit making a scene immediately and come with me. We are going home—as punishment you will not be going to the musical tonight. And I am calling the orphanage tomorrow first thing. It seems you are not a good fit with our family." She pulled at Ruthie and attempted to dislodge her from my lap.

"Noooooooo!" Ruthie screeched.

The headwaiter appeared by our side and attempted to mitigate the situation.

"Can I help you ladies?" he asked as he stretched out his gloved hand to me.

I ignored the waiter and arose standing nose to nose with the haughty woman before me. "This woman is leaving us right this moment. She is being abusive to this child."

"You have no right to speak to me in this manner! Who do you think you are?" the woman demanded.

"I am Billy Love Wolf Remington and if I have to call the police I will. This child is with me now. I will call Warren Grant at the orphanage and inform him of my actions. I am sure he will approve my actions when he finds out how you have treated Ruthie."

A portly man with thick jowls appeared and stood by the woman's side. He sniggered. "Darling we will take care of this unfortunate situation tomorrow. Come sit down. The *other children* are waiting and they are excited to be going to the Broadway show."

The woman huffed, turned on her heel and headed back to her life of privilege as if it was natural to discard a child who didn't fit her mold.

I lifted Ruthie's head and looked into her grief-stricken face. I spoke to her calmly. "Let's get you out of here Ruthie."

Ruthie and I stood up. We held hands and crossed the room to where Audrey and Ursula were seated. Ursula was rubbing her arms and tracing the scars…a habit she returned to when she became stressed.

"Ursula, Ruthie is okay. Tonight is your time and I expect you and Audrey to have fun at *Can-Can*. Can you do that for me?" I asked.

Audrey intervened. She reached across the table and clutched Ursula's hand. "Ursula and I will be fine, won't we?"

Ursula sat up straight and pulled the sleeves down to her wrists obscuring the silvery scars. I noted her resolve. Not long ago she would have melted down after observing Ruthie's trauma. But now she could cope. She and Audrey would carry on.

I gave them both a nod and guided Ruthie out of the restaurant. I grabbed a cab and she snuggled against me as the driver wove through the crowded streets of New York city. I knew Parker and Renata were out on the town with their own adventures tonight. My one-on-one time with Ruthie would allow me to gather my thoughts and make plans. First up was a phone call to Eva Braun. Ruthie needed her.

****

Parker and Renata entered the apartment. They were laughing together and recalling a street magician and his shenanigans. I put my finger to my lips instructing them to be quiet. I had just gotten Ruthie to sleep after a tear-filled evening.

There was reason to be optimistic however. I had telephoned Eva at her farm house in upstate New York. She immediately got on the line to Ruthie and assured her that she loved her and was working to cut strings that would enable her to adopt her.

I was attuned to Eva's plight. She was a woman living alone who had been one of the most notorious women in the world at one time—Adolf Hitler's mistress. Even seven years after the war ended and with nine previous years living in the United States away from the dictator, Eva still experienced discrimination. She had been threatened spit upon cursed and accused of despicable acts of treason.

I had heard all of the chatter. Eva Braun couldn't possibly raise a child. She was single, she was older, she was a consort of an evil dictator. There were many strikes against her, but those obstacles were not impossible to overcome. I would call the orphanage and ask to speak to Warren Grant who still served as a board member. There would be no excuses now—Eva and Ruthie needed to be together. There were three failed placements with families who had the audacity to return Ruthie to the orphanage. Like she was an item of clothing that didn't fit. I understood time was running out. She needed a stable and loving home. And Eva along with the support of family could provide it. The Wolfpack would stand strong by her side.

****

It was very early. The sky was lit with pastels as the sun made its way over the horizon. I buttered my toast and sipped hot tea as Parker and I recollected the event-filled crazy evening.

"I couldn't sleep, Parker. I just kept reliving my encounter with that horrible woman. Why was she allowed to take Ruthie into her home in the first place? It was obvious that she had no concern for her."

Parker slathered jam on his toast and sat back. I could tell he was gathering his thoughts.

"Billy Love, I must admit that for the longest time I thought you were exaggerating Ruthie's plight. I hope you will forgive me for even entertaining such a thought. I should have trusted your intuition. It is almost never wrong."

I paused letting his words sink in. He could admit to me when he was wrong about a situation. Very few men had that quality and I was lucky to call him my husband.

"Parker, intuition is a gift. I have it, Kat has it and so does Aunt Liz. It comes from within, but it also comes from experience. After the war ended and we discovered the horrendous circumstances that our children suffered I understood something profound— World War II may have officially ended but the healing had just begun and there would be many set-backs. Too many people in this country turned a blind eye and acted as if they could carry on their lives as if nothing of consequence had happened. They could adopt traumatized children and pretend they would be hunky dory if they provided them with fancy homes, clothes and elite schools."

"Darling, I understand you and your family are rarities. Precious jewels. Only a few people have your compassion and ability to transcend politics. You make a profound difference in people's lives."

I stood and kissed Parker on the cheek then went to the window.

"Eva's arrived. She's come to collect her child."

Chapter 24
Revenge

New York City and West Germany
1953
Katerina

The telephone jangled and I reached for it. "Kat, I'm afraid there was an incident today involving Wolfgang at the hospital." It was Nurse Phillips on the line. I barely recognized her voice—her vocals were high-pitched and her words were rapid and staccato-like. In all of our past interactions she had been measured and collected. I instantly understood something was off-kilter.

Wolfgang was late. He had failed to return home from his appointment at Bellevue. Jack and I had recently given him more independence…allowing him to take the bus to school and other activities. But he had continued to be furtive as to what he did with his free time. He seemingly had no friends. No one ever telephoned him. And his obsession with the novel *Frankenstein* continued. It was in his possession at all times.

Schnitzel lay on the floor beside me, whining. I sensed the dog knew that Wolfgang was in trouble. Where was he? I motioned for Jack to sit beside me as I listened to May Phillips. I sharply inhaled and struggled to manage my emotions.

"Kat, I have been concerned about Wolfgang for some time. Although he made headway in the first few weeks of treatment he has now slipped backward. He is sullen and refuses to share his thoughts and feelings with me. And then today his behavior escalated."

"For God's sake what did he do?" I blurted.

"You and Jack understand that he has been obsessed with laboratories and experimentation."

"Yes," I said. My impatience was growing exponentially. Nurse Phillips needed to get to the point. Jack placed a hand on my knee urging me to stay calm. I locked eyes with him.

"He broke into the lab and took some Petri dishes."

"And?" I asked.

"Those dishes are part of a massive experiment. They contain viruses that are extremely dangerous to people if they come in contact with them."

I was agitated. "Why would Wolfgang want to steal something so perilous? What would be his motive?" I tapped my foot as I waited for her response.

After a short pause as if she was pondering how to approach the situation, Nurse Phillips continued. "At this point I am uncertain. Let me read from his record. It is something he wrote the last time we met together." She began.

> *How many things are we upon the brink of becoming acquainted, if cowardice or carelessness did not restrain our inquiries? I resolved these circumstances in my mind and determined thenceforth to apply myself. I must observe the natural decay and corruption of the human body.*

I recoiled. It was one of the passages from the novel *Frankenstein*. The novel that Wolfgang continued to obsess over day and night. Now he had taken passages from the novel and internalized them. Where would this all lead?

It was too much. For months Wolfgang had made daily treks to the nearby cemetery. I believed his dark musings were but a phase—typical angst teenage behavior. But now he had stolen hazardous items from the laboratory. There was clearly a sinister component to his actions.

Tears streamed down my cheeks. What had happened to my precious boy? When did he come to harbor such destructive thoughts? And would he act further on his thoughts?

I cleared my throat and attempted to respond. My voice cracked.

"Nurse Phillips, Wolfgang has not returned home. I expected him several hours ago."

"Katerina, please contact me immediately when he arrives. Try to be calm. Don't alarm him in any way. Don't directly touch him or any of his belongings. He could already be contaminated. Isolate him in his room and lock him in if you must. Then wait for the research team to arrive and take over."

I handed the phone to Jack. I no longer was able to speak coherently.

Jack took over. "Nurse Phillips thank you for calling. We will be in touch immediately—as soon as Wolfgang returns home.

Jack slammed down the receiver and stared at me. His eyes were wild.

"What the hell is contained in that petri dish?" he demanded.

I whispered. "I don't know. Nurse Phillips refused to say."

We were living a nightmare.

Wolfgang failed to return home. He was gone.

****

I was sick with fear. And my reaction led to a horrific row between Jack and me. It was the most traumatic fight of our relationship which was fueled by Wolfgang's behavior and subsequent disappearance.

I had discovered a large amount of cash missing from my purse which was an indication that Wolfgang had planned to steal the petri dishes from the laboratory and disappear with their contents. How could I have been so blind to Wolfgang's ambitions?

Jack stood silently and stone-faced in the doorway of our bedroom. I studied his profile—his temple hair had grayed and his hairline had receded...but he was a handsome man with his strong jaw and chiseled face.

Finally, he spoke in a quiet voice. "Kat, I'm sorry. I should have been more understanding about your feelings."

"Me too Jack. Fighting does nothing to resolve the situation with Wolfgang does it?" I asked.

Jack crossed the room and reached me. I put my head on his shoulder and he stroked my hair.

"Billy Love is on her way over. She has some thoughts about where Wolfgang might have gone?"

"You called her Jack?"

"Yes. After our fight I decided that we needed a third person to help sort out our situation. Billy Love knows you better than anyone else and you can talk things through with her. Have a heart-to-heart conversation."

I kissed Jack on the cheek.

"I'll hop in the shower and you prepare us all some stiff drinks. Heaven knows Billy Love and I have a lot to discuss."

I grabbed a towel and headed to the bathroom then turned and looked over my shoulder at Jack.

He raised his eyebrows. "What else are you going to talk about with Billy Love?"

"Ruthie and Eva. There's a situation."

"Katerina Remington! What now?"

"You'll find out soon enough," I said coyly as I closed the door and turned on the shower. I smiled for the first time in several days.

Billy Love was seated curled up on the couch drink in hand when I emerged from the bathroom. I was flushed from the shower. My hair was still wet and my face was scrubbed clean devoid of makeup. I felt fresh...ready to tackle problems. Some of the animosity that I harbored toward Wolfgang had evaporated. He was still a child after all. Impulsive and thoughtless in his actions.

I grabbed my own libation and sat close to Billy Love as we clinked glasses.

"Billy Love, how do we get ourselves into these predicaments? Can't we be boring old women for once? I would love to be settled."

"Phooey, Kat you would be bored out of your mind."

Parker winked at us both and retreated into the kitchen to give us some privacy.

"Jack really is a hell of a good husband isn't he Kat? Your papa knew what he was doing when he insisted you go on that first date with him to Frankenstein's Castle."

I cringed at the word *Frankenstein*. Billy Love noted the expression on my face and realized that she had triggered a response. She popped her hand over her mouth as if to take the phrase back but then she plunged forward with the conversation.

"Kat, I have an idea where Wolfgang may have gone."

"Really? Out with it, Billy Love."

"Remember our conversation about Wolfgang's preoccupation with Prince Philipp Von Hessen. That first day at Bellevue when Nurse Phillips revealed the existence of his birth father to him?"

"Of course." I frowned as I pondered where Billy Love was headed with her train of thought.

"Well?" Billy Love asked.

I sat up straight and stared. "He's on his way to West Germany, isn't he Billy Love?"

"I am almost certain of it."

"But why would he steal petri dishes from Bellevue?" I asked. Billy Love took both her hands in mine and I instantly knew. *Revenge.*

****

"Jack, I got the plane tickets. We depart for West Germany tomorrow."

"Kat I am concerned. You don't know if you will find Wolfgang and if you do what his state of mind will be."

"I feel confident that Wolfgang is headed to Kronberg where the prince is now living. And since Nurse Phillips has insisted on accompanying Billy Love and me…she is the expert on the motives for Wolfgang's behavior. She can help talk him down if need be," I explained.

"There is still reason for caution. If Wolfgang is truly out for revenge, he could endanger everyone around him not just Philipp von Hessen."

"Wolfgang is a young teenager trying to find his way in the world. There is no other course of action I would be willing to take. I have no choice but to find him. He is our son Jack!"

"Whoa Kat I agree with you. I just don't want you to put yourself in harm's way if you don't have to do so," Jack said.

I became frustrated. "Your paternalistic military instincts are showing Jack. Do you believe three women joining forces are incapable of helping Wolfgang?"

Jack bit his lip and clammed up. As much as I loved him Jack had an overly protective side that irked me at times. I vowed to myself—there would be limited contact with my husband until I had Wolfgang safely in my custody. Jack needn't know when and where I would be located. If I told him, he would likely contact an old buddy from his time in the United States Army and ask him to accompany us to the prince's estate. Which would only create more chaos.

There were more secrets…each of us held—Billy Love, Nurse Phillips and I would reveal them as we tried to head off Wolfgang.

****

The plane touched down in Frankfurt. The three of us gathered our bags and descended down the staircase onto the tarmac. I shielded my eyes and squinted trying to find Papa, who was waiting to accompany us to his house in Darmstadt.

"There is Papa," I shouted. "Come on."

"Uncle Moody, thanks for picking us up," Billy Love said as she reached Papa's side kissed him soundly on both cheeks and mussed his wispy hair.

"My little Billy Love and darling Kat it is so good to see you both. Now who is this?" Papa asked as May Phillips, looking as prim and proper as ever, came up to greet him.

"Papa, this is Nurse Phillips Wolfgang's therapist. She has been working with him for the past year to help him cope with the impact of being held in the concentration camp."

Nurse Phillips stood eye-level with Papa and confidently shook his hand. "Very nice to meet you Mr. Wolf... I have great admiration for your daughter and your niece."

Papa brushed off the compliment and led us to his car. He tossed our bags into the trunk and put the car in gear. Then he turned around in his seat and addressed us.

"Wolfgang has been in Darmstadt."

Billy Love and I gasped. Nurse Phillips was stoic showing no reaction.

"Papa, what do you mean? How do you know?" My voice was thick with trepidation.

"I was in my yard and I looked out upon the forest bordering my property. I spotted him trying to hide in the dense underbrush. He looked haunted his eyes darted from side to side and he was disheveled. It was clear to me that he was spying on me."

"What did you do?" Billy Love asked.

"I called his name and walked calmly toward him to let him know that I wanted to talk with him. But the minute I got close he turned and ran into the dense foliage. That was two days ago—I haven't seen him since," Mood said.

"He is scared and uncertain. Mixed up," May said.

"Papa, I think he wanted to connect with you, but he got scared. He probably thought you would thwart his efforts to reach his birth father. So instead he changed his plans and headed straight to Kronberg where Prince von Hessen resides."

"Mr. Wolf, I informed Wolfgang a few months ago that Philipp was his birth father. Wolfgang is aware that Philipp sent his mother to Dachau solely because she was Jewish—to appease Adolf Hitler and his cronies. His mother subsequently perished in the gas chamber. Wolfgang was seven. He was old enough to remember the horrors of the camps," Nurse Phillips relayed in a matter-of-fact manner.

"So, Wolfgang wants revenge is that right? What do you think he is planning to do?" Papa asked.

"We are not sure, but he has in his possession some lethal petri dishes full of viruses," Nurse Phillips said. "He probably will attempt to contaminate the prince in some way."

"What kind of virus, May?" Papa asked. I knew with his background as a chemist he would try and probe for answers.

"I cannot tell you that. It is part of top-secret research. I will inform you that many of us have been working for years to find vaccines that will eradicate communicable diseases. We are very close to breakthroughs but bad publicity resulting from misuse of our research could lead to a catastrophe which could doom all of our successes. We can't let that happen."

"That's why we have to get to Wolfgang before he confronts Philipp," I explained.

"Agreed. We need to prevent an incident from happening and get Wolfgang to safety," Billy Love said.

"Mr. Wolf, I believe time is short. Kronberg is only ten minutes from the airport. I believe we need to go there directly. I have a feeling that Wolfgang is already there. Can you drive us?" Nurse Phillips asked with authority as she leaned forward in her seat and put her hand on Papa's shoulder.

Papa looked uncertain and looked intently at Kat and me searching for answers. Then without saying a word he made a sharp U-turn and headed toward the old castle where Phillip resided. What would we find?

****

Papa turned the car onto a gravel road and slowly approached the ruins of the Kronberg Castle and the tower where Prince Philipp von Hessen had retreated to live after the second war. In the distance we could see the family graveyard situated to the side of the castle.

"Stop the car Papa. We will walk from here—we don't want anyone to know we are coming," I whispered.

Papa cut the engine and looked at us expectantly.

"Uncle Mood, you stay here, we may need to make a fast get-away," Billy Love commanded.

Papa grunted and folded his arms as if reluctant to go along with our plans.

I looked at Billy Love. Her purse was open and she was fingering something. Dark metal. A pistol. What the heck? I knew Billy Love was a competent marksman but still, who knew she would bring a gun?

Nurse Phillips heaved a tote bag out of the trunk. What could be in the satchel? I became nervous—what did I really know about Nurse Phillips? She was being evasive in both her words and actions. Things could go very wrong. I concentrated on making my way toward the cemetery and pushed aside any worried thoughts.

Ahead I could make out the tall thin figure of a man working in the graveyard. He was righting tombstones and pulling tangled vines from their surfaces oblivious to his surroundings as he concentrated on the tasks at hand. To his left, hidden in the shadows of a giant elm tree was a smaller figure. It was Wolfgang. He was crouched motionless. He stared intently at the prince.

The three of us inched forward taking a circuitous route in order to stay out of sight.

"Let's split up. Come from behind Wolfgang," Nurse Phillips said.

Before we could reach him and without warning Wolfgang suddenly sprang forward toward the prince. He shouted and waved his arms. He clutched something in his hand.

"*Philipp von Hessen, Prince von Hessen*!" he sneered

Startled by the sound Philipp dropped his shovel and took a step back.

The prince's voiced trembled. "Who are you and what do you want?"

Wolfgang shook his head violently…his eyes were wild with rage.

"You killed my mother you bastard! You Nazi lover!"

"Stay back filthy child," Philipp demanded. He picked up the shovel and raised it in a menacing manner toward Wolfgang.

Billy Love entered the cemetery and stood directly in front of the prince. She held her pistol over her head. There was a loud cracking sound as she pulled the trigger.

Heads swiveled toward her. The prince flinched and turned ashen.

"Drop the shovel," Billy Love said. She pointed the pistol in the prince's direction and edged toward Philipp and Wolfgang. Standing between them she swiveled the gun back and forth. The prince looked grim –Wolfgang appeared defiant.

May addressed the prince in a guttural voice. "Ich warne dich! Zurüuckbleiben!"

I was shocked by Nurse Phillip's speech...spoken in fluent German. How had I missed the fact that German was clearly her native language? I immediately tucked away the information for later analysis then returned to the unfolding situation.

Philipp cringed and responded to both Billy Love's and Nurse Phillips' commands. He threw the shovel behind him held his hands in the air and shuffled backwards away from the gun barrel pointed in his direction.

Nurse Phillips ran toward Wolfgang even as she grabbed thick elbow-length rubber gloves from the tote bag and pulled them on. She quickly nabbed Wolfgang around his waist and tossed him to the ground. He kicked struggled and fought against her, but she managed to wrench the open petri dish from his grasp.

I came forward and watched the scene play out as Nurse Phillips dropped to a sitting position on an ancient tombstone and intently studied the petri dish.

"Wolfgang! It's okay now. Stay where you are and don't try anything else. We are all here to help you. We will handle the prince," I said.

Nurse Phillips stood and held up the glass petri dish. She smiled grimly then spoke with confidence. "It's okay. The virus is dead. No one can become infected."

Billy Love looked at me with confusion written on her face. I pulled a similar expression.

"Are you sure?" we asked in unison.

"Absolutely. There is a large *F* taped to the lid," Nurse Phillips replied.

"What do you mean?" Billy Love asked.

"Now is not the time to discuss any of this. Wolfgang come here." She crooked her finger to signal him. Wolfgang hung his head and shuffled to Nurse Phillips.

He broke into loud sobs. "But he k-killed my mother…he m-murdered my mother."

"What the hell are you talking about? You're just a young punk," Philipp said in a haughty voice.

I narrowed my eyes and spat my words addressing him. "You're wrong. Wolfgang is your biological son. And you are responsible for sending Anna to Dachau where she gave birth to him, lived a desolate existence and was eventually *selected* to be sent to the gas chamber."

Recognition flooded Philipp's eyes. He put his hands over his face and frantically rubbed his eyes as if to cast off the conjured up horrible images flashing over and over before him.

"While you and your royal cronies were having dinner parties and carrying on with the dictator and his motley group—Goebbels and Himmler among them—Anna and Wolfgang were struggling to survive conditions that no human being should have to endure," I said.

Wolfgang continued to lean against Nurse Phillips. His chest heaved as he muffled his sobs against her.

"I never discussed the Third Reich with anyone. How did you know?" the prince whispered.

"Samuel—who was a survivor of Dachau Concentration Camp—shared Anna's fate with us. You are despicable. Did you never wonder what had happened to Anna? She was your lover, your mate!" Billy Love shouted as she twisted the gun toward Phillip's head.

"Billy Love you can put the gun away. There is no further use for it," Nurse Phillips calmly said. She had slipped back into the consummate professional role: always in command of her emotions.

"That's right Billy Love. I have *Prince von Hessen* under my watch now." Papa had heard the commotion grabbed a shot-gun from the car's trunk and quickly moved across the graveyard to stand before us. His hand was on the trigger as he moved the barrel of the gun in position.

"Papa there is no need for you to be involved. Your F.B.I. days are over."

"Maybe so but the prince here is a scum bag and a scoundrel. He has been spreading his drivel in all of the German newspapers and pandering to the extreme right reactionaries...downplaying the atrocities committed by Hitler and his henchmen. Even romanticizing the past."

"It's over now," Kat said. "Wolfgang confronted Philipp and had his say and now it is time to move on."

The prince curled his upper lip. "Not so fast. I plan to report this sniveling boy to the German authorities."

"You will not," Nurse Phillips said quietly. "I will report you to the allies war tribunal for the crime of sending Anna to Dachau...for consorting with the Nazi regime to inflict genocide on the Jews. It you even think about turning on this young boy your life is over."

I turned toward Nurse Phillips. There was steel in her voice. I had never heard her speak in such a manner before. She was an enigma. On one hand a compassionate caring health professional whose mission was to minister to the mental health needs of children. The other side revealed a tough-minded woman who could and would stand up to anyone who threatened her work.

"Come to me boy," Papa said in a soothing voice. Wolfgang shot across the grass tripping over tombstones until he reached Papa's enveloping arms.

"Papa! Papa! Can we go back to Darmstadt now? Please?"

Wolfgang had reverted to young child-like mannerisms. He was but fifteen. His childhood memories would haunt him for years to come.

"Of course, Wolfgang," Papa said.

"And Papa, I want to go back to Frankenstein's castle. It's where mom and dad found me isn't it? They saved me, didn't they?"

"Yes indeed, Wolfgang."

Wolfgang looked at me with tears pooling in his eyes. "I'm sorry...so sorry, *Kat*. Can I go back to calling you Mom?" he asked.

"Yes," I replied as I ruffled my hand through his tangled curls. I tried to hold back my own tears.

"Mom, I had to try—to get even, to settle the score." Wolfgang looked up at the cloudy sky as if envisioning Anna caring for him as best she could under unthinkable circumstances."

I couldn't speak. My throat was closed.

Nurse Phillips filled the void. "Wolfgang, you loved Anna and she loved you so very much. Keep your good memories stored in your heart. Healing is a process. Sometimes it zigs and sometimes it zags but there are people around you who will always help you on your journey.

All of us turned together and watched the prince slink out the graveyard defeated. He was a broken man...a disposable man who would never again be part of our lives. He had squandered an opportunity for redemption.

Wolfgang and Papa trudged toward the car arm in arm. Papa had the shot gun slung over his shoulder. We listened as he whistled a beautiful haunting tune.

I thought to myself. Where would I be in this chaotic world without my family? My cousins, my aunts and uncles? My grandparents? I understood one thing. Very few people in life could fly solo and still survive unscathed.

Billy Love and I came together and hugged each other tightly. Wolfgang had closure...an epiphany regarding the tangled complications of relationships.

Our children—our precious children. Where would they lead us next?

When you begin a journey of revenge start by digging two graves, one for your enemy and one for yourself.

~ Jodi Picoult

Chapter 25
March 9, 1953

West Berlin and Perm Russia
1953
Elisabetha (AKA Velvet)

It was widely known that Josef Stalin was languishing in his villa outside of Moscow. He had suffered a series of strokes and although the Soviet Union propaganda machine was tight-lipped regarding his prognosis there were leaks that suggested his death was imminent.

The iron control that Stalin had exerted over his people was legendary. He had used terror and fear to hold power. After World War II ended the Cold War between the east and west commenced in earnest. People trapped in the eastern zones were living in misery and despair. For they were denied American aid in the form of the legislated Marshall Plan. There was no rebuilding of bombed-out structures, malnutrition was rampant and disease was left untreated. Further, Stalin manipulated the Soviet occupied eastern European nations and forced Communism on Poland, Hungary, Czechoslovakia and East Germany.

Massive numbers of people were sent to gulags for minor infractions of Soviet law and many died in the hard labor camps. Children were taken from their parents and sent to collective farms and put to work at a young age…to help the collective cause.

Leon and I had spent many long nights at UNICEF headquarters in West Berlin debating whether Adolf Hitler and the Nazi regime or Stalin and the Bolsheviks wrecked the most havoc on the world. This much we did understand. Both regimes deliberately portrayed Jews as threats to German and Soviet nationalism. Thus, they were targeted for annihilation…in the case of the Stalin and his leadership, the Jews—particularly those who were religious activists or Zionists were condemned for exposing capitalism which was the anti-thesis of communism tenents.

I looked around the warehouse containing box after box of supplies that had been stockpiled for the past two years. We were waiting to make a move and it appeared that time was imminent.

I recalled my conversation with Billy Love.

"We need you in Berlin. Can you come immediately?" I asked.

"Aunt Liz, I will make arrangements to be there as soon as possible. Look for a shipment of supplies out of New York City. It will be labeled *fragile*," Billy Love replied. She sounded evasive on the phone and I was immediately suspicious of her intent.

"Billy Love I need to know the contents of the shipment. So does Leon. We don't want to endanger any of the participants of our mission. It could doom all of the good we have accomplished since the end of the war."

"I'm not trying to put up roadblocks, but I cannot reveal any more than I already have. It is much too dangerous. You will need to trust me on my end."

"I do trust you Billy Love. Somehow I am not surprised by your demands."

"I know what I am doing. Even Kat is unaware of what is contained in the shipment."

"Kat is on her way as we speak and Audrey is with her. We are in process of securing the necessary transportation."

"Liz, enough said on the telephone. Wire taps are happening all over the world. Parker is particularly vulnerable because of his extensive travels to Germany and I of course have permanent links to Germany because of my relationship with Eva."

"I respect your wishes Billy Love. I do know something about espionage you will recall." I couldn't help but get a dig into my niece. After all I had the medals to prove my participation as an undercover resistance worker in Germany during the war.

"Touché. I will be there is a few days."

"By the way, Billy Love, how is Eva and her quest to adopt Ruthie?"

"I will fill you in on that development when I arrive there. I will tell you I am disgusted by the way Eva has been treated by people here in New York City. The board of directors has shown little backbone in their leadership at the orphanage. It is a travesty for both Eva and little Ruthie who yearn to be together."

My voice trailed off and I hung up the telephone without saying goodbye. I leaned against the wall and pressed my hand to my throbbing temple. Our foray into the Soviet Union was soon to be realized. We were prepared. There would be an opening and we would take it.

****

Josef Stalin was dead after suffering a massive stroke. The date was March 5, 1953. The Western newspapers all blared headlines.

The Evil Dictator is Dead! May the Soviet People Rejoice! The World is Free from the Ruthless Russian Leader!

I spread the newspapers out across the planked tables and studied them for details.

Stalin's body would lie in state for four days at the Kremlin after which a gigantic military funeral accompanied by parades and other festivities would take place in Red Square. The square would be festooned with huge banners and buntings embossed with red stars. There would be a series of lengthy speeches given by cronies of The Dictator after which military personnel would ceremoniously carry the casket to its final resting place—next to Comrade Lenin in the mausoleum.

The attention of the world and the Soviet masses would be fixated on Moscow. The huge Soviet military machine with its tanks and armored trucks would swarm the city in order to create an image of power and strength. And the state funeral would create a major distraction that would allow us to complete our UNICEF mission—a mission that had taken years to plan. Now that scheme had come to fruition.

There were only a handful of people who had a clear view of our plot and those individuals could be counted on to keep the plans airtight.

It was time. I locked the strategy room and waited for each person to relay their code name to gain entrance.

"Dolly."

"Lobo."

"Big Foot."

"Mad Hatter."

"Curly."

"Axel."

"Pixie."

"Hunter."

"Twitch."

They were all present…solemnly seated around the table with their hands folded in front of them ready to receive instructions.

I made eye contact with each one of the participants. They subtly nodded their heads in response.

"Let's begin. The name of our quest is *Operation Frosty*. From now on—until the end of our undertaking when everyone is safe and accounted for—when spoken to you will only answer to your code names and respond with reference to *Operation Frosty*. Do you all understand?" I commanded.

There was no need to wait for their answers. They were professionals. It was a rhetorical question.

I along with all of those involved in the operation had memorized the code names for each person.

Dolly Katerina

Lobo Billy Love

Big Foot Heinrich

Mad Hatter Walter

Curly Leon

Axel Babe Love

Pixie Audrey

Hunter Adam

Twitch Ryne

And I answered to *Velvet*.

There was one final participant who stayed behind in New York: *Flower Garden*. She would direct us from afar.

I lifted a pointer and moved across the room. "Would you please direct your attention to the map on the wall?"

Heads swiveled as they turned toward me. "We will discuss ground operations first. Be aware that this is a very treacherous assignment. You will travel from West Berlin all the way across the Soviet Union to the city of Perm. It is a 2,000 mile journey. There will be three of you who will take turns driving: *Dolly, Mad*

Hatter, and Hunter. You will not stop for any reason—is this clear?"

Three heads bobbed in unison.

"You will take the designated route highlighted in red. So as not to be detected you will travel south of Moscow where all of the funeral pageantry for Dictator Stalin will be taking place."

"And our papers, are they in order *Velvet*?" *Dolly* asked me.

"Yes, here they are. They look official. *Dolly* and *Mad Hatter* since you speak fluent Russian you are the designated spokespersons at all of the checkpoints. You will present yourselves as Soviet Union citizens."

"Will they be suspicious of a woman in a military vehicle?" *Dolly* asked.

"You will identify as *Mad Hatter's* wife assigned to accompany him on the journey. Your papers say you have clearance to enter the military base hidden among the Ural Mountains close to Perm. But in reality, you are headed toward a timberland outside of Perm. Your destination lies close to the gulag located north of the military base. There are children housed with their parents there and they are in bad shape—many are ravaged by disease created from close living quarters in the camp."

I raked the tip of the stick across the map and stabbed the exact location of the treacherous gulag. I continued. "A woman will meet you at the crossing of two roads. Her code name is *Ruby*. She will have men with her who will help unload the truck."

"*Velvet,* what are in those boxes we are delivering?" *Hunter* demanded. His right eye twitched. He was clearly nervous. I hoped he could hold it together as we needed him. He knew the Soviet terrain and he was a big burly man who could quickly help unload cargo. But he also was a defector to the West and we were all aware that if he were caught by the Bolsheviks his fate would be sealed.

"I can not reveal that information. Just know it will help the children. And *Hunter*, it is up to you to monitor the temperature of the trailer. It must be kept at forty degrees," I instructed.

Hunter was silent. He sat back and stared stone-faced at me waiting for the next instructions.

Dolly subtly raised one eyebrow at me. She knew. *Lobo* had informed her about the contents of the boxes.

I knew *Dolly* could be trusted to keep the secret. She had experience with covert operations in her past.

"The three of you leave in three hours. I trust you have all of the supplies you need for the journey… food, clothing?"

Mad Hatter got up, walked over to the map and retraced the route from West Berlin to Perm. He pointed his thick ridged finger at the location of Gulag 36.

He grunted. "After we unload what next? Where do we go?"

"You will not be returning to Berlin straightaway," I instructed.

"Oh?" *Hunter* asked.

I hesitated for a few moments then commented. "*Ruby* will get you to shelter where you will rest for two days. You will abandon your vehicle to her. She will then give you further plans for getting out of the Soviet Union and doubling back to West Berlin. Here are your papers. You three are dismissed. Good luck and God speed."

The three of them rose together—*Dolly, Mad Hatter* and *Hunter*. They took their identity documents and calmly exited the room.

I looked around the room. Phase one was in motion.

"*Axel* and I will be here at headquarters directing operations. The rest of you will be boarding a plane. It is a Soviet aircraft that was confiscated by the Americans at the end of the war. It has been repainted refurbished and labeled with the number Red 02 on the side of the plane. It is located in a camouflaged hanger in West Berlin…already loaded with supplies."

"You will drop those supplies in the forest surrounding the Gulag," *Curly* announced as he paced back and forth. "*Big Foot,* as pilot you will be in radio communication with headquarters here. You will be spoken to in Russian and you will respond in Russian. It is quite possible that the Russians will try and jam our airwaves if they suspect we are with the Western Allies."

Big Foot flicked a lighter and ignited the end of a fat cigar. He settled in, inhaled and then watched the smoke curl lazily in the air upon exhalation. He was a crusty guy—considered old at 40. In the chaos of the aftermath of World War II he made his way to West Berlin where had had lived in relative anonymity and comfort.

He had approached us and offered us his services after receiving information from relatives that the Bolsheviks were starving people and denying them a decent life. Leon and I had jumped at the chance to secure *Big Foot,* someone who spoke fluent Russian who could navigate a plane through Russian airspace.

Pixie and *Lobo* looked at me expectantly awaiting their assignments. *Big Foot* continued smoking as he pulled his scruffy beard and ignored the two women.

"Upon radio command you two along with *Curly* will push the sacks filled with food and other needed supplies out of the plane," I instructed.

"Phooey these two little women might be sucked right out the door. I can't have them in the plane. We need strong men," *Big Foot* commanded.

"See here *Big Foot!* We are perfectly capable—we know how to don our oxygen masks keep upright and gird as we unload parcels. You have no right to speak to us that way," *Lobo* said. She leapt out of her seat and planted herself directly in front of the pilot.

"Whoa there, Lady. Okay I surrender," he said as he stubbed out his cigar.

"Let's keep on task, shall we? *Twitch* will ride in the back as the waist gunner. Should any other Soviet planes threaten our air space he is authorized to blast them if we are attacked," I said.

I was giddy with anticipation that our mission was finally coming to fruition. Now if I could just keep all of the damn codes names straight!

"To summarize...the following people will be on the plane: *Twitch, Curly, Lobo, Pixie* and *Big Foot.* You will depart in two days and fly directly to Perm." I looked over at *Curly.*

"*Velvet*, there is another component to our mission. *Operation Frosty* has a dual purpose. I shall be operating a high-powered zoom camera as we fly over the Ural Mountains," *Curly* smirked. He looked like he had swallowed a cat.

Big Foot acted surprised. He poured a slug of whiskey and waited for further explanation.

There was none. Some secrets are best left alone—at least until the unveiling is imminent.

Chapter 26
Gulag 36

Perm Soviet Union
March 1953
Katerina (Dolly)

> *The old and the new, the liberal touch and the patriarchal*
> *one, fatal poverty and fatalistic wealth go fantastically*
> *interwoven in that strange first decade of our century.*
> ~Vladimir Nabokov, speaking about Russia in the early 1900s

I was exhausted. I shivered as I curled my feet up beneath me and leaned against the frost-caked window. We had traveled almost 2,000 miles across the Soviet Union on our journey to deliver the contents of the truck to a location near Perm. Perm—which translates to *Distant City*. It was 5 AM—the sun was starting to emerge behind the snow-capped Ural Mountains.

Josef Stalin's funeral had concluded yesterday morning. Throughout the day the state-controlled radio stations replayed the fanfare non-stop. The obnoxious over-bearing ceremonies were to our advantage however. There had been little interest at any of the check-points in what we were transporting or where we were headed. Indeed, the guards seemed impatient…waving us through the gates with only a glance at our identification papers.

We finally arrived at the last check-point leading into the city of Perm. *Mad Hatter* yammered in Russia and cracked jokes while trying to loosen up the Soviet guards. It apparently worked. They failed to notice me. The small woman curled up in the corner of the truck.

I rolled the window down and inhaled the sharp pine smell emitting from the heavily forested city. My imagination took hold as I envisioned my mother and grandmother's life in this remote area. I had few answers apart from the Russian treasures that were sent with my mother to Germany. My grandmother's letter indicated that our family was part of the Russian nobility whose people were persecuted and hunted strictly because of their heritage. It was even rumored that the Czarina Alexandra and her daughters briefly took refuge in the city as the Bolshevik revolutionary soldiers closed in on them.

My thoughts continued to be haunted with myriad questions. Why was my mother designated to immigrate to Germany? What happened to mother's family when the Bolsheviks took control of the country? Did they survive the violence that tore apart the country and that was targeted at the nobility? Were they still living in a remote area perhaps Siberia, where they were using aliases to protect themselves?

What was the meaning of the treasures found in the trunk?

The magnificent brooch was engraved *To Olga from Nicholas*. Olga was the name of the Czar's sister. Why would my family have it in their possession?

I shut the questions out of my mind and concentrated on the city. It was industrialized now with row after row of small brick houses stacked on top of each other. Much of the magnificent Russian architecture consisting of gilded cupolas and rotundas had been demolished by the Bolsheviks. The lavish structures were seen as symbols of greed and wealth. They were decimated.

"*Dolly*, hand me a slug of coffee from the thermos. I need it for the last leg of the trip. To keep my eyes from snapping shut," *Mad Hatter* muttered.

I handed the silver cup to him. "Here you go. We need to get *Hunter* out of the back of the truck. I can hear him stamping his feet and pacing, probably trying to warm up," I said.

Mad Hatter grunted. "We will be near the gulag in an hour. He will be fine."

We exited Perm and traveled on snow-packed winding roads into the countryside. Up ahead to my left the gulag appeared. I stared at the compound, horrified by the memories of Dachau that flooded back. It was like they had imported the German concentration camp to the Soviet Union—scrambled barbed wire encased the area—armed guards in watch towers—overcrowded stinking barracks stacked with people—young children detained with their parents. The prisoners were subjected to the harshest imaginable treatment.

Just like the Nazi regime. Had the world failed to comprehend the suffering imposed on people the trampling of humanity in the name of submission to power? I put my hand on my throat and looked away from the obscene picture.

Was there any relief from pain and death? I was acutely aware that the contents of our truck could save lives. The knowledge sustained me to continue the mission.

Mad Hatter veered the truck away from the gulag and plunged into the thick black forest that ringed the mountains. The trees formed a curtain of total darkness as we navigated the single lane before us.

A radio signal screeched and interrupted the silence.

"*Dolly*, come in, over." A clear female voice rang out.

I leaned forward and spoke into the receiver. "*Ruby* we are close. Direct us in."

"Turn left at the fork. You will see a cottage before you. Turn in. There will be a group of men waiting to receive your cargo."

Relief flooded through me. Our contact had everything ready for us. It was the Russian Ambassador's wife from Perm: Karina Petrov—code name *Ruby*.

Our truck rumbled up the lane and stopped. *Mad Hatter* exited the cab and jerked open the trailer. I slid out and stretched trying to still the cramps that wracked my body following the exhausting journey.

A tiny woman in a thick full-length coat stepped toward me with her arms outstretched. I folded myself into her even though I reeked with body odor.

"My *Dolly*," she murmured in Russian. "You are finally here."

I couldn't speak for the scalding tears clogging my throat.

"Come inside. You need a hot shower and some sustenance. Then we will discuss the next leg of your journey."

I nodded and followed her like a lost sheep into the safety of the cottage.

****

Refreshed from the sting of a shower and with my hunger sated I reclined on a thick pallet of pillows in front of the stone fireplace. The flames licked the stones and cast shadows on the cottage walls. I watched bulky men carry box after box of supplies into the basement of the cottage where a refrigerated room stood ready to house the contents.

I knew Karina was impatient...she could hardly contain herself as to what was in the boxes.

I addressed her. "*Ruby*, we have delivered a treasure to you...you are the first in the world to receive a shipment of this nature. For the captured children of Russia this is a gift that can prevent disease and save lives. Children can grow into healthy adults."

"Whatever is it?"

"Come let me show you."

We climbed down the rickety stairs to the basement. I sliced open one of the boxes and pulled out a vial along with a glass syringe.

I steadied my hand and held up the clear liquid container against the bare lightbulb. I contemplated the historic scientific breakthrough I was helping to introduce to the world.

"This contains the polio vaccine developed by Jonas Salk and his researchers—one of whom is our contact *Flower Garden*."

"But what? How?"

"It is a complicated story. But, *Ruby* it is a miracle treatment. Here is how it works. This vial contains the dead polio virus. When injected into the body of a healthy person the person's body reacts by forming antibodies against the virus. If by chance that person then comes in contact with a live polio virus the antibodies attack the virus and subdue it. This vaccine prevents the virus from attacking our neurological system."

Karina sat down heavily on a straight-backed chair. Her eyes glistened.

"I have seen so many children finally released from the camps…their bodies ravaged from polio—paralyzed, unable to function. Their brains impaired, spinal deformities. And the Bolsheviks have no way to care for these children. They are discarded like garbage left to languish. They die sordid deaths."

"But for some of the detention camp children now there will be a future. Provided you can get the children who have not yet contracted the disease immunized immediately after they are released. You can take them here to get the shots," I explained.

Karina stared at me. "But why did *Flower Garden* decide to send the vaccines to Russia of all places?"

"I haven't sorted out the whole story yet. We must accept and trust that her decision will benefit the children."

****

It was dawn when *Ruby* shook me awake.

"I have word that ten families were released from Gulag-Perm 36. Apparently immediately after Dictator Stalin's funeral—when the eyes of the world were upon our country—our Bolshevik government made a big show of publicizing the prisoners' release."

Ruby clicked her tongue and continued. "Of course, the radio program described the prisoners as robust from their years working in the labor camps. There was no mention of children and certainly no comment on how polio and other diseases had ravaged the camp and its occupants."

"Where did the families go after they were released?" I asked.

"They were dropped off in the middle of the town square. Our underground contact is bringing five of the families to the cottage today. We are keeping this operation as lean as possible. The fewer people who know about it the better."

"What is their physical condition?"

"Too many questions *Dolly*. Let's wait and see."

I arose brushed out my hair then donned coveralls and descended into the basement to await the arrival of our *patients*. I said a silent prayer to *Flower Garden*…my mentor, my hero, my nurse. *Be with me.*

Ruby called to me as she led the family of four down the steps into the dingy basement. I looked up and observed them. They visibly shivered as they pulled wool blankets around their shoulders. The mother had matted thin hair and haunted eyes and she carried a small girl in her arms. I noticed the girl's legs were dangling droopily. The father displayed a large visible hump on the left side of his back. He limped across the basement floor holding an older girl by the hand.

Instantly I knew that the *rib hump* was a sign that the father had contracted the polio virus. Nurse Phillips had shown me pictures of signs of polio virus. Both the younger girl and her father matched the images I had seen.

Nurse Phillips taught me that once someone contracts Polio they are immune from further infection. But I also understood that the results of the polio viruses destroying motor neurons in the body would lead to permanent life-long trauma and complications.

"*Dolly* take Father and younger daughter upstairs and give them a hot meal."

The mother looked at me with terror. I understood immediately and knelt before her.

I spoke in Russian softly modulating my voice to gain her trust.

"Please sit down. We are here to help you and your child. Your husband and your younger daughter will be okay. They don't need the shot."

The father kissed his wife on the cheek and gently extracted the child with the useless legs from her tight grip. Then he hobbled up the stairs behind *Dolly*. He had no energy to resist…he had completely given himself over to our commands. He was a shell.

The older girl wrapped her arms around her mother's waist and hid her eyes.

"What is your name little one?" I cooed as I gently touched her on the shoulder.

She flinched but whispered to me. "Irina."

"Irina," I said stopping on every syllable to draw out the name. "You have the most beautiful name in the world—it was my mother's name."

The girl looked at me shyly and our matching turquoise eyes met. My sparkling blue Russia eyes complements of the genes inherited from my mother.

The mother's shoulders relaxed but her spine was rigid. She was vigilant and I didn't blame her.

I removed a vial and syringe from the cardboard box and held them up to show the mother.

"This will protect you and your daughter from getting the polio disease. The disease that caused the hump on your husband's back and the made your daughter's legs stop moving."

Her eyes shifted back and forth. I could tell she was weighing the truth of my words. What if it was poison? She had watched as other inmates were given injections and then taken away… never to return to the barracks.

"Look, I received the injection myself. Right before I traveled to Perm.

I rolled up my sleeve and pointed to my upper arm.

"See the scar? I won't get polio now."

I waited several minutes.

"I won't force you to take the shot but it could save your lives."

"For Irina I will do it," the woman said capitulating."

Irina whimpered. "Will it hurt?"

"Darling your mama will hold you on her lap. You will feel a pin prick and then it will be over."

Irina knitted her brows and looked up at her mother. I watched as the mother-child bond tightened.

"Okay do it," Mother murmured.

After I scrubbed my hands with soap I extracted the syringe and vial from the labeled box then plunged the needle into the vial and withdrew an ounce of solution. I swabbed Irina's upper arm with the chilled alcohol.

"Pinch," I said as I inserted the long needle into her upper arm.

Irina stiffened but did not move as I pushed the plunger to release the medicine. Then I withdrew the needle and placed a cotton ball over the site.

"That wasn't too bad little one was it?" I asked.

Irina was stoic. "I want to watch Mama get her shot."

I smiled and repeated the procedure on Irina's mother. Maybe I would make a pretty good nurse one day. Or maybe not! Nurse Phillips would be proud of me though. She was a damn great teacher.

"I'm very hungry," Irina suddenly declared as she jumped off her mother's lap—revealing a spunky side to her.

"Of course, you are. Let's go see what there is to eat and then we will get you some hot chocolate and a warm bath," I said.

"Spaseeba, spaseeba, spaseeba," Irina's mother repeated. It was all she could manage but it was enough. She had accepted the vaccines.

****

Karina shut my bedroom door and perched at the foot of my bed. She patted the mattress and motioned for me to sit beside her.

She whispered. "Kat you will leave tomorrow at dawn. A member of the underground will drive you to your destination."

"And where am I headed?"

"We will tell you when you arrive. We are splitting the three of you up: *Mad Hatter* and *Hunter* will be transported to another location. For your safety. Our actions will keep the authorities guessing."

"I understand."

Karina continued. "Phase two is scheduled to take place later tomorrow. Even though the air drop of supplies will happen miles away from here it is imperative that you are gone from the region. If you were discovered there would be interrogations. The government would consider you to be a spy for the west: looking to procure military secrets that could assist them in the Cold War."

I became solemn. Billy Love and Audrey Hepburn would be airborne today. Attempting to complete Phase Two of the operation. And if the Soviet radars identified them as enemies the plane could be shot down. Danger continued to be imminent for all of us.

"One more thing Kat. The family—the one you inoculated today."

"Yes."

"They are traveling with you. It is not safe for them to remain in Perm."

I arched my eyebrows in surprise.

"The mother Svetlana is a distant relative of the Czarina Alexandra. The extended family has been living under assumed names for years but sooner or later they will be discovered and jailed again or executed. The Bolsheviks are ruthless. They believe that the Russian nobility will try to rise up again and defeat the communist regime. There are very few members of the nobility left in our vast country. Stalin was ruthless and was responsible for killing millions of people."

My mind traveled once again to the fate of my own family. What happened to my grandmothers, my aunts and my uncle? I only knew that they disappeared from Perm in 1911 and were never seen or heard from again.

I reached over and hugged Karina.

"You are putting yourself in peril *Ruby*. What would the authorities do to you and your husband if you were discovered in this role?"

"I am willing to take the risk. I can't turn my back. Too many others have chosen the path of denial. I won't be one of them. I couldn't live with myself."

"I will do as you order. After I am gone please send a coded message back to West Berlin as to my whereabouts. *Velvet* will keep the secret. And *Ruby* one more thing."

"Yes?"

"You and your people must learn to administer the polio vaccinations. It is really quite simple. I learned from the best nurse on earth."

"Of course, you did."

I continued to lecture. "Start with injecting yourselves. Keep healthy so that you can help others. You will build up antibodies that will ward off the infection that causes neurological damage."

"Okay lesson over. Now come on. Let's go downstairs and have us a celebration. Straight up Russian Vodka is in order don't you think?" *Ruby* asked.

"When with the natives partake of their customs is what I say."

"Ha, your mother was Russian so you ARE a native!"

"Half-native then? My other half is German Jewish." Even though I was bone-tired I managed a bit of humor.

"I will be down in a few minutes. I need to freshen up after being in a refrigerated basement all morning," I said.

Karina left the room and shut the door behind her. I examined my face in the mirror. New lines formed around my nose and along my mouth. Already this mission had taken its toll on me physically. And there would be hell to pay when Jack found out I was not in West Berlin but in Perm Soviet Union!

I could hardly worry about his reaction at the moment. And Jack understood when he married me that I was not a conventional 1950s housewife. No, indeed and neither was the rest of the Wolfpack which had continued to grow and expand over the years: Billy Love, Elisabetha, Babe and Bitsy Love, Eva Braun, Audrey Hepburn, Marlene Dietrich—and *Flower Garden*.

All of us. We stuck together. And we would not be deterred.

Chapter 27
The Drop

Perm Soviet Union
March 1953
Billy Love (Lobo)

The loaded spy plane equipped with a high image and high-resolution camera cruised at 65,000 feet above the Soviet Union. We were headed toward Perm: *Big Foot* the pilot handling the plane and *Twitch* the bombardier settled in the tail of the plane scanning for Soviet air fighters. *Leon, Pixie* and I crouched among the packages containing medical food and other supplies. We waited for a signal from *Big Foot* to open the side door of the plane and push them out.

Before we departed from West Berlin we had received a terse message from *Velvet*. Phase one of *Operation Frosty* was complete. The mysterious boxes had been delivered to a safe place in the forest surrounding the Ural Mountains. *Dolly* had been whisked out of the area and taken to a small town on the coast of Siberia. None of us were privy as to the exact location. If by chance we were shot down captured by the Bolsheviks and interrogated, we would be unable to tell them where *Dolly* was hidden.

Velvet had been in close communications with a network of spies within Moscow and other cities. Their role was to monitor military movement within the Soviet Regime. According to the spies in the week leading up to Dictator Stalin's funeral a massive number of troops had been moved to Moscow to show strength to the world and also to quell any likely protests.

This action thinned defenses in other areas of the Soviet Union, creating openings for espionage that would have otherwise been impossible. Phase Two of *Operation Frosty* was in progress.

Pixie and I were dressed in layer after layer of wool and even then, we shivered from the cold. My lips were blue. I watched

Pixie's breath cloud the air. She looked peaked and airsick like she might throw up at any moment. I placed my arm on her shoulder and silently asked her if she was alright.

I watched her shoulders stiffen as she pulled herself together. She was a movie star but her history as a survivor of the conditions of World War II made her determined. She swatted me away with a wave of her gloved hand.

The plane suddenly dropped several hundred feet and turned on its side making a sharp turn. *Big Foot* growled over his shoulder. "We're making a little detour before we drop those packages."

Curly raised his eyebrows and nodded toward me.

"What?"

"It's okay *Lobo*. *Big Foot* knows what he is doing. This is part of the operation."

"And why was I not informed? This is not acceptable."

"Look, *Lobo*, sometimes the fewer people who know the fewer people will discover our intentions."

"And you felt it was important to keep me out of the loop?" I demanded. My voice was rising even as I struggled to control its timbre.

"Yes, I did."

"Well?"

"Okay. Okay. We are zooming in on the Soviet manufacturing plant where it is rumored that missiles and atomic weapons are being produced," *Curly* informed me.

"And who gave the order for this? It makes our mission twice as dangerous. We are not just dropping needed supplies, are we?" I narrowed my eyes. *Pixie* looked up in alarm.

Big Foot ignored our conversation and concentrated on moving the plane over the designated area. I would be speaking to *Velvet* about this detour when we got back—IF we made it back to Berlin.

Curly was moving camera equipment around the cabin now. He climbed into the co-pilot's seat and settled in.

Through the treetops long tin buildings came into view. And there alongside them sat three gigantic intercontinental ballistic missiles. Everyone was silent for a few moments as we digested the scene. So, it was true. The Soviets were preparing offenses against the western allies.

It was an eerie scene. The area was deserted. Perhaps with the regime change created by Stalin's death there was a void in command. It looked like a still life on the ground—artificial and unreal.

"We only have a few moments. Hurry, *Curly*," *Big Foot* growled.

The camera clicked and whirred as picture after picture was taken.

Abruptly *Big Foot* pulled up on the stick shift and the nose of the plane angled upward. Within a few minutes we were once again cruising at 65,000 feet.

"So now are we going to drop the supply packages or is that too much to ask?" My voice dripped with sarcasm.

Big Foot and *Twitch* howled with laughter.

"It's a twofer don't you know?" *Twitch* cackled as he swiveled his machine gun from side to side. He knew I would be angry but apparently, he didn't care. It was obvious that a woman's opinion was unimportant to him.

The radio crackled and a Russian voice came over the airwaves.

"What are they saying?" *Pixie* asked.

"They are asking us about our reasons for being in the area. They think we are one of their own planes," I replied.

Big Foot was chattering away. But I was unable to interpret his remarks. My Russian was too limited. Finally, he stilled his microphone and turned to us.

"They are such fools!" he exclaimed.

Curly looked irritated at the pilot's outburst. "Come on, we still have another mission to complete. There is no need for you to be so arrogant."

Big Foot chuckled and slapped his ample belly. He studied the radar and directed the plane toward the forest surrounding the Ural Mountains where the drop would take place.

I couldn't help but admire his prowess. He certainly was a confident son of a bitch! I would dress him down after we landed in Japan for refueling.

I donned my oxygen mask and handed another to *Pixie*. We pulled them over our faces and I opened the tank spigot. I watched the bag fill and deflate with my breathing.

The site for the airdrop suddenly opened up. It was pitch black, but search lights dotted the area. We could see ant-like figures on the edge of the forest lighting flares and waving their arms at us.

I edged forward and *Curly* forced open the side door. The force of the wind knocked us backward. We held on tightly to the overhead straps and kicked the parcels forward and out the door with our feet.

It seemed to take forever but in reality, the plane was emptied within minutes. I looked down and watched as dozens of people pulled the packages out of the light into the safety of the inky black night.

Curly slammed the hinged door shut and we tore off our oxygen masks. We were spent with the exertion of our efforts.

Pixie and I leaned against each other. We did not speak. There was no need.

Tonight, the prisoners released from Gulag 36 might have a chance for a better life. They would receive sustenance warm blankets and clothing…bandages and medication coupled with immunizations from the polio virus and the epidemic that was spreading throughout the world. Their physical needs would be mitigated.

But would they ever recover enough to find spiritual peace within themselves? The deep cuts to the soul of humanity had been brutally delivered. The only hope was resilience.

Chapter 28
Coming Home

Toronto Canada
1954
Katerina

Our carefully planned trip had finally come to fruition—today Billy Love and I would be making the seven-hour journey from New York City to the small city of Cookesville, just outside of Toronto.

Jack had arranged for a Lincoln Town car which came complete with a uniformed chauffeur… thoughtful of him catering to our comfort. The car would arrive at our brownstone in an hour.

I was nervous yet excited to meet the woman who resided in the small brick obscure cottage. It was a miracle that she had even agreed to an audience with us. But I had enticed her by dropping hints that I had important family information to share. She had reluctantly agreed to see us.

A loud horn blared outside my window and I pulled the curtains aside to peer out. Billy Love stepped out of a yellow cab and looked up. She spotted me and waved with her prim white-gloved hand. I smiled and motioned her to come inside.

I stood in my slip and examined the crimson linen suit laid out on the bed. Lately there had been no occasion to dress in fine apparel. I had been consumed with our mission to Perm and all that it entailed including wearing the filthy drab olive uniform day after day on the truck ride through the Soviet Union. The uniform landed in the trash as soon as the operation was over.

Billy Love knocked on the bedroom door and entered without waiting for my response.

"Kat! We're really taking this trip. It's finally here isn't it?"

I enveloped Billy Love in my arms and inhaled her lavender scent. It was good to be reunited with my cousin again. The past year had been chaotic—monitoring the children and their mental health therapy sessions at Bellevue—particularly for Ursula and

Wolfgang who experienced a number of set-backs in their progress. It had been difficult. But we had persisted…ultimately both Billy Love and I believed Nurse Phillips and the other staff would guide them to a better place.

Then there was the UNICEF mission to Perm Russia which Aunt Elisabetha and Leon had masterminded. I had led the ground trip operation carrying the vaccines which would prevent polio: Billy Love was assigned to the second leg, dropping needed supplies to the released prisoners of Gulag 36.

Neither Billy Love or I understood at the time that high-resolution photos would be taken of the Russian missiles and turned over to the United States government. Proof that the Soviet Union had nuclear weapons that could be launched against our country.

To be honest neither of us would have agreed to participate in the trip across the frozen landscape of the Soviet Union if we were aware of the added assignment. If we had been captured by the Soviets we faced an almost certain long imprisonment that included torture and could have ended in our deaths. It was a precarious situation.

When Billy Love and I returned to New York City—mission completed—our husbands were furious. Jack gave me the silent treatment for weeks and Parker railed at Billy Love calling her reckless. We stood our ground though informing them both that they knew full well who they were marrying. The word *docile* was not in our vocabulary. Our efforts to smuggle Eva Braun out of Germany and onto the Oklahoma Ranch served as a reminder of our tenacity.

I sat on the bed and rolled my silk stockings up over my legs attaching the tops to lacy garter belts. Billy Love watched me.

She giggled. "Kat, we are a far cry from how we appeared a few months ago. Now we look like society ladies going to high tea at the Fairmont."

Billy Love jutted her hip and posed. Indeed, she could pass for one of the elegant ladies who lunched uptown. Her cobalt blue three-quarter sleeved jacket fastened with pearl buttons fit her lithe frame impeccably. Her a-line skirt fell just below her knee and the matching patent leather pumps gleamed. Carried in the crook of her arm was an alligator handbag which was all the rage this fashion season.

"Kat, how did you know to fashion your hair in a French twist today? Once again, we mirror each other. We are becoming more like my sisters Babe Love and Bitsy Love who can finish each other's sentences, aren't we?"

I stepped into my skirt pulled up the zipper and winked at Billy Love. "Of course. We think alike and act alike—it's just part of the Wolf personality."

Billy Love let the remark go and walked over to the metal trunk sitting on the floor. "So, you are taking it with us? To show her?"

"And to verify the authenticity of its contents."

I finished dressing and crossed the room. Taking out the key hidden in the false panel in my closet I inserted it into the trunk and flipped up the lid. On top lay the sapphire brooch which I gently withdrew and held in the palm of my hand.

"Billy Love, I want to wear it. I believe she will recognize it immediately and know that we are legitimate."

"That is a wonderful idea. I'll help you pin it on your jacket," Billy Love said.

I turned the brooch over and silently re-read the engraving on the back then I handed it to Billy Love. She secured the jewelry below the collar of my jacket.

The gemstone was icy and captivating and it demanded attention. I stepped before the mirror and examined it. Billy Love looked mesmerized.

I fingered the brooch lightly and murmured.

"It is the stone of wisdom and royalty...of prophecy and Divine favor. It is the gem of gems."

I came out of my trance as Jack's voice came through the bedroom door.

"Are you ladies ready? The town car is here."

After spritzing on a flowery perfume, I opened the bedroom door and emerged into the living room.

"Jack can you carry the trunk down to the car?"

I couldn't help but note the expression on my husband's face as he ogled me. Too bad there was no time for a romp in bed before our trip. I would make time when we returned. It had been too long—we needed to renew our marriage.

In his forties now with his sprinkle of reddish-brown freckles and boyish looks I desired him more than ever. *Later Katerina, later.*

Jack picked up the old trunk and carefully hauled it down the steep flight of stairs onto the street. He understood the contents were priceless.

The chauffeur tipped his hat and opened the back door of the town car as Billy Love and I slid in. Jack leaned over kissed me on the cheek and gingerly placed the trunk on my lap.

Billy Love and I held hands just like in the first days of our meeting each other.

The chauffeur put the car in gear and pulled out into traffic.

"You ladies sit back and relax now. Enjoy yourselves," he said.

There would be no relaxing. Billy Love and I were headed toward a visit that just might reveal answers to so many mysteries.

****

A modest red-brick home came into view as the chauffeur guided the town car through the town of Cookesville. Reflexively I placed my hands around the metal trunk as if to protect it from the unknown.

"Here we are folks. Are you sure this is the right address?"

"Yes, we are. Now please leave us and return in three hours. Go into Toronto and have a good meal."

"Thank you, ladies. Let me get the door. Do you need help carrying the trunk into the house?"

"No!" Billy Love and I answered in unison. No one could know what was hiding within the old trunk.

"Alright then. Good luck to you," he announced. He drove off and left us gawking at our surroundings.

"Come on Kat. No one will bite us," Billy Love proclaimed. She took off and headed up the small flight of concrete stairs. She stabbed the doorbell.

The screen was open. At the sound of the bells a small hunched over woman dressed in a faded housecoat and headscarf appeared before us. She lifted a cane and tapped the screen with it.

"Well, it's my visitors from New York City," she said. Her cultured accented voice belied her ragged appearance. "Come in, come in."

Billy Love held the screen door and I entered carrying the trunk.

"You can set that old thing down on the dining room table over there," the woman said as she pointed her cane. "Let's talk first, shall we? Would you like some refreshments before we begin?"

"Maybe later, thanks. Thank you for seeing us. I am Katerina, Kat Wolf Remington and this is my cousin Billy Love Wolf O'Rourke."

The woman narrowed her eyes as if thinking *What kind of name is Billy Love?*

"I'm Olga. Please, have a seat."

I looked around the small house. The furniture was thread-bare but everything was neat and tidy. Olga stared at my chest zeroing in on the brilliant sapphire brooch. She was momentarily coy remaining silent and not giving her emotions away.

"Now ladies I will get straight to the point. How did you find me and what do you want with me?"

"If you please, Olga, I want you to read a letter from my grandmother sent to her daughter Irina my mother."

Olga nodded but she looked uncertain. I unlocked the trunk removed a velvet drape and laid it beside the trunk. Then I reached in and withdrew the fragile letter from its envelope. I handed it to her and she began to read it aloud in a halting voice.

My Darling Irina,

Know that your papa and I had no choice but to send you to Germany. It was too dangerous for you to stay in Perm or even in the country for that matter. There is much unrest and upheaval here.

We know that you can have a life without scrutiny and fear of retaliation. Germany is a welcoming country and many of our relatives reside there. For now, however, it is my wish that you become anonymous. We have secured a factory job for you at the Merck Pharmaceutical company and you will live with Miss Hinders who runs a boarding house for single women.

Your sisters Olga and Viktoria, along with your brother Maxim are too young to travel...we must keep them with us for now. Someday we might be able to shepherd them to Germany so that you can keep them safe. The Bolsheviks are causing havoc, burning down country estates and looting properties. They are determined to destroy **Imperial Russia.**

Papa and I are needed here. We are a source of strength and inspiration for our extended family. We are chafing against the masses as they plot to control the running of industry and society. Lenin and his great socialism experiment is ruining the great Russian culture we have come to know and believe in.

We trust you will make us proud.

We lovingly let you go.

Mama

Olga paused as she dropped the letter on the velvet drape. She looked at me intently as if trying to make sure I was really Irina's daughter. Then she suddenly collapsed and slumped drawing her hand over her mouth. Anguished.

"Your grandmother *Aleksandra! My cousin!*"

Tears streamed down her face and she trembled.

"Yes, my grandmother. Here is mother's birth certificate." I handed it to her and she stared at it as if trying to memorize its existence.

Irina Maria
Born July 1, 1893
Parents: Aleksandra and Dmitri
Record of St. Stephen Russian Orthodox Church
Perm, Russia

Olga lifted her head and motioned. "Come here, *malenkiy*. Come here little one."

Upon hearing the affectionate Russian phrase, I became child-like. I responded to her command leapt to her side and curled my body into hers.

After all of the years without knowledge of my Russian heritage—suddenly part of the mystery was solved. I had a real person before me who was part of my extended family.

Olga traced her arthritic fingers over the sapphire broach. She understood its significance.

"Can I look at it more closely?" she asked

I sat back unclasped the pin from my jacket and handed it to her.

Olga turned it over and read. "*To Olga, from Nicholas. From your brother—the Czar of Russia.*"

She looked up at us as Billy Love blurted out. "The Czar who was killed by the Bolsheviks?"

"Yes, he was my older brother. I was the youngest in the Romanov family."

Billy Love continued to chatter unabated. "You are a princess then?"

"Technically yes, but the Russian monarchy ended when my brother and his family were killed by the Bolsheviks in 1918. Murdered. The entire family."

"What else is in the trunk?" Olga asked impatiently. She clearly did not want to dwell on the murders of the imperial family.

"A portrait of my mother Irina wearing a diamond tiara."

Olga scrutinized the painting trying to place it.

"I remember the day. It was your mother's birthday. We had invited her to the palace at St. Petersburg for the celebration. It was tradition for the young cousins coming of age to select a tiara from the vault to wear for the party and then sit for a portrait."

"What do you think happened to the tiara, Olga?" I asked.

"With the revolution the palace was looted of all of its vast treasures. When times were lean after the Bolsheviks took power, they sold most of the jewels to crooked dealers throughout the world. I have no idea what happened to the crown jewels."

I started to see a pattern regarding the objects I was removing individually from the trunk. Why had I failed to see it before? I needed Olga to guide me to clarity.

I selected the 12-centimeter-tall lacquered doll painted a brilliant red. Olga immediately recognized the stacking dolls. She quickly unscrewed each doll until she reached the final doll.

"There is another treasure within isn't there?" she asked.

I nodded and watched her open the mid-section of the wee doll. She gasped and pulled out the diamond ring.

"It's Alexandra's engagement ring from Nicholas. How clever to smuggle it out in the stacking dolls," Olga noted.

Olga abruptly stood up paced back and forth and then changed the conversation. "Did you know Czarina Alexandra was German, Katerina? Got engaged to Nicholas in Darmstadt the city in Germany where she was born?"

What? Did I hear correctly?

"I was born in Darmstadt— the city where my grandparents sent my mother to work in the factory."

"My Kat, don't you understand? The contents of this trunk belonged to my brother's wife Czarina Alexandra Empress of Russia. She must have sent her most precious objects to Perm to your grandmother, for safe keeping."

Olga stood and held the ring up to the lamp light. It dazzled and sparkled and threw light onto the ceiling.

Billy Love looked incredulous and I shivered.

Treasures belonging to *the Imperial Family* were hidden in my papa's basement and then in the back of my closet in a bedroom? For all these years?

"I believe the intent of the czarina was to send the treasures to her German side of the family in Darmstadt for safe-keeping. And Kat, your mother Irina was designated as the transporter," Olga said.

"Well the trunk did make it to Darmstadt, but my mother died in childbirth with me and my papa forgot all about the trunk until it was discovered in his bombed house after the second war. He sent it to me in New York without ever knowing its contents."

"Let's take a break. I'll get us some lemon pound cake and some tea," Olga declared.

"But there is one more item," I said.

"And I have an idea as to what it is. But before it is revealed I want to tell you and Billy Love a story about my brother Nicholas. Hear me out. History has painted him as a weak ineffective ruler who was easily influenced to take Russia into two wars, thus weakening the monarchy forever."

Olga moved into the kitchen and emerged balancing a tray laden with a teapot tea cups and cake. She heaved it onto the coffee table and sat down. She was winded with her effort.

"Where were we?" she asked rhetorically.

Her eyes bored into mine. "Katerina, Nicholas organized the first International Conference on Peace and Disarmament back in 1898. He felt peace was better for 'prosperity and progress of mankind'. Those were his exact words. He was nominated for Nobel Peace Prize. But unfortunately, he later fell under the influence of some war-mongering advisors."

I felt sick. Why does the notion of war seem to win out over forming lasting relationships and solving problems together? Why does greed and power dominate the world?

Olga continued on. "How do any of us know if we are successful in life? If we have wealth beyond belief, if people scrape and bow down to us, if we can eat rich foods until our bellies heave? None of these things appeal to me. Simplicity and the quest for peace will lead to serenity and happiness."

I was taken aback by Olga's philosophy. At one time she had wealth beyond belief, yet now she was fulfilled to live out her life in serenity and with simplicity. And I was grateful for her wisdom.

Billy Love went to the beat-up trunk and withdrew the last object—the *Imperial Faberge' Easter Egg*. Its stunning beauty could not be denied. Standing ten centimeters in length with its shell a gleaming pink color it was intricately decorated with gold leaf crisscrossing the egg in a harlequin pattern. Diamonds were encrusted along the harlequin repeat of the markings. Billy Love placed the egg on the solid gold pedestal and sat back.

Olga did not reach for it. Instead she circled around it as if to make certain it was real. Then she spoke.

"Lift the hinge. I want to see if the treasure is still within."

Billy Love opened the egg and withdrew a solid gold dove— the symbol of peace.

"Nicholas gave this egg to Alexandra in 1901 the year he received the Noble Peace Prize. It represented everything good about him, yet he succumbed to outside voices. He could not overpower them. He couldn't commit to his own value of integrity."

I started to speak but Olga held up her hand. She stood and shuffled to a table holding an old phonograph. Her trembling fingers lifted a dusty record. She blew away the film and placed it on the player then lifted the needle onto the record.

Waves of melodic sound encompassed the room. Olga shut her eyes and swayed. The piano music of the great Russian composer Rachmaninoff was magnificent—lush sparkling lyrical soaring emotional romantic. The music told a story—a rhapsody of Russian characters playing out the drama of their lives.

The final chords filled the room searing into our brains. I would never forget the impact of the music. It was part of me now.

We were silent for a few moments then Olga spoke.

"The past must be illuminated with the brightest lights of the world in order to create a future for our children. You must promote diversity of thought and action and protect your children and others. There is no other way of being."

With one swift movement Olga lifted the magnificent Fabergé egg and flung it to the floor where on impact it sounded like a scream as it exploded shards of glass and formed a carpet of pain stretching on and on.

"This egg was a symbol of materialism. We spend our time trying to accumulate more wealth and things. Greed is a cause of much destruction in the world."

Olga was keening now. Her grief for her Russian family was on display. She was the last remaining Romanov. Everyone else had been eliminated. And she had destroyed the egg—what she considered to be a symbol of evil rather than a gift of life.

The gold dove freed from the confines of the magnificent egg skittered across the room and landed at my feet. The dove—the symbol of peace. I clutched it to my chest.

Billy Love and I would keep Olga's secret. This crusade…the Fabergé egg never existed. But the dove within would survive. For the sake of our children. Our precious children. The future of the world.

Chapter 29
Epilogue

West Berlin/East Berlin
August 1961
Ursula

The early evening was sticky and sultry with no hint of a breeze. The four of us once orphaned by the ravages of the second world war, had reached adulthood. Our roots were German—two of us sisters who lived in the guard houses on the grounds of Dachau. The other two were Jewish survivors whose mothers were herded into the gas chamber and murdered.

Ruthie or Ruth as she wanted to be known was 17. I had just turned 18. Renata was 21 and Wolfgang was 22. Again and again our paths had crossed and tonight perhaps was a final reunion.

We sat cross-legged in the shadows that crisscrossed the top of the five-story building overlooking the Brandenburg Gate—which now served as a mockery of its own existence. Erected to be known as a symbol of peace! Now it served as a sign of division of our humanity.

From 1949 until this very evening 2.5 million fellow Germans had fled from East Berlin to West Berlin seeking to free themselves from communist rule. That liberty had now ended. With hollow eyes we surveyed the seemingly endless coils of barbed wire running along the divide between East and West. The Soviets had hauled heavy equipment to the site and were poised to begin laying the concrete piling for the fifteen-foot cement wall that would be erected.

Wolfgang laid back on his elbows and flipped on the aqua-colored transistor radio. He spun the dial until he found a melancholy jazz station and turned up the volume to its loudest level. I studied his profile. His dirty blonde curls defined him and framed his long thin face. He had a bad boy look to him which translated to an image of seeking out trouble, but I understood his behavior was an act. Underneath his sullen behavior was a boy who had been betrayed by an elitist father.

Wolfie lit a reefer inhaled the smoke deep into his lungs then exhaled. The air hung heavy with the earthy smell. He handed the joint to Renata, but she shook her head and passed it on to Ruth.

Renata. The good sister who never strayed—who did everything our parents asked. The honor student at New York University where she was studying and taking classes and planned to enter law school next year. To top it all off she was stunningly beautiful. Her glossy shoulder-length dark brown tresses laid perfectly in place. Her brilliant white smile lit up every room and she was the president of her sorority.

I should be jealous of Renata, but I wasn't. My sister was the reason I walked the earth: she was always on my side—always protecting me—always encouraging me. And she gave me unconditional love.

Ruth finished the joint and stubbed it out on the floor. She closed her eyes and tapped her feet to the music as tears streamed down her cheeks. None of us knew her well. From the time she was a toddler she had been shuttled back and forth between the orphanage and countless families who sought to adopt her only to send her back time and time again for failing to meet expectations as the perfect little angel.

Ruth was tall. She was a big-boned blue-eyed blonde and athletic: the perfect Aryan specimen. But she was rejected time and again by American families who desired dainty little dolls who they could dress in frilly dresses and rely on to remain silent. Who would only speak when spoken to and who would always display the perfect manners of an aristocratic female.

Eva had fought back against the orphanage rules against single parents and had finally been *allowed* to adopt Ruth. The two of them were quietly trying to build a life in upstate New York. But it was difficult after Eva garnered attention at the International Peace Conference---when she read Adolf Hitler's letters. And fascism once again reared its ugly head.

I stood in the consuming heat and bent over pressing my palms onto the cement floor. I arched my back and stretched my neck. My tiny cut-off denim shorts clung to my body and my tank top hugged my small breasts.

I began to dance to the jazz beat emitting from the radio. I inherently understood the others were watching: staring at my exotic cat eyes rimmed with glossy black mascara. My lithe pale body glistened with the silvery scars catching the fading light as I sensuously moved.

Each bleat of the saxophones corresponded with the rhythmic pounding of the concrete pillar pilings being installed to create the permanent concrete wall—dividing us—driving our fellow humans apart.

Boom! I angled my body and pointed my toe upward toward the sky. Each musical note sent a message coursing through me— I brought my foot down and pirouetted in circles until I became dizzy.

I failed to eat today. It was another example of my struggle to control my actions and emotions. If I didn't eat I would not have to vomit the food back up.

I raked my hands through my pixie cut. People told me I looked like a young Audrey Hepburn and indeed I was probably trying to emulate her. She was my godmother. I loved her.

The rhythmic clanking of the pilings continued as my body moved automatically in sync with the noise. I was in my own element now...failing to notice anything or anyone around me.

Sweat and tears clogged my vision and streamed down my face and onto my t-shirt. I was on the lip of the building. I felt nothing.

Wolfgang was suddenly behind me cradling me and pulling me backwards until I sat in his lap.

"No! Ursula! Leaving is not the answer. You have to stay with us. There is too much in this world that still needs to be done. And we are all part of being part of it—we are the next generation of the Wolfpack!"

My thin shoulders shook as I sobbed until I couldn't.

Wolfgang shoved something into my hands. It was a pair of binoculars.

"Look Ursie! Across the barbed wire. Look!"

He pulled me to standing and pointed me toward another building.

I adjusted the lens and trained the binoculars There stood four teenagers gazing at us. They formed a column holding hands and raising them in the air. Tears gushed down their faces.

Renata and Ruth came to our side as Wolfgang clicked off the radio. We stood in solidarity with our German countrymen. For we were all but children when our lives were torn apart.

The four of use bunched together and responded. We would not be silent. For silence was the hallmark of ignorance. And it was not an option.

"Zusammenhalten!" we yelled.

"Zusammenhalten!" The East German teenagers responded.

We stood together.

In the Author's Words

I retired from Grand View University after thirty-three years as a nurse educator. It was during my tenure there that I developed a penchant for policy and how it impacts people throughout the world.

Historical research is very important to understand the underpinnings of how policy is formulated and enacted. I completed extensive research for my novels *Billy Love's Wolfpack* and *Billy Love's Forsaken Children.*

The mix of immigration and discrimination is at the heart of my novels. American anti-immigration policies have existed since this country was founded—in my novels, the focus is on the plight of the Jews, before the World War Two, during the war and in the aftermath of the war. Following the war, thousands and thousands of German children from all walks of life were discriminated against and abandoned, left to succumb to the harsh forces of nature and the apathy of a weary nation. The children's struggle for survival is highlighted in *Forsaken Children.*

From my immersion in the health care field, I have come to understand the importance of physical and mental health in healing the body and the mind. My stories reflect the many assaults on people impacted by war—in particular, children as they experienced horrific circumstances resulting in behavioral challenges and worse...Post Traumatic Stress Disorder (P.T.S.D.), an unknown label in the 1940s.

I explore communicable disease, which was common where living conditions were crowded and people lived in filthy squalor. My novels are dedicated to bringing a myriad of issues to light, yet they also focus on the importance of relationships in bringing reform and light to a downtrodden world.

My definition of *politics is the art of persuasion.* I hope my passion and search for a complicated truth will keep the reader engaged and thoughtful.

I live in Des Moines, Iowa with my husband and two adult children. I am currently working on my fourth novel – *Ursula's Underground*.

Coming Soon

Billy Love's
Ursula's Underground World

Chapter 1

Greenwich Village
1961
Ursula

I slammed the door behind me and squinted—examining every inch of my tiny apartment. The minimal furnishings: a couple of straight-backed wooden chairs a single mattress butted up against the far paint-peeled wall, a rickety metal table where I ate rations standing up.

The one redeeming element in my abode was the large leaded glass window that overlooked a narrow courtyard. I crossed the room unlatched the hinge and flung it open, sticking my head outside and gulping in the frigid air as it seared my lungs.

My hands trembled as I ducked back inside and collapsed onto the hard-wood floor. I lit a joint and sucked eagerly on the reedy stem then released the earthy smoke into the stale air. It had been one hell of a day. I pulled a thread-bare blanket around me and attempted to lean back and relax. Impossible. My mind was reeling.

My thoughts traveled back to the fateful night where the four of us gathered to watch the Russians build the divisive wall—designed to sever relationships between East and West—the ultimate symbol of the so-called Cold War. 1961 was indeed a pivotal year. At eighteen I had reached an adulthood that I already wanted to erase.

If not for my dear, dear Wolfgang I might have jumped to my death that night on the rooftop in West Berlin. My thoughts were so bleak not even a crow bar could have pried them loose. The blackness came in layer after layer, glued together with thick molasses. Where the stickiness held your feet motionless locked into a permanent position.

When Wolfgang pulled me away from the ledge and talked soothingly into my ear I gathered the courage to emerge momentarily from my hollowness. He reminded me that there was important work waiting for us in the world. Nothing would be accomplished if I plunged into eternal darkness. He shoved binoculars into my hands and pointed me toward the German teenagers gathered on the communist side of the barrier. I looked. They appeared defiant yet strangely forlorn.

We had more in common than differences with the people on the other side of the barrier. It seemed logical that all of us were German youth born during the horrific years of World War II. Some of us were victims of the Jewish Holocaust— Wolfgang and Ruthie. Renata and I sisters…children of SS Dachau concentration camp guards. And the others segregated in East Berlin? Unknown.

What did the future hold for all of us?

I turned over on my stomach and pressed my check against the oiled pine floors. My coal-black dyed hair flopped into my heavily mascaraed eyes. Angrily I brushed my hair off my forehead and stared at the two side-by-side oil paintings propped at the foot of my bare mattress.

There was something hideous yet mesmerizing about the detailed paintings. One depicted a grotesque war scene with dead soldiers, their bodies in various stages of decomposition. The other picture revealed a street scene where crippled and disfigured war veterans begged for food. Both were signed *Otto Dix*. The *Impressionist* German painter with a mission to reveal the devastation of war.

I recalled what Nurse May Phillips had told me about the paintings. When the Nazis led by Adolf Hitler seized power in the 1920s, they banned Dix's work depicting distorted scenes from

World War I and burned many of his paintings because they were deemed *degenerate*. The Nazis only wanted to showcase artwork that exclusively reflected what they believed to be their finest images.

In the early nineteen thirties Nurse Phillips managed to purchase the two oil paintings in a small gallery in Dresden. She hid them away and eventually gave them to me—a gift she said. It was up to me to figure out their meaning. And to keep them safe for generations to come. I was designated the guardian of the work. A solemn responsibility.

Nurse Phillips. An enigma. There was no other person like her in the world—and I had been the fortunate recipient of her presence. Her intuitive, innovative behavioral therapies tailored for me. Her non-judgmental caring professionalism. Her constant challenges. Who else would assign passages from *Alice in Wonderland* and participate in group puppeteering with *White Rabbit and the Queen of Hearts*?

I had made so much progress under her tutelage. Even with multiple setbacks, I emerged stronger for her care.

I missed her so.

The strong weed I smoked tumbled my thoughts and hurled me back in time. It was 1955. Jonas Salk was on the cover of every major newspaper and magazine heralding the miracle of the polio vaccine. And Nurse Phillips was pictured by his side. Dr. Salk's research assistant…there she was smiling broadly…dressed in that familiar starched white uniform with her gray hair tucked into the round linen cap. The world was agog.

I was transported to the day I visited the Bellevue Hospital laboratory and observed the caged monkeys. Some of them had useless legs as they crawled around dragging their torsos across the cages with great effort. Now I understood that the animals were the recipients of experiments—injected with the polio virus to determine how the body would form antibodies against the deadly disease.

But then almost exactly one year following the breakthrough polio announcement, my heroine disappeared. There was no

313

warning. She was gone. Her apartment empty and scrubbed clean. Her wheelchair-bound husband missing along with her.

Mother had been frantic. I was too young to fully understand the implications. But then no one understood how Nurse Phillips could waltz into our lives and then—poof—vanish. Six long years passed. Wolfgang and I engaged in endless conversations about where she could be. But there were no clues.

Even father with all his covert work in the FBI was stumped—or if he knew where she was, he was honor-bound to silence. The great Dr. Parker O'Rourke, Professor of Economics at Columbia University. Decorated for his role in getting Eva Braun away from the clutches of Adolf Hitler and for his work related to the Nazi resistance in World War II.

And then there was Mother—Billy Love. With her crazy name and her unconventional *Wolf* family. She and Aunt Katerina with their scheming and plotting. Members of the *Wolf Pack*. Always with intentions to rectify and mitigate the evils of the globe.

Where was Nurse May Phillips? Life exhausted me. Yet I grudgingly acknowledged that the influence of my family and friends—especially the women—permeated my existence and gave me credence and hope.

I was fragile. I understood. My self-esteem fluctuated between none and a glimmer. And today was a reminder that people could easily ignore my presence.

I didn't exist.

I twisted the scratchy blanket around me and huddled in the fetal position. Darkness descended pulling me into its bony-fingered grasp.

There were no tears.

I was invisible.

The cool hipster today is your bearded laconic sage,
or schlerm, before a hardly touched beer in a beatnik dive,
whose speech is low and unfriendly,
whose girls say nothing and wear black.

~ Jack Kerouac
The Origins of the Beat Generation
Whose Girls Say Nothing and Wear Black

Billy Love's Wolfpack

Billy Love's Forsaken Children

Billy Love's Secret Crusaders

www.drjeanwolf.com

Resources

Carroll, L. (2015 edition). *Alice's Adventures in Wonderland*.
New York, NY: Sterling Publishing Company.

Shelley, M. (2003 edition). *Frankenstein*.
New York, NY: Penguin Books.